Ӄᶜ

It is almost dusk. He hears her calling to someone from the top of the path. He peers out through the dense branches as much as he dares, straining to hear what the voices are saying. Someone is offering Karen a ride home. He holds his breath, waiting for her response.

"Thanks, but I'll walk. I really need the exercise."

He takes this as a sign, and readies himself.

Soft, steady footsteps on the graveled path, a stone tumbles ahead, kicked by the toe of her shoe. She is deep in thought, her brows knitted together. What, he wonders briefly, is on her mind?

Mentally he shrugs off any concern. He knows that soon, very soon, it will no longer matter.

She passes close by, close enough that he smells her perfume. He counts her steps, knows exactly when to spring.

In a flash, he's upon her from behind, one arm looped around her neck. . . .

BY MARIAH STEWART

Dark Truth
Hard Truth
Cold Truth
Dead End
Dead Even
Dead Certain
Dead Wrong
Until Dark
The President's Daughter

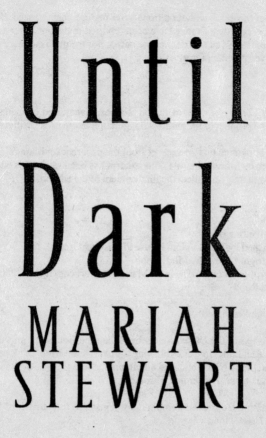

Until Dark

MARIAH STEWART

BALLANTINE BOOKS • NEW YORK

Until Dark is a work of fiction. Names, places, and incidents are either a product of the author's imagination or are used fictitiously.

This book contains an excerpt from the paperback edition of *Dead Wrong* by Mariah Stewart. This excerpt has been set for this edition only and may not reflect the final content of the edition.

A Ballantine Book
Published by The Random House Publishing Group
Copyright © 2003 by Marti Robb
Excerpt from *Dead Wrong* by Mariah Stewart copyright © 2003 by Marti Robb

Published in the United States by Ballantine Books, an imprint of The Random House Publishing Group, a division of Random House, Inc., New York, and simultaneously in Canada by Random House of Canada Limited, Toronto.

Ballantine Books and colophon are registered trademarks of Random House, Inc.

www.ballantinebooks.com

ISBN 0-345-44740-9

Manufactured in the United States of America

First Edition: December 2003

OPM 9 8 7 6 5 4

To Mel, with great affection—
Many thanks for sharing your knowledge of the
southern Arizona hills and for helping me to find
just the right place in which to set this story

PROLOGUE

He sat on the top row of the visitors bleachers, body pitched forward slightly, knees apart, arms resting on his thighs. A good portion of his face was hidden by sunglasses, much as the baseball cap covered his hair. He wore a dark blue T-shirt and well-worn jeans. He cheered when the visiting Patriots got a hit or scored a run, just like all the other parents seated around him.

But he was no one's dad, and applauding at the appropriate moments was merely another form of camouflage. An opportunity to watch without being seen. A chance to study without his quarry suspecting that every move she made was under scrutiny.

It was a method that, in the past, had always proven satisfactory.

Already this week he'd had ample opportunity to follow her, to get a feel for the rhythm of her life. Where she went, what she did. He knew where she shopped and where her kids went to school. When—and where—she was most likely to be alone, to be most vulnerable. The past week's surveillance had yielded much useful information, and hopefully, before the day was over, he'd know her even better.

He watched her move along the edge of the softball field from behind the batter's box to the concession stand, watched her disappear into the little cinder-block building thirty feet from where he sat and emerge several minutes later with a cooler with which she struggled momentarily. Most eyes being on the field at that moment, he recognized an opportunity that might not come again. Dropping off the side of the bleachers, he covered the ground between them in several long strides until he reached the building.

"May I give you a hand with that?" he asked, hesitating as if he'd just been about to join the line of customers waiting to buy snacks at the concession stand.

"Thanks. It's heavier than I thought." She smiled freely.

"Well, here, let me . . ." He lifted it with ease, surprised, having expected it to be much heavier, given her struggle to lift it. "That's heavier than it looks, all right. You must have had help carrying that from the car."

"Nope. I managed myself. Well, with a little help from my son." She looked up at the tall, good-looking, dark-haired man and smiled again.

He smiled back, even as he tucked away the new-found knowledge that she wasn't as physically strong as he'd expected.

Good to know.

He'd already figured out that she was a single mom. This was his third visit to this ball field in the past week. Experience, and careful observation, had taught him that, as a general rule, if the same woman drives the same kid in the same car to the same activity several days in a row, particularly on the weekend, and is never accompanied by a man, chances are she's a single mother.

Just his cup of tea.

"Which way were you headed with this?" he asked.

"Just over to the bench." She was still smiling.

She followed along behind him, then pointed to a spot near the bench where the Little League players sat watching the Deal, Pennsylvania, Red Sox battle the Patriots from nearby Gettysburg.

"Here is fine. Thanks again."

She looked up at him, squinting in the late-morning sun.

"Do I know you?" she asked. "Is your son on one of our teams?"

"No. My son plays for Gettysburg."

"Oh? Which position?"

"Third base." The first thing that came into his mind.

"Oh, Matt Gallagher?" Her smile brightened. "You're Matt Gallagher's dad?"

He nodded, uneasy and infinitely annoyed with himself for being so careless, so stupid. What had he been thinking?

"Do you know Matt?" he asked casually.

"No, no. But I know of him, of course, since he won the batting awards and all last year. That sort of news travels in Little League circles, as I'm sure you know."

"Well, I sure won't tell him that," he relaxed somewhat—after all, no harm, no foul—but reminded himself that such slips were worse than foolish. Loose lips and all that. "We don't want his head swelling more than it already is."

She thanked him again, and he returned to his place on the opposite side of the field, his heart beating wildly.

Her eyes were so blue, her hair so soft, so blond— there was just something about blue-eyed blonds. And her neck was so graceful and lovely, rising above the open collar of her blue-and-white-striped shirt . . .

Up close she was everything he'd hoped she'd be. He could barely wait to see her again. She'd serve his purpose quite nicely.

Of course, it would be a shame. She'd been friendly and courteous to him. He almost liked her. But he could not, must not, lose sight of his agenda, of the role she was to play. And that was, in the end, the important thing, he reminded himself. His agenda.

He glanced at his watch. Time to go. She wasn't the only fish in this week's sea. There were others to see, others to get to know a little better before his . . . *campaign* got under way.

He resisted the urge to walk past her again as he left the field. He could not risk further contact. At least, not until Tuesday.

On Tuesday, pretty blue-eyed, blond Kathleen Garvey, mother of Tim and Eddie, would be all his.

The trap would be baited, and the game could begin. . . .

CHAPTER ONE

The old man took two steps back, then two more, until he was close to the middle of the one-lane dirt road. There he stood, hands on his hips and a scowl on his face, watching the painters tuck the last of their scaffolding into the rusty bed of an old pickup truck of indeterminable color. The only vehicle in a twenty-mile radius that might have been older than the painters' was his own.

"So, what do you think?" The young woman stood on the bottom step of the front porch, the smile on her face a sure sign that she had a pretty good idea of what her elderly neighbor was thinking.

"Your grandfather be spinning in his grave, right at this very minute, that's what I think." He wagged a gnarled finger at her. "Old Jonathan be spinning out of control right down there where we laid him. Surely he is."

"Now, Mr. Webb"—Kendra Smith bit back a grin and forced her most earnest expression—"what is it that you think my grandfather might object to?"

"Well, since you ask, let's start right there with that purple door." The cigar that Oliver Webb held jabbed at the air in the general direction of the house that was the object under discussion.

"It's called aubergine. It means eggplant." She came down off the step to stand next to him.

"Fancy word for purple." He all but spit out the word. "What in the name of the Jersey Devil were you thinking? Painting the house *green* and the door *purple*!"

"I was thinking that the house has spent all of its two-hundred-plus years painted white." She tucked an arm through his. "I was thinking it was time for a change."

"Houses supposed to be white, maybe," Oliver Webb said, perhaps with a little less bluster. "If in fact they need to be painted at all."

"I like it, Mr. Webb." Kendra tilted her head as if to study the paint job that had just about all of the 147 residents of Smith's Forge, at the fringe of New Jersey's Pine Barrens, lingering at the counter in Mac-Namara's General Store for an extra ten or fifteen minutes just to talk about. "I like it a lot."

"Be suiting you, then," he grunted, and she knew he was softening, just as she'd known he would.

"Suits me just fine." She smiled, disarming him.

"Hmmph." Mr. Webb took a puff or two on his cigar. "Well, anyone come looking for you, you won't be hard to find, that's for sure."

He knocked the ash off his cigar and climbed into the cab of his 1976 Chevy pickup. The passenger door no longer opened, and the flatbed was riddled with cancer, but it ran, and as far as seventy-eight-year-old

Oliver Webb was concerned, running was all a pickup really had to do.

Still shaking his head, Webb made a U-turn and headed back toward the main road, which lay a mile or two through the pine trees. On his way, no doubt, to MacNamara's, where he'd tell one and all that yes, indeed, Kendra Smith had painted the old Smith house two shades of green and he'd seen with his own eyes that the front door was purple and that was a fact.

Kendra shoved her hands into the pockets of her worn jeans and watched the painters clear the last of the paint cans from the foot of the drive, then waved as they crowded into their truck and drove off in a cloud of dust. She took one last leisurely stroll around the side of the house, admiring the way the darker shade of green set off the windows from the pale sage of the clapboard. The afternoon sun sent shadows across the new roof—now a sturdy gray—and played up the clean new look of the ancient siding. Pleased more than ever with her decision to have the old house painted, she went up the back steps and opened the door.

During the months since her decision to return to Smith's Forge, to make the old house her own, she'd had the electrical wiring upgraded, the plumbing updated, and the pine floors refinished. She'd also toyed with the idea of central air-conditioning, but resisted rather than disturb the two-hundred-and-forty-year-old joists in the attic. There were some modern amenities that Smith House simply hadn't been built to accommodate.

The brick fireplaces had all been cleaned and relined, the kitchen spruced up just a bit, and she'd even had some insulation tucked into the attic. Bringing the family furniture out of storage where the pieces had languished for years had given her particular satisfaction. Seeing the rooms as they had been when she was a child had brought her the first bit of peace since her mother's death almost four years ago.

When Kendra's ill-fated marriage had fallen apart over the past year, there was no question of where she'd go to lick her wounds. Once having returned to Smith's Forge, she had no desire to leave, and so began the task of renovating the house to conform to her needs, just as her ancestors had done, each in their own time. Now that the last of the work was finished, she was ready, eager, to get back into the mainstream of life. She looked forward to once again feeling that zing when a new case caught her interest, the rush when she'd completed her task. The quiet satisfaction she got when her work helped some poor soul find closure.

She'd made a few phone calls earlier in the week, and late yesterday afternoon, her phone had rung with the request that she take on a job that was right up her alley. A packet of material would arrive within twenty-four hours, she'd been told. Could she begin work immediately?

Could she ever.

She slipped off her sandals and left them to one side of the front door, fighting back a slight twinge of conscience as she turned the lock. There wasn't one resident of Smith's Forge she wouldn't trust with her life, and locking the door felt as if she was locking it against them. To Kendra, that smacked of mistrust.

But years working as a sketch artist for various law enforcement agencies had given her an up close and personal view of the darkest side of human nature. Kendra had come to learn the value of taking those few basic steps to keeping all safeguarded and secure.

Step number one was keeping your home under lock and key, a sad but necessary commentary on modern times, even here, where in so many ways time had stood still. On her way out the back, she locked that door as well before slipping the key into her pocket.

The well-seasoned canoe that Kendra had dug out of the barn when she returned to Smith's Forge lay facedown on the ground where she'd left it yesterday at just this time. She flipped it over, then pulled it forward with both hands, dragging it over forty feet of scrubby grass and pale gray sand to the bank of the stream.

Wonder what Oliver will have to say when I paint the barn to match the house, she mused as she slid the canoe into the stream, then waded after it, climbed in, and pushed off in the shallow water.

The stream, at a narrow point behind the Smith property, both widened and deepened gradually as it flowed toward the lake deep in the woods. Miles of tributaries of this river or that snaked through the Pines, sometimes merging before going their separate ways again. There were endless ways of becoming disoriented and lost in any one of them. Once Kendra had known these waterways well. Her father had been raised in this house, had explored these woods and streams in this same canoe, and had shared the beauty and the mystery of the Pine Barrens with his wife and his children. Summer vacations, spring breaks, fall weekends, winter holidays—at every opportunity, Jeff Smith had brought his family here, to the million acres that made up the Pine Barrens, the landscape that had changed so little since the first Smith had settled there.

While still a child, Kendra had been taught by her father how to find her way around the Pines. Now, as an adult, a novice once again, she had to learn her way alone. Every day she repeated the previous day's run through the waterways, adding another mile or so to her trek, memorizing the natural landmarks. A right at the gnarled old cypress tree would bring her a mile and a half downstream from the next largest tributary of the river. Taking the left where the water forked would lead to the first of the lakes that lay beyond the marsh, one of several lakes that were born years ago when the river was dammed to create cranberry bogs. Once she had know it all as well as she knew the back of her hand. She was determined to learn it all over again, bit by bit, mile by mile.

Kendra reached her goal for the day—the point where the stream snaked past the old iron forge—and turned the canoe around to head back. It had been years since that last trip she'd made here with her father and her little brother. Ian had just turned four, and he'd amused himself by trailing his little fingers in the dark, tea-colored water as Kendra had helped paddle. Jeff Smith had been strong then, strong enough to paddle the canoe on his own, though he'd let Kendra lend a hand. Two months later, he was diagnosed with leukemia, and their whole world was turned on end.

Seven years later, Ian, too, was gone, lost forever. And then her mother, Elisa . . .

Kendra raised her paddle from the water and drifted for a moment. She'd come back to the Pines hoping to find that something of herself, something of her lost family, had remained here. Working on the house had immersed her in the past, filling the hours with memories that had to be worked through if she was to move on, and God knew the time had come for that. The last few months had taken their toll, but now she'd made her peace and was ready to put the past to rest and to find something meaningful to fill her days. For Kendra, that meant work.

Ten minutes later she saw the scrub pines that marked the edge of the Smith property. Just beyond the curve in the stream would be the clearing where she'd pull the canoe to shore. She slipped out of the small craft and into the water, preparing to drag the canoe up the slight incline, when she saw the figure of a man near the back of her house. Kendra froze, then slunk slowly down behind an outcropping of wild blueberry.

The man was tall and broad-shouldered with sandy hair cut close. He tossed a stick to the very large black dog that bounded across Kendra's backyard as if both dog and yard belonged to him. He wore khakis and a polo shirt of dark suede-blue that Kendra knew was the same color as his eyes.

She crouched in the creek for several minutes watching the man and the dog, hoping he'd leave. She blew out an irritated breath as it occurred to her that he was a man on a mission—why else would he have made the trip?—and as such he'd simply wait around until she showed up.

"Oh, hell," she muttered.

And then she splashed loudly to draw his attention, because only a fool would sneak up on the FBI.

"Nice dog," he called to her as she dragged the canoe to the barn and leaned it against the wall.

"Thanks, but she's not mine." Kendra braced herself for the dog's enthusiastic greeting. "She belongs to my neighbor down the road, though she does occasionally forget that, don't you, Lola . . . ?"

"What's her mix?"

"I've heard great Dane and cocker spaniel, though I have some difficulty imagining such a pairing."

Kendra stopped to pet the dog and sighed in resignation. Didn't it just figure that the day Adam Stark pulled into her driveway she'd be wearing old cut-off jeans—old and *wet* cut-off jeans—a shirt tied at the waist, no shoes, and her hair would be a frizzy tangle tied up without thought on the top of her head.

"How've you been, Adam?" She walked toward him with her hands on her hips. Fat lot of good it would do to worry about her appearance now.

"Great." He nodded. "How've you been?"

"Great," she said without much enthusiasm.

"You look . . . great," he said, and her eyes narrowed, thinking he was mocking her. When she realized that he didn't appear to be, she softened.

"Thank you, so do you." She stopped a few feet in front of him. "It seems that life is agreeing with you."

"No complaints."

They stared at each other, former more-than-friends not-quite-lovers, for a long minute.

"When John said he'd have a package delivered, I assumed he meant via some overnight mail service," she said to break the silence.

"Well, I was visiting my father in Pennsylvania when John called yesterday afternoon. He had the file delivered to me at my dad's before dinner last night so that I could look it over before bringing it to you."

"Why?"

"Because he wanted me to go over the case with you."

"I see." She walked to an outside hose and sprayed a thin veil of water over her sandy feet. Lola came closer to investigate, licking at the spray. "John said he's heading a special unit that focuses on serial crimes—abductions, rapes, murders. . . ."

"Right. I guess you discussed all this with him."

"Not to any great extent. He just said he had a case he wanted me to work on for him. He's pretty much a legend, you know, all those high-profile serial killer cases he worked on. So when you have a chance to work with him, you drop what you're doing." She resisted adding, *Which in my case was nothing.* "By the way, I did some work with one of your colleagues from the Seattle office while I was living in Washington state. Portia Cahill."

Kendra switched feet. Lola's pink tongue followed the spray.

"She's worked with John, too, she said." Kendra looked up at him and added, "She said she knew you."

"Portia and I were at Quantico together" was all Adam said.

Kendra shot him an amused glance that let him know that she knew there had been more to it than that. Having made her point, she continued.

"Anyway, I worked on a few cases with her while I was out there." Kendra turned off the hose and slung it over the water spout in a loose O. "She's working mostly with the terrorist unit now, did you know?"

"I'd heard that." Adam nodded. "Her sister, Miranda, was recently assigned to Mancini's unit."

"Portia said she had a twin sister with the Bureau." Kendra stood about five feet away from him, her hands on her hips, as if waiting. Finally, she said, "These cases, the ones John called about, they started as kidnappings?"

"I think the local agencies held out hope that that was all they were. Until the bodies were found. Three, actually, that we believe to be related."

"John said there'd been two." He had her total attention now, her wayward hair and wet cut-offs forgotten.

"The third body was found this morning. John called again right before I left my dad's."

"Three in how many weeks?"

"The first was found almost a month ago."

"He's been a busy boy," she murmured. "How were they killed?"

"Strangled. The body of the last victim showed evidence that she'd been roughed up a bit more than the first two before strangulation, but there's no question in anyone's mind that it's the same guy."

"Why?"

"Similarities between the victims, the nature of the crimes, the manner in which the bodies were disposed of, in such a way that it was clear the women had served their purpose, were no longer of any value to him. DNA from the first victim matched that found on the second. They haven't had time to finish testing the latest vic yet." He paused, then asked, "Did I mention that all three women had been raped?"

She shook her head no.

"The DNA was run through CODIS," he added, "but there were no hits."

"Which only means he hadn't previously committed a crime that would have put his DNA in the national database."

"True enough. Neither of the first two women had any other injuries, by the way. No excessive bruising, no marks that I could see from the photos, other than the strangulation marks at the neck."

"Interesting."

"Everyone seems to think so. Kathleen Garvey was found outside a little town called Deal, about twenty miles from Lancaster. According to the police report she'd last been seen talking with a man outside the sporting goods store in the center of town. Forty-eight hours later her body was found in the Dumpster behind the shop. An artist was brought in to prepare a sketch of the man she'd been seen with, but it isn't all that great."

"Can we get copies of the statements from the witnesses to see how they described him? And a copy of the sketch?"

"I have them."

Kendra glanced at the driveway and the shiny silver Audi sports coupe that sat there, sassy as hell with its top down.

"Not exactly standard issue," she noted.

"I had a lot of road to cover in a short period of time. Standard issue doesn't always cut it. Besides, I was on my own time when I left Virginia on Monday."

Kendra climbed the stairs to the back door, then paused on the top step.

"Get your files and bring them in. Let's see what you have." She stepped into the house, letting the screen door close behind her.

Adam crossed the yard in long strides, opened the trunk, and lifted out his briefcase. Lola, no longer distracted by the hose, followed behind, tail wagging, until a squirrel caught her eye and she took off in the direction of the dirt road.

"This is a really interesting place you have here."

At six feet four inches, Adam had to duck as he passed through the doorway between the back porch and the kitchen.

"Thanks." Kendra watched Adam's eyes gaze upwards as if to assure himself that he could stand up without the top of his head brushing the ceiling. "It was built by my father's family."

"Must have been at least two hundred years ago, judging by the height of the ceilings."

"Very close," she told him, "1768."

"Would it be rude to ask why anyone would have built out here in the woods, in the middle of nowhere, two hundred years ago? What was the attraction?"

Kendra laughed.

"Iron. My great-great-great-grandfather—there may have been a few more *greats* in there—had a forge that used bog iron to make cannon as well as cannonballs, some of which were used, the story goes, by Washington's troops at Valley Forge. Back then, this wasn't the middle of nowhere. Two hundred years ago, Smith's Forge was a town of over five hundred people, though there are fewer than one hundred fifty now. "

"I guess I blinked and missed the town on my way through."

"You didn't have to blink. After the iron industry moved from the area, many of the towns were pretty much deserted. Over the years, the woods took over."

"What happened to all the buildings?"

"Burned, many of them." Kendra took two glasses from a cupboard and a pitcher of iced tea from the refrigerator. "We have an inordinate number of forest fires in the Pines. It's just a fact of life here. And actually, some of the plant life here depends on it, needs the high heat to germinate. But once the fires start, they're often difficult if not impossible to control."

"What saved this house?"

"As the realtors say, location, location, location. We're on the outer edge of the Pines, and on the opposite side of a large lake from the woods." Ice clunked into the bottoms of both glasses. "We've come close a few times—that barn out back is actually the third one—but the house never caught. The one that's there now dates from 1847 or 1857, I forget which. Before the Civil War, I know, because this house used to be a stop on the Underground Railroad. There were a lot of places here in the Pines that served as refuge to the runaway slaves."

She stood at the window and looked outside. "When I was little, I used to stand at my bedroom window at night and think about what it was like to be slipping through those dark, narrow waterways at midnight, holding your breath, your life in the hands of so many strangers."

"You must have had quite an imagination as a child." He smiled at the thought of her in an upstairs window, staring into the night.

"It was well-fueled by my grandparents, I assure you," she said, laughing. "And once my little brother found the tunnel, he'd sneak in there and make all kinds of spooky noises to make us think there were ghosts in the house. So any imagination I had was cultivated by my family."

"There's a tunnel?"

"From the barn into the basement of the house, where there's a hidden room with dirt walls and floor. It's tiny and windowless, as I recall. I never went into the tunnel, myself. Too dark and creepy. Really creepy"—she hunched her shoulders—"spiders and mousies and bugs. Yuck."

Kendra poured tea into both glasses, then handed one to Adam. "Other buildings in the area weren't always as lucky as we were. But you can still see remnants of the town proper about a mile or so into the woods on the other side of the lake."

"Only remnants? You make it sound like a ghost town."

"As I said, we get a lot of fires in this area." She

leaned back against the counter, sipped at her tea, and tried to decide how she felt about seeing Adam again.

He was leaning against the opposite end of the counter, his long legs stretched out in front of him. She hadn't for a minute forgotten the set of his jaw or the lines that ran along the sides of his mouth, though those, it appeared, had deepened since she'd last seen him. The tiny lines that were just beginning to settle in around his eyes four years ago were deeper now, too, a testimony, perhaps, to the nature of things he'd done and seen since they'd last seen each other.

She raised a hand self-consciously to her own face, wondering how the stresses and strains of the past several years might now be playing out. Was he looking at her and seeing a different woman from the one he'd known back then? How much, she wondered, had they both changed?

Baggage best dealt with at another time, she cautioned herself, and tucked that bit of business aside.

"All right, then." Kendra gestured for him to take a chair at the square enamel-top kitchen table that sat in the middle of the room. "Let's see what you brought me. . . ."

CHAPTER
TWO

Adam placed his open briefcase on the table and thumbed through his files, looking for the envelope that contained the photographs of the victims.

"Before or after?" He asked when he found what he'd been looking for.

"Before, for now."

He slid a photograph of Kathleen Garvey across the table.

"She was so pretty." Kendra leaned over the back of a chair and touched the photograph with her right index finger. "How old?"

"Twenty-seven. Engaged to be married next spring to Tom Alspacher. Age thirty-two. Both Tom and Kathleen had been married once before, two children each." Adam didn't need to refer to the file. The facts had stayed with him.

"Where was he on the night his fiancée disappeared?"

"At his aunt's funeral in Rome, New York, hundreds of miles away. His children were with him, his parents were both in attendance as were numerous family members. Arrived in New York the day before

Kathleen disappeared. Got back to Deal four hours after her body had been discovered."

"Maybe it was somebody local," Kendra offered. "Maybe someone who knew he was out of town for a few days and thought she wasn't likely to be missed . . ."

"She was missed right away. She lived with her children and her younger sister, and apparently kept a tight schedule. Home from work no later than five forty-five every night. Dinner around six—her sister cooked and took care of the kids in exchange for room and board—and back out by seven three nights of the week. She was taking a course at the local community college. According to the sister, she always left work on time, always got home on time. Was never late for class."

"Why the stop at the sporting goods store?"

"She was picking up a baseball glove for her eight-year-old son. The sister said that Tom's son had given it to him but it needed to be restrung. Kathleen swung by on her way to school so that her son would have it for his game the next day."

Kendra studied the face of the woman in the photo, a woman with bright blue eyes and a brighter smile. A woman who could never have imagined what fate awaited her on a warm April evening when she would make what should have been one quick, routine stop.

"No mention to the sister of any unusual occurrence that day? Phone calls? Visitors?"

"No mention of anything in the report, but then there's no indication that the question was asked either."

"Do you have the witness statements?"

"Yes. Right here." Adam sorted through his folders searching for the one that held his copies of the faxed pages the FBI had received from the state police earlier in the week. "And here's a copy of the sketch their artist had done."

Kendra slid into a chair and began reading the report.

Adam watched her eyes flicker from line to line, watched her expression change as she progressed through the report. She leaned one elbow on the edge of the table and rested her chin in her open palm. She looked exactly the way she'd looked that first time Adam had met her. He'd been sent to pick her up at her hotel and accompany her to interview a key witness in a kidnapping case. At first he'd thought he'd knocked on the wrong door. He'd expected someone older, more seasoned. The woman who had stood in the doorway had been delicate-looking and just shy of petite. Her light auburn hair had been piled casually atop her head and her eyes had been green and serious.

Pebbles Flintstone, all grown-up had been his first impression.

It had taken less than an hour of watching her at work to replace that image with one of a woman who was totally professional, totally absorbed by her work, totally sensitive to the subjects she interviewed. After all, who better to understand what family members were going through after a loved one disappeared than someone whose own family had suffered that same relentless pain?

"So we have two witnesses who saw Kathleen standing in front of Fanning's Sporting Goods at a little before seven o'clock on a Thursday evening." Kendra spoke out loud as if to herself, as if she'd forgotten Adam was there. "Both witnesses describe the man she was with as a stranger, not someone from town. Tall, dark-haired. Black jacket, blue jeans. Glasses."

She picked up the sketch and studied it.

"One of the witnesses, an eight-year-old boy, was riding his bike on the opposite side of the street. He noticed Kathleen because he knew her son. They played on the same baseball team. The other witness, Mrs. Sims, had come from the pharmacy, which is apparently next door to the sporting goods store, while Kathleen and the stranger were chatting. She claims to have taken little notice of the man, she was in a hurry." Kendra tapped an impatient finger on the table. "So how did the artist manage to produce a sketch like this if it was already getting dark, the area was not especially well lit, one witness was across the street and the other admitted she barely noticed the man?"

"I'm guessing he belongs to the 'a poor sketch is better than none' camp."

She frowned. A poor sketch could only do more harm than good.

"May I see the rest of the photos now?"

Adam passed her the tan envelope. She tilted it to let the pictures slide out, then studied them carefully.

Kathleen Garvey no longer smiled for the camera. Black and blue halos rimmed her eyes, and her cheeks were abraided, with dried blood at one corner of her mouth. There was dirt on her chin and both arms, and the telltale bruising on her neck from her killer's hands. Her clothing was torn but the remains hung from her body in sections, as if her assailant had ripped at what was necessary for him to rape her and did not bother with the rest. The body lay in situ where it had been found, in the Dumpster, amid empty cardboard boxes that once held shiny aluminum base-ball bats from the sporting goods store and rotting produce from the small food market at the far end of the parking lot.

"Discarded, as you said." Kendra muttered when she reached the end of the stack. "Tossed out with the trash."

"Exactly. A statement on his part. She meant nothing. Her life meant nothing."

Kendra returned the photos to the envelope, then placed it inside the file, which she slid to her left.

"Let's take a look at the second victim."

"Amy Tilden. Age thirty-five." Adam had already pulled the file. "Mother of three, two daughters and a son. Divorced from Stan. Teacher's assistant in the lo-cal elementary school where her kids were in grades one, three, and six. Left her house on Monday evening for Home and School Night. Visited each of her kids' classrooms briefly—long enough to say she'd been there, but since she worked at the school, she stayed current with the teachers. She walked out the back of the building to get something from her car. Two days later her body was found dumped along the side of the road leading into town. No attempts had been made to hide it. The officers who found her said it looked like someone had pulled off onto the shoulder, opened the door, and shoved her out, as you'll see in the photos."

"No one noticed anyone strange hanging around the school that night?" Kendra asked as she reached for the file that Adam held out to her.

"No mention of anyone in the reports."

"The same lack of respect for his victim. And another pretty blond," Kendra observed. "I wonder if that's coincidence or preference. I guess we don't have a picture of victim number three yet."

"Not as of this morning."

"How long between the two murders?"

"Sixteen days."

"And between the second and the third?"

"Thirteen days."

"Cutting his time a little. Wonder how he's spending his time in between killings," she said in an almost whisper as she opened the envelope holding photos of Amy Tilden's body laying facedown and half off the shoulder of the road amid the newly green grass of early spring. A bag from a fast-food restaurant and an empty paper container that had once held french fries lay near her feet, which were still clad in shoes. The marks on her neck were identical to those on Kathleen Garvey's.

"The food wrappers here in the photos . . ."

"Had apparently been there long before the body arrived."

"He must have left something behind besides his DNA."

"There were fibers on both bodies, but none that matched."

"Meaning only that they were not assaulted in the same location. And he wasn't wearing the same clothes. And they may not have been transported in the same vehicle."

Adam nodded. "Maybe all of the above. There were a few hairs that matched, though, which by and of themselves, at this point, tell us only that the killer was a white male. Which we'd already figured out, since crimes such as these generally do stay within race."

"And the marks on the neck?"

"The same. Same distance from the marks made by the thumbs to the marks on the side of the neck. Bruising on the arms, bruising on the face. He worked them both over a bit before killing them."

"No witnesses this time."

"None that have come forward as yet, but they're still looking."

"I can't believe that no one saw him." Kendra shuffled through the reports provided by the local authorities. "With a school full of parents, people coming and going. How could no one have seen her leave the building?"

"She was seen leaving the building," Adam pointed out. "She wasn't seen again after the door closed behind her."

"Well, maybe they just didn't ask the right people." Kendra looked up at him. "I'm assuming you'll be doing your own investigation."

"The Bureau has been requested to assist in the investigation. There are several field agents on the scene as we speak."

"I'll need to meet with the witnesses that you have on the Garvey case if I'm to come up with a sketch. I'm going to want to go along with you on Tilden if witnesses are identified. If that's all right with you."

"That's why I'm here. John thought we should work in tandem on this."

A loud crack rattled the windows.

"Yow." Kendra turned toward the sound of the thunder, startled. "I wasn't aware we were in for a storm."

She rose to close the window as the wind whipped up, sending the curtains dancing and billowing over the sill.

"You might have just enough time to put the top up on your car before the rain starts," she said. "Unless you don't mind if all that fancy leather takes a bath."

"I'll be right back." Adam took off out the back like a shot.

Kendra stood in the window, the curtain pulled to one side, and watched Adam cross the yard to the drive where the Audi sat exposed to the rapidly approaching storm. His strides were long and quick with the crispness of the professional athlete he once was. Within minutes, the top was up on the car and he was taking the back steps two at a time to escape the storm's first wave.

"I can't believe how quickly the storm moved in," he said as he came through the screen door. "It's almost completely dark out now."

"Hopefully it will pass through before it does too much damage. If the wind keeps up like that, we'll likely see some trees down."

"As long as they don't take the electrical wires with them, I guess that's not the worst that could happen."

"Losing electricity isn't the worst thing back here. My ancestors lived a heck of a long time without electricity. But having the roads flooded out can be much worse than losing power."

"What's the chance of that happening?" He frowned. His assignment left no room for delays.

"Depends on how much rain we get and how quickly it falls." She stepped past him into the small laundry room off the back entry and returned with a white towel. "You might want to dry off before we get back into those files."

"Maybe we should put the Weather Channel on," he said as he dried off. "I was hoping to leave for Pennsylvania tonight. My schedule didn't take flooded roads into consideration."

"I'll be sure to pass that on to the Rain Gods." Kendra turned on the small television that sat on a counter opposite the sink, and watched the meteorologist of the moment discuss a storm moving into the southwest. Minutes later the local forecast followed.

"There you go." She turned to Adam as the forecast concluded. "Heavy rains and wind tonight, followed by clearing skies in the morning and . . ."

Another crack of thunder split the sky. The lights flickered and the picture on the television darkened.

Kendra leaned over and turned off the TV.

"It's dark as midnight here, and it's only, what,

barely six o'clock." Adam looked out the window and saw nothing except darkness.

"It does seem darker out here sometimes because there are no streetlights, no lights from other houses. My closest neighbor is almost a mile down the road. The storm is just making it worse."

She opened a closet door and took out a lantern, several candles, and a flashlight and set them on the counter near the television, just in case, then paused and asked, "Are you hungry?"

"I thought maybe we'd stop someplace and grab some dinner on our way to Pennsylvania."

"If we wait until we're on the road to have dinner we're going to get really, really hungry." She appeared mildly amused. "I wouldn't be surprised if the road is already flooded out from here to the highway."

"Are you serious?"

"It takes very little to flood out a dirt road. Fortunately, because the soil here is so porous, it will recede very quickly once the rain stops. Until then, I think we can count on being here for a while."

"Has anyone around here considered paving the road?"

"Sciencing," she grinned. "Back here, the old folks call that 'sciencing.' Hasn't been much call to pave these one-laners, though. Most of them are just access roads to someone's house. They don't actually go anyplace but into the woods a bit. People down here would never stand for their taxes to be used to pave what is, in essence, someone else's driveway."

"How many houses are on this road?"

"Three. This is the last. And no, we've never considered paving it ourselves."

She opened the freezer and poked around a bit.

"So, the question was, are you hungry?"

"Well, yes, actually, I am."

"Frankly, I could use a little break right around now. I'm for eating while we finish discussing Ms. Tilden, then maybe you can put a call in to Mancini and see what he's come up with on this most recent victim. We'll see what condition the roads are in after that."

"And if they're impassable?"

"Then you'll just have to sleep here and we'll leave in the morning. You can sleep in the study, if you don't mind spending the night on the sofa." She added apologetically, "The two extra bedrooms upstairs still have Ian's and my old single beds in them. I'm sure you wouldn't be comfortable in either, since you're so tall. My next project is going to have to be a real guest room."

"Where I sleep isn't much of an issue to me," Adam brushed off her apology. He'd hoped to be sitting in the office of the lead investigator on the Garvey case when the sun came up the next day. He hadn't planned on a sleepover and wasn't sure how he felt about spending a night under the same roof with her. "We'll have to leave really early to get an early start in Deal. We should be able to make good time if we leave before the morning rush hour."

"There is no morning rush hour around here, at least not until you head toward Philly or Wilmington. And if you're planning on driving that little number out there, no one would ever believe you're a fed. Now, we could take my Subaru. . . ."

"That old blue thing in the driveway? You really think that will make it all the way to Pennsylvania? How many miles on it?"

"It made it all the way back from Seattle, thank you very much." She ignored the last question.

"How many miles?" he repeated.

"Some."

"Over a hundred thousand?"

"Over a hundred thousand," she conceded.

"How many over a hundred?"

"Forty-seven something."

"One hundred forty-seven something miles?" He grinned. "I'd say you got your money's worth. What year is it, anyway?"

"1985."

"Maybe it's time for a new one."

"It was my mother's," she said.

"Oh."

"She only used it around town. She had a newer car that my stepfather bought for her as a present when she won her seat in the Senate." Kendra paused, then added, "The Subaru was the first car she'd ever bought for herself. She was so pleased with it. She'd ordered it new from the dealer with all the options she wanted. So it may seem antiquated, and next to that smooth little rascal you're driving it may not look like much, but as long as it runs, I'll drive it." Then, lest she sound too sentimental, she forced a smile. "Besides, down here where I live, my old car fits in just fine. Anything too flashy, too new, folks think you're showing off."

"Maybe I should have parked in the barn."

"Too late. It's probably the topic of conversation down at MacNamara's Diner as we speak."

"How did you know I stopped there?"

"The only route in to Smith's Forge is via Route 532 through Worth. And once you've passed through Worth, there is no other place to stop. I'll bet they told you to drive down the road here and look for the house with the purple door."

"As a matter of fact, they did."

"That must have made Oliver Webb one happy man," she mused.

"Who's Oliver Webb?"

"An old friend of my granddad's who's convinced that I've got all the ancestral Smiths resting uneasy since I had the house painted."

"Oh, thinks white would have been better?"

"Well, down here, depending on who you speak with, one might prefer no paint at all. At one time, in some areas deeper into the Pines, it was thought that painting the house would only invite higher real estate taxes."

"I guess a purple door is really asking for trouble, then."

"I had a hell of a time convincing the painters that I wasn't kidding. Now, back in Princeton, where we used to live, it wouldn't have raised an eyebrow." She opened the refrigerator and reached for the container of soup that her neighbor, Selena Brennan, had dropped off earlier in the day. "Down here, everything is grist for the local mill."

Lightning exploded outside and the thunder rattled the rafters of the old house.

"I think we might want to get this soup heated up just in case we lose power," she noted.

"Can I help with anything?"

"You can get two bowls and small plates out of the cupboard behind you"—she reached up to take a small pan from a rack on the wall behind the stove— "and maybe you could put some sandwiches together. I think there's some roast beef and some Swiss cheese in the fridge, rolls in the bread box there. And I'm sure there's some hot dogs, if you'd rather."

A look of something bordering on horror crossed Adam's face, much as she'd anticipated, and Kendra smiled to herself. He mumbled something about nitrates and searched for the roast beef.

The lights flickered several times while Kendra prepared soup and Adam made sandwiches. She replenished their glasses with fresh scoops of ice, some tea, a sprig of mint, and a thin slice of lemon before sitting down and, ignoring the torrent that slashed against the window behind her, asked, "Okay, where were we?"

Adam lay on the old leather sofa in the study that Jeff Smith had built for himself almost twenty-five years earlier. The room was large and square, with a ceiling higher than that found in any other room in the house, floor-to-ceiling library shelves on one long wall, rough-hewn rafters, and a bay window with a seat piled high with cushions. Adam plumped the pillow under his head and listened to the echo of Kendra's footfalls on the floorboards overhead and reminded himself that he and Kendra had, would probably always have, a strictly professional relationship.

Right.

At midnight the storm had still been shaking the trees that stood like sentinels around the old house, and Kendra had announced matter-of-factly that Adam would have to spend the night.

"My dad designed this addition himself," she'd told him as she led him into the darkly paneled room. "The sofa's extra long because *he* was, and he liked a sofa he could stretch out on without twisting up his legs. This was his favorite place in the house. I spend a lot of time here."

"It's a great room," Adam said, nodding his approval as if it had been expected. "Do you ever use the fireplace?"

"I've used it a lot since I've come back. It makes a cozy place to sit and read, or work."

Kendra opened a door to the right and said, "There's a full bath here, in case you want a shower. There are towels stacked on the shelves. Extra blankets are inside that chest next to the sofa in case it gets cool."

"Thanks. I'll be fine."

They stood awkwardly for the briefest of minutes, as if both of them had a sudden recollection of the last time they'd been in a cozy room together. Then, to banish the memory and avoid the moment, Adam lifted a photograph from one of the bookshelves. A tall, dark-haired man stood with his arm around a slender young woman with a mass of curly blond hair.

"Is this your father?"

"Yes," she smiled. "That was taken the summer he graduated from college."

"And the woman in the picture, is she your mother?"

"No, no. That's my aunt. My dad's sister, when she was still Lorraine."

"Who is she now?"

"Sierra." The sarcasm was unmistakable. "She took up with a somewhat wild crowd in college. Dropped out in the middle of her junior year, changed her name and bought herself a ranch in Arizona."

"How could she afford to do that?"

"She and my dad had trust funds that had been set up by their grandparents." She added dryly, "It was more than enough to pay for her ranch and to support the 'friends' who came and went over the years. And still do, no doubt."

"Sounds as if you disapprove of her."

"Disapprove?" Kendra pondered the word. "I hardly know her. I haven't seen her or heard from her since the trial. Not even when my mother died."

"The trial?" he asked, puzzled.

"Edward Paul Webster's trial. The man who kidnapped and murdered my brother and my cousin Zach."

"I'm sorry. I'd forgotten there had been two boys."

"Zach was Sierra's son." She turned her face so that he could not see her expression.

"Webster's still in prison, isn't he?"

"Serving two life sentences. The tax dollars of the good people of Arizona at work."

"I'm sorry. I didn't mean to bring up bad memories."

"I'm sorry, too. I didn't mean to get into ancient family history. Especially since it's so late in the evening and you're a guest in my home."

"Thanks to the storm." He gestured toward the window. "I think it's starting to slow a bit."

"It hardly matters at this point, since the roads will be flooded for hours yet."

"I appreciate your offer of a bed."

"Oh. You just reminded me. You'll need sheets. I'll be right back."

She returned in minutes with two pillows and a set of sheets.

"Thanks." He reached for them.

"You're welcome. I hope you'll be comfortable." She handed them over, then backed toward the door. "Well, I guess I'll see you in the morning. . . ."

"Yes. Thanks."

"If you need anything else . . ."

"No, no. I'll be fine. Thanks."

Adam watched her disappear down the hall, watched the house grow dark as she snapped off lights on her way to the stairs. He made up his bed and sat on the edge of it, thinking about the last time he'd seen Kendra.

She'd been burying her mother. Literally.

Though they'd only had a few casual dates, Adam had ached for her when the news broke about her mother's suicide. He'd known that she'd been devastated, but had no way of knowing just how lost she'd be in the aftermath. Kendra and her mother, the only survivors of the once happy Smith family, had been inordinately close. Kendra's father, Jeff, had died of leukemia when Kendra was thirteen. Years later, the loss of her brother had strengthened the bonds between mother and daughter.

Over dinner on their first real date, Kendra had spoken with great pride of her mother's accomplishments. Finishing law school in her late thirties, becoming an advocate for tougher prison sentences for those convicted of preying on the young and helpless, as well as establishing a forum for families to deal with the loss of a child. Later, with backing from her second husband, a onetime White House press secretary with rock-solid political ties, Elisa Smith-Norton ran for and won the Senate seat vacated when the incumbent was indicted for fraud. Adam and Kendra had had only three formal dates—hardly enough to have developed an intimate relationship—when her mother's sudden death took her back to New Jersey and out of his life.

Adam had attended the senator's funeral along with several other agents who'd worked with Kendra over the previous eight months. He'd spoken with her briefly—long enough to offer his condolences and little else—before passing through a seemingly endless line of mourners at the funeral home. Senator Smith-Norton had become a popular figure during her years as a public servant, and hundreds had shown up to pay their respects to her husband and her daughter.

Adam had left several messages for Kendra on her answering machine, but had never gotten a return call. He stopped leaving messages six weeks later when the news began circulating through the office that Kendra had married an old boyfriend who'd come back into the picture to comfort her when her mother died. The wedding had been small, Adam had heard from a friend of a friend, and totally unexpected by everyone who knew her. According to FBI gossip, even Kendra's stepfather had been caught off-guard. This last bit of news came from the secretary to the director, who himself was an old friend of Philip Norton, the senator's widower.

That had been nearly four years ago. Plenty of time, Adam figured, for his interest in her to have waned. Or so he'd believed, until John had called the day before and mentioned in that oh-so-nonchalant way of his that Kendra had returned to the East Coast, divorced and ready to resume business. And by the way, would Adam head down to southern New Jersey to pick her up and accompany her to Deal?

Casual though their relationship might have been, there was still an air of unfinished business that nagged at Adam every time he thought of her. And over the past several years he had thought of her more frequently than he liked to admit.

And now here he was, in her house, alone in the darkened room below her own, listening to the soft sound of her feet padding on the floorboards, the light sigh of the bed as she sat upon its edge, the low music from overhead. He closed his eyes and tried to pretend it wasn't her face he saw in his mind's eye.

As he lay in the dark room of the old house, where the barest wisp of aromatic tobacco lingered in the air, and counted sheep to the faint sound of the Dave Matthews Band, he wondered if this trip had been such a good idea after all.

CHAPTER
THREE

"Do you have everything you need, Ms. Smith?"

"Yes, yes, I'm fine. Is the little boy here yet?" Kendra unpacked the file from her briefcase and placed it on the table that dominated much of the small kitchen that served the dining needs of the Deal Police Department. She was anxious to spend some quality time with their young witness and knew from experience that casual surroundings might help eight-year-old Max Spinelli to relax.

Alan Ford, chief of police of the village of Deal, Pennsylvania, population 3,517, nodded from the doorway. He'd requested the assistance of the FBI under protest from several of his detectives whose last homicide investigation was seven years past and had involved a couple of bikers just passing through. They hadn't seen the need for outside intervention now that they had what appeared to be a bona fide serial killer in the area. Ford had expected the assistance to come in the form of a few agents. He hadn't expected the FBI to bring in a compositor. After all, their own sergeant had drawn up a sketch and that looked pretty good. On the other hand, this woman looked pretty good, too, so who was Ford to question the FBI's judgment?

The chief paused in the doorway and looked at Adam and asked, "By the way, why do you need a profiler?"

"What?" Adam looked up.

"A profiler. I'd heard that you specifically requested a profiler."

"Well, when you asked for us to assist, there'd only been two killings, possibly related." Adam leaned back in his chair. "Now that we have at least three, we have enough behavioral clues to start making appropriate inferences that can lead to a profile. She should be here soon."

"She?" Ford's eyebrows raised.

"She," Adam assured him. "And for the record, she prefers 'criminal investigative analyst' to 'profiler.' "

Muttering unintelligibly, Ford stuck his head out the door and called to someone down the hall, then opened the door wide enough for a frightened-looking young boy and his wary mother to enter the room.

"Max, Mrs. Spinelli, my name is Kendra Smith. I'm a sketch artist who occasionally works with the FBI. This is Agent Stark." Kendra turned slightly in her chair to nod to Adam, who extended his hand to both Mrs. Spinelli and her son.

"Agent Stark, my son has already told Chief Ford everything he knows. A sketch of the man who"—she swallowed hard—"a drawing, a good drawing, has been made. I'm not sure I understand why Max has to go through this questioning again."

"Kendra," Adam deferred the response to her, for which she was grateful.

"I appreciate that you and your son have been so cooperative. But in a case like this—I'm sure you are aware that the suspect is being sought in connection with two other victims—we just want to be sure that the sketch that was released to the media is as accurate as it can be."

"He told them everything he knows, and the artist drew a good picture." Mrs. Spinelli frowned.

"The picture is quite well drawn," Kendra chose her words carefully, "but it's a mistake to believe that the sketch is accurate just because the art is well-done."

She turned to address Max.

"I'm sure that the description you gave was as truthful as possible. But it's my understanding that you were given catalogs of photographs so that you could pick out features that looked right to you."

Max nodded. "The police had big books with faces in them. They told me to look at the faces and then they asked me, did his nose look like this? Or this?"

"And police artists often work that way." Not wanting to give the impression that she was critical of someone else's efforts, or worse, that she was questioning Max's veracity, Kendra smiled reassuringly at the child.

"But in order to refine the sketch, we'll need to have you tell us about that night, Max. No books this time."

"Okay," Max nodded.

"Now, according to the police report, you were

across the street in front of the video store when you first saw Ms. Garvey speaking with a man." Adam took over, hoping to re-create the scene so that Max might be better able to describe to Kendra exactly what he saw.

"Well, I was across the street when I saw Ms. Garvey talking to him, but I was crossing the street when she went into the store."

Kendra sat back in order to permit Adam to take over the questioning about the actual events of that evening.

"You were crossing the street from where, Max?"

"From the corner next to Fanning's, the sporting goods place, to the video store on the opposite corner." He glanced at his mother, then said somewhat sheepishly, "I'd forgotten to return a movie that my brother and I had rented. I wanted to get it back before my mom got home."

"The boys have been habitually late returning their movies," Mrs. Spinelli explained, "so the new rule is that they have to pay late fines from their allowance."

"Do you remember what you did after you left the house, Max?" Adam took a seat across the table from Max.

"Sure. I rode my bike right down Fourth Street and crossed Main right there at the corner where Fanning's is. Usually you can drop the tape right into a box outside the video store, but the box was full and I had to go inside. I parked my bike and went into the store and put the video on the counter."

"So how long do you think you were inside the store?"

Max shrugged. "Just a couple of minutes."

"When Ms. Smith and I drove into Deal this morning, we walked around town a little. I noticed that there's a parking lot behind Fanning's store. Did you pass the parking lot on your way down Fourth Street that night, Max?" Adam leaned back in his chair, a casual gesture that lent an air of informality to the session, as if he and Max were just old friends talking it over.

"Sure."

"Did you notice if there were any cars parked there that night? Any cars that you recognized?"

"Ms. Garvey's car was there, and Mr. Fanning's car."

"What kind of car does Mr. Fanning have?"

"A red Corvette." Max grinned. "It's hot."

"Were those the only cars parked there that night?"

"No, there was a van in the lot. I remember because it was parked over toward the back, and it sort of blocked Mr. Fanning's car. I had to look around it to see the Corvette."

"I guess when you go past Fanning's, you gotta see that 'vette." Adam nodded, man to man.

"Right. It's the only one around. You always look at it."

"So there was a van in the lot blocking your view of the 'vette, so you looked around the lot a little to see if the 'vette was there."

"Right."

"And where was the Garvey car?"

"On the other side of the van."

"What kind of van was it, did you happen to notice?"

"Nah. It was just a van."

"So, you don't know if it was new or old? Or the color . . . ?"

"It was sorta like . . ." Max appeared to be giving consideration to the van for the first time. "Sorta like . . . like Mrs. Alcort's van."

Max turned to look at his mother. "You know, the dark greenish blue one."

"What kind of van does Mrs. Alcort drive?"

"I think it's a Dodge," Mrs. Spinelli replied.

"Max," Kendra asked, "tell me what you saw when you looked across the street after you came out of the video store."

"I saw Ms. Garvey talking to a man."

"What can you tell me about the man? Was he tall? Short?"

"He's already told Chief Ford that the man was—" Mrs. Spinelli started before Adam stopped her.

"Let him tell Kendra."

"Was he as tall as Agent Stark?" Kendra asked.

"Uh-uh. Not near that tall."

"More like Chief Ford?" Kendra nodded to the door, outside of which the chief lurked. Chief Ford topped the chart at a solid five feet eight or nine.

"No, more like . . ." Max gave it considerable thought. "More like my dad."

"How tall is your husband, Mrs. Spinelli?"

"Just about six feet," she told Kendra.

"And what else did you notice about the man, Max?"

"Nothing. I wasn't close enough to really see him."

Kendra slid the artist's sketch out from the file, and pretended to study it. Finally, she said, "Does this look anything like the man you saw that night, Max?"

"I didn't see him close enough to say," Max told her. "I told him—the guy who drew that picture— when he was showing me faces. I told him that I didn't really know what the man looked like up close."

"Thank you, Max. You've been a very big help to me."

"But I haven't told you anything. I didn't really see him."

"Exactly." Kendra returned the sketch to the file. "Thank you, Mrs. Spinelli, for your time. And for bringing Max in."

Adam stood and took two cards from his wallet. One he handed to Max's mother.

"You ever want a tour of FBI headquarters, Max, you give me a call." Adam handed the other card to Max.

"Wow. Thanks!" Max took the card and studied it. "Wow, this says you're a *special* agent."

"That's right, son."

"Cool." Max tucked the card into his jacket pocket.

"Thanks again, Mrs. Spinelli." Adam opened the door for mother and son to leave, then paused and asked, "Max, had you ever seen that van before?"

"I don't know. Maybe at the Boys Club field. I think it might have been there on Sunday during the soccer tournament. At first I thought it was Mrs. Alcort's, 'cause it's sort of the same, but then I remembered that

the Alcorts went to Virginia because Jake's grandmother died."

"By Sunday, you mean the Sunday before the day you
saw Ms. Garvey with the man in front of Fanning's?"

"Yeah."

"Did you just see it that one time?"

"That's the only time I remember."

"Was Ms. Garvey at that game, Max?" Kendra
asked.

"Sure. Ms. Garvey was at all the games. She always
brought us snacks and stuff."

"Kathleen was one of the team mothers," Mrs.
Spinelli explained.

"Thanks, Max. If you think of anything else, would
you give me a call at the number on that card?"

"Sure."

Mother and son passed through the door into the
hallway, and Adam closed the door behind them before Chief Ford could enter.

"What do you think?" Adam asked Kendra.

"I think our sketch is a bit of a stretch on someone's
part. Of course, Mrs. Sims may have gotten a better
look at your suspect than Max did."

Adam was shuffling through the file that the chief
had given him earlier.

"I don't see a damned thing in here about the van
being at the soccer field on Sunday," he frowned.

"That's because it takes a *special* agent from the FBI
to ask all the right questions."

"All right, all right." Adam laughed good-naturedly.
"So I didn't tell Max that field agents are *special*
agents."

The door opened and Chief Ford stepped into the room.

"Was Max able to help you?" he asked.

"He helped," Kendra told him.

"Good, good. Are you ready for me to bring in Mrs. Sims, Ms. Smith?"

"Is she here?"

"Oh, she's been here for about twenty minutes or so. I didn't figure you'd be with Max for so long, so I told her to come in at ten-thirty."

"Bring her in then." Adam nodded.

Aretha Sims was a tiny, birdlike woman in her seventies. White-haired and with the small bones of a woman who has shrunken past her prime, her eyes were still lively and her gaze direct. She toddled into the room in her Sunday-best low-heeled shoes and introduced herself in a manner that told both Kendra and Adam that she was a woman who was accustomed to being *regarded*.

"Please, sit here, next to me." Adam pulled the chair out for her, and the elderly Mrs. Sims sat upon it delicately.

"Thank you, Agent Stark." She looked at Kendra and said, "You know, I've already spoken with the chief and with that other artist fellow they had here from the county. He drew a nice picture."

"Yes. I've seen it." Kendra folded her hands in front of her.

Mrs. Sims looked around the table. "Aren't you going to show me any books?"

"No, I'm afraid I don't work with visual aids."

"Then how can I pick him out?" Mrs. Sims's hands fluttered slightly.

"You will just describe to me what you saw."

"Just like that?" Mrs. Sims frowned.

"Yes. Just like that."

"Well, it doesn't seem very official." The elderly woman looked over her glasses at Kendra. "Are you sure you're with the FBI?"

"Actually, Mrs. Sims, I'm with the FBI," Adam told her. "Ms. Smith is a well-known compositor who often works along with the FBI. When we are lucky enough to get her."

Mrs. Sims looked at Kendra with no little bit of skepticism.

"You remember the case of the California carjacker?" Adam asked in confidential tones.

"Oh, my, yes. That woman with the gun who forced all those people to give up their cars? She went all the way from San Diego to Seattle." Mrs. Sims gave a shiver. "Shot those people, every one of them, right in the face. Made a body scared to death to drive to the grocery store."

"Ms. Smith was the artist who drew the sketch that led to the capture of the carjacker."

"You don't say?" Mrs. Sims regarded Kendra in a new light.

"If it wasn't for her, Carol Billingsly would still be out there, stealing cars and shooting people." Adam leaned close to Mrs. Sims. "Ms. Smith is the best at what she does. That's why the FBI called her in to work on this case."

"Oh, wait till I get home to tell Amelia." She looked across the table at Kendra. "That's my sister, Amelia."

"Was Amelia with you the night you saw Kathleen Garvey speaking with the man on the sidewalk outside Fanning's store?"

"No, no, Ms. Smith. She was at home. Amelia had taken a fall out in the garden a few weeks before—those pesky moles had the ground all uneven. She broke her ankle. I was on my way to the pharmacy to pick up a renewal of one of her prescriptions. Of course, I don't usually venture out after dark—my eyes aren't so good in the dark anymore—but the car had spent the whole day down at the Sunoco station having new tires put on, and they didn't get it back to me till almost six, and 'Melia was in such pain, well, I thought, just this one time, I could drive down to town by myself at night."

"Where did you park, Mrs. Sims?"

"Why, Agent Stark, I parked right out in front of Evans's, just like I always do. Mr. Evans had the package all ready for me and he was apologizing all over the place that he didn't have anyone working that night who could deliver the prescription—usually has that Parsons boy driving for him, but he was down with the flu and Mr. Evans doesn't close up at night till nine, which is way too late because we are in bed by nine every night, don't 'cha know?"

Mrs. Sims paused to take a breath and Adam seized the opportunity to continue his interrogation.

"The pharmacy is right next to Fanning's?"

"Yes. It sits right there in the middle of the block.

There's a dress shop on the other side, then Davis's Market."

"The police report says you walked past Ms. Garvey that night."

"It wasn't exactly *past* her. My car was parked at the curb, maybe two cars down from where she stood with that man, and she turned and waved to me when she saw me."

"So you didn't walk by where she was standing, facing her?"

"No, I was more to her side, on the left."

"And did the man turn when she did?"

"No." She paused, then said, "Well, not completely. He turned just a little to the side."

"So you only saw his profile."

"Yes. That's right."

"Was he wearing a hat?" Kendra's hands reached for her sketch pad and pencil though her eyes never left Mrs. Sims's face. "Glasses?"

"No hat, but he did have dark glasses. They covered his eyes all the way down to part of his cheeks. And he seemed to have a lot of hair. It sort of poufed out in the front." The woman held her hands near her forehead to demonstrate.

"Like curls, maybe?" Kendra's right hand moved across the paper.

"Maybe."

"What was the first thing you noticed about his profile, Mrs. Sims?"

"That he looked like my brother, Andrew." A hand flew to her mouth. "No, no, not that he *looked* like Andrew, but there was something about the way his nose . . ." Her fingers fluttered about her own nose while she searched for words. "It sort of tipped at the end."

"Turned up a little?" Kendra asked. "Or a lot?"

"Just a bit, there at the end."

"Like this?" Kendra showed her what she had drawn.

"My, you are fast," Mrs. Sims said admiringly as she studied the sketch. "Maybe a tad longer . . . yes, yes, like that."

"Do you remember what he was wearing?"

"A jacket of some sort, maybe. Oh, truly, I don't remember. I was unlocking my car, you see, and I was in a hurry to get back home, so I didn't really pay him much mind. I'm sorry. I wish I could help."

"You have helped. You've helped a great deal. Thank you for coming in, Mrs. Sims. We appreciate your time."

"I'm sorry I didn't pay closer attention." Mrs. Sims rose as Adam helped her with her chair. "Kathleen Garvey's grandmother was a dear, dear friend of mine. If I had known . . ."

"There was no way that you could have." Kendra stood and took the woman's hands. "There was no reason for you to think that this man was going to harm her."

"Yes, well." The woman took a tissue from her worn leather purse and blew her nose. "I hope you find him, Agent Stark. I hope the FBI finds him and shoots him, that's what I hope."

"We'll do our best to find him, Mrs. Sims." Adam walked her to the door and opened it, as he had for the

Spinellis. His hand on her elbow was a gentle touch, his voice low as he walked her into the hallway.

"Okay, so you want to tell me what that artist was thinking when he sketched that face?" Adam said when he returned to the room.

"Beats me." Kendra shook her head. "Max admitted he couldn't see the man, and Mrs. Sims only saw him from the side from a couple of car lengths away."

"Then how did anyone manage to come up with a full frontal sketch?" Adam folded his arms across his chest.

"That would appear to be the question for the day." Kendra tucked her drawing into the folder. "Perhaps a chat with Chief Ford will enlighten us."

Chatting with Chief Ford brought little to the table, except to confirm that the artist, who had taken several art classes at the local college, had brought several books with him. Adam had determined that there were witnesses in the third and most recent case, and Kendra was hopeful that interviews with them would add to her own sketch, maybe complete it. As it was, she left the Deal police station fearing that the drawing that had been circulated throughout the media would, in the end, prove to look nothing like the object of their search. Assuming, of course, that law enforcement caught him.

"One thing I'm sure of," Kendra told Adam as they walked to his car, "is that wherever he is, he's laughing his ass off. And he's probably feeling pretty cocky right about now."

"You mean because he knows he'll never be identified from that sketch?"

"The drawing shows the man from the front, which of course means that you don't see that he has a little ski jump at the tip of his nose. Even if other witnesses had seen him from the front, why was there no sketch done from the side? I just don't understand what this artist thought he was doing, throwing stuff like that to the newspapers. Not that I think he intentionally released a bad sketch, or that he intended to mislead anyone. But for my money, those damned visual aids serve no purpose except to confuse the witness."

"Maybe sometimes . . ."

"I don't use them. Ever. Look, the witness is the only one who knows what he or she saw. His or her memory is evidence. You don't tamper with evidence." She swung her bag over her shoulder, her brow furrowed. "Once you've spread out a bunch of mug shots or catalogs filled with facial features in front of a witness, you've already created a certain amount of confusion in his or her mind. After looking at hundreds of pairs of eyes, do you really think a person can then accurately describe the shape, the color, the set of the eyes they actually *saw*?"

They had reached the car and Adam had opened the trunk, setting her briefcase alongside his own.

"Would you mind if I put the top down?" he asked as he removed the jacket of his obligatory dark suit.

Kendra shook her head. "It'll feel good, maybe help clear my head a little."

"I apologize," she said as she got into the car. "As

you can probably tell, this kind of carelessness always sets me off."

"Ummm. I seem to recall that," he said as he started the engine. "I seem to recall another case, in Virginia, a few years back."

"Oh, don't even remind me," she said through gritted teeth. "That was the most blatant case of . . . I don't even know what to call it. Ineptitude?"

"You were pretty hot, as I remember."

"You know what made me angriest about that sketch? It wasn't necessary to have done it. There was a witness who clearly saw the suspect's face. *Clearly* saw it, as clearly as I can see you. So why use visual aids, when the best visual is right there? The witness's memory."

"Sometimes the emotions of the witness play into it."

"That's exactly why it's important not to flood the person's mind with too many images. The more acute the trauma, the more the witness might sometimes want to forget what he or she has seen. By giving the witness so many different features to look at, you've created a situation where you are offering an alternative, one that he or she may grab on to, to replace one image with another."

"You mean create a face that's inaccurate so the witness doesn't have to 'see' the real suspect again."

"I don't think anyone consciously does that, but yes, I think that's exactly what happens. It's a means of banishing the bad memory and replacing it with something that isn't quite real, and therefore less threatening."

"Which I guess explains why there are so many

composites floating around that ultimately are found to look so little like the criminal."

"That's my theory." She leaned back in the seat as Adam accelerated. "I don't mean to imply that there's no one out there who does this the right way. There's a woman on the West Coast who has literally written the book on this subject and has raised the art of compositing to a whole new level. And there are plenty of fine artists who insist on doing their own interviewing and who do not use mug shots and who are really careful about what they do. I'm sure that the person who drew that sketch of the man you're looking for didn't set out to do a bad job. But he made mistakes, and his mistakes may have cost the investigation. And may end up costing another young woman her life if he gets the urge to kill again soon."

They rode in silence, both of them knowing that it really wasn't a matter of if, but when.

Finally, Kendra spoke up.

"And that is why I think we need to speak with the witnesses from this third murder before anyone else can shove photographs or sketches under their noses, ask them leading questions, and otherwise distort their memories of what they really saw."

"I've already called our agents on the scene and instructed them not to let anyone get to the witnesses until we have an opportunity to speak with them."

"What time are we expected?"

"I told the chief we'd be there between three and four," Adam said as he picked up Route 30 and headed east. "Which means we'll have time to stop and grab a late lunch. Breakfast was a long, long time ago, and once we hit Walnut Crossing, we'll be tied up for hours."

"We passed a couple of fast-food restaurants on the way out of Deal."

Adam looked at her as if she'd sprouted fangs.

"You don't still eat that stuff, do you?"

"You mean, salty fries, fried chicken . . ."

"And here I thought you'd mended your ways." Adam shook his head. "After that homemade soup you served me last night, I figured you'd had an epiphany."

"Sorry to disappoint you, but the soup was made by my friend, Selena. Lola's owner and organic from the ground up, if you'll pardon the expression."

"Maybe you could learn a thing or two from her."

"Oh, right. How could I forget?" She grinned at him across the console. "Mr. Let-nothing-impure-pass-my-lips."

"Exactly." He nodded, amused in spite of himself. "That stuff you eat will kill you. Seriously. Fat. Sodium. High cholesterol. And God knows what kind of meat those fast-food places really use."

"Oh, but those three eggs you had this morning were okay, right? And all that butter you put on your toast?"

"There's nothing wrong with eggs. And butter won't hurt you. Margarine, on the other hand, is pure yellow death." Adam changed lanes to pass the car in front of them. "I'm surprised that a smart woman like you doesn't keep up with this stuff. That you prefer to remain unenlightened."

"You mean I don't subscribe to all those alternative health journals that you used to read."

"Still do. And may I add that I believe I'm a better person—a *healthier* person—for it."

"I guess you keep in shape lugging around all those vitamin bottles that I saw you stashing in your briefcase after breakfast this morning."

"Absolutely." He glanced in the rearview mirror, then pulled back into the right lane. "There's a restaurant up here that looks like it might do. There on the right. Let's give it a try."

"But it's part of a chain." She feigned horror. "Who knows where they get their meat from?"

"If it worries you, order a salad." He smiled. "Foreign as the concept might be to make a meal out of a bowl of greens with no chemical aftertaste."

Kendra recalled the last restaurant meal she'd had with Adam. It had been two nights before her mother's death.

"I think I'll have a BLT—heavy on the bacon, heavy on the mayo—and a diet cola."

"Ugh," he muttered something under his breath— Kendra thought she heard the words *pig fat* and *unnatural*—as he parked the car close enough to the front door that he could keep an eye on it. "I'd hate to see what your arteries look like."

"Smoking or non?" The hostess met them at the door with a smile.

"Non," Adam replied, then hesitated. Turning to Kendra, he asked, tongue-in-cheek, "Unless you want to sit in smoking?"

Kendra rolled her eyes at him. "I may eat junk food, but I draw the line at cigarettes."

"Nonsmoking," he nodded to the waitress, who gestured for them to follow her.

They slid into a booth that faced the front of the restaurant, where Adam could happily keep an eye on his car.

"Why did you ask if I wanted to sit in smoking?" Kendra asked after they had made their selections and ordered. "You know I don't smoke."

"That's funny," Adam replied, "I could have sworn I smelled pipe smoke last night."

"Where?" She leaned back to permit the waitress to pour their water.

"In the study. But it's okay, you don't have to hide the fact that you smoke . . . or that you entertain men who do."

"I don't smoke. And I haven't had a man in my house since . . . well, I guess since I moved back. Unless you count Oliver Webb, who's seventy-something, or Father Tim, whose interest in me is strictly as a supporter of his homeless shelter."

"Why the smell of tobacco, then?" Adam did his best to mask his relief that there'd been no entertaining in the study other than himself.

"My dad smoked a pipe."

"Your dad?" His eyebrows raised. "But I thought your dad has been dead for . . ."

"Seventeen years."

"Are you saying that your father has . . . stayed on in the house?"

"No, no," she laughed. "It's not a ghost. But for

some reason, every once in a while, you get a whiff of tobacco in that room. Sometimes I can't tell if I really smell it or if it's just a memory. A trace of him. I find it comforting."

He nodded thoughtfully. If believing that a bit of her father had stayed within the house gave her comfort, what was the harm? He knew what it was like to bury a much loved parent, and as she'd already buried everyone she'd loved, Adam figured she was entitled to this bit of fancy.

"A trace of your dad's scent left behind. A memory of sorts."

"Yes, that's what I think. Now," she brushed the subject aside and picked up a triangle of her club sandwich, "how do you think this guy is getting around as easily as he is?"

CHAPTER
FOUR

Adam stepped aside to admit Kendra into the sitting area of his hotel room. It was a little past two in the morning and they'd just returned from Walnut Crossing, where they'd spent the past nine hours speaking with the witnesses who had been the last to see Karen Meyer alive. As soon as they could, they would move on to Windsorville, to speak with possible witnesses relating to the disappearance of Amy Tilden. Keyed up after hours of interviews, neither of them could sleep.

Kendra took a seat on one end of the sofa, pulled a sheaf of notes out of her folder and asked, "What did you think of the police investigation in Walnut Crossing?"

Adam sat on the other end of the sofa, his long body angled to face her.

"I thought they did a good job, if not a great one. Which is what I told Mancini when I called in earlier this evening. By the way, he now has several more agents working with the state police to track the van and assist with the processing of the prints they found on some of the debris in the Dumpster where they found Kathleen Garvey's body."

"So sad. All Karen Meyer had done was go to a concert in the town square so that she could be there when her daughter played in the school band for the first time, then stayed to watch her son's ball game. Those simple, selfless acts of a loving mother somehow put her in the path of a killer."

"Founder's Day." Adam pulled the police report from the folder and skimmed over it, hoping to find something they might have missed. "The entire town was there."

"The entire town, plus one," she said pointedly. "One with a dark van parked at the farthest end of the lot, where the park begins. The park Karen Meyer would walk through to get home."

"Doesn't it ever strike you how crazy it all is? How one small thing—one tiny, random decision—can end up making the difference between life and death?" Adam said. "So many 'if only's.' If only one of her children had gone with her. If only she'd accepted the ride home that her neighbors offered. If only she'd walked home on the main streets, or left earlier, instead of choosing to stay to see her son's game."

"No question it's the same guy?"

"Not in my mind. We'll know for sure once the DNA matches up, but in my mind it's a given. Tossed by the side of the road where she'd be certain to be found." Adam paused, then added, "Only thing different with Karen Meyer is that her clothes were damp, which has yet to be explained, since it hasn't rained here in a week. But I'd bet everything I have that he's been watching her, just waiting for the most opportune time.

"And watched her closely enough that he knew that whenever she walked home from town, she took a shortcut through the park. I think he was waiting for her. But if she hadn't gone through the park that night, he'd have been waiting for her somewhere else at some other time. He wanted her. I think he just waited for her in the woods."

"Like the Big Bad Wolf," Kendra noted. "What do you think the autopsy will show?"

"Strangulation. He was a lot rougher with Karen than he'd been with the other two, but I think it was a strong emotion that he hadn't planned on—anger, most likely—that drove him to want to hurt her."

"Because she fought him?"

"I'm thinking that they'll find traces of skin and blood under her nails, which the others did not have. Which leads to the question of why she would have been able to fight him, even unsuccessfully, when the other two showed no sign of a struggle." Adam leaned forward and sorted through a stack of photographs that he'd taken from the folder marked TILDEN in wide black letters. "A question to which I believe I have the answer. . . ."

When he found the photo he was looking for, he pushed it to the center of the table, his jaw set squarely. Amy Tilden's body lay on the shoulder of the road, surrounded by litter. From the folder marked GARVEY he removed another set of photos from which he pulled out several close-up shots. He placed them side by side on the table, facing Kendra.

"You're looking at those little marks on their arms. Any idea what might have made them?"

"Stun gun."

"A stun gun? You think he—"

"Stunned his victims? Yes, so they could be easily and quietly tucked into the van. They work by giving an electrical charge to the victim. If the charge is strong enough, it can knock a grown man to his knees, but not necessarily knock him out. So you can be rendered totally helpless but be conscious, or semiconscious, depending on how high the current is. The current runs between two prongs that hold the electrodes, and if the prongs come in contact with the skin, they can leave small marks that look like burns. Like these on the backs of our victims' arms." He shuffled through the stack of photographs. "Which explains why neither Kathleen Garvey nor Amy Tilden appeared to have struggled. Of course, we'll have to wait until the Meyer autopsy is finished to see if there are similar marks on her."

"But there won't be, will there? That's why he roughed her up so badly. He hadn't been able to stun her."

"My guess is that he might have taken her by surprise, and she could have reacted before he did."

"You mean, kicked him or punched him . . ."

". . . or possibly knocked the stun gun out of the way. He isn't used to having to fight for what he wants. He's been taking the easy way, and it's been working quite nicely for him up until now."

"I guess that could have made him angry enough to

work her over the way he did." Kendra sighed. "Sometimes I hate this job."

"Why do it, then? Don't you have a degree in art history and a minor in communications?"

"I'm lucky. I've always had a talent for drawing faces. I took some studio courses when I was in college, and even flirted with the idea of becoming a painter for a time."

"Then surely there are other ways for you to make a living."

"Yes, but nothing that would give me the same sense of satisfaction I get when a sketch I've made results in a good arrest. I remember very clearly how I felt when my brother's murderer was brought to trial and was convicted. Sentencing Webster to life in prison would not bring back Ian and Zach. But at least their killer would pay a price for what he'd done to them. To what he'd done to the people who loved them. Every victim deserves justice," she said quietly. "Everyone who has lost someone they loved deserves to have all the doors closed behind them, so that they can get on with the rest of their lives. Everyone deserves closure. This is the only way I know to help others to find it."

Closure of a kind, Adam knew, that had eluded Kendra for years.

"My mother went to her grave not having found my brother's body. We never knew what really happened to him. How he died, or where. A man had been tried and convicted of his murder, but he never admitted a thing, never gave us a thing." She looked up at Adam from across the table. "One of the reasons why I've never believed she committed suicide. She wouldn't have chosen to leave this life while his body was still out there."

"What were the others?"

"The others?"

"The other reasons."

"She wouldn't have left me. My mother and I were very close. She was my best friend. We had gone through so much together. My father's illness . . . his death . . . my brother's murder, the trial . . ." Kendra swallowed hard. "She used to say that we were survivors, that our grief bound us as much as our love and our blood. There is no way in hell she would have chosen to leave me behind to deal with the pain of losing her. She and I had been to that well too many times together. She would never have made me go alone. She never would have taken her life and left me to wonder why."

"What do you think happened, then?"

Kendra shrugged.

"I have no idea. I was hoping the police could tell me. That was their job, to study the evidence, then tell me what happened."

"I'm sure they believed they did that, Kendra."

"They were wrong," she snapped. "She wouldn't have left me, wouldn't have left her husband. She and Philip were very happy together. He was the one who encouraged her to run for office—financed her campaigns and pulled in every old political favor he could think of to help her get elected. Not because she was his *wife*, but because he *believed* in her." Kendra shook her head. "After so many years without my father, so many years of believing that the best was in the past, she'd finally met a man who made her believe in the future, to believe in herself and her ability to do great things. There was nothing that Philip wouldn't have done for her—nor her for him. She wouldn't have left him. Wouldn't have left me. I tried to make the police understand that. . . ."

"But even the FBI came up cold, Kendra," he reminded her gently. "And you know, better than I, that your stepfather's connections ensured that the best the Bureau had had looked into her death."

"They missed something. They all did," she insisted. "There was no note, Adam. If my mother killed herself—put a gun to her head and pulled the trigger—she would have written a note first. To me. To her husband. But there was nothing."

"Nothing found."

She looked at him sharply.

"There was nothing *found* because there was nothing *to be* found. My mother was not a quitter. If you'd known her, you'd have known that taking her own life would never have been an option for her. She would have considered it cowardly. After all the terrible times she survived in her life, why, when things were so wonderful, would she have killed herself?"

"And what does your stepfather think?"

"He agrees with me completely, of course. Neither of us has ever accepted the official version. Neither of us ever will."

"And assuming that you're right, what are your chances of ever finding out what really happened that night?"

"Less than a snowball's chance in hell. Philip and I both know that." She picked at a cuticle so that she had someplace to look other than at Adam. She didn't want to see what was in his eyes. She suspected that he believed that she—and Philip, too, most likely—was in total denial where her mother was concerned. It was a conversation she did not want to have with him.

"Why these women, Adam?" she asked, changing the subject. "Why did he choose them?"

"Well, let's look at what we learned about them today. Mancini always says you have to study the victim to find the killer. We know that Amy Tilden had arrived late to school for Home and School night because her son had a soccer game and her youngest daughter had Brownies that afternoon. She'd watched the game, picked up her daughter, then headed home for dinner. According to the statement of the next-door neighbor, with whom she shared a driveway, Amy and the kids arrived at the house right around six-fifteen and Amy's ex-husband, Stan, arrived shortly thereafter."

"Ex-husband?"

"He came over to watch the kids while Amy went back to school. He said he had dinner with them and she left at seven. He was the one who called the police when she didn't return home."

"How'd she do that? Get everyone fed and be back out the door in less than an hour?" Kendra frowned. "He bring a pizza home with him?"

"Nope. The extremely efficient Amy Tilden apparently had put something in her slow cooker before she left for work in the morning. By the time she left her home after dinner to go back to school, she had the dishes in the dishwasher and all three kids lined up doing their homework."

"The Amy Tildens of the world humble me with their ability to organize, to keep everyone's life in order. Why would someone want to harm a woman like that? And not just harm her, but humiliate her by tossing her onto the road like a piece of litter? What was he trying to prove?"

"When we figure that out, we'll be close to finding him. Though I suspect it's tied into the manner in which he rapes. Except for Karen Meyer, he has exhibited surprisingly little violence for so violent an act. Almost as if the rapes, too, were meant to prove a point. To humiliate and shame these women, to show his power over them."

"Wouldn't it take a great deal of control to commit a rape in such a way?"

"Absolutely, and there's no question that he's a very controlled individual. He wants a minimum of resistance, hence the stun gun. Wants to exercise his power and make certain that his victims know that he holds the power." Adam hesitated, then added, "Except, again, for Karen Meyer, where things apparently did not go according to plan. Now, do you have a copy of the statement from the guy who was parked next to the Tilden van in the lot behind the school the night Amy disappeared?"

"Yes. Jack Wilson. Forty-three years old, turkey farmer." Kendra shuffled through her notes. "He was late arriving at school to meet with his son's teacher, couldn't find a spot in the visitors' lot so he parked in the employee lot."

"And just happened to be returning to his car after his appointment in time to see a man coming from around the back of the dark van that was parked on the other side of Amy's car."

"And just happened to get a glimpse of him in his headlights before he hopped into the driver's side." Kendra read her notes aloud. "Longish dark hair, curly in the front . . . a nose he described as a 'ski jump' . . ." She glanced up at Adam. "Which isn't a terribly unusual feature, by the way. All the Smith men had one."

She studied the sketch she'd made as she slipped off her shoes and pulled her legs up onto the sofa.

"Mr. Wilson actually got a better look at our suspect than anyone so far, but he was out of town when the investigation started and only spoke to the police on Thursday afternoon, when he returned. I think that's one reason why the original sketch is so far off the mark," Kendra murmured. "They didn't know they had a good witness."

"And then we had those kids come forward—the boys who played on the opposing soccer team that afternoon—to report that a dark van had been parked near their bus at the field."

"It's too bad the boys didn't get a better look at the driver."

"Well, their general description matched Max Spinelli's. About six feet tall, dark hair."

"Which probably describes about half the men in Windsorville."

Kendra lined up the photos of the three victims side by side on the table in front of them.

"But why these women?" Adam frowned. "So often, you see serial killers targeting prostitutes. But these women are about as far from being hookers as you can get. Devoted mothers. Single women, all of whom worked, contributed to their communities, were totally involved in their kids' activities. The ultimate soccer moms. None of them women whose lives should have ended this way."

"No one's should." Kendra stared at the photos. "Do you think their physical appearance was a factor in their being chosen as victims?"

"You mean because they are all tall, slender, and blond?" Adam nodded. "Hard to believe that could be a coincidence, isn't it?"

He slid the photos into a small stack, like a deck of playing cards.

"Miranda Cahill is joining the investigation," he told Kendra. "She should be here by tomorrow afternoon at the latest."

"Is she the profiler—excuse me, the criminal investigative analyst—you spoke of earlier?"

"No. That's Anne Marie McCall. Miranda's joining the investigation to help with the interviewing process; specifically, to interview the families. One thing we're looking to determine is whether these women knew each other or were connected in some way. I'll be interested in seeing what she comes up with."

"So will I." Kendra leaned back against the sofa, her eyes half-closed with fatigue. "She'll want to take the sketch. Maybe someone will recognize him."

"I'm one step ahead of you," Adam said as he returned the photographs to their respective folders. "I also want to speak with the state police about replacing that first sketch that was circulated with the one you did this evening."

When she did not respond, he turned back to her, and found her head resting against the back of the sofa. Her eyes were closed and her breathing rhythmic, her face soft with sleep.

"Kendra?" he asked softly.

Her eyes flickered slightly beneath the lids but did not open.

Adam went into the bedroom and returned with a blanket he'd taken from the bed and one of the pillows. He spread the blanket over her carefully and tucked the pillow under her head, then turned off the light. He put the safety chain on the door, and went back into the other room to go to sleep.

Kendra awoke in the night, mildly disoriented and more than a bit chagrined to find that she'd fallen asleep in Adam's room rather than her own.

"Oh, hell," she muttered as she struggled to free herself from the blanket that she'd wrapped partially around her midsection as she slept.

Stumbling to the small desk that sat along the far wall, she peered at the phone for the read-out of the time. Three forty-seven A.M. She wondered how long she'd been asleep.

Berating herself for dozing off in the middle of a conversation, Kendra folded the blanket neatly and left it on the sofa. In the dark, she paused, debating whether or not to turn on the light so that she could gather her notes and whatever else she had left on the coffee table. From the next room, Adam's breathing was rhythmic, steady. Turning on the light could awaken him, something she wanted to avoid at all costs. It was bad enough she'd fallen asleep when she did. Advertising that she was sneaking back to her own room in the wee hours would only embarrass her more. She stood next to the sofa and allowed her toes to search for her shoes. Finding them, she slipped them on, then quietly walked to the door, unlatched it, and stepped out into the hush of the hallway.

It was hard to believe that people were sleeping behind the doors that lined the hall, the floor was so quiet. She found her room, six doors down from Adam's, and as carefully as she could, slid the card in the lock to open the door. Closing it behind her, she set the safety lock and turned on the light switch. The light in the bathroom to her left came on, giving her enough visibility to find her way to her bed. Stripping off her clothes and searching through her suitcase for a nightshirt, she reached for the phone to call the desk clerk to request an early wake-up call. Knowing that Adam would want to get an early start, and still feeling sheepish about falling asleep in his room, she reached for the phone on the table next to her bed.

It was then that she noticed the message light was blinking.

Adam was the only person who knew she was here. Had he called her room after she'd fallen asleep to leave some smart-mouthed message for her to find when she returned? She wouldn't put it past him.

She lifted the receiver and pushed the button to retrieve the message.

"Hi," a male voice greeted her cheerfully.

Definitely not Adam.

"Heard you were in town and, well, I just couldn't resist giving you a ring. It's sure been a long time, hasn't it? Sorry we won't be able to get together just yet—you know, places to go, people to see. But you can expect to hear from me again. I will be in touch. You can bet your life on it."

Kendra frowned and hung up the phone. Obviously the call had been intended for someone else and had been mistakenly directed to her room. She called the desk and requested a six-fifteen wake-up call, ordered coffee to be delivered at six-thirty, then, remembering the message, said, "Oh, by the way. There was a message on my phone that should have gone to another room."

"Which other room?" the desk clerk asked.

"I don't know which other room. A man left a message that was clearly intended for someone else. I have no idea who he was or whose room he thought he had reached, but the message wasn't for me."

"Hold on, please."

Kendra yawned, sorry she'd even brought it up. She rested the phone between her cheek and her shoulder while she turned down the bed, then sat at the edge of the mattress, wanting nothing more than to fall straight back onto the pillow and return to sleep.

"Ms. Smith, there's no record of an incoming call being placed to your room."

"How is that possible? I just listened to the message. . . ."

"The call must have been made from inside the hotel."

"Oh." Kendra's tired brain pondered momentarily, then gave up. "Well, in that case, I suppose the two parties could have already met up. Thanks."

Kendra turned off all but the small light in the bathroom, then dropped into bed, grateful to stretch out her legs. The call forgotten, she was sound asleep almost as soon as her head touched the pillow.

CHAPTER
FIVE

"How many do we have?" Kendra looked across the conference table in the State Police Barracks at Lieutenant Al Barker, who'd been instrumental in providing copies of the most up-to-the-minute details of the investigation into the death of Karen Meyer. "How many witnesses actually saw the suspect?"

"Well, there were seven people who stepped forward, but only two actually gave what appears to be a credible account." Barker leaned forward, resting his forearms on the table. "Caucasian male, approximately six feet tall, early to mid-twenties. Dark hair, dark glasses, dark clothing, dark van. Nothing that we didn't already have from the priors."

"I'll need to speak with them individually," a frustrated Kendra told him, wondering what had happened to Adam's directive that no one speak with the witnesses. Lieutenant Barker apparently thought it applied to everyone except him.

"We're having a list typed up for you and will bring in whomever you need." Barker paused, then added, "We'd like to run that sketch of yours in tomorrow morning's paper."

"If it holds up against the witnesses, it's yours."

Adam entered the room accompanied by a tall, leggy woman with ice blue eyes and dark hair neatly pulled back from her face and clipped at the nape of her neck.

"You must be Miranda Cahill." Kendra smiled.

"Since we've never met, I'm going out on a limb here and guess that you know my sister." The woman extended her hand to Kendra.

"I know that you and Portia are identical twins, so it sounds silly to even comment on how alike you are, but it is amazing. Even your voices are similar. The two of you must have had some good times when you were younger."

"Actually, we're mirror-image twins. And yes, we did have some fun with it. Still do, actually." Miranda grinned. "Just because we're mature, responsible individuals entrusted by our government to carry guns doesn't mean we're above sometimes impersonating each other when circumstances dictate."

"Well, as one who fell victim to the infamous 'Cahill switch,' I suggest we change the subject." Adam pulled out a chair for Miranda, then one for himself.

"Oh, forgot about that one." Miranda turned to Lieutenant Barker and explained, "Portia, Adam, and I were at the Academy together."

Lieutenant Barker nodded slowly, contemplating the havoc two beautiful, identical women could create if they set their minds to it.

"Miranda's part of the posse, sent to help us out," Adam explained. "She'll be visiting with the families of the victims over the next few days to see if there are any common threads."

"Kendra." Miranda turned to her. "I've seen your sketch. I'd like to take it with me."

Kendra hesitated. "I'm not certain it's complete."

Adam frowned. "What do you think you're missing? All of the descriptions we've gotten so far have been the same. Dark shock of hair falling over the forehead. Face partially covered by dark glasses. Height, build, age, all the same . . ."

"I guess I was hoping to lock into a few distinguishing facial features." Kendra tapped her pencil on the table.

"You can't draw what no one has seen."

"Well, I keep hoping to find someone who has seen him up close and personal."

"Three did," Lieutenant Barker reminded her. "Part of what we're trying to do here is to prevent him from getting that close to anyone else again."

"All right. But could you not release it publicly until we've spoken with the witnesses here? Someone might give us something that can help me refine the sketch."

"I'll check back with you at the end of the day," Miranda agreed.

Kendra handed over her sketch. "Can you have some copies made?"

"I'll be right back with them." Barker took the drawing that Kendra had completed the day before and left the room.

"I take it there're still no leads?" Miranda asked after the trooper had left the room.

"Nada." Adam shook his head. "But he's sure left his DNA everywhere."

"Now why would he do that?" Miranda pondered. "Why would he be so careless about leaving DNA when he's gone to so much trouble to set up his kills so carefully? From what you've told me, Adam, he's invested a good deal of his time just studying his victims. So why leave behind something that could potentially lead right to his door?"

"Maybe he's confident enough to believe we'll never catch him. If we can't catch him, we can't positively match him to the DNA that's been recovered."

"How often does that happen? That a killer like this is never caught?" Kendra looked up at Adam over the notes she'd taken the day before.

"You would not want to know the answer to that question." Adam looked grim.

"Another thing," Miranda noted, "he's going to have to dump that van soon and look for something else, if he hasn't already done so."

"The state police are, as we speak, responding to a report of an abandoned van about seven miles from here." Adam passed on the information he'd been given.

"Then we can probably expect to hear about another stolen vehicle real soon."

"True enough. He'll need transportation. Unless, of course, he has something hidden away somewhere." Adam considered the possibilities.

"Do you think he's from this area?" Kendra asked.

"He'd almost have to be. If he's not, he's studied it pretty damned thoroughly," Miranda offered. "You know, killers all have a comfort zone. It's pretty clear he's in his here. He'll stay as long as it's comfortable for him."

"Well, since we haven't even come close to him, I doubt he's left the area," Adam noted. "I'd expect him to stick around and watch, see how we're doing in terms of the investigation."

"And keep an eye on his next victim," Kendra said softly.

"Chances are he's already doing that. We just don't know where he'll strike this time." Adam swiveled slightly in his chair. "I think the sooner we get the word out on this guy, the better off everyone will be. Kendra, if your sketch can give one woman a heads up . . ."

"Just give me till this afternoon. Just let me speak with the witnesses who claim to have seen him around the park in Walnut Crossing. If there's nothing new, we'll hand over the sketch for the six o'clock news."

"Fair enough. But I still want Miranda to take this one with her. I think we can trust the sketch to resemble our man closely enough that it might spark some recollection in someone who's seen him. Maybe one of the victim's kids or neighbors might recall having seen him hanging around."

"Since all three of the victims have been single mothers with kids on sports teams, I've asked the locals to give me a list of all those teams, complete with players' and coaches' names and phone numbers, so we can start interviewing them." Adam looked directly at Miranda. "You're going to be a busy girl."

"I'll have help from the locals, plus we have three more agents on board now," she told him.

"And as you identify others who have seen the UNSUB," Adam told her, referring to the as-yet-unknown subject, "we'll bring them in to talk with Kendra. Show her sketch and see if they can add anything. Getting his face out there is one of the best ways I can think of to throw him off schedule."

"Assuming I can come up with an accurate sketch," Kendra agreed. "I almost hate to give Miranda the one I did this afternoon. Maybe it could be more accurate . . ."

"If you need to refine your drawing later, that would be fine. But I think Miranda needs something to work with, and so far, your sketch is all we have. And who knows? Maybe she'll come back to us later today with some good news."

Unfortunately, Miranda's news hadn't been all that good. Other than the previously reported sightings at soccer and baseball games, no family member of any victim had noticed a stranger, or strange events, within weeks or days of the abductions. Even the agents who canvassed the ball fields and tracked down teammates of the murder victims' children had little to add. The ball fields and bleachers were always filled with men the age of the suspect. Many of them were around six feet tall with dark hair and wore baseball caps and dark glasses while watching their kids' games on a sunny day. So far they had nothing that distinguished this tall, dark-haired man from any other.

But while most of the witnesses who met with

Adam and Kendra had nothing new to add, at the end of the day one resident of Walnut Crossing had proved to be the witness they'd all prayed for.

An amateur boxer in his youth, Joe Tursky took pride in the fact that he worked out on a daily basis. Early in the morning, on Founder's Day, Joe had parked his station wagon at the edge of the woods while he and his German shepherd jogged the path that traced along the entire circumference of the park.

"What time had you arrived, do you recall?" Adam had asked.

"It was right around eight in the morning. Before the festivities started. I run that park every day with my dog, usually in the afternoon, but with a dog that big, you know, people get nervous, so on days when I know there's something going on, I try to get out early."

"When you arrived at eight, were there other cars in the parking lot?" Adam continued his questioning.

"Only up in the area toward the square, you know, people setting up for the concerts and that sort of thing, but no one down around the ball fields or the park areas." The middle-aged Tursky shook his head. "Not when I arrived."

"So take us through what happened, what you saw." Adam rolled his chair back from the table to directly face the witness.

"Well, Casper and me—that's my dog, we call him Casper, like the ghost, because he's a white shepherd—anyway, we did our run along the path and stopped halfway at the spring. There's a creek there with a natural spring, water's pure as you can find anywhere.

People come with plastic bottles and fill 'em up to take home. Anyway, I stopped there for a drink, and to let Casper drink, too. It was already getting warm. Then, all of a sudden, Casper goes on the alert, you know what I mean?" Joe Tursky turned to face Kendra. "He just went still as a stone, like he was watching something down the path. And then before I knew it, he just took off. Like a shot."

"He wasn't on a lead?" asked Kendra.

"He had been—you just can't let a dog like that run free—but I'd dropped the lead while we were drinking. So I took off after him, calling him, but he's a lot faster than I am, you know what I mean? You try to keep in shape, but . . ." He shrugged.

"But you caught up with him . . ." Adam gestured for Tursky to continue.

"Yeah, a minute or two later. He was barking his head off. Had some guy backed up against a tree and Casper was barking like nobody's business."

"What did you do?"

"Well, I apologized all over the place—the guy was obviously scared shitless. I grabbed Casper's leash and the guy just took off. White as a sheet, he was, and shaking like a leaf."

"Can you describe him?" Kendra opened the file in front of her so that she, but not Joe Tursky, could see the sketch that lay within.

"Six feet or a little better. Dark hair, curly in the front. Wearing dark jeans, dark shirt, like a polo shirt." Tursky paused to recall.

"Had you seen him before?" Adam exchanged a glance with Kendra. So far it sounded like their man.

"Not before, but I saw him again on the way out of the park. I had Casper on a short lead coming up that last ridge, where all the paths converge, that's where I saw him. I don't know who was more surprised, him or me. He jumped near out of his skin when he saw Casper."

"Mr. Tursky, does this look anything like the man you saw in the park?" Kendra slid a copy of her drawing across the table.

Pulling a worn brown eyeglass case out of the inner pocket of the light jacket that lay across the arm of the chair, Tursky put them on and studied the sketch.

"Yeah, that's him." Tursky nodded.

"Please. It's very important that you look at the sketch very carefully." Kendra tapped the image. "What can you add to it? Where does it seem not quite right?"

Tursky held the drawing up in front of him and stared at it for a long moment.

"The lips are a little too thin, maybe. I think his bottom lip was fuller. And of course, he wasn't wearing these glasses, so his eyes . . ."

"You saw his eyes?" Kendra's head snapped up.

"Well, yeah," Joe Tursky shrugged, "he was lookin' right at me."

"What color, did you notice?" Kendra forced back the rash of questions she was dying to ask, knowing that bombarding the witness with too much all at once could cause him, in the end, to overlook something.

"Dark. Dark brown. Thick lashes. Thick brows."

"Were they close together?"

"Not really." Tursky's own eyebrows knit together as he tried to recall. "Seems they were wide-spaced."

"Shape?"

"Round." The witness nodded. "Round, wide dark eyes."

"Lines around the corners?" Kendra had picked up her sketch pad, the pencil moving across the paper rapidly.

"No, I don't think so. But there were some around the mouth, like a crease here." Tursky drew an imaginary line down the side of his own face, from just to the side of his nose to just past the corner of his mouth.

"Anything else? Anything else you can remember?" The pencil paused. "Scars, a mole . . . anything that would distinguish his face?"

"No. No, I don't remember anything else." Tursky shook his head. "Oh. One thing I did notice that I thought was odd."

"What's that?"

"His clothes were wet. Like he'd been swimming in them."

"Is there a pool or a pond in the area?"

"Just a stream down there at the foot of the path."

"Mr. Tursky, can you approximate his age?" Kendra asked as Adam added to his notes.

"Early to mid-twenties."

"Are you sure there was nothing distinguished about his face?"

"No. I'm not one hundred percent certain. I'll tell ya the truth, the first time I saw him, I was more concerned about getting Casper under control, and the second, I was just surprised to see him. I didn't look for scars or anything like that, if that's what you mean."

"Is this the face?" Kendra showed him the sketch.

"That's amazing." Tursky whistled in admiration. "That's just what he looked like. How can you do that?"

"You're the one who did it, Mr. Tursky, by describing the man so accurately."

"Mr. Tursky," Adam spoke up, "you said you were surprised to see him the second time. Why was that? Because you'd thought he'd left the park?"

"No, because of where he was coming from."

"Where was he coming from?"

"There's an area that's off limits, it's marked off with a chain-link fence. 'Course, the kids do get down there from time to time to party, so I hear, but it's a tough way down and a tough way back up again."

"What's down there?"

"Couple of caves. They flood every time it rains, and since the township doesn't have the manpower to patrol the area, they keep it secured."

"Mr. Tursky, can you take us through the park and show us both places where you saw this man?" Adam asked.

"Sure." Tursky nodded. "Be glad to."

"I'll be right back." Adam rose to leave the room to gather the necessary investigators to search the woods for any trace evidence their suspect may have inadvertently left behind.

"Agent Stark, this is him, isn't it?" Tursky asked as Adam reached the door. "The man who's been killing those girls?"

"We believe it is."

"If I'd known that," Tursky said quietly, "I'd've let Casper have at him."

"That's him?" Lieutenant Barker looked over Kendra's shoulder. "That the son of a bitch we're looking for?"

"That's him." Kendra handed the state trooper the sketch. "All ready to make his debut on the local six o'clock news. Compliments of our new best friend, Joseph Tursky."

"Looks like a cocky bastard, doesn't he?" Barker studied the drawing. "Cocky and full of himself."

"He'd have to be." Adam walked through the open door. "To do what he does, in the manner in which he does it. He'd have to be damned confident. And bold as brass, as my grandmother would say."

"I'll pass this on to the press. A few of the local stations got wind that the FBI was called in and have had vans hanging around the parking lot all day. Let's make it worth their while." The trooper started to excuse himself, sketch in one hand, the other hand smoothing back his hair for the cameras, when he turned back and asked Kendra, "Would you be willing to come out to meet the media with me? Maybe just let me introduce you, show your sketch . . . ?"

"Sure. Just give me a minute."

"I'll meet you out front," Barker said as he left the room.

"What's next?" Kendra asked Adam.

"Well, we're going to be heading out to the park. We'll meet the evidence team down there. There's a lot of ground to cover down there, and only a few hours of daylight left."

"State, local, and federal investigators, I take it."

"As many hands as we can get."

Kendra finished packing her folders into her briefcase and closed the cover with a snap of the lock.

"Kendra, the sketch you did ... it really is remarkable."

"I had good information from a great witness." She smiled as she picked up her purse and slung the wide strap over her shoulder. "Fortunately for us Mr. Tursky has a good memory. Let's see what happens once the sketch is made public. Hopefully someone will recognize him and call in, and you'll find him before he finds another victim."

"Nothing's ever that easy."

"Maybe this time you'll get lucky."

She paused, feeling like the guest whose welcome has just worn out. "I think I'll call for a cab to take me back to the hotel. I know everyone is anxious to get down to the park, and there's really nothing more for me to do here once the press conference is over."

"Why not take my car? I can grab a ride with Barker or Miranda."

"I don't really see any reason for me to stay in Walnut Crossing. My job was to sketch," she reminded him. "I sketched."

Adam stood with his hands on his hips, as if pondering some unexpected bit of news. He hadn't thought about her leaving just yet.

"What if we get another good witness?"

"I don't know what someone else could add to

what Mr. Tursky gave us that would change the sketch. He said there were no distinguishing features. And if something really important came up, I can always come back, you know."

"Yes, but you still have to get home, right? Why not drive my car back to Smith's Forge and I'll pick it up on my way back to Virginia?"

"Then what will you drive while you're here?"

"I'm not worried about getting around."

"I don't know if I'm up to such a racy little number." She crossed her arms over her chest. "It might be too much car for me."

He studied her stance, the amused expression on her face.

"I doubt it." He tossed her the keys. "I seriously doubt it."

CHAPTER
SIX

Kendra left the highway, opting for the back
roads that wound around the hill on which Walnut Crossing was built and led back to the main road
on the far side. She wished she'd asked Adam to show
her how to put the top down, though she suspected it
wouldn't be all that difficult, since it was automatic
and there must be a manual somewhere. But having
the windows down and all that lovely country air
rushing through was just fine. Especially for someone
accustomed to driving a car that had to be coaxed to
go over fifty, and had long ago lost its ability to provide heat, air-conditioning, and music. The Audi could
chew up her old Subaru and spit it out in less than
thirty seconds.

A green station wagon pulled out of the hotel's back
parking lot as Kendra slowed to pull in. The driver
beeped his horn in greeting as he sped past. Kendra
waved idly, with little more than a cursory glance in
his direction.

"Guess he's admiring my wheels," Kendra said under her breath as she parked as close to the front door
as she could.

"And such nice wheels, they are." She nodded while she locked the door, then stepped back to admire the saucy car. "Very, very nice. Though sadly not mine. I am tempted. I have to admit."

In spite of the grind of the past few days, she felt . . . lighter, might be the best way to describe it, she thought as she got into the elevator and pushed the button for the fifth floor. Could be the car.

Could also be the car's owner.

Kendra was pondering this as she unlocked the door to her room and dropped her briefcase in front of the closet, recalling her brief relationship with Adam four years ago and what had happened to bring it to an end before it even had a chance to begin.

Her mother's death had happened, for one thing.

Greg Carson had happened, for another.

Kendra had only recently begun to acknowledge the relationship between the two.

In the aftermath of her mother's death, Kendra had been totally unanchored, numb with grief, with only the haziest memory of her mother's funeral and none whatsoever of going to the cemetery, of placing flowers on her mother's coffin.

For weeks after, Kendra had floated through an unreal landscape that was barren and unfamiliar. Greg, her college boyfriend, had brought the known, the dependable, back into her unstable life. An assistant in the local district attorney's office, Greg had heard about Elisa Smith-Norton's suicide at almost the same time that Kendra was being notified. He'd rushed to the senator's home, and finding that Kendra was living in Smith's Forge, drove there himself to bring her back to

Princeton so she would not have to be alone through the ordeal until her stepfather arrived. Greg helped them to deal with the funeral home, the press, and the florist, and made phone calls to family and friends on her behalf. He'd held her hand in the receiving line at the funeral home and offered his shoulder as often as she needed it. When a mere six weeks later he'd been offered the opportunity to start a firm with a class-mate from law school, only the thought of leaving Kendra alone made him think twice about moving to Washington state. His solution was to offer marriage. Kendra, still shell-shocked, had said yes.

The wedding had been small and intimate, attended only by a few close friends and the groom's family. Kendra's reluctant stepfather had given her away. While he liked Greg and held him in high regard, Philip Nor-ton had made no secret of the fact that he believed the marriage was a mistake, that Kendra was in no condi-tion to make such an important decision. He feared that, feeling adrift, Kendra reached out for whatever mooring she could find. Time had proven him right.

Greg had been a fine husband, had tried everything he could to help Kendra overcome her grief and to find some happiness in life again. She was the first to praise his efforts. And the first to admit that she'd been a poor excuse for a wife.

Gentleman and genuinely nice guy that he was, Greg had never blamed her for being less of a mar-riage partner than he deserved. It was to his credit that he'd let Kendra go when she insisted that his life would be better in the long run with a woman who loved him with her whole heart. It hurt Kendra terribly to know that she'd never be that someone, but they were close enough as friends that she believed she owed him her total honesty. It had been with much regret that she'd left Washington to begin the long ride back across the country, alone.

On her way east, she drove into Montana, searching for the place where her family had camped during the last trip they'd made together before her father succumbed to his illness. Jeff Smith had wanted one last wilderness trip with his wife and children, had insisted on it, and Elisa, understanding that this would be their last time alone as a family, had made certain that he'd had that trip. They'd hiked into the hills and made camp along a stream that moved smartly over rock, underscoring the time there with a constant rippling of water rushing around stone.

They'd lain under the stars together, lined up like sentries beneath the big sky that rose over the landscape, before retiring to the tent they had shared. They hiked and fished for trout in mountain streams and told ghost stories around the campfire at night. They followed cougar tracks—from a distance, of course— one afternoon and awoke one morning to a rainstorm so fierce the hail blew a hole in the roof of the tent. Every day, Jeff grew a little weaker, and every day, Elisa remained determined that he have the best of his family while he could still enjoy them. It was only when she knew he would only have a few more days to make it home that she agreed to leave.

Their ten days had been filled with poignant moments, many of which Kendra had caught in photographs. But few were more touching than the one capturing Elisa's struggle to help her husband down the mountain. Years later, when she ran for the Senate, those photos had surfaced, and the image of the small, fiercely determined dark-haired woman supporting the tall, gaunt man down a dusty trail, his arms around her shoulders, had said all there was to say about Elisa's strength and courage. Later, the picture had appeared in the local papers, and later still on the cover of a national newsmagazine in their issue on women in the Senate. The framed original now stood on the mantel in the front room of Smith House, where Kendra could see it daily, along with other beloved family photographs.

Driving into the hills had been a lonely journey for Kendra, but a necessary one. It was there that they'd last existed as a family, there that she'd first begun to understand the bonds between herself and her parents. Coming back so many years later had the feel of a sad pilgrimage. She couldn't remember exactly where they'd camped or what streams they'd forded, but with the weather just starting to change, it wouldn't have mattered. She'd have had to have a death wish to venture up into the mountains alone when the first of the winter storms was brewing. She went far enough to find a winding stream, sat on an outcropping of rock, and watched the water rush below her feet. The sun had been warm on her back and shoulders, and she tried to remember everything she could about that last trip. The way the coffee smelled and tasted first thing in the morning. The way the breeze blew up from nowhere and cast the scent of wildflowers from the hills across the meadow where she and Ian, still a toddler, chased butterflies. The stories her father had told them at night, huddled together around the fire as the air chilled, about his youth, about his hopes and aspirations, about his love for his family and the Pines where he'd grown up ... about his dreams for his children ...

And Kendra realized that the last thing her father, or her mother, would have wanted for her, would have been half a life. And that was exactly what she'd been permitting herself.

Survivor's guilt, Kendra's friend Selena, a psychologist, had suggested after she'd returned to the Pines the previous October.

"Not anymore," Kendra had vowed on that autumn day, and she set about to renovate Smith House to accommodate her taste and her requirements. At the same time, she vowed to restructure her life, to set a new agenda for herself, one that would focus on her work and her personal commitments.

Her house was a joy to her now, she reflected as she stripped off the navy suit jacket she'd worn that morning and dropped it onto the bed that housekeeping had so neatly made up while she was gone. It had been worth every bit of time and effort and money she'd put into it. Smith House was truly her home now.

And working again was a joy as well, she acknowledged. She'd felt more alive over the past few days than she had in years.

Working with Adam Stark seemed to be just the icing on the cake.

She debated on whether to take him up on his offer

for her to drive his car home, which of course would then require Adam to make a visit to the Pines to pick it up. Kendra lay back across the bed and closed her eyes. She had no trouble calling up his face. It was right there, in the forefront of her mind. Strong jawline, sculpted cheeks, and wide-set blue eyes. A mouth that drifted easily into a smile, a deep dimple on the left side. Dark hair just slightly longer than the Bureau liked.

The last time she'd gone out with him, they'd had dinner at a small Thai place that Adam had found in Georgetown. He'd brought her back to the hotel room she'd been staying in while she worked the case the Bureau had given her, and had kissed her goodnight, cupping her face in his hands and moving his mouth across hers as if he owned it—

The ring of the telephone startled her, and she sat up with a jolt and reached for it.

"Hello?"

"I'm sorry," the pleasant male voice on the other end of the line apologized. "I must have dialed the wrong room number."

"That's all right." Kendra hung up the phone, then looked down at her watch. It was close to six.

She snapped on the remote and pulled up the channel menu, searching for the local news. She wanted to see how the case had been presented and how her sketch looked.

The pretty blond reporter led with the story, and, Kendra nodded, did a fine job with it.

There was the press conference with the state police, the FBI, and the chiefs of police from several local towns who'd been brought in to assist in the search of the park in Walnut Crossing. Kendra could see Adam standing off to one side, slightly behind Miranda Cahill. He leaned over and whispered something in Miranda's ear, and she tilted her pretty head slightly, nodding solemnly without taking her eyes from the speaker.

A little surge of something—something mean and green—shot through Kendra. She swatted at it and tried to ignore it as best she could.

Adam doesn't owe me anything, she reminded herself sternly. *We're friends. Just friends. We work on an occasional case together. That's all.*

"Damn it," she couldn't help but add aloud.

The tape that had been shot earlier of Kendra holding her composite drawing now took center stage, and she pushed aside her pique and leaned forward to see the face she'd drawn as others would see it. She was grateful that the camera had not lingered on her. She hadn't realized how severe, how businesslike she appeared in her dark blue suit and crisp white cotton shirt. Only the small gold cross resting in the hollow of her neck lent any touch of warmth to her image.

It was a good sketch, though, she acknowledged, and true to the images the witnesses had presented to her. As true as her art could make it. And that, not how she looked on camera, was the only thing that really mattered.

She wondered if he—the man whose face was held on the screen—was watching, wherever he was. If he recognized himself in the sketch. If he was surprised by the accuracy of the likeness. If it frightened him to know that his secret—his *face*—had been revealed for all to see. Would it make him careless now? Angry?

The joint task force that had been formed to investigate the matter was announced. Four FBI agents were named. Adam and Miranda were the only ones Kendra recognized.

She turned off the television and picked up the phone, dialing the front desk, and requested assistance in renting a car.

"Yes, tonight . . . whatever you can get on short notice would be fine. Yes, I'll be here."

Next she called Adam's room and left the message that she'd rented a car to drive home and had left the keys to the Audi at the front desk in an envelope.

"Thanks anyway," she added, lest she sound too strident. "I appreciate your offer, but it's probably a waste of your time for you to drive all the way to my place just to pick up your car. It isn't as if you don't have other things to do. Well, I guess I'll see you next time. Thanks again . . ."

What was the point in staying another night? she asked herself as she began to pack her things. The job she'd been hired to do was done. And Adam? Well, he had more important things to do. Driving his car to Smith's Forge *was* silly when he'd have need of it here. The fact that she had gotten the impression he wanted to see her again, well, she could be wrong about that. So all in all, it was better that she leave, alone, now, before she got in the way of the investigation.

And besides, she thought as she tossed her belongings into her suitcase, if Adam found his way back to

Smith's Forge, she wanted it to be for a reason other than to pick up his car.

"Hey, Selena!" Kendra called from her kitchen window. It had been less than forty minutes since the rental agent had picked up the car and less than twenty since she'd phoned her friend and neighbor Selena Brennan to let her know she was home.

Selena waved to Kendra at the same time she whistled for Lola. The dog had taken off for the stream behind Kendra's house and was eagerly investigating something on the ground.

"I told you that you didn't have to bring the mail down, that I'd walk up later and pick it up," Kendra said as she came out into the yard.

"I know, but I have appointments this afternoon in town and wanted to leave a little early to run a few errands, so I thought I'd drop your mail off before I started getting ready to leave. Besides," the young woman grinned as she tucked a strand of brown hair behind her ear, "Lola missed you. She made a beeline down the road as soon as I opened the door."

"Where's Lola?" Kendra frowned, looking around. She spotted the dog down near the edge of the stream. "What's she got there?"

"Oh, who knows? She's always picking up something." Selena and Kendra walked across the yard to where the big dog stood, sniffing happily and wagging her tale with anticipation.

"What is that thing?" Selena bent over and picked up the remains of a sandwich, Lola lunging to grab a bite or two in passing. "Looks like one of the canoeists threw away their lunch."

"Here, give it here," Kendra reached for it, "and I'll pitch it in the trash, unless you're going to let Lola have the rest of it."

"No, I don't like her eating people-food. She gets plenty of doggie treats at home and, I dare say, here as well." Selena followed Kendra to the back of the house where she lifted the lid of a trash can and dumped the sandwich in. "I did notice the box of extra-large Milk Bones on your counter."

"Lola's extra-large, aren't you, girl? She's my buddy." Kendra rubbed the dog behind the ears, and Lola's sorrow at watching the sandwich disappear vanished. "So what's new in the neighborhood?"

"There were some canoes through last night. Several in a group, and later, one loner passed the back of my house, though I doubt he'll be back anytime soon, since Lola took off after him something fierce."

"She must have been having a guard-dog moment."

"Well, she'll have to get over it. It seems that every weekend there are more and more visitors."

"A sure sign of spring, when the canoes start again in force." Kendra nodded. Starting in the spring, weekends brought a steady stream of nature lovers to the Pines to explore and to enjoy the scenery. Kendra had never minded sharing the woods and the waterways with others who admired them, but her welcome ended at her property line. "I guess it's time to put up new 'No Trespassing' signs, just in case someone else decides that my yard would make a good picnic area."

"Actually, I think someone may have been down

here the other night." Selena paused, remembering. "Lola was barking to beat the band after dinner, but I couldn't tell exactly where she was. I whistled for her, and eventually she came running back from this direction. I figured someone might have been passing by on their way back to the car lot up by the lake."

"I'll make a new sign and nail it up this afternoon. In the meantime, come on in and have some tea with me."

"Can't. I have patients coming at one and I'm booked steadily through till six." Selena had a thriving therapy practice. Not only was she very good at what she did, but she was a Piney, born and raised, and proud of it. Troubled locals who would never dream of seeking help from a stranger would agree to counsel with Lem and Ida Brennan's daughter in the office she had built off the back of the family home if they couldn't get to her office in Reedsboro, the nearest real town.

Like Kendra, Selena had left the Pines to go to school, and like Kendra, as an adult, she had been drawn back to the simplicity and beauty of the Pines, and chose to make her life there. The two women had known each other since childhood, and had, with Kendra's return to the Pines, rekindled their friendship.

"By the way, I saw Father Tim on Monday. He wanted me to remind you about dinner at the shelter on Tuesday and that he was hoping for something a little more than salads and chicken sandwiches from the fast-food restaurant out on Route Nine."

"I will never live that down, will I?" Kendra laughed. "I guess the fact that my new stove was late in being delivered and installed wasn't a good enough excuse for not showing up with a home-cooked dinner."

"It made for a good story." Selena was laughing, too.

"One Father Tim still enjoys telling, apparently."

"You can redeem yourself by showing up with something really good next week."

"I was thinking simple, like spaghetti and meatballs and a salad. Something good for dessert."

"Great. I still have about two dozen jars of sauce that I made last summer. We can use some of that," Selena offered.

Kendra rolled her eyes.

"Of course you do. And I suppose you have some homemade pasta in the freezer as well?"

"Don't ask unless you really want to know." Selena grinned.

"Okay, I guess I can pick up some garlic bread and dessert. No, I'll make dessert. I'll bake a cake." She frowned. "How many cakes should I make for . . . how many men in the shelter this week?"

"There were twenty-two as of last night, but as you know, that changes from day to day. Plan on two cakes—something not too sugary, maybe a pound cake—and a fruit salad."

"Does pound cake come in a mix?"

"Yes. So does fruit salad, but I recommend that you make that yourself."

"I promise I'll go to the market Tuesday morning." Kendra laughed good-naturedly. "Can you think of anything else we'll need?"

"No, that should be fine." Selena glanced at her

watch. "If I don't get moving I'll be late for my one o'clock. Now, where is that dog . . ."

"She's around somewhere. Why not leave her here? You can stop back to get her after your appointments. Maybe have dinner with me."

"Sounds like a plan. I should be back around seven."

"Perfect. I'll see you then."

Kendra watched Selena pull out of the drive, then walked around the side of the house, calling Lola's name. She heard her, coughing and sputtering, before she saw her.

"Here, girl." Kendra patted her thigh, and the dog came to her, wagging the ever-moving tail, to sit at Kendra's feet and gaze lovingly at her. "Did you hear Selena mention that new box of biscuits?"

Lola thumped her tail on the grass, then stood and coughed again, a great hacking cough.

"Are you all right, Lola? Need some water? I'll run in and get a bowl. I'll even bring a treat, if you wait right here. . . ."

Kendra grabbed the old crockery bowl that she left just inside the back door, and filled it with water from the hose. "Come on, now, and take a drink."

Lola drank from the bowl, then sat on her big haunches and focused on the biscuit that was being held up for her. She took the treat, but laid it on the ground and choked yet again.

"What's wrong, girl?" Kendra frowned, becoming more concerned. But just then a rabbit darted out from under the holly bush and Lola felt compelled to give chase.

Kendra watched the dog take off, then walked to

the front of the house to check on her newly emerging gardens.

It wasn't until Kendra rounded the side of the house less than five minutes later, after stopping to pull dandelions from a newly planted bed, that she found Lola laying on the grass in the backyard. At first she'd thought the dog was sleeping.

But when she walked past, she saw that the dog's eyes were open and her tongue was hanging out one side of her mouth, her chest rising and falling rapidly and unevenly.

"What's wrong, girl?" Kendra bent down on one knee.

The tail thumped weakly.

"Oh, Lola," Kendra said under her breath. "You're sick, aren't you?"

Whimpering slightly, Lola tried in vain to stand. Her legs lacked the strength to support her nearly one hundred pounds.

"You stay, girl. Stay." Kendra paused. The dog was too big for her to lift. "We'll have to get Dr. Mark to come for you. Stay right there. . . ."

Kendra rushed to the house for the phone.

It was a long twenty minutes before Mark Traub, the young veterinarian from the local animal hospital, pulled into her driveway. Kendra sat on the ground next to Lola and rubbed the back of her head and tried to reach Selena on her cell phone. The only message she could think to leave was "Call me. Now."

"Hey, Lola," the vet said softly as he approached. "No, no, girl. Stay right there. Kendra, let me take a look at her. . . ."

"Mark, I think she just had a seizure," Kendra told him, her voice shaky.

After a quick examination, the vet looked up and said, "I need to take her into the clinic. You're going to have to help me get her onto the gurney."

"Of course, whatever you need." Kendra bit her lip and looked down at the big sweet dog, whose eyes were now closed, her breathing more erratic. "What do you think happened?"

"I'll need to run some tests to be sure, but off the top of my head," Mark said as he headed to his van, "I'd say it looks like she's been poisoned."

CHAPTER
SEVEN

Adam stood to one side of the entrance to the cave and watched as the crime scene investigative team prepared to move their equipment on to the next. The sun had just started to come up, he'd been there since the day before, and couldn't remember for certain when he'd last eaten. And to make his disposition just a little more sour, he'd called Kendra at the hotel to see if she wanted to grab some breakfast with him before she left, only to find out that she already had.

He rubbed the back of his neck hoping to erase some of the tension that had grown out of fatigue and frustration. The hours spent in the park had yielded little that appeared promising. Cigarette butts and beer cans littered the area, likely remnants from the last teen party to have been held here but nothing that could be connected with their UNSUB. There were footprints up and down the path that, in the absence of rain, could have been there for days. So far the caves had given up nothing of any substance.

"You think maybe he was scoping this place out to

use in the future?" Miranda asked as she walked toward him and peeled off her gloves.

"No. I think he killed Karen Meyer here. We just haven't found the right cave."

"You look pissed off," she noted.

"I'm starving and have a massive headache and pretty young women who should be around to dance at their children's weddings are dropping like flies. Other than that, things are swell."

"I heard they were bringing in some sandwiches, up in the park. Why don't you run up and grab something to eat? You can grab something for me while you're at it." She glanced at the sun rising over the trees. "At least we'll be able to work without those damn floodlights in our faces for a while."

"That might help the headache," he grumbled.

"I have aspirin in my car. Help yourself." She searched her pockets, then handed him her keys. "Look in the glove box. And if the food wagon is more than a rumor, bring me something really good."

"Preferences?"

"Protein. And something to drink. Anything wet will do. Within reason, of course. You know what I like."

Adam pocketed the keys and headed up the narrow path that rose gradually to the main walk above, ever conscious that he was following in the footsteps of a killer. At the top, he stepped under the yellow tape strung between trees and looked over his shoulder, back down the path. There was no way their killer could have spent time here without leaving something of himself behind. Unfortunately, finding it and separating it from the bits and pieces left by others was time-consuming. It could take days to distinguish a cigarette butt tossed by the killer from those tossed by the junior high kids who sneaked down to split the six-pack that someone had stolen from an unsuspecting parent. There was simply too much debris in the area.

Adam snagged a bottle of water from the van that was just setting up to dole out food and drinks to the weary investigators and continued on to Miranda's car for the aspirin that he hoped would dull the pounding between his ears. He leaned against the side of the car while he tossed back the capsules and watched the gathering news crews, ignoring the attempts of several reporters to get his attention. He polished off the water and flipped the bottle end over end into a trash can that stood about ten feet away before returning to the van to grab a couple of sandwiches and a few cold cans of soda—diet for Miranda.

As he descended the path to the caves, he recalled how, years back, when he'd been at the Academy and dating Portia, the Cahill sisters had pulled the old twin switch on him—more than once. He'd always found them out, though, before he'd caught on to the mirror-image thing, because Miranda would not touch sugared sodas, and Portia could not tolerate artificial sweeteners. In the end, the three had become friends, and he'd come to admire their skills as agents as much as he'd once been taken by their beauty. He'd personally requested that John include Miranda in the team he was sending up from Quantico to work on this current investigation. She was one hell of an investigator, he was thinking as he walked back down the path toward the caves.

A small scrap of fabric clinging to the low branch of a shrub caught his eye and he leaned down to inspect it. It was pale green, nearly the color of the new leaves, and may have escaped notice for that reason. He called to one of the investigators who was headed toward him, and watched while the tiny scrap was picked from the branch with tweezers and placed into a plastic bag that was then marked.

Adam had just started back down to the caves when the cry went up.

"In here!"

It had been over an hour before Adam made his way into the cave. Due to the confined nature of the area, the crime scene investigators had closed it off to all except the most necessary personnel. In a case such as this, where there had been little physical evidence to date beyond the bodies of the slain women, contamination was not to be risked. So Adam waited along with his fellow FBI agents and members of the local police department until the scene had been carefully processed. Once inside the cave, he'd been grateful that the investigators had been concerned more with thoroughness than with appeasing the feds.

Blood was splattered on both the walls and the ceiling of the cave, so much so that in the glow from the lights, the walls almost appeared to be on fire. Pools of red, still sticky, covered the floor like a ragged carpet. Droplets were found toward the back of the cave, but nothing near the savagery close to the entrance.

"How do you read it?" one of the local homicide detectives asked Adam as the photographer began to do his job, the flash from his camera sending jolts of light through the narrow space.

"None of our victims had wounds that would account for all the blood you see in here. The smaller pool of blood on the floor at the back of the cave, that could have come from Karen Meyer. But the blood on the walls, the floor, the ceiling . . . that didn't come from any of the three victims."

"So you think that . . ."

"Yeah," Adam said wearily. "We're missing a body."

The body didn't stay missing for long.

Before the day had ended, Julie Lohmann, or what had remained of her, was found beside the stream that flowed through the back of the park.

"She just doesn't fit the pattern at all," Miranda had noted. "Nineteen years old, unmarried, no children. No connection with any of our previous victims. No similarities either. What are the chances there's more than one killer?"

"None," Adam said, shaking his head. "It's the same guy."

"What do you think happened here?"

"My guess would be that Julie was in the wrong place at the wrong time," Adam replied. "I think maybe she stumbled onto our man while he was in the process of either killing Karen Meyer, or while he was preparing to dispose of the body."

"It must have really pissed him off. It takes a lot of rage to do what he did to her. I never saw so many stab wounds," she said softly, then, almost as if thinking aloud, asked, "What would she have been doing here alone?"

"Meeting someone," Adam supposed.

"Her boyfriend," one of the officers told them as she walked past. "They just picked him up and took him to the station. He called to report her missing a few hours ago. We're on our way to his apartment right now."

"It wasn't him," Adam said.

"I guess we'll need a little evidence of that, won't we?" The officer tossed over her shoulder.

Adam shook his head and turned back to Miranda. "You might want to take part in that. Don't let the poor guy get railroaded. This is our man, Miranda. This was his spot. His killing ground. He'd be territorial. I'd bet my life on it."

"Then I'm on my way." Miranda turned to leave. "You staying here?"

"Yes." He gazed back down to the stream. "There's something I want to check out."

Adam picked his way down the steep, stony path, then paused, midway from his starting point, and tried to imagine the scene that had played out here just twenty-four hours earlier. Tried to imagine what would have been going through the killer's head after he'd finished with Julie Lohmann.

Up until now, he'd been so organized. Methodically stalking his victims, learning their habits, so that he'd know the best and most expedient time and place to strike. He'd been efficient in his taking, efficient in his killing, never losing total control. Until he met up with Julie Lohmann.

The more Adam thought about it, the more certain he was that the young girl's murder had been little more than an impulse their UNSUB couldn't resist. She'd clearly been in the wrong place at the wrong time. Had she perhaps arrived on the path as he'd been carrying Karen Meyer up toward the parking lot?

Adam retraced his steps back to the parking lot, looking for a spot where Karen Meyer's body may have been dumped while Julie Lohmann was dealt with. He stood near the shrub where earlier he'd found the shred of fabric. Stepping off the path several feet to the left, he knelt down and studied a soft impression on the new growth of weeds that had sprung up over the past month. He leaned forward to study small drops of red-brown that speckled the ground. If, as he suspected, the killer had been surprised on the path by Julie while carrying Karen's body, he might have tossed his burden in an effort to catch his new prey. Later, after killing Julie, he'd have come back to get Karen to finish carrying her to his car so that he could dispose of her at what Adam suspected was a previously determined spot.

Returning to the top of the trail that led down to the stream where Julie's body had been found, her chest slashed open by an unknown number of wounds, her face battered beyond recognition. Adam closed his eyes, trying to see what the killer had seen.

Had he stood right here, on this very spot, holding her in his arms, before making his way down the path to the stream? Adam followed the path down toward the water, stood near the blood-covered rock where Julie's body had been left, like an offering. Why would he have brought her here? Why not leave her in the cave? Had he planned on using the cave again for his future victims, his *chosen* victims? Did he see Julie's murder as an aberration, a distraction he needed to clear out from his space?

Why carry her all the way down to the stream? Why not dispose of her when he disposed of Karen?

Too much blood, Adam thought. There had been too much blood.

Had he carried her down to the stream to wash her off? But she'd been covered with blood when they found the body.

Ah, but maybe he'd washed off himself. Maybe the trip down that steep path was to serve a dual purpose. To dispose of Julie's body in a place that hopefully wouldn't be found for several days. And to clean himself of her blood.

Adam walked downstream until he reached a spot where the water pooled. There, on the flat rock that overlooked the deep water, he found traces of pale pink water still in the shallow crevices. Closer inspection found several other rocks with similar pools containing darker pink liquid. Their UNSUB had washed off after he'd carried Julie Lohmann's bloody body down to the stream. And unless Adam was mistaken, he had washed his clothes as well.

Which would explain why Karen Meyer's clothes were damp when they found her.

Adam sought out a CSI and directed her down to

the rocks to take samples of the pink water. Then taking a sample of water from the stream in a vial he borrowed from the investigator, Adam set out for the medical examiner's lab.

Well, damn her. Damn her anyway. She shouldn't have been there. It was her own fault. She shouldn't have gotten in my way.

He stared at the live picture on his television while unconsciously rubbing his elbow where he'd scraped it on the rocks in the stream where he'd washed up after he'd dropped her there. The blood actually came out of his shirt quite nicely—he had soaked it good right away—and the jeans had washed up okay, too. It had been so convenient, having a source of running water right there.

Still, he didn't like having his plans disrupted. It confused him, threw him off course. Made him lose control.

Things never turned out well when he lost control.

But what a lovely kink she'd thrown into the mix. She wasn't his usual type, but he had to admit, change was good every once in a while.

And the television coverage had been outstanding, especially considering that this was, after all, a rural area and shouldn't be expected to present the news with the same level of excellence that one would demand from the networks. But that little redhead from the station in Lancaster, well, she was a real pro, wasn't she? He was tempted to write to the station to congratulate her on a job well done.

He chuckled out loud now and increased the volume as he watched the lead investigator from the FBI drone on and on about the case and what it all meant, then swelled with pride watching the lovely Kendra display her sketch. She'd done quite a good job. Perhaps a bit too good, he noted, not above giving credit where it was due. But it was only as he'd expected. After all, she was the best, wasn't she?

Still, as accurate as the portrait was, did she not know him?

The news anchor spoiled his reflective mood commenting that this latest victim did not fit the established profile of the Soccer Mom Strangler.

The Soccer Mom Strangler!

Was he serious?

"Oh, this is too rich."

That they had to give him a name, well, that's what those media types did, wasn't it?

The Boston Strangler. The Green River Killer.

The Soccer Mom Strangler.

It made a man proud.

And wasn't it lovely? Wasn't it fun, to have so many scrambling around? Sort of like a reverse game of Hide and Seek, where he was It, but instead of him doing the seeking, all the other players were out looking for him.

Of course, they'd never find him, of that he was certain.

Perhaps it might be time to think about raising the stakes a little. Give them all a little something to think about.

He leaned back in his chair, pondering the best way to do that.

He needn't rush. He had all the time in the world. Something clever would come to him.

It always did.

He changed the channel but turned off the sound, though his eyes remained fixated on the screen upon which a commercial for some exotic piece of exercise equipment was being hawked by a woman wearing little more than a bikini. He barely saw her.

In his mind, a different kind of drama was playing out. As he stared at the screen, he visualized darker scenes that were running over and over and over in his head.

Karen Meyer coming down the path, taking her customary shortcut through the park to her cul-de-sac on the other side of the woods as he watched from behind a stand of laurel.

Would tonight be the night?

It is almost dusk. He hears her calling to someone from the top of the path. He peers out through the dense branches as much as he dares, straining to hear what the voices are saying. Someone is offering Karen a ride home. He holds his breath, waiting for her response.

"Thanks, but I'll walk. I really need the exercise."

He takes this as a sign, and readies himself.

Soft, steady footsteps on the graveled path, a stone tumbles ahead, kicked by the toe of her shoe. She is deep in thought, her brows knitted together. What, he wonders briefly, is on her mind?

Mentally he shrugs off any concern. He knows that soon, very soon, it will no longer matter.

She passes close by, close enough that he can smell

her perfume. He counts her steps, knows exactly when to spring.

In a flash, he's upon her from behind, one arm looped around her neck, the other positioning the stun gun.

And then she jabs him, *hard,* with her elbow. The unexpected blow knocks the gun from his hand. She spins, karate-style, preparing her defenses. With one punch to her jaw, he takes her out.

Panting from the unexpected exertion, he stands, hands on hips, and stares down at her.

Then he bends and lifts her, carries her over his shoulder down the path. Down, down, to the cave that he's prepared for her arrival.

His nerves are on edge. She wasn't supposed to do that. He was going to have to show her a thing or two.

He closes his eyes, remembering . . .

Then, later, the scene on his imaginary screen shifts.

It is dark now, and it's done. Karen has paid the price and is of no further use to him. She's to be disposed of. He's left her in the cave while he goes up the path to the parking lot to see what's going on. He gets to the top of the path, then stands quietly, sniffing the air like a dog. There are no cars in the lot now, no one about at all. Pleased, he moves the van close to the path, then returns to the cave for Karen.

He is halfway up the path, Karen slung over his shoulder, when he sees the light. He pauses, then steps off the path into the shadows. The light is a small dot on the ground, moving toward him. He stares, motionless, as the flashlight approaches, curious at first. Slowly, he lowers to the ground, still holding his burden, and crouches in the dark, watching the light move closer.

She is almost past him, when the light falls to his side of the path.

She opens her mouth to scream, but no sound comes out. He tosses Karen like a sack, leaps for his new prey.

He closes his eyes, remembering . . .

The knife in his hand, though he had no recollection of having removed it from its sheath. The knife at her throat. He could almost hear his own voice warning her to be quiet. To settle down and she'd live to tell about it.

Not that he'd considered for a minute not killing her, but she didn't need to know that at that moment.

But had she listened to him? No. No, she started to scream for help. So what could he do?

He slit her throat, then carried her to his cave.

But there he'd lost control, something he'd never done before. Not ever. The knife had slammed down, over and over and over. . . .

He takes a long, slow breath, and stares at the screen, bringing back the images, savoring every one.

CHAPTER
EIGHT

"Selena, I'm so sorry." Kendra looked up with eyes red from crying as Selena entered the room. "I am so, so sorry."

"It wasn't your fault." Selena, her own eyes brimmed with tears, hugged her. "If you hadn't called Mark when you did, we could have lost Lola. I owe you for saving her life."

"Mark thinks she was poisoned. They're still trying to determine what it was."

"That's what he said when he called me. He said it could have been an insecticide, but he isn't sure."

"Lola's too smart to eat something with insecticide on it."

"Lola is a dog. If the chemical was strong enough, maybe even licking it could have made her sick. I just can't figure out where she could have gotten into something that strong. I don't have chemicals around my house."

"Neither do I. And as far as I know, she didn't eat anything except the dog biscuit that I gave her—"

"And the sandwich she found in your yard," Selena said slowly.

The women stared at each other in silence. Then Kendra stood up and walked toward the door.

"I'll be back in twenty minutes," she told Selena. "The trash men don't come until Thursday."

"Why would anyone lace a sandwich with insecticide?" Kendra asked.

"And then leave it in your yard?" Selena shook her head. "Makes no sense at all, does it?"

"Well, turning it over to the police was a good idea. And thank God, Lola's going to be all right. It's lucky that you took the sandwich from her before she had a chance to finish it off."

"Lucky that she's as obedient as she is. Any other dog might have gobbled it down." Selena leaned over the railing of her back porch to look down at Kendra, who stood on the grass below. "But I still don't understand why someone would do something like that. I mean, spray insecticide on a sandwich."

"Could have been an accident."

"How do you accidentally get insecticide on your lunch?"

"Maybe someone was making the sandwich and sprayed at something—bees, maybe, or a fly—and maybe the window was open and wind blew the spray back and it landed on the bread."

Selena stared at her.

"How do you come up with this stuff?"

"I'm trying to think of a logical way that this could have happened. That's the only logical thing I can think of."

"Even you would have to admit that that's pretty

remote," Selena said dryly. "And how would this accidentally tainted sandwich end up in your backyard?"

"Maybe the person with the sandwich was canoeing downstream and eating at the same time. Maybe just as he was passing my place, he took a bite out of the sandwich and realized it was contaminated and he tossed it"—she flung her arm as if throwing away the imaginary sandwich—"without thinking."

"I'm trying to remind myself that you're actually an intelligent woman."

"What other explanation could there be? Unless someone was trying to poison, say, the raccoons . . ."

"No one around here would do that, regardless of how annoying the raccoons are. No one around here would deliberately try to poison an animal."

"Which means it had to have been accidental."

"Well, accidental or not, I'm lucky to have my dog coming home tomorrow. Are you still willing to have her stay with you over the weekend while I run up to Trenton to see my brother?"

"Are you still willing to leave her with me, after what happened?"

"Kendra, I'd trust you with my life." Selena smiled for the first time in hours. "And with my dog's. Besides, what are the chances of someone tossing another poisoned sandwich into your backyard?"

Kendra wasn't expecting to find another poisoned sandwich, but she did give the yard a thorough going-over before Selena dropped Lola off on Friday afternoon. Her ordeal apparently forgotten, the dog did her best to plant a few sloppy kisses on Kendra's face before racing off after a chipmunk.

"You'd never suspect we almost lost her just a few days ago, would you?" Selena observed.

"She certainly doesn't appear worse for having spent two days in the doggie clinic," Kendra agreed. "Even so, I'm not letting her out of my sight all weekend."

"That may be tough. She isn't one to stay in one spot for long."

"I intend to do my best to keep her amused and close to the house, all the same."

Selena slid behind the wheel of her car and closed the door. "You have my cell phone number if you need me, but I don't expect you'll have any problems. Mark promised me that, except for a possible sore throat from the chemicals, Lola should be as good as new."

"Oh, that reminds me. I got a call from Ray Kilmer at the police station this morning. They got the results back from their lab. It seems the chemicals used were your basic household variety of spray insecticide, just as Mark thought. You know, Bugs-Away, or whatever they call that stuff."

"Curious," Selena said as she began to back her car out onto the road.

"Selena," Kendra called to her.

When the car stopped, Kendra walked to the open driver's side window and asked, "Did you have any . . . feelings, or anything about this?"

"No." Selena shook her head. She paused, then added, "But there was something . . . I don't want to call it a premonition . . . on Tuesday afternoon. Before you came back. It wasn't anything I could put my finger on.

Just a, well, a chill would be the best way to describe it. I have no idea what it meant. If, in fact, it meant anything. You know that it's sometimes hard to tell, sometimes hard to interpret . . . and you know how hard I've tried all these years not to have premonitions."

"I know you've never been comfortable, well, *knowing* things."

"And I know people like to think that, because I'm a little sensitive, I can always see the future or predict things. It doesn't always work that way. Sometimes things just pass you by."

"That's because you try to ignore your gift."

"I don't know that I'd call it a gift, Kendra. I've never been able to decide how I really feel about it."

"Must make your counseling sessions interesting, though."

"It might, if I let it. I am very, very careful not to 'hear' my patients unless they are speaking out loud." Selena waved and completed her turn, then honked her horn as she drove off down the road.

"Come on, Lola," Kendra called, not wanting the dog too far out of sight. "Let's go inside and get a cool drink, would you like that?"

Lola, who'd been investigating some scent at the edge of the woods, loped across the lawn at the sound of her name. Though a bit slower than normal, one would be hard pressed to tell that she'd been so ill just forty-eight hours earlier.

Kendra filled Lola's water bowl and set it on the kitchen floor, and the dog drank eagerly.

"Lola, you're a mess," Kendra said as water

dripped onto the floor. She reached for the paper towels to mop up. "Now, we're going to have a nice, quiet weekend. After the week I've had, after dealing with everything from a serial killer to a sandwich poisoner, I want no more excitement in my life than what I get from paying my bills and reading the book I picked up at the drugstore last night."

And for the most part, the weekend was uneventful, the only moment of note coming on Sunday morning when Kendra opened the barn door. Having missed her daily canoe trips into the Pines, she'd decided the time had come to resume her forays. She'd take the larger of the two canoes so that Lola could accompany her. But after she'd swung back the unlocked door, and before she could step inside, Lola began to growl, a long, low, threatening sound from deep inside.

The hair on the back of Kendra's neck stood straight up, and she took several steps back.

"What is it, girl?" she whispered. "What's wrong?"

Even as Kendra stepped back, Lola advanced slowly, sniffing the air and growling as she entered the barn and paused as if listening. Kendra stood in the doorway and took stock.

The two canoes stood up against the right wall, and toward the back of the barn was an old lawn mower and a new bicycle. Several rakes and a shovel or two stood near the door, and a row of paint cans stood in a neat line awaiting proper disposal. Light from the open door spilled onto the floor, and it was plain that there was nothing there that shouldn't have been.

"Do you smell a fox, maybe, or a raccoon?" Kendra

patted the dog on the head. "There's nothing here, Lola."

Confident that the dog must have caught the scent from an animal that somehow had found its way in—and out—overnight, Kendra dragged the canoe out through the double doors and down to the stream. She'd had to clap her hands to get Lola's attention, though, and was tempted to leave the dog at the house when Lola, still visibly agitated, finally arrived at the stream.

"Oh, that old fox or whatever it was is long gone now," Kendra said as she pushed the canoe from the side of the stream. "You just sit back there and relax, and we'll see what's going on upstream today."

Kendra paddled as far as the first big lake, noting that the number of early-morning canoers seemed to increase with every mile. That the Pines had become such a popular place was a good thing, she reminded herself. The more people who enjoyed the protected areas, the more likely it was that those areas would remain protected. But still, for one accustomed to having endless stretches of waterways to herself, she regretted having to share this Sunday morning with strangers, friendly though they might be. After the violence that had engulfed her over the past week, she needed the healing serenity that she always found in the rhythmic paddling on her solitary ventures into the heart of the Pines.

Lola, who'd been obediently sitting at the front of the canoe and taking in the sights, stood up and began to fuss at a flotilla of kayakers. Kendra waved at their greeting, admonished Lola to sit back down, then reluctantly acknowledged that it was time to start back to Smith House. In an effort to buy herself a bit more peace, she sought the more remote branches of one of the rivers on her return. But even here, in the more far-reaching tributaries, she met the occasional soul who'd ventured from the established channels to seek the calm of the woods, much as she was doing. Usually, Kendra was happy to share the beauty of the Pines with others who sought this same refuge. Today wasn't one of those times.

Easing her canoe into the narrow waterway that would take her home, she tried to focus on the gentleness of the morning, the soft bird sounds, and the greening up of the undergrowth. Last night's rain had left behind a slight mist that the morning sun had all but burned off, and the patches of sunlight and shadow on the water pleased her eye and soothed her spirit. In spite of her disappointment at finding so much activity in the Pines that morning, she felt refreshed. The muscles in her arms stung slightly from not having worked a paddle for close to a week, but other than that bit of discomfort, she was feeling refreshed by the time she approached her property line.

The first thing she'd do was to make that sign she'd promised herself.

She dragged the canoe onto the soft bank, stepping aside as Lola jumped past her and took off, returning reluctantly at Kendra's command. The canoe resting against the side of the barn to dry, Kendra unlocked the back of the house. Insisting that Lola accompany her, she went inside, refilled the dog's water dish and grabbed a bottle of chilled Deer Park from the fridge while on her way into the study.

She'd prefer a more permanent wooden sign, but for today, she'd have to be content with something makeshift. Temporarily, a message in black marker on a piece of cardboard nailed to the tree would do. She searched the closet and found a cardboard box from which she cut the lid. In block letters she printed NO TRESPASSING on the cardboard and held it up to admire. It would serve the purpose just fine.

She found a nail and hammer in the tool box she kept in the back entry, and tucking the sign under her arm, went back outside, Lola at her heels. The dog cast a wary eye at the barn, but stayed close by Kendra, even when Kendra waded into the shallow part of the stream to nail the sign to the section of tree trunk that would be most visible from the water.

"There," she said to Lola. "I'd say that's pretty clear, wouldn't you?"

She waded back toward the narrow clearing when something fluttering in the light wind caught her eye. A scrap of fabric had been tied to a low branch of one of the shrubs that grew along the bank. Knowing that it was not uncommon for the canoers or kayakers to mark their way along the streams by tying something onto the trees or bushes so that they could find their way back, and harmless as the scrap was, she left it there, thinking that whoever had tied it there, could have picked a more noticeable color. That pale, slightly faded green would be difficult to spot. Had the wind not brought it to motion, Kendra wouldn't have seen it at all.

She flipped on the small television in the kitchen while she made lunch, after which she discovered Lola had a fondness for green grapes. She was just tossing one into the air for the dog to catch when "News Week in Review" came on. The opening segment promised news about the Soccer Mom killer who was stalking women in eastern Pennsylvania. Kendra's sketch was featured as part of the teaser.

She pulled a chair out from the table and sat down to watch as the reporter went through the killings that had dominated the news for the past week. An FBI spokesperson appeared to give an update, followed by film of the scene in the park where the last victim had been found.

". . . and in spite of the fact that this latest victim did not fit the pattern the killer had established, the FBI believes the same man is responsible for all four murders." The reporter stood at the point where the two park paths joined, the exact spot where Joseph Tursky said he'd seen the man in the composite. "Police think the murderer had lain in wait here," she pointed behind her to a heavily shrubbed area, "until Karen Meyer started through the woods on a shortcut to her home, which is in a small development just to the south of the park. They believe the killer overtook her, perhaps knocking her unconscious, then carrying her to a cave down this path."

She stepped aside and pointed to the path beyond the yellow tape.

"Then, after raping and murdering the young mother of three, the killer apparently carried her body up the path toward the parking lot I'm standing near, possibly intending to leave his victim elsewhere. It is believed that it was during this trip back up the path that he encountered nineteen-year-old Julie Lohmann. Police think the killer attacked Ms. Lohmann, then returned to the cave with her, where she was viciously murdered. Her body was then taken to the stream that runs through the park, left on the bank while, sources tell me, he may have washed up in the swiftly moving water. . . ."

A photograph of Julie Lohmann flashed on the screen. Her high school senior photo, Kendra suspected, that of a pretty, dark-haired girl whose smile confided her belief that a life brimming with endless possibilities lay just beyond graduation.

The image on the screen switched back to Kendra's sketch, and the reporter repeated the phone numbers to call if anyone thought they'd seen the man in the picture.

Kendra clicked off the TV, wondering if anyone had called those numbers with reliable information. Had he been sighted? Identified? She had Adam's cell phone number in her wallet. She could call.

Then again, so could he . . .

The sound of the car pulling into the drive drew Kendra's attention as well as Lola's, who knew the sound of that car and couldn't get outside fast enough to greet her mistress.

"Hey!" Kendra called from the top step. "How was your visit?"

"Great." Selena got out of the car and slid her sunglasses onto the top of her head. "The christening was fun, except that they had me seated at the table with my sister Christine, who has the worst case of self-congratulitis I've ever seen. She just can't tell you frequently enough just how good she is, and at how many things she does, in fact, excel."

"Ah, yes," Kendra nodded sympathetically, "there are few things more boring than listening to someone toot their own horn."

"I've had to put up with it all my life," Selena grumbled. "We all thought she'd grow out of it. But how's my doggie? How's Lola?"

Lola barked a greeting, jumped up to cover Selena's face with a big slurp, then barked again.

"Was she good?"

"She was great," Kendra answered honestly. "She's wonderful company. I'm thinking I should get a dog myself."

"Did you ever have one?"

"We always had dogs when I was growing up. My mother was never without one. Her last dog . . . the one she had . . . at the house in Princeton . . . died about two weeks before she did." Kendra hadn't thought about Job, her mother's dog, in several years. "I didn't realize how much I missed having one until I had Lola here for a few days."

"The local animal shelter always has wonderful dogs," Selena noted.

"That's what I'm thinking."

Lola jumped at the side of the car.

"Well, I guess that's pretty clear." Selena laughed. "Someone wants to go home."

"And I was starting to think she liked it here."

"You know what they say, there's no place like

home." Selena gave Kendra a quick hug. "Thanks so much for letting her stay with you. I really appreciate it. Especially since, well, since this week."

"It was my pleasure," Kendra said as she returned the hug. "I really enjoyed the company. Maybe I've been alone long enough here. Maybe it's time to get a dog."

"Or a man." Selena grinned as she started the car.

"Oh, sure. Lots of them around." Kendra laughed. "I think I'll have better luck finding the right dog."

The sound of the ringing phone drifted through the open kitchen window.

"I better get that. I'll see you on Tuesday at Father Tim's."

"Want me to pick you up?"

"That'll be great." Kendra waved as she ran up the back steps. She caught the phone right as the answering machine picked up.

"Hello?" she said, breathless from the sprint.

There was just the faintest hint of music in the background.

"Hello?" she repeated.

When the silence continued, she hung up.

"Grrrr." She growled and headed back for the kitchen when the phone rang again.

Tempted though she was to pound it with a hammer, she lifted the receiver.

"Now listen up. I don't think you're the least bit—"

"Kendra?"

"Adam? Did you just call here and hang up?"

"Why would I do that?"

"Someone did."

"Wasn't me. Maybe a wrong number?"

"I guess. It's happened several times this week, though." She relaxed. "Tell me, how's the investigation going? I was just wondering if you'd gotten any response at all to the sketch. Other than the usual 'I think I saw this guy with Elvis at a bar on the outskirts of town the other night' . . ."

"Oh, there's been a reaction, all right," Adam said, his voice weary. "They found another body this morning in Newkirk—that's near Lancaster. Everything fits, except the description of the last person she'd been seen with."

"What's different?"

"It seems our killer has shaved."

"Shaved? But he didn't have a beard."

"No, but he did have a full head of hair."

"He shaved his head?"

"Apparently so." Adam paused, then asked, "Can you meet me at the police department here in Newkirk? Looks like your work might not be quite finished on this one."

"You can always computer generate—" she started, but he interrupted.

"John wants you back on the case. He doesn't believe a computer can capture the nuances of expression that you do. And neither do I."

"All right. It will take me a few hours to get there, though."

"I'll be here," Adam told her. "I won't be going any place any time soon."

CHAPTER
NINE

"I should have paid more attention. I should have watched out for her. I should never have let her walk out the door with that man. . . ."

Grace Tobin covered her face with her hands and sobbed.

"There was no way you could have known." Kendra rubbed the back of the woman's shoulders to comfort her. She looked across the room to where Adam sat, and shrugged slightly. The witness had to get through this part—the grief, the self-recrimination—before she could give them any information at all. Only after Grace had built some emotional fences would she be able to recall the events clearly. Where she had pulled back from Adam, Kendra willingly stepped into the role of comforter and willing shoulder to facilitate the process.

"He just seemed so nice, so sincere. Annie was taken with him from the minute she met him, I could tell."

Kendra handed Grace a tissue and asked, "How could you tell? What did he do to get her attention, do you remember?"

"He was very quiet, very soft-spoken. Respectful, I'd say." Grace sniffed. "He bought us both drinks and asked her to dance. . . . Annie loves to dance. She started taking lessons about two years ago, right after her divorce. It was the only thing she did for herself, you know? Everything else she did was for her kids."

At the thought of Annie's two children, Grace burst into tears all over again.

"What was his name, did he say?"

"Jeff. He said his name was Jeff."

"Last name?"

"If he gave one I didn't hear it. I was busy talking to someone else when he came up to us. Then he and Annie started talking, and they moved to a table. They talked for a couple of hours. Actually, it looked as if she was doing most of the talking. A couple of times I looked over and he was nodding, like he was agreeing with something she said, you know the way you do when you're interested in the conversation. . . ." Grace's eyes spilled over once again.

"Adam, perhaps you could get Grace a glass of water." Kendra glanced in the direction of the kitchen. Due to the stress of the witnesses, they opted to interview her in her own home, hoping that the familiar surroundings would go a long way toward helping her to relax.

It had seemed like a good idea at the time, Kendra thought wryly as she patted the sobbing woman on the back.

From her seat on the sofa in Grace Tobin's living room, Kendra could see straight across the street to Annie McGlynn's town house, where media and law enforcement vehicles all but blocked off the street entirely. As Adam returned to the room with water for Grace, she nodded in the direction of the window. Her message received, Adam closed the blinds.

"I guess Chris will take the kids now," Grace hiccuped. "God knows what will happen to them."

"Chris?"

"Annie's ex-husband."

"I take it you don't care for him?" Adam commented as he sat on a chair facing the two women.

"He ran around on her the entire time they were married. He never had time for the kids when she was alive." She shook her head. "Annie did everything for those kids. She was the perfect mother."

"You mean, involved in their activities? Sports, school, that sort of thing?" Adam asked.

"There was no part of their lives she didn't care about. Annie had grown up in foster homes. She was determined that her kids would have every advantage she hadn't had. Including a mother who was always there for them, a mother who always listened . . ." Grace accepted another tissue from Kendra. "She had never had anyone to pay attention to her, you know? So when I saw this guy sitting there, listening to her, being so respectful of her, I thought, 'Wow, isn't this great? Maybe Annie's luck is finally changing.' . . ."

She hiccuped again.

"Well, it changed all right." Grace's jaw tightened. "Shit, you just can never tell, can you? I mean, he was a guy anyone would be interested in. Good-looking, tall . . ."

"How tall?" Kendra interrupted, trying to get to the business at hand. "As tall as Agent Stark?"

"No, not quite. But I'm not a good judge of height, and besides, mostly he was sitting down, except for when he first approached us and later when they were dancing. Shit. He looked nothing like the picture on television."

"Then we'll make a new picture, one that looks the way he does now."

"Then you think it's the same man who killed those other women?" The question was directed to Adam.

"It's a possibility."

"The police report says that he was bald." Kendra jumped in before Grace could ask questions of her own.

Grace nodded. "But bald like he'd shaved, not like he'd lost his hair, you know what I mean? You know the difference? Like perfectly smooth."

"The shape of his head"—Kendra's hands reached into her bag for her sketch pad and pencil—"more round than oval?"

"Just . . . nice. Not too anything. Just . . . oh, maybe rounded, not pointy, if that's what you mean."

"Like this?" Kendra's fingers had floated over the paper. She turned the sketch pad to Grace.

"A little less round maybe on the sides there . . . yes, like that."

"And his ears, what were they like? Did they protrude . . . ?"

"Oh, no, they were pretty close to the side of his head, flat like . . . yes." Grace nodded as Kendra moved closer to her so she could see the sketch as it was being made.

"His jaw . . . the shape of his face . . ."

Grace traced her finger on the paper. "Lean. I remember thinking he was lean . . . not just his face, but everything about him."

Adam's cell phone rang, and he walked into the kitchen to avoid breaking the concentration of the victim or the artist. When he returned several minutes later, Kendra glanced his way.

"That was Chief Rosello, Newkirk PD. He's across the street." Adam folded the phone and returned it to his pocket. "He was wondering when you'd have a sketch for him. They're anxious to display the suspect's new look to the media."

"I'm done, I think, unless Grace has something else to add?" Kendra handed Grace the sketch.

"His eyes were a little darker, maybe. Maybe there were more lashes . . ."

Kendra made the appropriate changes.

"That's better, yes." Grace nodded confidently. "That's him. That's the man Annie met at the bar."

"Did you notice what time they left?"

"No, I'm sorry. I didn't even realize she'd left the bar until it was closing time and she was nowhere to be found."

"Was that unusual for her?"

"Annie never left bars with a guy she didn't know. Never. She just wouldn't." Grace shook her head sadly.

"But she did this time."

"I don't know that she meant to leave with him."

Grace frowned. "I mean, she might have just stepped outside with him, maybe, like if he was going to show her something."

"Like what?" Kendra stood. "What would she want to see badly enough that she would go outside with a stranger?"

"Two weeks ago she met a guy with a Corvette at Huskers—that's the bar we were at last night—and we both went outside to take a look. That was one sweet car," Grace told them. "So maybe it was a car. Annie's a real car freak, especially sports cars. She just loves sports cars."

Grace dabbed at her face, seemingly unaware that she still spoke of her friend in the present tense.

"Whose car was that, do you know? The Corvette?"

"Some guy from Harrisburg—no, I know what you're thinking, but he looked nothing like this guy. Nothing at all. That guy was short, paunchy. The type of guy who *needs* a great car, if you catch my drift."

"If you think of anything, if you remember anything else, any distinguishing marks, anything at all, you can call me at this number, or you can call Agent Stark." Kendra handed her a card.

"Thanks, I will." Grace sat the card next to Adam's on the coffee table, then rose to walk her visitors to the door.

"Ms. Tobin, could you think back to the night you and Annie went outside to look at the Corvette?" Adam turned as he reached the second step outside the Tobin town house. "This man, Jeff, was he there that night?"

"Not that I remember," she told him.

"Anyone at all that you remember maybe paying attention to Annie? Anyone who was staring at her? Did you notice? Or did she maybe mention that someone was watching her?"

"No, I'm sorry." Grace shook her head. "If there was, she never mentioned it. And I didn't notice. I'm sorry."

Grace Tobin's attention was drawn to the scene across the street, where a tall thin woman was getting out of the police car that had just pulled up.

"That's Annie's sister, Molly. Do you think it would be all right if I went over . . . ?"

"We'll walk you over, sure." Adam reached a hand up to her from the step upon which he stood, waited while she checked her pocket for her keys, then closed the door behind her.

"Thank you," she whispered as she took his hand and walked with him and Kendra to the foot of Annie McGlynn's driveway, where the media that had earlier gathered now descended upon them.

"Would you mind taking her inside, Kendra?" Adam asked. "Then when you come back out, might be a good time for you to show off the new sketch and talk to the media."

"You got a good description?" Jim Rosello of the Newkirk, Pennsylvania, Police Department, called to Adam.

"Good enough," Adam nodded. "The witness is pretty sure of herself. Kendra's sketch reflects that."

"You think she'll be willing to show the sketch to the press herself, maybe say a few words about it? If she's ready."

"She's ready." Adam turned to watch Kendra come down the front steps. She always managed to draw his attention. Always . . . no matter where he was, no matter what the circumstances.

"Kendra," he called to her.

When she approached, her leather envelope tucked under her arm, Adam introduced her to Chief Rosello, adding, "The chief agrees that now is a good time to show off Jeff to the media."

"Jeff?" the chief asked.

"That's the name the suspect gave to Annie and Grace at the bar," Kendra told him. "Which is probably not his real name, but maybe one he's used before. It's worth mentioning. And something else that might be worth mentioning," she touched the chief's arm as they walked in the direction of the yellow tape that cordoned off the media. "He might be driving a stolen sports car. At least temporarily."

Kendra faced the cameras like a pro, holding up both sketches to show the contrast.

"At first glance, they hardly appear to be the same man," she told them before one of the reporters could make that observation on their own. "You can see how the hair, the glasses, the baseball cap, all combine to make the subject appear older than he looks in the more stripped-down, bald version of himself. There's nothing for him to hide behind here."

"What are the chances that in the first sketch he was wearing a wig?" one of the television reporters asked.

"Chief Rosello?" Kendra stepped back to allow him to respond.

"He could have been," Rosello agreed. "No one

was really close enough to him to be able to make that distinction. And we have no way of knowing that he isn't wearing a wig today. He's not going to be easy to identify. He's clever and he's demonstrated that he will alter his appearance and very well may have again. Keep in mind that facial hair doesn't take all that long to grow for some men. A week from now, he could be sporting a mustache. And now you've seen him with and without hair."

"Do you think it'll be that long before he strikes again?" someone asked.

"The FBI is steering the overall investigation," Rosello turned to Adam, "so I think I'll let Agent Stark respond to that."

Adam spoke with the press for almost ten minutes before he decided to pull the plug on the discussion. It still had not been determined how much information would be released to the public.

Before stepping back from the microphone, Adam added, "One more thing. The suspect may be driving a sports car. He—"

"What makes you think that?" the reporter closest to Adam's right asked.

"There's a possibility that he might have used that as a lure to draw Annie McGlynn into the parking lot. He clearly watches his victims long enough to know their habits, what will draw their attention."

The press digested this bit of news silently before erupting with a barrage of questions.

"Anything else pertaining to this particular case, you'll have to go through Chief Rosello." Adam waved aside the flood of questions.

"Thanks," the chief muttered under his breath as Adam escaped.

"Don't mention it." Adam smiled as he passed.

"Stay and have dinner with me." Adam grabbed Kendra's arm as she was about to get into her rental car.

"Is it dinnertime already?" She looked at her watch.

"Well, it will be, in about an hour or so." He tugged on her sleeve. "Don't leave yet."

"I'm finished here and . . ."

"Okay, so you're finished. I'm not finished." He did a poor job of keeping the exasperation from his voice. "I'm going to be here for a few more days, so I can't offer to drive down and pick you up for dinner. You're here now. I'm entitled to one meal a day, dammit. And I want to have that one damned meal with you."

"Oh," she said, startled by his outburst. "Okay."

"Thank you." He ran a hand through his hair. "I apologize for the tantrum. I usually handle rejection much better."

"That wasn't a rejection. And for the record, I understand there's a lot of pressure associated with this case."

"Pressure from the locals, pressure from my boss, pressure from the press, the families . . ." He leaned back against the car.

"And pressure from yourself to find him before he kills anyone else," she said softly.

"Knowing that unless we get very lucky, he will most likely find his next victim before we find him." He met her eyes straight on.

"How lucky do you feel?" she asked.

"Not lucky at all," he told her. "And very, very tired."

"Then I'll drive," she said, pointing to her rental car, a sensible, late-model sedan.

"Nah." He smiled and pointed to the Audi that was parked two houses down from Grace Tobin's. "I'm not *that* tired."

"Now, that was entertaining." The man grinned broadly. "Very entertaining, indeed."

He tapped his fingers on the arms of the chair and processed all the information that had just fallen into his lap.

Such a lovely pair they made, Kendra and Adam.

Kendra and Adam, he mused. Adam and Kendra.

He'd have to play with them a bit more. Perhaps it was time to give them something more to think about. He'd come up with something.

She is a clever thing though, he'd noted as he'd watched her speak with the press. Her sketches were so accurate. He shook his head, once again admiring her ability. Of course, he'd known just how clever she was.

Still, he couldn't help but feel just a tad bit disappointed in her.

But wasn't she a pretty sight, in her black-and-white checked suit, her hair—his mother used to call that color strawberry blond—swept up off her neck, that thin gold chain and the delicate cross that dangled from it and rested in the hollow of her slender throat.

The thought came to him so suddenly that it startled him, causing him to all but gasp.

Smiling, he put his feet up on the hassock and rested his arms over his chest, feeling quite smug and more than just a bit pleased with himself.

Now, perhaps he'd see just how smart his Kendra really was.

CHAPTER TEN

"You look exhausted," Kendra said after they'd been seated in the small, pleasant restaurant overlooking a golf course, where spotlights glowed here and there to illuminate the greens.

"I am exhausted. Thanks for noticing."

"Hard not to," she smiled gently. "Dark circles under the eyes, difficulty concentrating . . ."

"My concentration is just fine."

"Of course it is. You keep looking back at the specials listed on the blackboard there to see if maybe they've changed it from one minute to the next."

"Very funny. I already know what I'm having."

"What's that?"

"Catfish."

"Ugh. Bottom-feeders." She pretended to shudder.

"I beg your pardon."

"Catfish. They're bottom-feeders." She smiled and leaned forward to add, "And we all know what sinks to the bottom, don't we?"

"Oh, and pray tell, what healthy little number will you be ordering?"

"I'm having the steak. Rare. Baked potato—lots of butter."

"You need a vegetable," he frowned.

"I'll have a salad."

He shook his head. "Someday, when your arteries are so clogged the blood can't pass through, you'll think of me and wish you'd have taken better care of yourself."

"I do take care of myself."

"Kendra, you eat crap."

She grinned and looked up at the waitress who appeared to take their orders.

"How do you argue with a woman like this?" he asked rhetorically.

"I think a better question might be why," the waitress winked at Kendra as she took their orders. She was still smiling when she returned with Adam's beer and Kendra's club soda.

"How can you lecture me on what I eat when you're drinking beer? It's loaded with carbohydrates."

"Carbohydrates are my friends." He sipped at the beer gratefully, hoping to wash away the dust from the crime scene and the tension of the afternoon's interview. "And after the two days I've had, I need all the friends I can get. I earned this beer."

"It's been that bad, then?" she asked softly.

"As bad as anything I've ever seen."

"The woman you found near the stream . . ."

"She was nineteen years old, and he slaughtered her. Brutally raped and slaughtered her."

"That wasn't the way he handled the other women, though. Why are you so sure it's the same man?"

"He was there. We've established that. He was there with Karen Meyer, he killed her there. And there's evidence to show that after he killed his second victim, he washed up in the stream afterward, then, his clothes still wet, carried Karen out of the park. Her clothes were still damp when they found her, from her body being held up against his wet clothes when he carried her. And the lab is testing her clothes and water from the stream for traces of marine life that might match."

"You think it's a mother-thing?" she asked. "I mean, except for this young girl, all of his victims were single mothers. Maybe he has a screwed-up relationship with his mother. Maybe he's killing her. Maybe he thinks it's okay as long as it's done neatly."

"Could be. It will be interesting to see what our profiler has to say when she joins us."

"What do you think?"

"I've thought about the mother angle. All of his victims, with the exception, as you noted, of the young girl at the park, were all mothers of young kids, all single mothers. Not just mothers, though, almost professional moms. Super-moms. The moms who go season to season, from softball practice to soccer games to hockey camp. You know how law enforcement hates it when the press comes along and tags these guys with cutesy nicknames, but Soccer Mom Strangler pretty much sums it up."

"You think he had a super-mom? Maybe one who pushed him into sports or whatever, things he didn't want to do?"

"I think it's just as likely that he had a mother who

didn't give a shit. Or maybe one who directed her energies elsewhere, making him feel that everyone was more important than he was. Maybe he still resents her for it."

"So maybe he's killing women who were the type of mother he never had?"

Adam shrugged. "We'll see what McCall thinks when she gets here."

Kendra sat back to permit the waitress to serve their salads, then set about pouring the dressing over the bowl of greens. When she'd been quiet for longer than he thought was necessary, Adam asked, "What?"

"Nothing."

"There's something," he prodded. "What are you thinking about?"

"How mothers do what they think is best for their kids, and how sometimes it can turn out that what she did might have been the worst for that kid."

"Where's this coming from?"

"This whole thing has just made me think about my mother. She was one of those mothers who always had you moving, always had you involved in something. Ian, even more so than me. She had hoped that keeping him busy would settle him down a little, but it seemed to just make things worse."

"What things?"

"Ian had . . . issues, when he was in grade school. Mom thought it had something to do with our dad dying when he did, with having to grow up without a father. Whatever it was, he went through a stage, starting when he was around nine or ten, when he was a real handful."

"What do you mean?"

"Oh, you know, getting in trouble in school . . ."

"What kind of trouble?"

"Oh, fights. Not doing his homework. Lying." She paused, then added, "He'd gotten pretty defiant toward my mother."

The admission appeared to embarrass her.

"How long did that last?" Adam asked.

"It never ended." She averted her eyes, toyed with a piece of radish with her fork. "My mother almost canceled the summer thing that last year."

"What was the 'summer thing'?"

"Every summer, starting when he was about eight, our cousin Zach would come east and stay with us for two weeks, then Ian would go spend a few weeks in Arizona with Zach and my aunt. But my mother almost didn't let him go to Arizona that last summer. Somehow, in the end, he managed to convince her that it would do him good to get away from home, to be with Zach. Spend some time outdoors, that sort of thing. Ian worked on her for weeks to let him go, to the extent that he did a total about-face. He seemed to change his attitude, picked up after himself, stopped sneaking out at night. . . ."

"He was sneaking out at night as a young child?"

Kendra nodded.

"No wonder your mother was concerned."

"She was beside herself, worrying about him. And then he did such a turn around, that she agreed to let him have his summer. It seemed to mean so much to him." She blew out a long breath. "I guess I don't have to tell you that she never forgave herself."

"She had no way of knowing what was going to happen to him."

"I guess we're back to the old wrong-place-at-the-wrong-time thing again."

They ate in silence, then she asked, to change the subject, "So, what do you think of his latest victim? Annie McGlynn? You think this shows departure from his past MO?"

"Not really. He obviously watched this woman, obviously knew where to go to find her, how to approach her, and how to get her to step outside with him. Something a woman like that wouldn't do under ordinary circumstances.

"So he created circumstances that weren't ordinary." Adam stabbed at a tomato. "Wonder what kind of car he told her he had outside in the lot?"

"You really think that was it?"

"It makes as much sense as anything else. Miranda's going back to the bar tonight to interview several of the regulars. We'll see if anyone noticed something special in the parking lot night before last. She'll show around the sketch you made of the suspect before he shaved his head, see if anyone noticed if he was there the week before. By the way, did I mention that Annie McGlynn had little red marks on the back of her arm?"

"He used the stun gun on her." Kendra set her fork down on the side of her plate.

Adam nodded. "She never knew what hit her. At least not for a while."

"This whole thing is making me sick." Kendra pushed her salad plate to one side. "All of these women who wanted nothing more than to live their lives, raise their kids . . ."

"It is pretty sickening," he agreed. "No one will be happier than I when we finally catch up with him."

"You really think you will? Catch him?" Kendra asked after the waitress served their entrées.

"Yes, I do." He looked at her levelly. "He'll make a mistake. He'll screw up. Sooner or later, he'll do something stupid, because he's been very successful so far and that kind of success will make him cocky. He's a man who wants to be noticed. Men like that always go one step too far. He can't help but call attention to himself."

"Let's hope you're right," she said. "And that it's sooner rather than later."

"Can I interest you in some dessert?" The waitress asked a few minutes later when she passed by the table and noted that both Adam and Kendra had finished eating.

"We'll take a look at the menu," Kendra said, and brightened.

"Of course you will," Adam muttered, recalling that, once upon a time, he'd taken great delight in teasing Kendra about her sweet tooth.

She made a face at him and studied the menu the waitress brought her.

"In addition to the items on the menu, we also have fruit salad," she noted.

"I'll have that," Adam told her.

"And I'll have the Chocolate Overdose," Kendra said, smiling up at the waitress.

"Oh, God." Adam shook his head, and Kendra laughed.

"What is a day without a little chocolate?"

"*Overdose* implies more than a little."

"And with any luck, it will deliver."

He groaned as the chocolate concoction, served in a brandy snifter, was placed before her. Cups of coffee were offered, along with his fruit. He stared blatantly at her dessert: two brownies separated by a layer of chocolate ice cream and covered with hot fudge, topped with whipped cream.

She loaded the spoon with ice cream and hot fudge, waved it in front of him, saying, "You know you want a bite."

"I'll stick with the strawberries."

"Bleh." She wrinkled her nose. "Don't you ever want something you know isn't good for you?"

"Yes," he said quietly, the mirth fading. "Yes, I do."

"Don't you ever just say, the hell with it, and go for it anyway?" she said, oblivious at first to the solemn note that had crept into his voice. Too late, she caught it.

"I'm thinking about it. I've been thinking about it a lot."

She hadn't intended on having the conversation turn serious, and was unprepared for it when it did.

"Sorry, Kendra. But since it's come up, I'm going to have to admit that I never did get you out of my system."

"I wasn't aware that I was in your system."

"Neither was I, until you left."

"I didn't mean to leave." She put her spoon

down, dessert unimportant now. "I got caught up in something—"

"You got married," he reminded her. "I'd say that was caught up in something."

"I never meant for that to happen either. All of a sudden, I was so alone. Everyone was gone." For a brief moment, a shadow passed across her face, laying bare the raw bewilderment, the terror, that must have followed her mother's unexpected death, and suddenly Adam was sorry he'd opened the door onto what was obviously a painful episode in her life.

She swallowed hard. "And Greg was there. We'd gone together in college, he'd moved away, then moved back right before my mother's death. He helped me out so much . . . dealt with things I couldn't deal with. Took care of things for me. When he was offered a position in Washington and asked me to go with him, my first thought was, great. It's the opposite side of the country. I can have a different life there. And maybe if I leave, maybe this numbness will go away. Maybe I'll be able to feel something again."

"Didn't love enter into this at all?"

She looked him squarely in the eyes. "I depended on him a great deal. Cared about him so much—I still do. He's a very good man. But no, I wasn't in love with him, and it occurred to me that I never would be. Once I realized that, it seemed that the best thing I could do for him was to leave while we were still friends."

She toyed with her napkin, realizing that she'd never put it into words so succinctly before. She wondered if

Adam thought she was shallow and callous, and was just about to ask, when she looked up at him.

"What did he say, when you told him you were leaving?"

"He said okay, he understood."

"That's all?"

"Pretty much."

"Just, okay? You can leave?"

She nodded. "Why?"

"If you were my wife," he said as he reached over and touched the tips of her fingers with his own, "you'd have to do a hell of a lot better than that. I would never give up on you that easily."

His hand tugged on hers, then covered it. "I would move heaven and earth to prove that you were wrong, if you were my wife."

"Adam . . ." she whispered, surprised by his admission.

"Sorry." His face colored slightly as the waitress appeared with the check and handed it to him. "I probably shouldn't have said that. And I shouldn't have asked about your marriage. It's none of my business. I'm sorry. I shouldn't have pried."

"I didn't think you were prying," she said in his defense. "Look, I probably should have gotten in touch with you and explained what was happening back then but everything happened so quickly and—"

"No explanations owed—then or now. I shouldn't have brought it up." His smile was terse as he removed several bills from his wallet and left them on the table. "You ready to go?"

She followed him to the cash register, waited while

he paid the bill, and politely thanked him for dinner as she followed him out into the cool April evening.

"Adam, I really want to . . ." she said as he opened the car door for her.

"It's okay, you don't have to. . . . Look, we'd only had a few real dates. I didn't even know if you were interested back then."

"I should have called you. I wanted to call you. It sounds weak and stupid now, but I just got swept up in everything after my mother's death. I was depressed and scared to death, and as hard as it is for me to admit it now, I needed someone to take care of me, Adam. I was at a very low point in my life."

"I would have happily done that." He was close to her now, close enough that she could feel his breath on her face. "I'd have taken care of you."

"No, you wouldn't. At least not for long. It's not a healthy kind of relationship. I know. I've been there. Not just with Greg, but with my mother. After my brother's disappearance my mother just collapsed emotionally, and hung in that state for months. I took care of her, totally, for all that time. It was as if our roles were reversed. As if I was the mother and she the child. I grew very dependent on that role, Adam, and it wasn't healthy. I almost resented her when she started to come out of it and do on her own, for herself. It was hard for me to go back to being the child again. And let's not talk about how I felt when she told me she was going to law school, or that she was getting married again."

She reached her arms up and drew him closer. "That's not the kind of relationship I would have wanted with you. It's not a relationship that can grow into anything good."

"So you're saying it's either a good relationship or no relationship?"

"Well, why would anyone want to get into a relationship that—"

His mouth silenced hers, softly at first, then more insistently. She remembered what it had been like to kiss Adam. Had never forgotten. And he didn't disappoint.

When she could catch her breath, Kendra leaned back and said, "And just for the record, I was interested. I was very interested."

"You were?"

She nodded. "I still am."

"Well, then"—he bent down and kissed her again, more gently this time—"I guess that's a start."

He held the door for her and she eased onto the cool leather seat, her heart still pounding and her head still swimming.

"I guess we'll have to go back and pick up your car," he said as he slid behind the wheel. "Where are you staying tonight?"

"Home," she told him.

"Home?" He frowned. "Why would you drive all the way back there tonight?"

"It's only a few hours," she reminded him, "and besides, my day is going to start early and I have a big dinner date tomorrow night."

"It figures," he grumbled, his good mood swinging south.

She laughed. "I volunteer to provide dinner to Father Tim's shelter for homeless men once a week."

"They let you cook?"

"Smart-ass. Tomorrow's my night."

"Father Tim must be pretty desperate."

"Please. Anyone can put together a spaghetti dinner." She rolled her eyes. "But if the truth were to be known, I am having a little bit of help."

"Ha!"

She laughed in spite of herself. "Selena offered a few jars of sauce that she made last summer."

"Selena who made the wonderful soup?"

Kendra nodded.

"If her spaghetti sauce is as good as her soup, these guys are in for a treat. Think anyone would notice if I sneaked in for one night?"

"Not a chance. Father Tim will feed anyone who comes and sits at his table. No questions asked."

"How do you know you've made enough, if you don't know how many will show up?"

"Somehow it always works out that there's enough." She shrugged.

"Sort of like the loaves and fishes."

"Sort of."

"How did you get involved in that?"

"Through Selena. She met Father Tim when he was first starting up his mission over in Reedsboro to help homeless men and was looking for volunteers. One thing she could do was cook. So she started a program where meals would be served every night of the week and she got others to sign up to take one night. Pretty soon she had enough volunteers to have each person responsible for only one night out of the month. There are beds for a few who have no place else to sleep, and he helps to get medical care for those who need it. There's a shop there where the men can trade hours of service, working on the house or the grounds, for clothing if they need clothes. Residents get three meals a day. . . ."

". . . more than I've gotten lately," Adam noted under his breath.

". . . and there are volunteers to help the men look for jobs. And there are opportunities to earn a few dollars working around the Mission."

"Father Tim sounds very ambitious."

"He is"—she nodded—"and very successful. He's helped hundreds of homeless men over the past few years."

"Can't that prove to be dangerous?" Adam asked as he pulled up alongside Kendra's car on the street near Grace Tobin's house. "Aren't some of those men potentially unstable?"

"There have been no problems that I know of. And Selena is a psychologist. She has provided some counseling services over the years."

"She sounds like quite an interesting woman."

"She is. Did I tell you she's psychic?"

"I thought you said she was a psychologist."

"She is. But she's psychic, too."

"For real?"

"The only real one I've ever met."

"Does she read your mind?"

"Sometimes I think she does, though she doesn't mean to, and tries to hide it when she does."

"I'd like to meet her sometime. I've never met a real

psychic. Ask her if she can help us solve this case, why don't you?"

"It doesn't work like that with her."

"How does it work?"

"I'm not really sure. I think things just come to her."

"Well, see if something will come to her before another woman loses her life, will you?"

"She knows about the case. If she was getting anything on him I wouldn't have to ask. She'd tell me. She just doesn't always know. She tries not to know things."

Kendra thought back on the incident with Lola, and related the story to Adam.

"Someone left a poisoned *sandwich* in your backyard?" His eyebrows raised.

"It was an accident, I'm sure."

"How do you accidentally leave a poisoned sandwich someplace?"

"I can't think of any reason why anyone would have done it intentionally. I think it was a mistake. That it got tossed there somehow by mistake."

"Oh, out of a passing car, perhaps?" he said sarcastically.

"No, but by someone passing by in a canoe maybe. People canoe and kayak back there all the time. Every day."

"Did you tell the police?"

"Of course. They identified the poison as one of those over-the-counter spray insecticides."

"How's the dog?"

"Oh, she's fine. She totally recovered within two days."

"Well, I guess your friend won't be letting her dog run loose anymore."

"It's tough to keep her from running off, Adam. Selena's yard is small and fenced, and Lola likes to run. She often comes to visit with me when Selena is at work or when she sees patients at the house."

"She sees patients at her house? Alone?" Adam frowned. "Are you all nuts back there in Smith's Forge?"

"Nothing ever happens in Smith's Forge, Adam. Nothing ever has. Probably never will."

"Well then, we'll have to see what we can do about that," he said as he drew her to him.

"Why don't you come and see for yourself over the weekend," she suggested. "If you can get away, that is."

"I'm tied up this weekend," he told her. "My father's getting married on Saturday. There will be hell to pay if his only son—and best man—is among the missing."

"Your father is getting married again?"

"Yes."

"Well, don't look so happy about it. Do you know the bride?"

"Sure. Clare was an old friend of my mother's."

"I see."

"Actually, I don't see, but my sister tells me I'm being immature and shortsighted and keeps reminding me that my father deserves to be happy, and that he's been alone for a long time. Which isn't quite true, since he started dating Clare within six months of my mother's death. They just didn't admit to it until last year." He shook his head. "I think it would be easier to accept if they hadn't been so deceitful about it."

"And if he was marrying someone other than your mother's friend?"

"That, too. It feels too much like a betrayal to me."

"If I could give you some unsolicited advice?"

He gestured for her to go right ahead.

"Whatever your feelings are for her, he's still your father. Be grateful you still have him. Be grateful your sister is still a part of your life. Be grateful for any bit of family you still have. Any one of them can be taken from you like that." She snapped her fingers.

"I'll work on it," he said with a nod. "Now, are you sure you won't change your mind and stay over tonight? I'm sure we can get you a room at the hotel where I'm staying."

She shook her head.

"Not this time. I really need to get an early start to-morrow," she said, thinking of cakes to be baked and fruits to be cut up for salad. "I'm not used to cooking for crowds, you know. I have no idea how long all this prep work is going to take."

"I'll walk you to your car then, since I can't talk you into staying over."

"Thanks," she said as she got out of the passenger side.

He opened the back passenger door of her car after she'd unlocked it.

"Sorry," he told her. "Force of habit. Just checking the backseat."

"With everything that's been going on, don't bother to apologize. I appreciate the gesture."

"Keep your doors locked."

"Don't worry about me. I'll be careful. And in a few hours I'll be home, safe and sound in my own house." She leaned up and kissed him soundly on the mouth. "Now you go back to your room and get some sleep. You look like the walking dead."

"Careful, too much flattery could turn my head."

"Go then." She got into her car. "Don't set the alarm, don't ask for a wake-up call. Just sleep."

"That sounds like a good idea." He closed the door for her, then stepped back and watched her turn the car around, waving as she passed. Adam walked back to his own car, got in, and headed for the hotel, praying that tonight there would be no new body, no new call.

CHAPTER
ELEVEN

Selena Brennan had met Father Tim shortly after she purchased the house on Main that had once belonged to her grandparents in Cole, the next town over, and soon became involved in his work of feeding, clothing, and providing a home for indigent men. Before the doors had opened to their first residents, Selena had organized a network of volunteers who would, once a month, provide dinner for whomever needed a good meal. Her network helped to feed Father Tim's flock three hundred sixty-five nights of the year.

Food for the Mission was donated by individuals or by local corporations looking for tax write-offs. The residents could stay as long as they needed to, no questions asked, and in return, they offered their services in accordance with whatever abilities they might possess. Some might paint porch railings or repair a ceiling damaged by a leaking pipe, others might help with the landscaping or volunteer to work in the Mission's thrift shop, where clothing donated by various churches throughout the state was sold.

The residents changed from month to month, week to week. Some would come seasonally, as did the man who worked the cranberry bogs, then sought a bit of a respite before moving south when the cranberry season was over. He would stay at the Mission and offer his services as a mechanic, tuning up whichever of Father Tim's vehicles needed work. Over the years, the Mission had been the recipient of the charitable donations of two pickup trucks, a sedan, a van, and a station wagon. While used mostly for the Mission's needs, there were times when a resident who held a valid driver's license might need transportation to a job interview, or to visit an ailing relative, and Father Tim always made a vehicle available under such circumstances.

The Tuesday dinner crowd at the Ministry of Hope generally numbered around eighteen. When Kendra and Selena arrived with the provisions for the spaghetti dinner they'd volunteered to provide that night, several of the men had already arrived and claimed their places at the two tables that ran the length of what had once been the living room of the old house. Furnishings were intentionally sparse, so that additional tables could be brought in as needed. A serving table was placed at one end of the room, and it was here that plates and flatware could be picked up and taken to the place of choice. Several large bowls of salad and baskets of bread were already on the table.

"How many tonight?" Kendra asked Father Tim when he stuck his head into the kitchen.

"Looks like we'll have maybe nineteen or so." The balding, middle-aged man stepped into the room and lifted a pile of plates. "I'll take these out for you."

"Thanks." Kendra smiled.

"Smells good." The priest nodded toward the large pot of spaghetti sauce.

"Selena's secret recipe," Kendra told him.

"So secret it's on the back of the tomato paste can," Selena said as she came in through the back door, tying an apron around her waist. "Here, Kendra, I brought one for you, too."

Kendra held still long enough for Selena to slip the apron over her head.

"I see Paul is back," Selena said to Father Tim.

"Yes, he didn't have much luck in Baltimore, I'm afraid."

"And Alex, I noticed, is here."

"Same story." Father Tim shrugged. "For some, it's a tougher world than others."

"Who's the man in the red-and-black-checked jacket?" Kendra asked, looking out the window. "He looks familiar."

"Could be," the priest nodded. "He's Cal Lukins's ex-son-in-law. Lost his job in Virginia and tried to move back home, but his family isn't having any of it, since he had all those problems with drugs last year."

"Is he clean now?" Kendra frowned, remembering Cal as the teenager who used to follow her and Selena to the lake when they went swimming, often standing behind the trees at the edge of the lake to watch.

"Would he be here if he wasn't?" Father Tim pointed out. "They all know the rules. No drugs, no alcohol, no women."

"Everyone washes up for meals every day, and no one starts eating until everyone has been served and grace has been said," Selena added.

"That pretty much sums up the rules of conduct," Tim nodded.

A car door slammed in the driveway just beyond the open window, and Selena turned to stare at the four men who got out and stopped to chat with Cal. Then, all five walked toward the house.

"Are they here for dinner?" she asked the priest.

"Yes, they're residents. Ted, he's the tall one with the beard, arrived about a month ago. The two men in the middle there, John and Albert, have been here for most of the winter. Peter, he's the one with the glasses and the ponytail, he's been here on and off for several weeks."

Her eyes narrowing, Selena continued to stare, until Kendra poked her.

"What?"

"I said, do you want to put the pasta on now?" Kendra waved a hand in front of Selena's face.

"Oh, yes, sure . . ."

"I'll go make sure everyone who's eating with us tonight is at their place." Father Tim left the room, a pile of white stoneware plates in hand.

"Is something wrong?" Kendra asked.

"No." Selena shook her head. "Here. Take the rest of these plates in and come back for the flatware. Let's get this show on the road."

Dinner was a civilized affair since Father Tim insisted that the residents bring their manners along with their appetites. Following tradition, Kendra and Selena ate with the residents. Twice, Kendra looked over at her friend to find her sitting quietly, her hands folded in her lap, as if she were meditating. On two other occasions, she'd noticed Selena's eyes moving from man to man, as if searching for something.

"Okay, spill," Kendra said on the way home. "What was going on back there?"

"What do you mean?"

"You know what I mean. The eyes roaming around the room like you were . . . I don't know, expecting something to happen." Kendra frowned.

"No, I didn't expect anything would happen."

"Then what was it?"

"More like . . . a sense of something. Someone. I don't know." Selena put on her left signal to make the turn onto the dirt road. "Like someone . . ."

She struggled for her words.

"Out with it," Kendra sighed.

"Something made the hair on the back of my neck stand straight up tonight and I can't put my finger on what it was," Selena admitted, "or who it was who made me so uneasy."

"You're kidding. One of the residents?"

"It would have had to have been. The only others there were Father Tim and the two of us. I can't explain it. It was a . . . a foreboding, I guess is the best word. A dark . . . something." She shook her head. "I tried several times to identify it, to focus on the source, but I couldn't. There were too many people there, too close together. I just couldn't separate one from the other. And I've ignored these . . . sensations . . . for so long now, that I don't even know if I could identify the source even if I tried."

Selena passed her own house and drove another mile down the road to Smith House.

"That's a little scary," Kendra said as the car pulled into her driveway. "Maybe you should say something to Father Tim."

"Something like what? Oh, by the way, I got bad vibes from one of your guests at dinner the other night, but I don't know which one it was or what it meant, if anything?" Selena shook her head.

"Father Tim knows that you're, well, sensitive. He respects that."

"I don't know how 'sensitive' I am anymore. I tried so hard for so long to push that part of me away, that I don't know how reliable my 'feelings' are. I may have pretty much destroyed or distorted any sensitivity I may have had at one time. I don't know when, if, to trust what I feel anymore." She shrugged. "In any event, the evening's over and if anything should have been said, the time is past. I imagine it was nothing anyway."

"Maybe, maybe not." Kendra opened the passenger door and got out, then leaned back in the window. "But if you get any more of those feelings, pass them on, would you? I for one would be interested in knowing what's behind them. And besides, you know what they say about safe being better than sorry."

Stretched out on the single mattress on the bed in the second room to the left of the stairs, he crossed his legs in the dark and went over the entire evening, from the minute he realized that she was there, in the Mission. There for him to see, to speak with. He could have reached out and touched her if he'd wanted to. No one would have thought it odd or unseemly.

She hadn't suspected. Not for a second.

He was at once elated, and at the same time, disappointed.

She hadn't known him at all.

And hadn't it been such a rush, seeing her here, under the same roof? She'd passed him his cup of coffee, smiled at his conversation, chatted graciously.

It had been a risk, he'd known, to stay, knowing she was there. But it was a risk he simply couldn't resist taking.

She'd been right there, inches away from him.

But she never really *looked* at him. And had she really looked, might she have known?

Unlike that friend of hers, he frowned. That one had scared him a time or two. Something in the way she stared at him had set off his internal alarms. He hadn't liked it. He hadn't liked it one bit.

And she'd sicced that dog on him, he was certain of it, sending it down to the water's edge to frighten him.

He smiled in the dark, wondering how the dog had liked the sandwich he'd left for her.

He turned over onto his side. If he moved up on the pillow just a little, he could see the woods there in the moonlight. From the room's other window, he could see the lake in the center of the town. He liked it here, as much as he had liked any place. Too bad he couldn't stay on and on.

The time would come, soon enough, when he would have to leave and not look back, lose himself again, become someone else again. The thought made him sad. But he'd never forget the kindness of Father Tim and his Ministry of Hope. Father Tim had been good to him. Someday, he vowed, when he had gotten what he'd come for, he'd give something back. Anonymously, of course, but he would show his gratitude. After all, look at all Father Tim had done for him.

Fed him when he was hungry. Offered him shelter, a place to sleep. A place to hide.

Allowed him the use of that old van so he could travel about. Letting him work in the thrift shop so he could earn the money he needed for gasoline and tolls. Not to mention that the shop provided him with a source of clothing so he could always replace what he'd had to dispose of.

No questions asked, ever.

Yes, the Ministry of Hope had been very, very good to him. He was grateful to have found it.

He yawned and pulled the blanket up over his shoulders, ordered himself to sleep. After all, tomorrow was going to be another busy day.

He smiled in the dark. He could hardly wait.

CHAPTER TWELVE

When Joanne Jacobson left her house at five-thirty on Wednesday evening, she never suspected it would be the last time she would ever pass through her front door. She'd paused momentarily to flick a tent caterpillar off the mailbox, then grimaced in disgust as she found another one crawling across the brick walk that she, with the help of her two brothers, had just laid the weekend before.

The thirty-four-year-old mother of two honked the horn of her station wagon impatiently, then gave it another blast just for good measure. Within seconds, the door flew open and her son flew out. If he didn't hurry, she'd told him, he'd be late for the pregame warm-up for the first game of the new baseball season. Besides, she reminded him, she'd volunteered to man the refreshment stand that night, and she still had to pick up all those cases of soda, all those boxes of chips.

Ten minutes later, she pulled into the parking lot at the ballpark, and after winking at him for luck—at twelve, he was too old to publicly kiss—she drove to the local beverage distributor. After having the cases of soda stacked into the back of her car, she returned to the ball field and drove around to the far side, where the stand was located, to park behind the small building that was constructed out of concrete block.

There was another car already parked there, another station wagon—late model, light silvery blue in color, its back gate standing open—in the single parking space. Not having time to search for the owner to ask that the car be moved, she parked next to it, mumbling curses under her breath that she'd have to carry all these heavy cases by herself, from the back of her car, around that car, and into the back of the refreshment stand. She unlocked the back door, then returned for the soda.

"Let me give you a hand with that," said a gentle voice from behind.

She turned to offer her grateful thanks, but the word never had a chance to pass her lips.

She collapsed like a balloon with an air leak, right into his arms.

He merely turned around and dropped her neatly into the back of the wagon, where he quickly bound her wrists and ankles with the rope that had already been measured and cut for that purpose, and taped her mouth. He threw a blanket over her unconscious form, tossed the stun gun into the cargo area next to sweet Joanne, and whistled on his way to the driver's side door. He ducked into the car to avoid being seen by the boy who, completely unaware of what had just transpired, walked leisurely in the direction of the snack hut.

"Mom?" He heard the boy's confused call as he drove away. "Mom?"

Joanne Jacobson was found seventeen hours later, sprawled in a field not far from the tracks of the Strasburg Railroad, a popular tourist attraction outside of Lancaster. A group of Amish children, taking a short-cut through a cornfield on their way to school, had found the body and gone running off in different directions in terror at the sight of the young nearly naked "English" woman, at the same time obliterating any other footprints that might have been present. The father of the group, once summoned, alerted the authorities. Within an hour, the fields were overrun with police officers, state troopers, and FBI agents. It was unclear to Amos Stolzfus, the man in whose field the body lay, just who, exactly, was in charge.

Adam Stark stood near the body and stared, taking in the scene and mentally comparing it to the scenes where the other women had been found. What was the same? What was different?

This place was more secluded than the others had been. In the past, the killer had dumped his victims in prominent places, places where they'd be found sooner rather than later. But he'd taken no time to arrange them, pose them, as some killers might do. He'd merely dropped them off, and they landed as they fell, as had this one, as if they were no longer important, no longer held his interest. Adam knelt down next to the body and stared into lifeless eyes that sat in a face too swollen for him to know if she'd been pretty or not. He guessed that she had been. All of the other victims were.

The sunlight glittered off the gold cross that hung around her neck and the flies buzzed around her, as if claiming their rights. He hoped that the crime scene technicians were quick in gathering their evidence. He hated when bodies had to remain in the sun for too long. It seemed disrespectful not to move them to shelter, to not take them away from the heat and the beetles and the flies.

"He's getting really bold," Adam said to no one in particular. "He took that woman literally from under the noses of about seventy-five people, including her own son."

"He's getting quicker, too," a uniformed officer responded in passing. "We've already found the car."

"Wiped down, of course." Adam nodded.

"Of course. From stem to stern. Wiped down, washed off. Not a print to be found anywhere except for those from the guys in the car wash. I'm guessing he had a sheet or something under her to eliminate trace evidence."

"Description from the car wash?" Adam asked.

"White male, six feet one, baseball cap over longish brown hair."

"Another disguise."

"Sure. Why not? Look how successful he's been, changing his appearance. Changes his cars." The officer shook his head. "The owner of this last car didn't even know the car had been stolen, that's how quickly this guy works. Steals the car, steals the woman, does his thing, dumps the woman, dumps the car, and *poof!* He disappears into thin air and leaves nothing behind."

"Nothing but another dead woman." His hands on his hips, Adam watched the crime scene investigators move in, then jammed his hands into his pockets and walked away.

And less than thirty-six hours later, yet another body was found.

Adam stood at the head of the conference room table in the state police barracks outside of Lancaster where all involved law enforcement agencies convened to meet with the profiler handpicked by John Mancini to join his team.

In her mid-to-late thirties, wearing a stylish suit of pale green with a matching top under the open jacket, her short blond hair curled softly around her face, Anne Marie McCall was all business. Her impatience to get on with it was well known within the Bureau, and Adam was not the only one who had to suppress a smile as she barely hesitated before introducing herself rather than wait for one of the other agents to do the honors for her.

"I've studied your evidence." She launched right into it, walking around the table and making eye contact with everyone there in his or her turn. "I've studied your photos, your reports, your witness statements, your victims, the autopsy reports. I've spoken with the homicide detectives and I've visited the sites where the bodies were found. Let's talk about what conclusions I've come to."

McCall stepped back from her chair, her hands on her hips. She was getting into the groove, and would wander around the room, putting together her profile of their killer as she mentally reviewed the notes she'd made while going over all the case data.

"Based on the range of ages of the victims—and I'm not counting the nineteen-year-old here, she was an aberration—we're looking for a man between the ages of twenty-three and thirty, though I believe he's probably at the lower end of that range. He's white, he's physically strong, capable of lifting and carrying up to at least one hundred thirty-five pounds, the weight of his heaviest victim."

She stared at the back wall for a long minute.

"Socioeconomic status? Tough to call." McCall nodded thoughtfully. "He has a great deal of mobility, which could suggest that he's self-employed, but more likely unemployed. The abductions occurred on different days of the week as well as on a weekend. The victims were all found within twenty-four hours or less following their disappearance. So far, they've all been from neighboring communities, some driving time involved, so we know he's mobile. He's stealing cars to get around. Stealing and then returning cars. So we know that he has mobility and flexibility in his employment, if in fact he is employed, and in his lifestyle. He is either single, or living with someone who doesn't keep tabs on him. He's very, very organized; he knows everything he needs to know about his victims before he strikes. He apparently doesn't like surprises."

"Julie Lohmann surprised him," one of the officers noted.

"And we'll get back to her in a few." McCall nodded. "Okay, we know he studies his victims carefully before he goes after them. He follows them, maybe occasionally even speaks to them. It would excite him, knowing that she has no idea of what he's planning on doing to her. So it follows that he's a low-key kind of guy, the kind who doesn't set off any alarms, doesn't call attention to himself in any manner that would cause suspicion. He fits in wherever he is."

McCall paused at the window, looked out across the rolling fields and up at the sky, barely noticing that the gathering clouds threatened a sudden storm.

"Where and how does he find his victims?" she asked, then answered, "At ball games. Soccer, softball . . . where he can get close enough to study without anyone being aware that he's watching. When the game is over, he can even follow his prey closely from the field to the parking lot without drawing any notice at all, maybe hear her voice, catch her scent. He fits in, age-wise—probably looks like any other dad, there to watch his kid."

She turned to the group and asked, "Who would suspect? Who would know?"

No one sitting around the table moved.

"Now, we've concluded that he's highly organized," she continued, "methodical, coolly efficient. Determined. He is highly controlled. The rapes, the strangulations, appear to be committed in an almost passionless manner. Perfunctory. Emotionless. The clothing disturbed only enough for him to complete his task. With the exception of the rope marks, there's little bruising, no bites, no excessive vaginal tearing. The intimacy is all superficial. That's his comfort zone. No investment of himself here. Some rapists, as you are all aware, really enjoy the act, enjoy inflicting pain and fear. This guy, on the other hand, appears to be wanting to get it over with."

"Then why do it?" someone asked.

"Oh, I think it's a power thing. He's proving that he's in control. He can—and will—do whatever he pleases to them and they are powerless to stop him. He's *the man*. And he needs to prove that. Maybe to an authority figure. Someone he feels treated him badly. Maybe his mother." She hesitated, then added, "Probably his mother. He exercises his power over her, but still treats the victim with a certain amount of reserve."

"Showing his respect?" a trooper asked sarcastically.

"Possibly. And remember, there's evidence that all of his victims, except for Julie Lohmann, were stunned twice. I think he stung them the first time to initially subdue them. To gain control over them."

"And the second time before he raped them, so they couldn't fight back," one of the Deal detectives said.

"True. But it also rendered them powerless. Making the humiliation of the rape that much more complete. And then he strangled them. Again, apparently with little emotion. The marks on the necks of the victims show precise placement to make the killing as swift as possible. There was no dragging out of this act either."

"So you're saying we have an UNSUB who rapes and murders but doesn't enjoy it?" A skeptical young state trooper sat back in his chair, arms folded across his chest.

"Yes, that's what the evidence tells us."

"Why would anyone do that if he doesn't enjoy any of it?"

"I didn't say he didn't enjoy any of the process." McCall leaned on the back of her chair. "Let's look at his behavior for a moment. Certain aspects of these crimes were high risk. Abducting women from parking lots. Amy Tilden from her children's school, where several hundred parents and teachers met in classrooms that overlooked the lot. Two of our victims from public parking lots in their towns. One from the snack stand at a crowded Little League field in broad daylight. What does this suggest?"

Before she could answer her own rhetorical question, Chief Ford said, "He's arrogant, confident, thinks he's so much smarter than we are that he can flaunt himself and we'll still never be able to find him."

"That's right. He exposes himself to a high risk of being identified, even caught. But he does it anyway, because it excites him. It's the risk that excites him. Judging from the emotionless way the actual rapes and murders were committed, one would wonder if the planning and the risk-taking weren't perhaps more enjoyable for him than the actual acts."

"Then why do it?" someone asked. "Why risk so much to commit crimes that don't really turn you on?"

"Maybe the risk is the turn-on," McCall said with a shrug. "Or maybe the crimes are merely a means to an end. A way of calling attention to himself."

"Yet he takes pains not to get caught."

"But he lets himself be seen," the lead detective from Walnut Creek reminded them. "Closely enough that we were able to get a good sketch. Does he want to be caught?"

"I don't think he wants to be *caught*," Miranda Cahill spoke up for the first time. "I think he wants to be *noticed*."

"I believe that may be the key," McCall agreed.

"Noticed by whom?" an officer turned to ask.

"Perhaps by someone connected to the investigation."

The gathering of law enforcement personnel gazed around the table at each other.

"Who?" someone asked. "Someone here?"

"Quite possibly," McCall agreed. "Of course, if we knew whose attention he's after, we'd probably be well on our way to figuring out who he is, wouldn't we?"

"So, in other words, he's showing off for someone?"

"In other words, yes, possibly. But I don't think this is the first time."

"Not the first time?" Adam asked. "You're saying he's killed before?"

"Yes, several times I'd venture to guess. He's way too smooth for a beginner." McCall shook her head. "And the precise manner in which he's conducted the crimes, choreographed, scripted. Novices rarely kill in so highly disciplined a fashion."

"Except for Julie Lohmann," Chief Ford noted.

"Ahhh, this young girl." McCall shook her head, her eyes showing real emotion for the first time since she began speaking. "This is different. He totally lost it with her. Who knows which of them surprised the other, but she was definitely a surprise. She probably tried to run, maybe screamed. That would have excited him. The autopsy showed a violent rape, a lot of vaginal tearing, bite marks on her breasts and neck, an excessive number of stab wounds. He simply hadn't planned on her. There was no script, and so he just went with his emotions with this one."

"Emotions?" an officer asked.

"Everything he's suppressed with the others. Everything he held back." McCall turned away. "This poor girl took the brunt of it."

"So where do we go from here? I'm throwing this open for suggestions"—Lieutenant Barker stood to one side of the table after Anne Marie McCall sat down—"because I don't have a clue, folks. This son of a bitch has walked past us like a phantom. He comes and goes as he pleases. He abducts his victims at will, kills them and drops them into our midst, then vanishes. We have seven dead women and no credible leads. He's the invisible man. He's not leaving much behind."

"He may have left something behind these last two times," Adam spoke up.

"You mean his DNA? He's been leaving that all over the place," Barker growled.

"More than his DNA. As you all know from studying the scene or the photos, Joanne Jacobson was found wearing a gold cross on a chain around her neck."

"So what?" a detective from Walnut Crossing asked.

"So her sister claims never to have seen it before," Adam said, turning to him.

The detective shrugged. "Maybe she has a boyfriend."

"If she does, then Leslie Miller, last night's victim, was seeing the same guy." Adam tossed photos of both women onto the table. "Same cross, same chain. And Miller's ex-husband swears she never wore anything around her neck."

The eleven men and three women seated around the table moved forward in unison toward the table for a closer look.

"The earlier victims weren't wearing these." Miranda was the first to speak up. "So why now? He's sending us a message, but what is it?"

"Maybe he found religion," a uniformed member of the Dale Police Department offered.

"It feels more like a taunt, somehow," Adam said, a thought niggling at the back of his mind. What was it that seemed so familiar about the cross? He stared at it, trying to remember.

"Maybe he's asking us to pray for his victims?" the chief of the Windsorville Police Department ventured as the photographs were passed around the table. "Or for him."

"Yeah, I'll pray for him, all right," the trooper nearest the door muttered. "Pray that he burns in hell."

Hours later it hit him.

Then, even as his blood turned cold, Adam left his hotel room, his cell phone in his hand, dialing as he walked though the lobby.

"Rosello," the Newkirk chief of police answered his private line.

"Can you get me a copy of the tape that one of your local stations made of our compositor showing off the sketch she made outside of Annie McGlynn's last week?" Adam asked after identifying himself. "There's something I want to check out. Can you arrange it? Yes, as soon as possible. I can be at your office in less than an hour. Thanks, Chief."

Adam disconnected the call, slapping the phone on his palm without even realizing he was doing so, and walked to his car. He dialed Kendra's number, then started his engine, pulling out of the parking lot as he counted the rings. She picked up on the fourth ring, just as the answering machine came on.

"Hey, Adam, hi." She sounded out of breath. "Hold on, let me turn off the machine . . . how are you?"

"Good. I'm good." He hesitated, then asked, "How are you?"

"I'm fine. I was just faxing my report to John. I figured my work on this case was done." She paused, then asked, "My work is done on this one, isn't it?"

"I think so. It's almost pointless now to try to keep up with his disguises. He has a full, thick head of dark hair, he's bald, he has a brown ponytail, he has a blond crew cut. He's driving a Taurus wagon, a Chevy pickup, a Pathfinder, a sports car . . ."

"He's very, very clever, isn't he?"

"Very." Adam bit the inside of his bottom lip. *It's just a theory,* he reminded himself. And he could be wrong. He prayed he was wrong.

"Where are you?" she was asking. "Are you still in Pennsylvania?"

"Yes. I'm in Spring Glen, but I'm on my way to see Rosello in Newkirk."

"Oh?" Curiosity caused her voice to perk up just a bit. "Something come up?"

"Just want to compare notes on something."

"You going to tell me?"

"After I speak with Rosello." He accelerated as he pulled onto Route 30 and eased into the fast lane.

"Are you going to make it to your father's wedding?"

"Oh, shit," he swore. "That's tomorrow afternoon. Damn it. If I'm not there, he's going to think it's because I don't *want* to be there."

"I'm sure if you explain what you're working on . . ."

"My future stepmother won't care. She'll see it as a slight."

"Is it possible to take an afternoon off?"

"Tough to do in the middle of an investigation like this. But, maybe I can squeeze out a few hours." He sighed, wondering if, in fact, his father would understand.

Adam changed lanes, darting around a tractor trailer to get to open road. "Kendra, tell me again about the dog being poisoned."

"What?" He could almost see her frown.

"Tell me about the dog. . . ."

He kept her on the phone for as long as he could, on the one hand soothed by the connection, however remote, on the other, worried that he'd soon learn that his crazy idea wasn't so crazy after all.

When he arrived at the Newkirk Police Station, Rosello had the videotape already in the VCR.

"I've watched it twice already," the chief told

Adam, "and I can't for the life of me figure out what it is you're looking for."

Adam caught the remote that Rosello tossed to him and rewound the tape, then hit play. The tape ran for almost forty-five seconds before Adam froze the tape.

"There." Adam leaned closer to the screen. "That's what I'm looking for."

From his briefcase, Adam removed a folder. He dropped it in the chief's lap, then watched for a reaction as Rosello thumbed through the pack of photos.

"You're looking at the cross." Rosello looked up. "The one your compositor is wearing."

"It's identical to the ones placed around the necks of the last two victims, apparently by the killer. The families of both of these women swear they'd never seen the victims wear such a cross."

"Why do you suppose he did that?" Rosello looked back at Kendra's image, motionless on the big screen. "Unless he's trying to get her attention."

"God knows he's got mine," Adam said, hitting the eject button and pocketing the tape. "I'll get this back to you."

"It's a copy of the copy." Sensing that Adam was in a hurry, Rosello stood up to walk him to the door. "I figured if the tape was so important that you'd drive all the way back here to watch it, that you'd want to be taking it with you."

"Thanks." Adam saluted as he headed for the exit. "I owe you one."

"I just don't get it," Kendra yawned, then excused herself. She'd been reading in bed, had fallen asleep only to be awakened by Adam's call. "Why would the killer be doing this? Because I did the sketches of him? My sketches certainly haven't cramped his style at all, not as far as I can tell. If anything, he's escalated his activity since that tape was first shown on television. And I'm not his customary victim of choice. I'm nobody's mother. I'm not blond. I just don't get it."

"I'm not certain I do either, but it seems like too much of a coincidence. You're on TV wearing a cross around your neck, he starts putting them on his victims."

"Well, if he's sending a message, it's gone right over my head." She stifled another yawn. "What does your profiler say?"

"She's already said she believes he's trying to get the attention of someone connected to the investigation."

"I wonder why he didn't do something sooner, like with the other victims. There weren't any similarities with any of them, were there?"

"None that were readily noticeable, but Miranda is already checking on that. And think about this: Maybe it's someone who was caught and convicted because of a composite that you did in the past. Or someone who loved someone you sketched."

"Adam, I don't know the whereabouts of every convicted criminal I've drawn since the beginning of my career."

"No, but that would be easy enough to check. Can you give me a list of names?"

"Actually, I can do better than that. I can give you their names and copies of their composites. I've kept every one. But I can tell you that if I'd ever sketched this man before, I'd remember the face. It's an intimate thing, drawing someone's face. And I know I've never done this man before."

"All the same, I'd like you to fax those sketches down to Mancini first thing in the morning."

"Sure."

"Kendra, what are your plans for the weekend?" he asked abruptly.

"Don't really have any. Why?"

"Come with me to my dad's wedding."

"Wait a minute, I thought you said earlier that you wouldn't be able to go."

"I spoke with John after I left Newkirk, gave him an update. He thought I could spare a few hours."

There was silence on the phone.

"Adam, John would never tell you, or any other agent, to leave a major investigation, even for a few hours. There has to be more to this than you're telling me." She bit her bottom lip, then said, "You don't think he's going to come after me, do you?"

"You may well be the party whose attention he's trying to get. Someone has to keep an eye on you until we figure out why, and who. It might as well be me."

Another silence.

Finally, she sighed heavily.

"What time will you be here?"

CHAPTER THIRTEEN

"Look down in that valley," Kendra said as she stared out the car window at the blurred scenery whizzing by the Audi's window. "There's another one of those pretty little towns, with the white-spired churches and all the pretty houses."

"I don't know that, up close, they're all that pretty," Adam replied.

"Why wouldn't they be?"

"A lot of those towns were coal mining towns," he told her, never taking his eyes off the road. "And when the mines closed up, so did a lot of the towns."

"You mean the towns are abandoned?"

"Not entirely, but many of them have very little going on these days. No industry moved in to replace coal."

"How do you suppose they make a living, then?" She turned back to him. "The people in those towns?"

"Any way they can."

"When did the mines close up?"

"Most of the anthracite mines were closed by the 1920s. After that, there was a lot of strip mining, but this country was weaning itself off coal and turning to oil and gas." He pointed off to the right. "If you look up that hill, you can see the scars the strip mines left behind."

Her gaze followed upward, where a deep gash, like a ravine, seemed to cut the hill in two.

"There wasn't a kid that I knew growing up in Hopewell who hadn't been touched by coal, shaped by it, one way or another," Adam added.

"How were you shaped by it?"

"Oh, I come from a bit of a mixed bag." His mouth turned up at one side in a sort of half-smile. "On my father's side I had a great-great-uncle who was in the Molly Maguires, and on my mother's a great-grandfather who was one of the Pinkerton agents hired to infiltrate the group and bring them down."

"Your family gatherings back then must have been interesting," she noted, leaning back against the headrest.

"So they tell me." He smiled, recalling the stories his grandfather used to tell.

"I guess you take after the Pinkerton side."

"I admit to having been inspired by an old photo of my great-great-grandfather. I never really wanted to be anything except an FBI agent."

"But you played professional football for all those years."

"Eight years." He emphasized the eight.

"And then you just stopped?"

"Yep. That was the plan."

"Would it be too personal if I asked what the plan was?"

"The plan was to retire from football before I got

so banged up I wouldn't be able to pass the FBI physical."

"But I thought playing professional sports was supposed to be every little boy's dream."

"It wasn't mine."

"Then why did you do it?"

"You grow up in coal country and you play sports because that's what you do. Don't get me wrong, Kendra, I love football. Loved playing it in high school. It was the best." His voice softened. "And it was my way out. It was my ticket to Penn State. And around here, playing football for Penn State is as close to heaven as a guy can get. Not just for you, but for your entire family. My father got to wear the Penn State jacket, the sweatshirt. Everyone knew that Frank Stark's son played linebacker for Penn State. It was a huge feather in his cap."

"Did you enjoy it?"

"Penn State?" He laughed. "My God, you'd have to be dead to not love playing ball for them. I was grateful for the opportunity to go there, to play there. It had been one of my prime goals, to go there. And from there, to the FBI Academy."

"But you decided to play professional football instead."

"That was never really on my agenda." He shook his head. "But my junior year, the defensive coach took me aside after a game and introduced me to the scout from the Cleveland Browns. Then a few weeks later, from the Patriots. Then the Raiders. The Steelers . . ."

He flicked on his right-turn signal and headed for the exit.

"And then I was drafted by the Steelers and on my way to Pittsburgh."

"You must have been excited, though."

"Oh, of course I was. Who wouldn't be? The thought of being able to play for a few more years—and to get paid a lot of money to do it—well, that was amazing. It had all come as a bit of a surprise to me, that's all."

"I guess your dad was proud."

"My dad was almost hyperventilating when I told him." Kendra noticed Adam wasn't smiling. "Any thoughts I might have had about turning down the offer went out the window. There was no way I could have disappointed him like that."

"But surely he would have understood."

"No. He would not have." He slowed down as he started down the exit ramp. "The town I grew up in was—is—very working class. The kind of neighborhood where people still hang their laundry out back and stores will still give kids credit because the owner has known the family for generations. No one from Hopewell had ever played football for Penn State. No one had ever been drafted to play a professional sport. There was no way I could have, or would have, walked away from the opportunity."

Adam pulled up to the self-serve pump at the first gas station he came to.

"Don't misunderstand," he said, opening his door, "I have no regrets. I was damned lucky, and I know it. I made the kind of money I know I'll never make again. I wouldn't take those years back for anything.

But the whole time I was playing, I felt as if I was looking over my shoulder. I was so afraid I'd get hurt, that something would happen and I wouldn't qualify for the Academy. I just wanted to get through that, to get to this. This—working for the Bureau—is what I was meant to do. What I dreamed of doing when I was a kid."

He filled the tank, paid for the gas with a card, and got back into the car, glancing at his watch.

"It's already two," he said. "The wedding is supposed to start at three. We're going to go directly to my grandmother's. You can change there, if you like."

"I would appreciate that." Kendra looked down at her khaki pants and light blue sweater. Comfortable traveling clothes, but not wedding attire. Adam had told her there'd be a place for her to change before joining the rest of the family at his sister's house for the festivities.

The signpost at the corner of the street Adam turned on to was bent at an odd angle, as if recently struck by a car and not yet repaired. The street itself was narrow, the cars parked on either side allowing easy passage of one vehicle at a time. The houses were all bungalow-style one-and-one-half-story structures dating from the early 1900s, some with enclosed porches, all with narrow driveways and cement walks leading the short distance from front steps to the street. Adam made a slow right into the drive of a small shingle house that was identical to those on either side except for the fact that its cedar shakes remained their original brown, while the house to the left had been painted white, and the one on the right had been recently re-sided with a cream-colored vinyl. There were hydrangeas and azaleas in bloom beside the open porch, and cement urns at the base of the steps were crowded with pansies. White curtains hung at every window, and in the doorway stood a plumpish woman who looked to be in her mid-seventies.

"Hi, Gran!" Adam called to her as he got out of the car.

"How in the world does a big boy like you fit into that little bitty car?" The old woman stepped out onto the porch, her arms crossed over her chest.

"I just fold myself up, and slide in." He waited for Kendra, then took her elbow, whispering, "Ah, by the way, she thinks you're my girlfriend."

"Why did you tell her that?" Kendra murmured, smiling at the woman who had moved to the top step.

"It was that or tell her I'm trying to keep you out of the clutches of a serial killer."

"You couldn't have just said we were friends?" She nodded.

"No one around here would believe that."

She was about to ask why not, when his grandmother called a greeting from the porch. They had reached the end of the walk and Adam dropped her arm to take the steps two at a time and embrace his grandmother.

"You look wonderful, Gran." He kissed her soundly on the cheek.

"Thank you, son, so do you." She patted the sides of his face with her hands, all the while peering over his shoulder to get a better look at the young woman who'd accompanied her only grandson on this trip home.

"Gran, this is Kendra Smith." Adam draped an arm over his grandmother's shoulder. "Kendra, this is my grandmother, Alice McGovern."

"Good to meet you, Mrs. McGovern." Kendra flashed her best smile.

"Good to meet you as well." Adam's grandmother smiled back. "Now, come in, come in. I thought we'd have time for tea before we go over to Kelly's."

Alice McGovern opened the door and waited for them to enter the dark, cool foyer.

"Come on back to the kitchen"—Mrs. McGovern bustled past her visitors—"the water is all ready. And I made some of those raspberry cookies you love, Adam."

"Gran, do you think we have time for tea?"

Alice turned and glared at her grandson.

"Oh, right." Adam nodded. "Tea it is."

Kendra followed into a small, all-white kitchen that was surprisingly modern and equipped with all new appliances.

"I had to hide them from Alex and Melanie, of course, those two buggers are always into my pantry."

"Alex and Melanie are my sister's kids," Adam explained. "They live a half-dozen doors down on the opposite side of the street, which is where the wedding is going to be."

"They stay here after school until Kelly or her husband, Scott, gets home from work, whoever gets home first gets the kids. They're only here for two hours or so in the afternoon, but they do keep me moving. I spend my days resting up for three o'clock when the school bus lets them off."

The entire time Alice McGovern spoke, she was in motion, albeit somewhat slow motion, pouring tea into the teapot and then into the cups that had already been arranged on the kitchen table, set for tea for three, with porcelain cups and saucers and matching plates.

"Adam, you pull that chair out for your lady friend and show your manners," she instructed.

"Yes, ma'am." He grinned, then held a chair out for her as well, and remained standing until both women were seated.

"Now, then, we can have a nice little chat and get acquainted before we go to the wedding." Mrs. McGovern nodded. "Kendra, Adam tells me you're an artist."

"A sketch artist, yes."

"Lovely." Alice passed Kendra the plate of fruit-filled sandwich cookies with hands distorted by arthritis. "Do you do landscapes or portraits?"

"I guess you could call them portraits."

"Kendra does composite drawings, Gran. For law enforcement agencies. She'll interview witnesses and then make a drawing."

"Oh, like that one I saw on the news the other night? That man who's been killing all those poor girls down near Philadelphia?"

"Yes, exactly like that." Adam sipped at his tea, which he never drank, except when he was here. He wasn't particularly fond of the beverage, but tea with his gran was a ritual left over from his high school days, and he'd never let on.

"Actually, that was my sketch," Kendra said, wondering why Adam had neglected to add that.

The woman's face went white. "Why, I can't believe they'd let a pretty little thing like you get that close to a monster like him."

"No, no, Mrs. McGovern, I don't have to get anywhere near him. I just talk to people who have seen him, and they tell me what he looked like, and I try to draw him from their descriptions," Kendra assured her. "I never get close to him."

"She tries to make the picture look enough like the suspect so that if someone sees that person, they will recognize him and call the police."

"Well, that's a relief." Adam's grandmother did look relieved. "I'd hate to think about you having to meet face-to-face with those awful people. I used to worry something fierce about Adam, until they gave him that nice desk job."

Desk job? Kendra mouthed the words silently.

Adam winked.

"Now, tell me how you learned how to draw faces like that? It's an odd profession for a woman," she frowned, then added hastily, "though I'm sure you're quite good at it."

"I've always been interested in faces." Kendra suppressed a smile. "And I've always liked to draw. It just seemed natural to combine the two."

"Did you go to art school, to learn how to draw faces?"

"No. I did have some formal art courses in college,

but I really taught myself. I used to sketch the people sitting near me in class, and my neighbors, and the girls in the dorm. I'd go to Ocean City—that's on the New Jersey shore—and sit on the boardwalk, and draw the people who walked by. When I got older and was looking for a career, I was lucky to be able to find one that let me use that ability." Kendra left out the parts about her brother and the fact that her well-connected stepfather had opened the door for her first freelance job for the FBI. She had completely understood that while his influence had gotten her the opportunity, subsequent assignments would not be forthcoming if she didn't get the job done. But there was no point in going into any of this with Adam's grandmother. She merely said, "I was lucky to get referrals to other law enforcement agencies, but most of my work has been for the FBI."

"Gran, we're going to need to change for the wedding." Adam touched his grandmother on the arm. "I'll run out to the car and get our things so we can leave on time. I don't think Dad would appreciate his best man being late."

"I do appreciate punctuality," Alice McGovern said to Kendra as Adam left the room. "Especially for an occasion like this. Why, I expect I'll see some people I haven't seen since Lynnie died."

"Lynnie?"

"My daughter. Adam's mother."

"Oh."

"Seven years come August, it will be. Can't hardly believe it's been that long, myself, but there it is."

"Did you have other children, Mrs. McGovern?"

"No, just the one daughter." The woman's face brightened. "But she was enough. She was a treasure. A joy, every day of her life. It was the saddest day of my life, the day I buried her. Sadder than losing my husband, and he died when I was only thirty-one."

"So you raised her alone, for the most part."

"She was seven when her father died. Mostly, it was just me and her, until she married Frank. I missed her from the day she left to get married. I still miss her. She was my best friend, Lynnie was."

"I know exactly how you feel." Kendra touched her arm gently. "I lost my father when I was young. And my mother and I were very close."

"And she has passed on?"

"Four years ago."

"I'm so sorry." Mrs. McGovern took Kendra's hands and folded them within her own.

"Thank you." Kendra fought back the lump that had unexpectedly formed in her throat.

"Kendra," Adam called from the front of the house, "I have your things here. You should probably run upstairs and change now. Gran, is the guest room all right for Kendra to use?"

"Yes, dear," she called back to him, "it's always ready for company."

Kendra stood, her teacup in hand. "Thank you for the tea, Mrs. McGovern."

"It was my pleasure, dear."

The old woman watched approvingly as the younger woman rinsed her teacup and saucer at the sink, then set it upon the counter before leaving the room. She heard Adam's voice in the foyer as he gave Kendra instructions on which room upstairs she could use and where the bathroom was, and she smiled to herself. Adam was the undisputed apple of her eye. It had been so very long since he'd brought a girl home, and it was time he settled down. The whole family was eager to meet her. And Kendra did seem like such a nice girl, Alice thought as she rinsed her cup and Adam's and placed them on the counter next to Kendra's.

The arthritis in her hip had been acting up again, and she'd decided that she'd use her cane this afternoon. Not that the hip was that bad, but as an accessory, the cane served more than one purpose. She wasn't above seeking a sympathetic audience when she could get one, and today, for certain, she'd have all the attention she could hope for.

"Gran, I'm just going to duck into your room to change if that's okay." Adam peered around the door frame.

"Go right ahead, dear." Alice nodded, then went into the dining room where she straightened a bowl of roses, killing time until she heard him open the door and step back into the hallway. She called to him to join her. She'd been hoping for a few minutes alone with him to speak her piece on an issue that she felt needed discussing.

"My, don't you look handsome in that dark suit." She smiled as she fussed about the knot in his tie, which, while perfect, was never too perfect that she couldn't fuss over it all the same. "And I'm so happy that you agreed to be your father's best man. It means a lot to him, son. He wants so badly for you to be all right with his marriage to Clare."

"Being his best man doesn't necessarily mean that I approve, Gran."

"He's your father, Adam. He doesn't need your approval."

"Ouch." He smiled in spite of himself. Few people had the ability to put things into perspective the way his grandmother did.

"Tell me, son," she leaned upon her cane, "would you feel the same way if your father was marrying someone other than Clare?"

"Maybe not. I guess it does bother me that she was friends with Mom for all those years." He hesitated for a moment. "All those months she was around when Mom was sick . . ."

"Do you think she had an ulterior motive, then? All those times she stopped in to see your mother, you think she was just waiting for her to die so she could move into her life?"

"Gran, that's a terrible thing to say!" Adam stared at his grandmother in disbelief.

"Well, that appears to be your implication."

"Are you happy about this wedding?"

"It doesn't matter whether I am or not. The only person who has to be happy is your father. I personally never cared much for Clare, but I'm not the one marrying her. If she can make your father happy, share his life in a way that matters to him, that's what counts."

He started to reply when he heard Kendra coming down the steps.

"We're in here, dear," Alice called to her before Adam could open his mouth. "In the dining room."

She moved closer to the china cupboard, where all manner of objects were displayed.

"Now, are you a Hummel collector?" she asked Kendra.

"Hummel?" Kendra looked through the glass door of the cupboard at the rows of cherub-faced figurines, then shook her head. "Oh, no."

"Oh, good." Alice pretended to fan herself with one hand to show her relief. "I already promised them to Kelly, you know. But I have some lovely Depression glass that you and Adam might like."

Alice opened the cupboard door and reached for a pale pink glass sherbet dish. Kendra, wide-eyed, turned to give Adam a questioning look, which he pretended not to notice.

"We don't have to divvy up the McGovern heirlooms today, Gran," Adam teased. "Besides, it's almost three. We need to get moving along here."

He pulled the curtain back from the window.

"The wedding guests are already arriving," he pointed out. "I saw Mrs. Dowell and Mrs. Eberly."

"Oh, well, then, let's do get moving." She closed the china cupboard door. Her step was spry as she went into the hallway in search of her handbag, with the cane, apparently forgotten, tucked under one arm. "Come along, Adam, you'll have to help me down the steps, but I dare say I'll be fine from there."

The home of Kelly and Scott Lister, Adam's sister and brother-in-law, was a short walk away, though the uneven sidewalk required a bit of care on the part of Alice McGovern and therefore the walk took a few minutes longer than it might otherwise. Adam's sister's bungalow was similar in design and construction to that of their grandmother's. Today the house was decorated, from the front porch straight through to the backyard, with white and yellow streamers, white crepe paper wedding bells, and white and yellow balloons. A yellow-and-white-frosted cake sat on the dining room sideboard next to a stack of white paper plates adorned with yellow roses. Bowls and vases of yellow roses abounded.

"I take it Clare is fond of yellow," Kendra noted.

"Apparently," Adam said out of the corner of his mouth as they made their way through the dining room to the kitchen, where his father nervously peered through the curtain that hung on the window over the sink, giving him a clear view into the backyard.

"Adam!" his father exclaimed, putting down the water he'd been drinking from a clear plastic cup to embrace his son. "Just in time! I told Kelly you'd be here on time!"

Frank Stark was a full head shorter than his son and outweighed him by a good thirty pounds. His light brown hair had thinned over the years until he was almost bald on the top and front of his head. He wore wire-framed glasses, a crisp white shirt, and dark navy suit. Looking at him, Kendra could see Adam in twenty-five years, less the paunch.

"I was afraid you'd be too busy down there with that Super-mom Strangler to stand for your old man."

"I'd never be too busy to stand for you, Dad." Adam hugged his father, then leaned forward to whisper, "Er, Dad, Gran thinks I have a desk job, and actually, I think they're calling him the Soccer Mom Strangler."

"She thinks you . . ." Frank stepped back, frowning.

"She was worried about me getting shot, like the FBI agents do on TV sometimes, so when she asked me if I couldn't ask for a desk job, I said sure."

"But this new serial killer down there in the southern part of the state, you're working on that?"

Adam nodded and accepted a hug from his sister, who greeted him with a peck on the cheek before introducing herself to Kendra.

"Wow, you are pretty. Adam didn't exaggerate. Love that shade of lavender, it's perfect with your hair." Kelly nodded. "You know, the whole family's just dying to meet you."

"They are?" asked Kendra. "Why?"

"Oh, you know." Kelly nudged her with an elbow. "Everyone's curious."

"About what?" Kendra frowned.

"Ah, I think the bride is here." Adam tapped Kelly on the shoulder. "How 'bout if I take Gran out to the garden and seat her, and try to get everyone else seated as well?"

"Good idea. I see Father Patrick has just arrived." Kelly paused at the back door. "Doesn't the yard look beautiful? We planted a dozen new rosebushes just so Dad and Clare could have their rose garden wedding."

"You did a wonderful job, sweetheart." Adam kissed his younger sister on the temple. "The arbor looks spectacular. And the house looks great."

"Thanks, Adam." Kelly beamed, then snapped to. "Okay. Take Gran out. You might want to take

Kendra out, too. Where's Uncle Joe? And the kids . . . where are the kids? Alex? Melanie?"

Kelly hustled herself out the back door in search of her family.

"Gran?" Adam offered his arm. "I think they're almost ready."

"Well, then, Kendra, if you'd hold the door open for me, and Adam, if you'll let me lean a bit, I think we can navigate the back steps . . . yes, that's just fine. . . ."

When all had gathered in the garden and taken their seats on the folding chairs set up for the purpose, someone played a taped version of the traditional wedding march as Clare Tilton, in pale yellow chiffon, joined Frank Stark at the rose-covered arbor where they exchanged vows in a brief ceremony. The couple turned to greet their guests and were showered with yellow rose petals, which seemed to signal the end of the solemnity of the day.

Almost immediately, a band set up in one corner of the yard, a bar in another, and the party began.

By the end of the evening, Kendra's head was spinning. She'd met most of the residents of Hopewell, held most of the babies under two, and fielded incessant questions about her and Adam's nuptial plans. She wanted to strangle him.

Once she'd acknowledged that she had no family, Kendra found herself at the mercy of Adam's aunt Jackie, Frank's sister, who insisted on helping to plan the "wedding," "Since your mother—God rest her soul, I'm sure—isn't here to help." Within minutes, Jackie was searching her handbag for a small notebook, writing up the guest list and offering suggestions for the reception to a startled Kendra.

Adam's brother-in-law was passing out plastic flutes of champagne for a toast right about the same time that Jackie began hinting that Jessica, her three-year-old granddaughter, would make the most adorable flower girl.

"I think everyone is gathering to toast the newlyweds," Kendra noted, infinitely grateful for the opportunity to escape Aunt Jackie and her lists.

"We'll chat later." Jackie patted Kendra's back. "You'll need to know which halls have the best caterers. . . . I'm assuming of course that the wedding will be here, since you said you have no family."

"Everyone, quiet," Kelly announced unceremoniously, "Adam is going to make a toast."

"Friends, family," Adam began, meeting his father's eyes. His grandmother's words played over inside his head, and he knew that she was right. Whatever brought his father happiness should be accepted for what it was, without judgment. He couldn't change the events of the past few years, couldn't bring his mother back, couldn't stop his father from falling in love with another woman, regardless of when that happened. And he, Adam, didn't have to love Clare. But he did have to respect the fact that his father did.

"We're here to celebrate a happy occasion," Adam said solemnly. "After all these years of chasing her, Dad finally caught up with Clare. We suspect she may have had to slow down a bit for him . . ."

Chuckles from the crowd.

". . . but we're glad that she did. Dad, we're happy

that you found someone to share your life with. Clare, welcome to the family." Adam raised his glass, as did all gathered in the room. "Long life, love, and much joy."

"Here, here . . ."

"Thank you, son," Frank Stark said softly as the well-wishers sipped at their champagne. "I appreciate what you said . . . for Clare especially. It means a lot to me . . . and I know it means a lot to her."

"She's a fine lady and a welcome addition to the family." Adam looked beyond his father to his grandmother. "Life is short. You've been alone long enough. Spend the rest of your life with someone who loves you. God knows you're entitled. We all are."

"Thank you, son," Frank repeated as his brother, Ed, stepped forward to make another toast.

Ed's toast was followed by one from a neighbor, then others from Frank's cousin, Clare's brother, and the parish priest. Before long, many of the adults were giddy with champagne and emotion and most of the small children were cranky. Kendra wandered into the house and busied herself looking at the photos that covered all but one wall in the living room. She stepped closer, her eyes going from frame to frame, following Adam's football career through pictures, from Pop Warner to Penn State right on through the pros, like a shrine. All it lacked was a few candles in the wall sconces.

From across the room, Adam signaled to Kendra to join him on the front porch.

"By the way, what exactly did you tell these people?" Kendra asked as he opened the front door and stood aside to permit her to step onto the porch.

"What do you mean?"

"You know what I mean. They seem to think there's going to be another wedding in the family."

"Oh, that." He nodded grimly. "I probably should have warned you about my aunt Jackie. She can be a bit, ummmm, domineering, at times."

"Domineering." Kendra pondered the word. "What a gentle way to put it."

"Was she tough on you?"

"Naw. But I think now might be a good time to tell me exactly what you told your grandmother about me. About us."

"Oh, well, just that I was bringing a girlfriend home to meet her."

"How does that translate into 'Do you like Hummels?' and 'What colors are you planning for the wedding?' "

"I guess Gran might have read a bit more into it than I'd intended."

"The way your family is reacting, one might think you never brought a girl home before and that . . ." She paused. "When *was* the last time you brought a girl home?"

"A few years ago," he admitted sheepishly.

"How many?"

He appeared to be calculating. "Well, I guess it must have been, oh, maybe eight, because my mother was still alive, and she had wanted us to announce our engagement to the family at Christmas."

"You haven't brought a girl home in *eight years*?" She almost choked. "And she was your fiancée?"

"That was the only time I was engaged." He leaned forward and confided, "I haven't had a lot of other long-term relationships."

"No wonder they all think this is serious. But I'd hardly call our relationship a long-term one."

"I'm working on that." He cupped her face in his hand. "When you consider what's been happening these past two weeks, there hasn't been much time left over for romance. Not if one wants to do it right, that is."

"Perhaps you'd like to share that thought with some of your relatives," she said, her voice softening, wondering what Adam's idea of doing a romance right might be. "They're all under the impression that a wedding is in the near future."

"I guess there could have been a bit of embellishment between the time I told my grandmother I was bringing you home and the time it passed from her to one aunt, then to another, to my cousins . . ."

"Are you aware that your aunt Jackie has already planned our wedding—Church of the Savior, by the way—as well as the reception, which we're having at the Union Club? That would be the old, original Union Club, not the new one on Tenth Street."

Adam laughed at Kendra's accurate mimic of his aunt.

"She gave me a list of which florist to use, the name of the best caterer, and which of your cousins I should consider for the bridal party. Your cousin Ellie should be included because she's twenty-six and quote, without apparent prospects and maybe Adam has a friend in the FBI, end quote."

"I'm really sorry." Adam put an arm around Kendra. "It never occurred to me that things would get so out of hand."

With his index finger, he slid a long curl back behind her ear, where it had earlier been.

"You've been a really good sport. I'll make it up to you, I promise."

"How?"

"What would it take?"

Before she could respond, his cell phone began to ring. Frowning, he reached for it, answering with a curt, "Stark."

Adam moved away from her, almost imperceptibly, the humor now gone from his face. In its place was what Kendra had come to think of as his FBI face. The face he wore when something serious needed his attention.

"We're on our way . . . a few hours. Where do you want us to meet them?" He leaned back against the porch railing. "Tell them we'll be there."

He slid the phone back into his jacket and took her by the hand.

"That was Miranda Cahill."

"There's been another one," she said flatly.

Adam shook his head.

"Not another body, but some new information."

"What information? Information about the killer?"

"She needs for us to get back to the Lancaster area as soon as possible for a meeting." He deftly avoided her question.

"She wants me to come, too?"

"Yes."

"But my sketches are done." She paused in the doorway. "Why would she want me at this meeting?"

"I guess we'll find out when we get down there." He held the door for her. "But right now we have apologies to make and miles to go."

CHAPTER
FOURTEEN

Kendra suspected that Adam knew exactly why they'd been called back, why someone felt the meeting couldn't wait until the morning. Her suspicions were confirmed when, after arriving at the state police barracks, Lieutenant Barker greeted her with, "As Miranda told Adam on the phone, we're hoping you can shed some light on this situation."

"Ahhh, Lieutenant, I haven't discussed the phone conversation with Kendra."

She turned and looked up at Adam, frowning. "You knew what this meeting was about, and yet we drove all the way down here without you saying a word about it?"

"I thought it would be better if everyone was here to go over everything that's come up."

"What has 'come up'?" Kendra asked pointedly. "And what does it have to do with me?"

"I think I should probably start this thing rolling," Miranda Cahill said almost apologetically as she came into the room. "And please don't be angry with Adam. I asked him not to tell you what we'd found. I thought it would be better to show you."

Miranda opened her brown leather briefcase and nodded to Lieutenant Barker. "If you'd get the door, please? We can't be sure who might be sneaking around, trying to get information."

"Why all the secrecy?" Kendra did little to hide her annoyance.

"Kendra, if you'd sit here, next to me." Miranda gestured to the chair to her left. "There are some things I need to show you."

With some reluctance, Kendra sat down.

"Adam told me about the crosses that the killer began to put around the necks of his victims after you appeared on television at a news conference wearing a gold cross quite visibly around your neck." Miranda spread photographs across the conference table. "Here's a still shot of you, Kendra, from that video. And shots of his next victims. See the gold crosses?"

"Yes, I saw them before, and Adam and I discussed the fact that possibly the killer had started doing that to get my attention, though I can't imagine why he—"

"Oh, but he was trying to get your attention long before that," Miranda stopped her.

"What are you talking about?" Kendra's voice dropped slightly and her eyes narrowed.

From the briefcase, Miranda lifted a second folder.

"Adam asked me to go back over those first murders to see if there was anything we hadn't noticed previously. Anything at all, but particularly, anything that the women might have had in common, something they'd been wearing or had in their possession that was identical to the others. And what we found," Miranda said as she removed a series of photographs from the folder, placing them upon the table as if dealing cards, "what we found, was that all of the women had little tiny plastic tortoiseshell hair clips."

Kendra leaned forward to look at the photos that were being spread before her.

"Now, it wasn't apparent at first, because the coroner had removed the clips from Amy Tilden's hair and placed them in the evidence box. Kathleen Garvey and Karen Meyer, however, still had the clips in place. They're so tiny, so seemingly unimportant, that they really didn't make much of an impression on anyone. At least, not until we started looking for them."

Kendra placed a finger on the nearest photograph, a close up of blond hair pulled back and held with a tiny, brown plastic clip in the shape of a butterfly and asked, "This is the clip?"

"Yes."

"Everyone wears those little clips," Kendra frowned. "You can buy them at any drugstore, a dollar or so for a bunch of them. They come in clear and lots of different colors besides tortoiseshell. I have some myself. . . ."

"We know." Miranda placed another picture on the table.

In this photo, an unsmiling Kendra's head was tilted slightly to one side. Small clips held her hair back from her face. The next picture was a close-up of the small faux shell butterflies.

"Where did you get this?" Kendra stood up suddenly. "That picture is over two years old. It was taken at a press conference in Seattle after the police caught a bank robbery suspect I'd sketched."

"It ran in one of the Seattle newspapers. I found it on the Internet," Miranda said. "Right now, we're checking with the Seattle police and NCIC to see if there are any unsolved murders where the victims had similar hair clips."

"You think he did this . . . that he . . . the killer . . . put these clips in their hair? You think he's been watching me for two years?" Kendra whispered, disbelieving. "Why would anyone be watching me?"

Miranda looked up at Adam, who nodded slowly.

"Lieutenant Barker?" Miranda drew him into the conversation.

The state trooper approached the table, a small brown evidence envelope in his hand. He unhooked the clasp designed to keep the contents from spilling out and passed the envelope to Kendra.

Something in the envelope was round and heavy, and she shook it to slide the object onto the table. She stared dumbly at the shiny silver watch with the leather strap that landed on the wooded surface with a faint *clunk*.

"Kendra," Lieutenant Barker said, "do you recognize that watch?"

Her hand reached for it, then she paused, looking up at Barker.

"It's okay," he told her. "It was already dusted for prints. There weren't any."

Kendra picked up the watch and studied it warily. On the face was the raised impression of a Gothic-style building, around which letters spelled out PRINCETON ACADEMY. Her hands began to shake as she turned it over to read the initials engraved on the back.

IJS

"I don't understand." She pressed her fingers to her temples. "I don't understand."

"We checked with the school," Miranda said gently. "The only student who ever attended Princeton Academy who had those initials was—"

"My brother, Ian." Kendra finished the sentence. "Ian Jefferson Smith. Where did you find this?"

"You recognize this watch as having belonged to your brother?" Barker asked.

"Yes, yes. My mother bought it for him. Ian was so pleased." She looked across the table at Adam. "As I told you, Ian had been in and out of trouble for about a year. That last summer, he seemed to turn the corner. Stopped sneaking out, never missed a curfew. So my mother gave him the watch and a matching key chain for his birthday."

"What were the keys for, do you know?"

"There was one for the front door of the house in Princeton," she fingered the watch, remembering, "and one for the back door there, too."

"Only those two?"

"Yes," she nodded.

"Do you know where the key chain is now?"

"I'm sure it's in a box someplace. My mother kept that after Ian died. It had represented something to her. It had been an act of faith on her part, giving him his own keys after all he'd done that year."

"Do you know where it is now?"

"Yes. It's still in the safe-deposit box where I put it, along with her jewelry after she . . . after she died."

She turned to Adam. "It's still running. The watch is still running."

"I noticed. Kendra," Adam asked, "do you remember where and when you last saw this watch?"

"Yes, I do. It was on his wrist when he boarded the plane for Tucson. It was the last time I ever saw him." Kendra watched the second hand tick around the face of the watch.

"Are you positive?" Adam asked.

"Absolutely positive. One hundred percent positive."

"And you're certain it was this watch, not another one." Barker leaned on the back of the chair at the head of the table.

"It was the only one he had. Now, is someone going to tell me where it was found?"

"It was under the body of the last victim," Adam told her.

"*What?*"

"It was underneath Leslie Miller's body," Adam repeated.

"Well, that makes no sense." Kendra frowned. "How could that possibly be? Ian had taken it with him to Arizona. . . ."

"That's what we're trying to figure out," Lieutenant Barker said. "We were hoping you'd have some ideas about that."

"Not a clue." She shook her head, not comprehending what she'd heard. "I don't have a clue, unless it was stolen. But he almost never took it off, and when he did, he would put it in his pocket, or in his backpack."

"Kendra, we need to talk about what you remember about your brother's disappearance." Adam took both of her hands in his own. "We need to walk through the whole thing, start to finish, whatever your personal recollections are."

"Of course." She nodded, her head pounding unmercifully. She'd heard every word that had been spoken since coming into the conference room that evening, but somehow she felt as if she couldn't connect the dots.

"Lieutenant Barker," Adam turned to the trooper, "if you wouldn't mind, I think we'll take Kendra back to the hotel so she can get something to eat before we start this process."

"Sure," Barker replied. As if he'd expected anything more from the FBI. After all, since when had they been willing to share?

Adam and a still-dazed Kendra met Miranda in the lobby of the hotel where she'd been staying for the past several days. Anticipating that they'd be needing a place to meet and discuss their strategy in private, Miranda had reserved a suite for Adam that had a well-appointed sitting room. She handed him the key as the three got into the elevator.

"I'll give you a few minutes to get settled," Miranda told Kendra. "Unfortunately, I wasn't able to get you a room to yourself. There's a quilters' convention in Lancaster this weekend, so I was lucky to get anything for Adam, and the only reason why he merited a suite was because it was a last-minute cancellation. I hope you don't mind bunking in with me tonight, Kendra."

"No, no, of course not. It's generous of you to offer to share your room."

"We'll be joining you in a minute," Miranda told Adam when the elevator stopped at the sixth floor. "I just want to give Kendra a minute or two to get settled. Your room is one floor up. Why not order dinner from room service for all of us, and give the kitchen a head start. It's almost eleven o'clock. I can't speak for either of you, but I'm famished."

"Will do. What do you want me to order for you?" Adam put his hand out to stop the door from closing.

"Anything is fine," Kendra said absently.

"Chicken-something for me." Miranda stepped off the elevator.

The two women walked the short distance to the room, and Miranda swiped the key in the lock to open the door. She held it open to allow Kendra to pass, then let the door close behind her. The room was spacious, with two double beds separated by a small table upon which sat a lamp, a telephone, a menu from the hotel restaurant, and a copy of the current issue of *Lancaster County Today* magazine.

Kendra paused and turned to Miranda.

"Which bed?"

"I've been sleeping in this one." Miranda pointed to the one closest to the door.

Kendra swung her bag onto the bottom of the other bed and unzipped it.

"I think I need to freshen up," she said as she took a small plastic case out of the travel bag.

"Go ahead," Miranda smiled gently, "take all the time you need. You must be tired after all the driving you two did today."

Kendra went into the bathroom and turned on the

light and the fan, then sat on the edge of the tub and covered her face with her hands, which had begun to shake the moment she had closed the bathroom door behind her, and tried to make sense of what was happening.

How could Ian's watch, lost with him almost ten years ago, have turned up here, in Pennsylvania, beneath the body of a dead woman?

The only plausible explanation was that the person who dropped the watch had somehow been in contact with Ian—before or after his death. He would have had it with him when he left the ranch the morning they left for their camping trip, wouldn't he? He'd taken everything else in his backpack, surely he would have taken the watch he treasured, wouldn't he?

Which meant that maybe someone knew where the remains of Ian and Zach lay hidden. But how, unless they stumbled across the bodies? Search teams had gone days without finding them. The only living soul that Kendra was certain knew where the bodies had been left was Edward Paul Webster, who was currently serving two life sentences for the murders of Ian Smith and Zachary Smith. Webster, an admitted pedophile, had adamantly denied ever having seen either of the boys, and all throughout the trial, had sworn his innocence, had sworn that someone else was responsible for their disappearance. Could Webster have taken the watch and passed it off to someone else, someone who was now on a killing spree of his own?

Or could Webster have been telling the truth all along?

* * *

"Miranda, here's your salad." Adam lifted the cover from the large bowl of greens topped with slices of grilled chicken and offered Miranda a seat at the round table near the windows. "And Kendra, for you, and against my better judgment, I might add . . ."

With a flourish, he lifted a second lid.

"A hamburger, rare. Onion rings. Fries."

"Lots of fat, lots of fried. Just the way I like it." She tried to smile but failed. "You're entirely too good to me."

"I do my best."

The trio made small talk while they ate, tension hanging over them like a storm cloud. They all knew it was about to burst, but ignored it for as long as they could.

When they'd finished eating, Adam leaned back in his chair, and asked Kendra, "Have you had any thoughts about who might have had access to your brother's watch?"

"Ian must have dropped it somewhere, maybe on the trail. And someone found it."

"That watch is sterling silver. It would have tarnished if it had been laying out in the elements for any length of time. It was in perfect condition. And it's still running, which means that not only has it been taken care of all these years, but someone's been changing the batteries."

"Maybe someone found it shortly after Ian lost it." Miranda poured a cup of coffee from the large carafe and offered it to Kendra, who accepted gratefully. This night promised to be a long one.

"That camping area was swarming with law enforcement and search parties for a week after the boys disappeared," Adam reminded her. "I find it hard to believe that someone would find something clearly marked with the initials of one of the missing boys but would fail to turn it over to the police or the FBI."

"Maybe someone wanted a souvenir," Miranda added with a shrug.

"Maybe someone had taken it from Ian and held on to it all these years."

"And then accidentally dropped it under the body of a woman he'd killed a few days ago? Are you suggesting that the same person who killed Ian and Zach might have killed these women?" Kendra made a face, shook her head. "I don't believe it. The man who killed my brother and my cousin was tried and convicted of the crimes. I sat in the courtroom every day during that trial. I believe Webster was guilty of many, many things. Including the murder of my brother and my cousin."

"Tell me everything you remember about that summer. Start at the beginning of the summer, earlier if you think it's relevant. Tell us about Ian's trip." Adam rose and opened his briefcase. "If you have no objections, I want to record this, so we have something to rely on other than our own memories. Unless you object?"

"No, of course not. It's a good idea."

"And maybe we should move over to the sitting area, where you can be more comfortable. Come on," Adam held out his hand. "Take a seat there on the sofa and put your feet up. Miranda, I'd be forever grateful for a cup of that coffee, if you wouldn't mind fixing it for me while I put a new tape in the recorder. . . ."

Kendra sat in the far corner of the sofa and toed off her shoes. It did feel good to relax. She sipped at her coffee and watched Miranda add cream to a cup, which she handed to Adam before pulling a club chair closer to the table, kicking her shoes off, and taking a seat.

"Let's start with the beginning of the summer, shall we?" Adam said after identifying the parties and the date, time, and place of the interview for the tape. "And for the record, what summer are we talking about?"

"This was the summer of 1990. Ian had just turned eleven," she began.

"How old were you, that year?" Miranda asked.

"Twenty."

"So you were nine years older than your brother?"

"Yes. I wasn't home a lot that summer. I came back from college in May, spent a few weeks at home, then visited my roommate in Maine for a week. We did some hiking with a group from school. I didn't arrive at home until the middle of July. Zach was already there when I got home."

"That's your cousin, Zachary Smith," Adam stated for the record.

"Yes. He's the son of my father's sister, Lorraine." Kendra smiled wryly. "Excuse me, *Sierra*."

"You've mentioned her before. I take it you and your mother were not close to her?"

"Sierra wasn't close to anyone. She certainly wasn't close to my father. But when the boys were about eight or nine—Zach was a year older than Ian—Mom started having Zach come East for a visit every summer, and Sierra reciprocated by having Ian out at her ranch. Mom felt strongly that the boys should know each other. Regardless of what she may have thought of Zach's mother, my mom felt a responsibility to Zach."

"In what way?"

"She thought Zach should be aware of his heritage, should know his family. He was my dad's only nephew."

"What about Zach's father? And his family?" Miranda asked.

"We never knew who Zach's father was," Kendra said as she shook her head. "No one's ever talked about him. When Sierra was young, she was a bit . . . free-range, my mother called her once."

"Promiscuous?" Miranda offered.

"I think that may be an understatement, but we'll settle for promiscuous." Kendra's jaw hardened visibly. "At one time she lived a really free and easy lifestyle."

"Of which your parents disapproved?" Adam asked.

"I don't think they cared what she did with her own life, but I think they felt that she should have provided more structure for Zach." Kendra curled her legs beneath her and settled back into the sofa cushions. "I should explain here that both my father and my aunt came into a great deal of money when they each turned twenty-one, then more when they turned thirty-five. Sierra used a bit of hers to buy the ranch in Arizona.

Free spirit that she was, she had a steady stream of visitors, some who stayed for months, years, maybe."

"And she supported this group?" Miranda asked.

"Yes, food, shelter, and later, we found out, all the drugs they could consume."

"Sounds like a commune from the 1960s." Miranda put her feet up on the end of the table.

"Except there was no contribution from anyone except Sierra," Kendra said. "Several of the women who showed up had children of their own, and my aunt supported them, too. Most of those kids, we learned at the trial, were younger than Zach. All in all, I think he was a really lonely kid."

"He must have had friends from school," Adam noted.

"Zach was home-schooled."

"I guess he must have looked forward to coming to stay with your family in the summer. If for nothing else, the change of scenery," Miranda said.

"Yes, as much, I suspect, as Ian looked forward to going to Arizona. He was fascinated by the terrain, by the culture. The lure of the Old West." Kendra smiled, remembering. "Ian was always fascinated with the whole cowboy thing. Wanted to live a rugged life on a ranch, like his cousin did. In a way, I think he envied Zach as much as Zach envied his lifestyle."

"If your aunt was doing drugs, as you say, why would your mother permit him to go there and stay for two weeks every year?"

"At the time, Adam, we had no idea. Sierra had sworn that she'd been clean and sober for years, and was just living the simple, natural life in the hills,"

Kendra told them. "She was apparently fine whenever my mother spoke with her on the phone. If Mom had known the truth, she never would have permitted Ian to go."

"Did they communicate? Sierra and your mother?" Miranda asked.

"Only by phone. And then only when they were making arrangements for the boys' trips. After the trial, my mother washed her hands of my aunt completely. Once she found out what had really been going on out there—the drugs—my mother severed ties completely. It sickened her that she'd let her son go there, year after year. She never forgave Sierra—or herself, for that matter—for what happened."

"And your brother never said anything about what was going on out there?"

"Not a word. You know, my mother really believed Sierra had cleaned up her act. Afterward, we figured both boys had probably agreed not to tell Mom the truth, because they knew she would put an end to Ian's visits out there."

"So they got along really well, Ian and Zach?" Miranda asked.

"As far as I could tell. They were close in age, and there was a strong resemblance between them. People often thought they were brothers. I'm assuming they got along well. I spent as little time as possible with them," Kendra explained. "After all, I was a college junior that summer. Adolescent boys were beneath my notice. Except for the second week that Zach was at our house, I barely saw them at all."

"Let's go back to early in the summer." Adam glanced

at a notebook upon which he'd obviously prepared some notes. "You had mentioned once that Ian had been having trouble in school that year."

"Yes. He'd been defiant . . . his grades had been poor. He was in real danger of not being permitted to return in September." Kendra rested her elbow on the arm of the sofa. "My mother was at the end of her rope. She'd told Ian she was sending him to some kind of boot camp instead of Arizona and he changed both his behavior and his attitude practically overnight. I think that was when we first realized just how much those weeks in Arizona with Zach meant to him."

"What do you suppose the attraction was?" Miranda leaned forward. "What was it, do you think, that mattered so much to him?"

"I always thought it was the freedom. The hiking into the hills, the sleeping out under the stars. So different from life out here. And Ian was really into Native American artifacts. He had several things that he found in the hills, plus some items he bought with birthday money every summer."

Kendra paused, then added, "As a matter of fact, that last summer, he'd taken quite a bit of cash with him. Zach had told him about an old man who lived in the hills who claimed to be a descendant of Cochise and who was getting ready to sell some of his ancestor's things. Ian thought he'd be able to buy something really terrific—like a bow and the quiver that Cochise kept his arrows in. I gave him money to buy something since I'd been away on his birthday."

"How much money did he have with him?"

"I don't know. Whatever Mom gave him, plus his allowance, plus what I gave him."

"A hundred dollars?"

"More than that, probably. I gave him fifty dollars toward the bow and quiver. Mom usually gave him spending money. And I have no idea how much of his own money he took." Kendra looked at Adam. "Ian could well have had several hundred dollars with him."

"None of it was ever found?"

"No," she told him. "At least not that I know of. Of course, it could have all been in his backpack when they left for their camping trip."

"So your cousin was here for a two-week visit after which time your mother put the two boys on a plane to Tucson," Miranda reiterated. "How long were they there before they disappeared?"

"Less than a week," Kendra told her. "Ian apparently was anxious to meet the old man and see what he had for sale. I think it was the fourth or fifth day that the boys set out on their hike."

"The plan was to hike up into the hills, buy some things from this man, then hike back down? How long had they planned on being away?"

"Adam, from what I remember, my aunt said they left on a Tuesday morning. Early, like six or so. Before the heat of the day. They would have walked several miles to the foothills, then camped someplace overnight. I think we were told that the old man's cabin was up in the hills someplace."

"And no one saw them after they left the ranch?"

"No one. Except Edward Paul Webster," Kendra said bitterly.

She paused, then added, "And Christopher Moss."

"Who is Christopher Moss?" Adam asked.

"Christopher was one of the kids who lived on the ranch, the son of one of Sierra's friends who'd come for a weekend and never left. He was younger than Ian and Zach, maybe seven at the time." She looked up at Adam and added, "I think at trial it came out that he suffered from fetal alcohol syndrome, he had a lot of problems. Anyway, he had seen the boys leave, and followed them. Several of the other kids said that they'd seen Chris sort of sneaking along behind the boys. Apparently it was something this boy did often. Just follow behind the other kids."

"How had he escaped the murderer?" Miranda frowned.

"Actually, he didn't. The police pulled Webster over because the car he was driving had been reported stolen; Christopher was in the front seat. That's how the police first realized something was wrong. The boy was sobbing hysterically and babbling incoherently. The police ran a check on Webster and learned that he'd only been released from prison three weeks earlier. He'd served eight years for assaulting a child." Kendra got up and poured herself a glass of water. "Once the police realized that Chris had followed the boys, they started searching for them."

"And they were never found," Adam noted.

"Not a trace. And Christopher couldn't help a bit. He had a breakdown and was placed in a home for children with severe emotional problems. Webster said he'd found Christopher wandering by the side of the road, crying and talking garble, and that he'd picked him up and was taking him to the next town. Which was, incidentally, eighteen miles in the opposite direction."

"So Webster's credibility was in question from the start. What evidence had been presented against him, I wonder," Adam murmured.

"I don't recall, frankly. I attended the trial, but so much of it was a blur. The only thing I remember is that Ian's jacket was on the front seat when the police pulled Webster over. He said that Christopher had had it in his hands when he picked the boy up, but no one believed that."

"And Webster is still in prison?"

"Yes." Kendra nodded.

"Well, it's obvious that there's some connection between the deaths of those two boys and the killer who's trying so hard to get Kendra's attention. Ian's watch showing up after all these years can't be an accident. The little hair clips in the victims' hair that are identical to those Kendra wore, the gold crosses . . ." Adam leaned forward, his arms resting on his knees. "Someone's getting real personal with you. The question is who? And why? Kendra, how do you feel about a trip to Arizona? Starting with a trip with your aunt?"

"I'm not sure I could even find her ranch," Kendra admitted. "I've had no contact with her in over ten years."

"It's well documented in the FBI file, and we should have a copy of that by seven tomorrow morning. The Bureau has booked two seats on a flight to Tucson that leaves at ten from Philadelphia. Miranda, maybe you'll do the honors and drive Kendra and me to the airport?"

"You've got it." Miranda stood up. "Come on, Kendra, it's almost three A.M. You don't want to have dark circles under your eyes when you see your aunt for the first time in, what's it been? Ten years?" Miranda tucked her shoes under her arm and started for the door. "Thanks for dinner, Adam. We'll be back at seven for breakfast and a look at that file before you take off with it."

CHAPTER
FIFTEEN

"I thought I remembered there being more desert." Kendra looked out the window as Adam sped onto the interstate. "I don't remember there being so many hills."

"There's plenty of desert. But Arizona has its share of hills, too," he said, checking his rearview mirror before hitting the gas and jolting the rented sedan up to seventy-five miles per hour, twenty miles over the speed limit on this section of Route 10.

The rental car had been awaiting their arrival at Tucson International Airport, and while the sedate model would not have been his first choice, Adam was determined to make it to Bisbee in as close to an hour as possible. The sedan would just have to rise to the occasion. He had an agenda.

"It's getting late." Kendra glanced at the clock on the dashboard. "Are you sure this sheriff . . . what was his name?"

"Cole Gamble."

"If that doesn't sound like a western sheriff, I don't know what does." She leaned back against the headrest and grinned. "Can't you just see him, in a wide-brimmed hat and dusty boots?"

Her voice dropped an octave or two.

"Howdy, ma'am. Sheriff Cole Gamble at your service."

Adam laughed, wondering when she would begin to react to the fact that the last time she'd made this drive from Tucson to Bisbee had been for the trial of her brother's murderer.

"Are you sure Sheriff Gamble will wait for us?"

"He said he'd be there. He was really intrigued by my questions, and seemed to be willing—eager, might be a better word—to meet with us."

"I wonder why."

"He said he grew up in the area, and remembers the boys' disappearance, Webster's arrest and trial. He knows the area well, and will take us wherever we want to go."

"I wonder if he knows where my aunt's ranch is."

"I'd bet on it." Adam took advantage of a long stretch of road to increase his speed. "You're going to stop there, aren't you?"

"Well, I guess we'll have to, though I'm not looking forward to seeing her. On the one hand, I feel obligated. On the other hand, I haven't heard from her since the trial, not even when my mother died. It's hard to believe she didn't know about Mom's death. The story made the news everywhere. I received cards from all over the country." She added with a touch of sarcasm, "The suicide of a senator is big news, you know."

"That is odd, especially when you consider what

they went through together, as mothers of children who went missing together."

"One would think. But Sierra was always a very self-centered, self-indulgent woman, at least my mother thought so. As long as something didn't directly affect her, it didn't have any relevance in her life. I doubt she gave my mother's death more than passing notice."

"Well, I'd like to speak with her, as well as with some of the people living at her little commune. Assuming she's still there."

"You can bet on it. Sierra's lived on that ranch with her merry little band for years now. She's like the queen bee, you know? Queen of all she surveys? Everyone defers to her. That little world just revolves around her." Kendra's voice held a touch of bitterness. "The only way she'd leave would be in a pine box."

"And I think it's important that we speak with the boy who followed Ian and Zach the day they left, and with his parents."

"There was only his mother, as I recall. I don't think his father was ever around. Another fatherless boy, just like Zach. Frankly, my mother always felt Sierra treated Zach like an afterthought." Kendra looked out the window, at the lights that sparkled here and there out among the hills. "I didn't remember how open it is out here either."

"It's open all right. It's pretty empty, actually, outside of the cities. There are a lot of ranches in this part of the state, cattle ranches and some cotton farms."

"We haven't passed many towns."

"A lot of the towns down here are no more than

dots on a map, places where the ranchers pick up their mail. And of course, a ghost town or two."

"Cochise County," she murmured, reading the sign they'd just passed. "Cochise was the Indian whose bow Ian wanted to buy."

"Think that was a scam? What are the chances it was an authentic Cochise artifact?"

"I don't know. Zach was pretty certain, said he'd seen something that made him think it was the real deal. I don't recall exactly what, though. Of course, Zach was twelve, so what had seemed credible to him could have been anything. And truthfully, at the time, I wasn't terribly interested in what the 'kids' were doing."

"I'm assuming the old man was questioned after the boys disappeared."

"There'd be a statement in the sheriff's file, wouldn't you think?"

"You'll be able to ask Sheriff Gamble in about ten more minutes." Adam followed the signs for Bisbee.

"We're here already? That didn't take long."

"Seventy-nine minutes." He grinned. "But who's counting?"

Cole Gamble of the Cochise County Sheriff's Department was looking out the window when the dark blue sedan pulled into the parking lot. He'd been looking forward to this meeting ever since John Mancini, who was head of some special investigative unit of the FBI, had called him the day before and asked that he cooperate with a field agent who'd be visiting the following day. If Mancini's polite request hadn't caught his attention, the case they were looking into surely did. Cole Gamble had vivid memories of the Smith case. Two boys disappearing in the hills, no trace ever found. A third boy found hysterical in the clutches of a convicted child rapist, who was promptly arrested for the murder of the two missing boys. A sensational trial. A conviction that was based, some legal purists argued, on the thinnest of circumstantial evidence and an overabundance of emotion.

Cole Gamble remembered every bit of it. He'd been fifteen years old at the time, three years older than Zach Smith. And until Edward Paul Webster had been tried, convicted, and locked away forever, Cole's mother had barely let him out of her sight.

The car's headlights still illumined part of the lot, then dimmed just before a tall man got out from behind the wheel. He was met in front of the car by a small, slender woman. The lot was too dark to see either of their faces, but he knew the woman was the sister of one of the boys, the one from back East, and the man was some hotshot FBI agent who used to play pro football. Mancini had mentioned his name, but right now Sheriff Gamble was focused on the woman. He'd seen her years before. The newspapers had been filled with her picture, and that of her mother, back during the days of the trial. He'd even seen her in front of the old courthouse a couple of times. He remembered how fragile she had looked, yet how steadily she'd supported her mother to the waiting car.

"Sheriff Gamble?" The agent now stood in the doorway.

Stark. Right. Adam Stark. Played for the Steelers.

Retired to join the FBI. Who in their right mind did a thing like that?

"Yes. Agent Stark, Ms. Smith." The young sheriff greeted them both with a smile.

"I hope we didn't keep you too late." Kendra took the hand he extended to her.

"Not at all. You're actually earlier than I'd expected."

"Agent Stark drives like a . . ."

Adam coughed.

". . . like the wind." She smiled.

"I'm sure he does," Gamble nodded and shook the agent's hand. "Come on into my office. I already have the old files out. As you would expect, a lot of investigation went into this case. There were boxes of interviews, records, reports . . ."

Adam and Kendra followed Gamble into a room where several open boxes containing manila files sat on the floor, three chairs were arranged around a small round table, and fresh coffee dripped into a waiting pot. The sheriff offered mugs to his visitors, and when everyone was settled, he rested his arms on the table and said, "Agent Mancini gave me a rundown on the case you're working, and the reasons why you wanted to revisit this one. But I'm not certain I understand exactly what you're looking for."

"Something that could connect our killer to the disappearance of my brother and cousin." Kendra explained that Ian's watch had recently been found. "Someone, at some time, had to come in contact with him—or with his body—for them to have gotten his watch."

"Maybe he dropped it on the trail," Gamble offered, "and someone picked it up."

"With all the publicity surrounding the case, don't you think that anyone finding such a thing would have brought it right to the police?" Adam pointed out.

"Not necessarily. Maybe someone wanted a souvenir. You have to understand that this was the biggest happening in Cochise County since the Earp brothers took on the Clanton clan at the OK Corral." Gamble sipped at his coffee, then added a bit more sugar. "And there's always the possibility that the watch had been dropped but not found for several years. Maybe someone finding it years after the fact wouldn't have made the connection."

"We'd thought of that," she admitted, "but the watch is perfectly clean of dirt and tarnish. And it's still running."

"See, like I said, someone had themselves a souvenir."

"Be that as it may, Sheriff, how did that souvenir end up under the body of one of our victims on the opposite side of the country?" Adam asked.

Gamble shook his head. "Now, you've got me there. How do you think it got there?"

"We thought perhaps if we looked over some of the statements from the old case, spoke with some of the witnesses. Maybe someone who was living at my aunt's ranch at the time . . ."

"Well, I'm happy to offer you whatever help you need." *Though I don't see what good it will do or what you think you're going to find,* he could have added. "Where do you want to start?"

"I guess we'd like to read through the file, maybe we'll get some ideas," Kendra told him.

"And we're going to want to visit with Kendra's aunt. Kendra hasn't been out here since the trial and doesn't remember how to get to her ranch." Adam took off his jacket and hung it over the back of his chair. "Maybe you know where it is."

Sheriff Gamble put his mug down on the table and stared at Kendra for a long minute.

"I guess this means you don't know."

"Know what?"

"Sierra Smith died almost five years ago."

Kendra's jaw dropped.

"How?"

"Her body was found out in a gully about eight miles from her ranch. Looked like she'd taken a bad fall from the rocks, cracked her head, broke her neck, on one of the rocks below."

"Oh, my God. I had no idea," Kendra whispered.

"I'm sorry, I thought you'd have known. Being her niece and her not having any other living relatives."

"There was no way we would have known," Kendra told him. "I mean, there wasn't anyone who'd have known to get in touch with us."

"And she was alone when this happened?" Adam asked.

"Yes. Apparently she'd been in the habit of taking long walks into the hills early in the mornings, but she was usually back by eight or nine o'clock. When eleven rolled around and she still hadn't returned, some of her friends from the ranch went looking for her. She was already dead when they found her."

"Then the ranch has been sold?"

"No, no, she left the ranch to several of the people she'd been living with. Three or four women friends who'd been out there with her for a long time. She'd set it up somehow with her lawyer. She had some money that she left to them to pay the taxes and the upkeep on the property."

"Who was her lawyer, do you know?"

"Not offhand, but I can find out for you." He turned back to Kendra. "I'm really sorry, Ms. Smith, for not being a little more delicate."

"That's all right. You wouldn't have known. Can you give us directions to the ranch? It's been so many years, I'd never find it."

"Sure. I can draw you a map, if you like." Gamble patted his pockets, looking for a pen.

"What happened to the other boy?" Kendra asked as the sheriff began to draw his map. "The third boy, the one they found in the car with Webster?"

"Oh, Chris Moss?" Gamble looked up from his sketch. "The last I heard he was still in that institution up around Benson. Why?"

"He's one of the people we want to speak with," Adam told him. *And one other, but that conversation can wait.*

"Well, I don't know that that's going to be possible. Last I heard, he still wasn't talking. He hasn't, far as I know, since this thing happened. Nothing but babble, anyway. But you can ask his mother. She's one of the ones your aunt left the ranch to." Sheriff Gamble handed his map to Adam and, pointing to the files, asked, "Now, which box would you like to start with?"

It was almost two in the morning when Kendra stretched out on the bed in the motel where the sheriff had thoughtfully arranged for rooms for her and Adam for the night. Exhausted from the trip and overcome with more emotions than she could deal with, she was grateful for an opportunity to sort it all out. Adam and the sheriff had both walked her to her door, and while she would have been grateful for Adam's company, she could not very well have invited him in and closed the door in Sheriff Gamble's face.

It was just as well, she rationalized as she washed her face in the bathroom sink. She'd been feeling increasingly uneasy, almost claustrophobic, since they got off the plane in Tucson. She'd done her best to mask her unrest from Adam because there were so many emotions at war within her.

The memories of the trial and her mother's difficulty getting through it.

They'd sat day after day in the courtroom, not only hoping to see justice served, but hoping against hope that, before the trial ended, the accused would break down and tell where he'd left the bodies. By the time the trial had ended, all Elisa Smith had wanted was to bring her son home and bury him next to his father.

But Webster had never admitted his guilt, and Elisa and Kendra had returned to New Jersey with aching hearts that would never heal.

And then there was the matter of her aunt's death.

Kendra slipped into a nightshirt, as she tried to decide how she really felt about that. Her last living blood relative had died a year before her mother had, and they hadn't known. What might she have done if she had? What might Elisa have done?

"Nothing," she whispered to the room as she turned out the lights. "I don't think we would have done a damned thing."

That Kendra still harbored animosity toward her aunt had much to do with the fact that her mother had gone to her grave blaming Sierra for what happened to the boys. Between her drug use and her apparent inattention to her son's activities, Sierra had, in Kendra's own opinion, left the door wide open for disaster. And when disaster had occurred, Sierra had merely shrugged and told Ian's grieving mother and sister that "sometimes these things happen."

Kendra felt the tide of bitterness rise within her again, and let guilt flow over her as she realized the truth: She could not mourn for Sierra Smith.

It hadn't even occurred to her to ask the sheriff if he knew where they'd buried her.

CHAPTER
SIXTEEN

He sat in the worn, overstuffed chair, restlessly punching at the remote control with his thumb, skimming past daytime dramas, quiz shows, and reruns of old detective shows. He hadn't missed a news broadcast or a newspaper in days, yet there'd been no comment about his sly little reference to Kendra. And surely someone had noticed, for heaven's sake. This was the FBI he was dealing with, wasn't it? You'd think that *someone* would have noticed by now that all of his ladies had one thing or another in common with Kendra.

He wondered if she appreciated all the trouble he'd gone to, getting all those little mementos exactly right. He sincerely hoped she did.

After all, imitation was the sincerest form of flattery.

Funny there'd been no mention, though. He frowned.

And then there was the matter of last night's press conference. Kendra hadn't been there. Nor had Adam Stark. The only member of the team he recognized was that tall dark-haired Agent Cahill. Now *there*, he smiled broadly, was a dish fit for a king.

He amused himself thinking about Miranda Cahill

and wondering if he should add her to his list of potentials. He'd have to think about that. There just may come a time when he'd need to get the FBI's attention in a way they couldn't ignore.

And the way they were ignoring his little gestures on Kendra's behalf was annoying. More than annoying. It was insulting. The more he thought about it, the more he knew for certain that it hadn't been overlooked. They had chosen not to acknowledge it, and that in itself was an insult. It simply wasn't fair play.

He searched his jacket pocket for a cigarette, then leaned over to tie his sneakers. He'd have to go outside to smoke. It was a rule. It was okay, though. He didn't mind. If that was what Father Tim wanted, he didn't mind at all.

Now, on the other hand, he played devil's advocate to himself as he walked through the peaceful gardens, wasn't there always the chance that maybe no one had caught on yet?

Nah, he rejected that thought as he blew a long trail of smoke from one side of his mouth. How could that possibly be? How could they miss something so obvious? Aren't we dealing with some of the best criminal investigative minds in the country here?

And yet he had them all stumped, didn't he? No one had a clue. He guessed that made him one of the best criminal minds in the country.

The thought cheered him, and his chest swelled with pride, that he could best the best.

Even her. Especially her. She had always been too smart for her own good.

But where was she? He frowned again. Were they

hiding her? He wanted her here, to watch. Here, where she could watch up close, where she would be able to understand, to appreciate, his cleverness. Sooner or later, she was going to have to admit just how clever he really was.

Tires crunched on the stone drive, and a car door slammed. He turned in time to see the pretty young woman get out of her car and take several bags of groceries from the backseat. With one foot, she closed the door, took several steps, then stopped, warily, looking around as if testing the air. She stood for several long moments in the same spot, her head slightly tilted to one side, as if trying to decipher something that eluded her, then turned her back, and went about her business.

He watched from behind a low stand of mountain laurel, and it suddenly occurred to him that should ever the need arise, there was one sure way of getting Kendra's attention.

He wondered why he hadn't thought of it sooner.

CHAPTER
SEVENTEEN

Adam rested a reassuring hand on Kendra's shoulder.

"How do you feel, coming back here after all these years?"

"I don't feel much of anything," she told him honestly. "I thought maybe I'd have a sense of some emotion, or, oh, something relevant. But I don't."

"Are you ready to go down and see if they'll speak with us?"

"Yes."

"Come on then." He gave her shoulder a squeeze. "We'll have to leave the car here and walk down, since the gate's locked."

He ducked under the fence, waited for her, then held his hand out for her. She took it, and hand in hand they walked down the slope that led to the ranch house a quarter of a mile ahead.

"Think we should have called first?"

"I don't know what I would have said."

"Well, you better think of something." Adam gestured in the direction of the house. "Someone just came out onto the porch."

"Wonder if she's one of Sierra's heirs."

"Guess we'll soon find out."

The air was warm for just past nine in the morning, and the sun, still on the rise, cast the shadow of the barn across a clearing that separated the house from several outbuildings. The woman who'd come out of the house sat quietly in a rocking chair, watching their approach. Except for the gentle rocking, there was no other motion that Kendra could see.

Their footsteps making a scuffing sound in the dry gravel, Adam and Kendra walked toward the thin figure hunched in the rocking chair. They were within twenty feet of the porch before she acknowledged their presence.

"Something I can do for you?" she called softly as she stubbed out a cigarette on the wooden floor of the porch. The aroma of marijuana was unmistakable.

"Hello," Kendra called back. "Are you one of the ladies who owns this ranch?"

"Yes," she responded somewhat warily.

"I'm Kendra Smith." She stopped at the bottom step, still holding Adam's hand. "My aunt, Sierra, owned this ranch at one time."

"If you've come to try to take it away from us, we'll fight you. We'll all fight you." The woman's eyes narrowed suspiciously and she stood. Her voice began to rise shrilly. "It was all legal. There was a will. Sierra wanted us to have—"

"Whoa, I'm not here to take anything from you. I just came to talk, that's all."

"Talk?" Dirty fingers pulled nervously at a long strand of unkempt brown hair.

"Yes. That's all. I'm just looking for some information."

"Information about what?"

"Years ago, my brother died out here, along with my cousin, and I was hoping to speak with someone who was living here at the time. Were you living here then, when Sierra's son and my brother were lost?"

"You're Ian's sister?" The woman's eyebrows raised slightly.

Kendra nodded. "Yes."

"I was here then. I remember Ian." She lowered herself back into the chair. "He was a beautiful boy. Spoiled, though. He had too much. He didn't like to share. He was mean sometimes."

"Mean to whom?" Kendra's brows knit closely. Ian had been a handful, true, but mean?

"To Zach. To some of the other kids. He liked to bully."

"What's your name?" Kendra asked.

"Emmy Moss."

"Are you Christopher Moss's mother?"

"I am."

"How is your son?" Kendra sat on the top step and looked up at the woman, who looked barely old enough to have had a child who would be well into his teens by now.

"He's the same. Same as he was. Same as he's been." She rocked herself back and forth.

"Do you visit him often?" Kendra leaned back against the railing, and Adam stepped aside as if to step out of the picture. Kendra was doing fine on her own for now.

"No." Emmy picked at a fingernail. "It makes me too sad to go. He never says anything but that same garble and I never know what it means. I can't stand it."

"It must be very difficult for you."

"Chrissy has always been difficult for me. They said it was because . . . because I used to drink a lot. Before he was born. But whatever, he was never right."

"My aunt told my mother that the day the boys, Ian and Zach, disappeared, Christopher followed behind them. Do you think they knew that he was following?"

Emmy shrugged. "Maybe. He always was trailing on behind the other kids. He just wanted to be noticed. Just wanted to be included."

"Did you see them leave that day?"

"I was sitting right here when they came outside." She nodded. "Zach and Ian. They had backpacks and some food in a small cooler. You have to keep your stuff cool out here, you know, otherwise things spoil so quickly with the heat."

"Did you see them leave, Emmy?"

"No. I went back inside to make breakfast for Sierra. She always let me cook her breakfast for her. She liked the way I cooked."

"I guess you miss her." Adam sat down on the step next to Kendra.

"Sure. She was more like a sister than a friend. She let me live here, let me keep the ranch. Me and Rosie and Sarah. We were like sisters, the four of us . . ." Her voice trailed away.

"Did the boys mention to you where they were going that morning?"

"Someplace out toward the Chiricahuas." Emmy

pointed to the mountains in the distance, beyond the barn. "They were going to camp for a few days."

"Did Sierra know how far they were going to go?"

"Sure. What difference did it make?"

Because when they ran into trouble, they were too far away to get help, that's what difference it made, Kendra wanted to shout.

"So they set out that way . . ." Kendra gritted her teeth, and pointed in the direction of the mountains, "and then Christopher followed?"

"A few minutes later." Emmy shook her head. "It was a few minutes later that Chrissy left. He never went off on his own, Chrissy didn't. Never left the ranch by himself. He didn't know his way around. Just couldn't remember things well. That's why he followed the other boys."

"Who else saw the boys leave? Who else was out here that morning?"

"Just me."

"Emmy, would it be all right with you if we went to see Christopher?" Adam asked.

"He won't know you're there, chances are."

"We'd like your permission to stop by anyway," Adam said.

"Sure, whatever." Emmy shrugged.

"Thanks for your time, Emmy." Kendra rose and dusted off the back of her khakis.

"You want to wait around to see Sarah and Rose? They sleep late sometimes. . . ."

"Not this time, I'm afraid."

"Some other time, then." Emmy continued to twist the long tangle of dark hair and began to rock again.

"Bye," Kendra waved, suddenly anxious to leave. She barely said a word until they were beyond the gates and in the car.

"Wow," she said, "the sixties are alive and well outside of Chaco, Arizona."

"What a way to spend your life." Adam shook his head as he started up the car. "Getting high on your front porch and watching the buzzards fly by."

"She was pretty much out there, wasn't she?" Kendra turned sideways in her seat and rested her arms on the window.

"What are you thinking?"

"I'm thinking about how desolate it is out here. What if everyone believed that the boys went in one direction, and they actually went in another? I mean, with spaced-out Emmy as the only witness, how reliable was the information? Maybe they didn't search for them in the right place."

"Kendra, you read the reports last night and this morning. This place was swarming with law enforcement agents and volunteers, twenty miles in every direction. There wasn't a sign of either of them."

"But they didn't start looking until the boys had been gone for almost two days. They could have walked more than twenty miles in two days, Adam."

"From what I read in the files, those hills were scoured. But we can always go over the files again with Sheriff Gamble. Maybe there's something we missed."

"Maybe."

Kendra leaned closer to the window to rest her chin on her arms. "The ranch looks smaller, shabbier.

When I was here before, there were more people. More activity. It's so quiet out here now."

"Maybe it was your aunt who kept things moving."

"No doubt. Mom always said she was a lightning rod, that things always happened when she was around." Kendra looked back at the hills as Adam started the car. "Strange to think that she died almost a full year before Mom and that no one called us."

"Do you think it would have occurred to Emmy?"

"I don't think there's much that occurs to Emmy," she said dryly.

"Shall we see if her son has anything meaningful to add?"

"To Benson." She pointed straight ahead. "But I doubt Christopher will be of any more help than his mother was."

It appeared that Christopher would be no help at all.

The small private hospital that Christopher Moss called home sat at the edge of the desert. Out front, the pink blooms of the barrel cactus were just beginning to open. Hummingbirds darted around the feeders that hung from the low branches of the cottonwoods. The hospital was mission style, with arches and tiles set into the stucco walls. The grounds were manicured and neat. The overwhelming impression was of money, exclusivity.

"I wonder if my aunt paid for this," Kendra said in a low voice as she and Adam approached the courtyard.

"Emmy didn't appear to be a lady of means."

"It would have been good use of Sierra's money," Kendra told him, thinking of some of the ways she was putting the Smith money to work. Father Tim's Mission was only one beneficiary. "Better to take care of Christopher than to have Emmy and her gang smoke it away. Or worse."

The hospital was cool inside, the staff cordial. Kendra and Adam were taken to Christopher's room by a young male orderly who had a buzz cut, several tattoos, and a friendly manner.

"Chrissy, you have some company," the orderly announced as he led the visitors into the room. He opened the drapes to let in the scenery, then pointed to a chair next to the window.

The man in the chair appeared to be in his thirties, though Kendra and Adam were well aware that he couldn't have been more than eighteen. His pale hair was long and pulled back in a ponytail held with a red rubber band. He wore a shirt that buttoned down the front and cotton pants with a drawstring at the waist of the same color blue as the shirt. He stared out the window, and it wasn't until Kendra spoke that his eyes shifted to look at her face, though his head never moved. His left hand moved to one of the buttons on his shirt, which he began to stroke, holding it between his thumb and his index finger.

"Hi, Christopher," Kendra said as she took a few steps forward, then stopped. "Is it okay if I sit down in the chair there, next to you?"

"He doesn't talk," the orderly said, as if Christopher was deaf as well as mute. "He never talks. Well, rarely, anyway. Sometimes you can get him to write or draw pictures, but that's all."

"Christopher, my name is Kendra. I'm Ian's sister. Do you remember Ian?"

Christopher looked past her, to some place beyond the window.

"We saw your mother today, Christopher. Emmy. We went to see her at the ranch. Do you remember the ranch? You used to live there."

Nothing, not so much as the blink of an eye.

"Do you remember Zach? Zach was my cousin. You lived on the ranch with him, with your mother, Emmy, and Zach's mother, Sierra, and lots of other people. Do you remember Zach?"

Christopher's head turned slightly but still, he did not look at her face. Kendra continued to chat with him in a low, soothing voice, hoping that something would reach him, but nothing appeared to have gotten through. He simply stared out the window.

"I guess that's that." She looked up at Adam, still speaking softly.

"What were you hoping for?" he asked.

Kendra shrugged. "I have no idea what I thought I'd find."

She turned back to Christopher and took his hands in her own, patting them gently. "You take care, Christopher. Maybe we'll get to see you again before we leave Arizona."

Kendra quietly returned her chair to its spot against the wall, and turned to leave.

"Be . . . ca . . . ca . . ." The voice, little more than a whisper, was raspy from disuse.

"What?" Stunned that he'd spoken, she turned back to Christopher. "What did you say?"

"Be . . . ca . . . ca . . ." he stuttered.

"Because? Because what?" She knelt in front of him, and found that fat tears were pooling in the corners of his eyes. "Because what, Christopher?"

"Be . . . ca . . . ca . . ." he repeated, his eyes not meeting hers.

She quickly searched her handbag for her Daytimer, where she knew she'd find at least a small piece of paper and a pen. She placed the paper in front of Christopher and held out the pen. When he made no move to take it, she put it in his hand, wrapping his fingers around it.

"Here, Christopher. Can you write it for me? Whatever it is you're trying to tell us, can you write it for me?"

Christopher Moss stared for long minutes at the pen before his gaze moved slowly to the paper on the table, then back to the pen. Kendra had all but given up hope that he'd use them, when Christopher moved the pen to the paper and began to write. When he dropped the pen, Kendra picked it up and handed it back to him, but his gaze had changed, as if he was no longer aware of her presence.

Kendra slipped the pen into her pocket and lifted the paper.

BE CAUS

"What in the devil do you suppose that means?" Adam whispered.

Kendra shook her head and reached behind Christopher to grab a few tissues from the box that sat on the windowsill. She wiped his face dry of tears, then tucked the paper into her purse.

"Let's see if this means anything to Sheriff Gamble." Kendra tossed the tissues into the trash. "Thank you, Christopher. I know this means something important to you. We'll do our best to try to figure out what."

"So, how'd you make out?" Cole Gamble asked when Adam and Kendra walked into his office later that afternoon. "Was Christopher able to tell you something you didn't already know?"

"We don't know," Adam told him.

Kendra took out the narrow sheet of paper and laid it on the desk in front of the sheriff.

"This is what we have. Any idea what it might mean?"

Gamble picked up the paper and studied it.

"*Because?* Is that what he was trying to write?" Gamble shook his head. "*Because* what?"

"No clue," Kendra told him. "I told him that we'd seen his mother at the ranch this morning—"

"How'd that go, by the way?" the sheriff interrupted to ask.

"Okay, I guess. Emmy's not a font of credible information. She seemed more concerned with the rhythm of her rocker than anything else," Kendra told him.

"Sad but true." Gamble nodded. "Sorry. You were saying?"

"Just that I was telling Christopher about seeing his mother, and talking about the ranch and Zach and Ian, and he started crying and he said something that sounded like this. *Be* . . . *ca* . . . *ca*." She mimicked the sound the boy had made. "I gave him the paper and pen and asked him to write down what he was trying to say, and that's what he wrote. It could be *because* . . . but that doesn't really mean anything by itself."

"I'd like to make a copy of that paper, if I could. Maybe it will mean something to someone."

Kendra handed over the paper, waited while Gamble made a copy, then folded it and put it back into her bag when he returned.

"Shame he's the way he is," the sheriff was saying. "Might have had something meaningful to tell us about that day. Sorry you made the trip all the way out here for nothing."

"It wasn't a wasted trip. We got to see the files on the investigation, and look over the trial notes." Adam rubbed his chin. "Which reminds me. Kendra said that Ian might have had several hundred dollars with him when he left New Jersey. That Zach had told him about an old man who claimed to be a descendant of Cochise who was going to sell some items to Ian. But I didn't see where he was interviewed."

"There's a mention in the file that one of the boys from the ranch did say that Ian and Zach were going to see some old Indian, but no one knew who or where. I believe there was a search made for this man, but there's no indication that any such person was ever found. Who knows, maybe he didn't exist. Could be that Zach had made it up."

"Why would he do that?" Kendra frowned.

"Hey, who knows why kids do half the things they do, make up the stuff they do. You should hear some of the stories I hear." Gamble paused to answer his ringing phone, gave a few instructions to the person on the other end, then hung up. Turning back to Adam and Kendra he asked, "Now, where will you go from here?"

"I guess the next logical move is to talk to Webster."

"As in, Edward Paul? Are you serious?" Gamble raised an eyebrow.

"As long as we're here, we might as well." Adam turned to Kendra, who was trying to look as if she was not as startled by Adam's comment as the sheriff was. "Why leave a stone unturned?"

"You won't learn a damn thing from him. One of the assistant county DAs was out at the prison two weeks ago on another case. Says Webster is still insisting he's innocent."

"Maybe he figures if he continues to profess his innocence, sooner or later someone will listen."

"Who knows?" Gamble looked up from his desk and met Kendra's eyes. "I'd be happy to call the warden out at the prison and arrange for Agent Stark to see Webster. I'm assuming that you won't be going with him."

"No, no, I'll go," Kendra told him. "I'll go."

"You don't have to do this, you know," Adam told Kendra as he pulled up to the gatehouse and gave their names to the guard.

"I know I don't have to. There, Adam, he's waving us through. Thanks," she called out the window. "I want to. I mean, I may never again get this close to him. I want to hear what he has to say. And who knows, maybe he'll slip up and say something."

"Something like what? Something like, okay, I confess. I killed your brother and your cousin, here's where the bodies are, and oh, yeah, I gave your brother's watch to some guy I passed on my way back out of the hills?"

"Hey, it could happen."

"Ready?" Adam asked after he'd parked the car in the visitors lot.

"As ready as I'm going to be." Kendra opened the door and got out. The sun had already warmed things up to a toasty ninety degrees, but on the advice of Sheriff Gamble, she wore long pants to keep her legs covered and a camp shirt that covered any shape she might have.

"You don't need to hear some of the things the men might be yelling, if they see you," Gamble explained. "So my advice is to cover it all up and pretend not to notice them."

Kendra had taken the advice, and as a result, was overly warm by the time she reached the prison door. Gratefully, the interior was air-conditioned, though claustrophobic, with an endless series of doors that locked with a heavy, solid sound, and narrow, endless, colorless halls that led farther and farther into the depths of Arroyo State Prison, halfway between Benson and Tucson. The plan was to stop at the prison, meet with Webster, and go directly to the airport for the flight back to Philadelphia.

The guard paused in front of a dark green door that had a large screened window set in the middle.

Through the glass, Kendra could see a table, painted the same green as the door, and several mismatched chairs.

"The prisoner will be brought in as soon as you're ready," the guard told them. "I'll be right here the entire time you're in there with him."

"Thanks," Adam nodded.

The guard ushered the two of them into the room, and pushed a button that resulted in a muffled buzz somewhere behind the door, which was set to one side of the back wall. The door opened, and Edward Paul Webster, in ankle shackles, his hands cuffed behind him, shuffled in. He looked over his visitors without comment, then seated himself opposite Kendra and stared at her from lifeless brown eyes.

Finally, she said, "Do you know who I am?"

"They told me that you're the sister of one of the boys they say I killed." His face, pale and pocked with old acne scars, was without expression. "I did not kill him or that other boy, let's get that out of the way right up front."

He turned to Adam and sneered, "Hear that, Mr. FBI?"

"You were tried and convicted by a jury—" Adam pointed out.

"It was all bullshit," Webster interrupted, the surface of his raw anger scratched. His fleshy lips curled upward on one side and his face distorted into an ugly mask. "There were no bodies, no evidence to even link me to either of them. I was railroaded. My biggest crime that day was being in the wrong place at the wrong time. Well, that, and stealing that car . . ."

"What about Christopher Moss?" Kendra asked with a touch of sarcasm. "Have you forgotten about him?"

"No, I haven't forgotten about him," he singsonged his response, mocking her. "That kid was a basket case when I picked him up on the side of the road. He was crying and shaking and babbling and clutching that jacket, just like I told the police then. I'm telling you the same. I never saw your brother or that other kid, I never touched the Moss boy. I stopped to give him a ride because he looked like, well, he looked like he'd seen a ghost or something, okay? Like something had spooked him big time."

"The police thought maybe you had spooked him, Webster." Adam rested his arms on the table. "The jury believed that you were responsible for Christopher's hysteria."

"That kid hadn't been in my car for more than five minutes when the police stopped me."

"The car was reported stolen from one of the campsites that was located in the immediate area where the boys were hiking."

"Yeah, I stole the car. I never denied that. The keys were in the ignition, I was tired of walking, it was hot, I figured what the hell."

"What were you doing up there? Up there in the hills?" Adam continued his questioning.

"Well, Mr. FBI, I'm willing to bet if you thought it was important enough to make this trip, that you've already read the file your boys have on this case."

"You were hanging out with friends," Adam said dryly.

"That's right."

"The police were never able to find those friends to talk to them."

"Maybe they didn't want to be found."

"Maybe they were underage boys."

"Maybe they were." Webster shrugged. "So what?"

"Wouldn't that have been a violation of your parole?" Adam asked.

"Maybe so." Webster smirked. "So, what's the point of this?"

"I was hoping you'd . . ." Kendra sighed.

"What? Confess?" He laughed out loud. "Lady, I have nothing to confess. Not about those boys, anyway. I said when I was arrested, I said when I was tried. When I was sentenced. When that lady came out here—the mother of one of those kids later became a senator or something and she made my life a living—"

"She was my mother," Kendra interjected.

"She still a senator?"

"She died a few years ago."

"Gee, I'm real sorry to hear that," Webster said with neither sympathy nor sincerity.

"I can see that you are."

The two stared at each other for several long minutes. Neither of them blinked.

"Look, we were just hoping that you'd give us an idea of where the bodies were—" Adam began.

"You deaf, buddy? I don't know anything about those boys. And what's the big deal now, anyway? Why's this coming up again now?"

"There've been a series of murders out East," Adam

told him. "Young women. Seven of them, in a short period of time."

"What's that got to do with me?"

"Ian Smith's watch was found under the body of the last victim," Adam told him.

"So what?"

"So Ian would have had the watch with him when he was killed, and—"

"And you think I took the watch, maybe gave it to someone?" Webster snorted in disgust. "I don't know how many times I have to say it. I never saw your brother or his stupid watch. And just for the record, most of my friends don't do women."

Kendra looked up at Adam. Webster was not going to give them an inch on this.

"Look, I will tell you what I told the cops who arrested me. I done a lot of things in my life. Things that don't fit your idea of what's, well, let's just say that things maybe you wouldn't do. But that's my business and I ain't in here for none of that." He looked at Adam. "But I never killed no one. I never saw those two boys. I didn't touch that kid—Moss."

"Then why was he crying hysterically when the police pulled you over?"

"I don't know, and frankly, at this point, I don't give a shit." Webster stood up. "I got nothing more to say."

Without looking back, Webster walked to the door at the back of the room and the guard on the other side of the glass opened it as he approached.

"Well, that was enlightening." Kendra sighed and stood up. "Let's get out of here."

* * *

"I can't remember the last time I was so happy to see sunlight," she said after they'd signed out and walked through the front doors of the prison. "And what an ugly man he was. I don't mean just physically. I mean everything about him. Smirking, creepy, mean-spirited . . ."

"I agree," Adam said as he unlocked the car. "And I hate to say this, but maybe we should consider the possibility that he's telling the truth."

"Are you crazy? That is one mean son of a bitch in there."

"I agree. But being a mean son of a bitch doesn't necessarily make him a murderer."

"He was convicted—"

"On purely circumstantial evidence. From what I read in the reports that were in Gamble's file, emotions were running pretty high about this case. Two boys missing and presumed dead, the only witness the killer and an emotionally disturbed young man who was found in the company of a man who'd been convicted in several states, over several decades, of raping and beating young boys."

Kendra stared straight ahead as Adam slowed on his approach to the gatehouse, where he returned their guest passes to the guard.

"Frankly, I believe Edward Paul Webster should spend the rest of his natural life behind bars," Adam continued. "He's done some heinous things in his day. He's a predator and nothing will ever change what he is and what he'd do again if he got the chance. If they let him out tomorrow, I'd bet my last dollar that the first thing he'd do is look for some young boy to assault. I've yet to see a reformed pedophile. But I don't know that he's a killer. I don't know that I believe he killed Ian and Zach. Why not admit it? He isn't going anywhere, either way. Ever. Life without parole means just that. So it shouldn't matter. He's already been convicted. Why wouldn't he admit it if it's true?"

"But if Webster didn't kill them," she swallowed hard, "that would mean . . ."

She hesitated, the thought incomprehensible to her.

"Yes," Adam said. "That would mean that the person responsible for Ian and Zach's deaths is still out there."

CHAPTER
EIGHTEEN

"Do you realize what you're saying?" Kendra's eyes had widened at the thought. "It never occurred to anyone that Webster could be telling the truth. That all these years, he's been in prison . . ."

"Where he does undoubtedly belong," Adam muttered, "if not for this crime, then for all the others."

"While someone else has been free, all this time."

He'd been silent for a while then, his mind quickly processing the possibilities. He hadn't liked what he'd come up with.

Adam's earliest opportunity for a bit of privacy hadn't come until they reached the airport in Tucson. He used it to first call John Mancini, then Miranda Cahill. After a brief chat, he'd tersely asked her to meet their flight when they landed at Philadelphia International Airport later that evening.

"Something important?" Kendra asked when she emerged from a trip to the ladies' room to find Adam standing as if in a trance, staring out the window, his cell phone still in his hand.

"What? Oh, maybe. Look, they're letting passengers on board our flight. Let's get ourselves settled in, maybe we can grab a little rest between here and Philly." He took her arm.

"Is that your way of telling me that you're not going to tell me what's going on?"

"It's my way of telling you that I will tell you once I've put it all together."

She'd been tempted to ask, but didn't. Once seated on the plane, she closed her eyes and tried to relax. When she fell asleep, her dreams were a murky collage of faces, of mouths moving but no words emanating forth. Edward Paul Webster and Christopher Moss. Her brother, her mother, Emmy Moss. Father Tim. Adam . . .

It wasn't until they arrived in Philadelphia and Kendra saw Miranda Cahill waiting for them at the gate that she began to sense that Adam was keeping more than his suppositions from her.

"Where did you leave your car?" Adam asked Miranda, the appropriate greetings having been exchanged.

"Right outside the terminal door."

"I thought no one was permitted to leave cars unattended in the airports anymore," Kendra noted.

"It's not unattended," Miranda told her. "One of Philly's finest is standing guard waiting for us to claim it."

They entered the concourse, Kendra walking between the two agents, trying to keep up with their long strides, wondering when Adam was going to tell her what was going on and why Miranda was waiting for them when their plane touched down.

"Is this it?" Adam asked, pointing to a Taurus sedan next to which stood a uniformed police officer.

"Yes." Miranda nodded.

When Adam asked "May I have the key?" Miranda tossed it to him, then paused to have a few words with the officer who'd been watching the car.

Adam unlocked the passenger side door, and held it open for Kendra, then went around to the driver's side. Once behind the wheel of the car, Kendra in the front seat next to him, Adam asked, "How would you feel about a little company for a few days?"

"Company? At my house?" A smile tilted her lips. After the intensity of the past few days, a little down time with Adam in the midst of the Pines could be just what the doctor ordered.

"That's right."

"You mean, you?"

"No, I mean Miranda."

"Oh," she said, trying not to let her disappointment show. *Whoopee.*

He was watching Miranda chat with the police officer she'd left in charge of the car.

"Adam, would you please tell me what's going on?"

"Roll your window down and tell her time's up, will you?" was all he said.

She did, and moments later, Miranda was sliding into the backseat, waving good-bye to her admirer.

"Did you pack a bag with clothes for a few days?" Adam asked.

"Yes, it's in the trunk. Now are you going to tell me what's going on?"

"You don't know either?" Kendra turned in the seat, somewhat hampered by her shoulder restraint.

"No. All he said was to pack for a few nights and get a rental car and meet your flight."

"Miranda's going to stay with you for a few days," Adam told them both.

"I already got that much. Why?" Kendra demanded.

"Because I don't like the way this whole thing is playing out." Adam drove onto I-95 and headed south. "Let's start putting things into perspective, shall we?"

He accelerated, passing a white stretch limousine, before continuing.

"Six months ago, Kendra moves back East. A few months later, a serial killer starts leaving bodies all within the area she'd be covering if the Bureau called in a compositor. And she was called in. She's seen on television wearing a small gold cross around her neck. Within twenty-four hours, corpses start showing up wearing similar crosses. And then Miranda does a little investigating and finds that the earlier victims all had tiny plastic tortoiseshell butterfly clips in their hair, which their nearest and dearest have confirmed they never saw these women wear, by the way." He paused, trying to gauge what effect his words were having on Kendra, but her face was inscrutable.

He went on. "A little deeper investigation on Agent Cahill's part turns up a photo of you that ran in a West Coast newspaper a little more than eighteen months ago, showing you wearing those tiny plastic butterflies in your hair. All this information was relayed to John Mancini. Guess what he found."

"I'm afraid to ask." Kendra's voice was just barely above a whisper.

"There are four unsolved murders in the area between Seattle and Redding, California. The first victim was found almost a year and a half ago. Four beautiful blond women. All single mothers. All were raped, then strangled. All were found with—"

"Small plastic butterflies in their hair," Kendra completed the sentence.

"You got it. Now, let's see if you can guess when those killings stopped?"

"I'm almost afraid to." Kendra's eyes grew wide.

"The last one was in December of last year. Right after you moved back East. The first one here was four months later."

"What are you saying?"

"I'm saying it took him a few months to figure out you'd left the West Coast, and another month or so to figure out where you'd gone."

"And you are positive it's the same man?"

"All signs point to it," Adam said, following the signs for the airport. "The only difference is that in the West Coast killings he left no DNA. He must have used condoms for the rapes, and was careful not to let the victims scratch him."

"Why do you suppose he got careless after he moved east?"

"I don't think he got careless. I think he got cocky. There's a difference. I think he believes we will never be able to find him."

"Adam, what are you doing?" Kendra protested. "You're headed right back in to the airport."

"That's where my car is," Adam told her as he drove into the garage and pulled the sedan directly behind the Audi. "Now, which of you ladies is going to drive to Kendra's?"

"I can drive, since I know the way." Kendra turned to Miranda.

"I don't mind." Miranda shook her head. "But Adam, I think we need to finish the conversation."

"First let me fill you in on where Kendra and I have been for the past several days."

Adam told her all that had happened from the time he and Kendra met with Sheriff Gamble right through their meeting with Edward Paul Webster.

"So the question remains," Adam concluded, "if we suppose for a minute that Webster is telling the truth, who killed Ian and Zach?"

"The someone who's trying to get Kendra's attention now," Miranda said without thinking.

Kendra frowned, the phrase ringing in her ears. Someone had said that recently.

I've been trying to get your attention. . . .

"The phone call," Kendra said aloud. "At the hotel. He said something about trying to get my attention."

"Who did?" Adam and Miranda both asked at the same time.

"The man on the phone, the first night I stayed at the hotel." She looked at Adam. "The night I fell asleep on the sofa, and woke up and went back to my room. There was a message for me, some man whose voice I didn't recognize. All friendly, as if he was chatting with an old friend. And the message was exactly what you'd leave for an old friend." She frowned. "I can't remember what else he said, but that was the tone. I just didn't pay that much attention because I assumed he'd left the message on the wrong extension. But when I mentioned it to the desk, they said there was no record of the call, that it had come from inside . . ."

"I'll have someone check that out with the hotel," Adam said. "It could have been our killer."

"Who may hold the key to Ian's death as well as these most recent killings," Miranda noted. "He may have you in his sights now, Kendra."

"Isn't that a bit of a leap?" Kendra turned around in her seat to glare at Miranda. "Even if you assume that there's a connection between my brother's death and the death of all these women, why would it follow that he's after me?"

"Let's start with the fact that he's definitely fixated on you, and has been for years. The murders out on the coast stopped as soon as you left the area. And then, there's the matter of Ian's watch," Miranda reminded her. "If we can figure out why, we can figure out who."

"He might be fixated, as you say, in some way, but the women he's killing, they're nothing like me. I'm not blond, I don't have children, so I've never done the super-mom thing . . ."

"That may just be a part of it. Maybe he's trying to get your attention by attacking women of a certain type for a reason that has nothing to do with you."

"What do you mean?"

"We all agree that he wants to get your attention,

but the means he chooses to do that may mean something only to him. Obviously his choice of victim is personal to him, he's deriving great satisfaction from killing these blond mommies. But the fact is, he's committing acts that are going to draw you into his world, regardless of who he kills. Since he's obviously been following your career, odds were that the Bureau would bring you in to work the case, which would bring you into his drama."

"I agree with Miranda, and so does our profiler." Adam nodded. "Which is why I asked Miranda to stay with you for a few days."

"What makes you think I need a baby-sitter?"

"Think of me as a house guest," Miranda offered. "One who just happens to carry a Sig Sauer semiautomatic."

"You think he's going to come after me, don't you?"

"The phone call I had while at the airport, that was Anne Marie McCall. I'd called her earlier and left a message for her, told her everything we learned while we were in Arizona. She's convinced that the messages the UNSUB is sending are directed to you. The hair clips, the crosses, he's telling you that he's watching you, that he's been watching you, very closely. That he notices every little thing about you."

"But why? Why me?"

"I don't know. The truth is somewhere in this jumble. We just haven't figured it out yet. And until we do—or until we find him—you and Miranda are going to be new best friends."

"Then you really do believe that Webster is telling the truth. That someone else killed Ian and Zach."

"I think it's a possibility we simply can no longer ignore."

Kendra got out of the car and walked around the front to the driver's side. Adam caught her hand.

"I'm not willing to risk your life while we find out," he told her. "It took me too long to find you again."

"Where are you going?"

"To Virginia. I have a meeting with John in the morning." He leaned down and kissed the side of her face.

Miranda cleared her throat; when she met Adam's eyes her expression was one of amusement. He raised an eyebrow, as if waiting for her to comment. When she did not, he smiled.

"A wise move on your part," he murmured. "You two keep in touch."

Adam closed the car door behind Kendra and waited until Miranda had moved from the backseat to the front before stepping back from the car. He waved, then stood in the parking lot, until the sedan disappeared around the first curve on its way toward the exit, praying that Miranda's presence would prove in the end to have been unnecessary. Kendra hadn't seemed wild about the idea, but sending her home alone was a chance he hadn't been willing to take.

"Can we stop at a market or something?" Miranda asked, after Kendra announced that they were nearing Smith's Forge. "I want to pick up a bottle of shampoo and some conditioner."

"Sure. There's a market right up ahead."

"Do you need anything?" Miranda asked. "Anything I can pick up for you?"

"Nothing that I can think of."

"I'll just be a minute." Miranda hopped out of the car as soon as Kendra stopped in front of the store.

Miranda had been more than a minute. By Kendra's calculations, it had been closer to twenty by the time she wandered back out of the store, several plastic grocery bags hanging from her wrists.

"I hope you don't mind." Miranda opened the back door on the passenger side and put the bags on the floor. "I picked up a few things to munch on."

"It was Adam, wasn't it?" Kendra glared as Miranda got back into the car. "He told you that all I'd have to eat in my house would be junk food, didn't he?"

"Why, no." A slow smile spread across Miranda's face. "But I wish he had. I could have saved a few bucks."

"What do you mean?"

"I mean, I just figured that you and Adam . . . I mean, it's plain to see that you and he are more than . . . what I mean is, that your relationship is moving toward something. Not that there's anything wrong with that," she hastened to add, "and not that it's any of my business—"

"But . . ." Kendra waited for her to continue.

"Well, I figured if you were anything like Adam, when it comes to food, I'd starve to death by the time he gets back here. So I just stocked up on a few staples."

"Like what?"

"Salsa, tortilla chips," Miranda said, then added, "But I picked up some strawberries, popcorn, and some of those little carrots, too."

"The little tiny snack carrots?"

Miranda nodded.

"Did you happen to pick up any dip?"

"Ranch, of course," Miranda said, a laugh in her voice. "What good are carrots without Ranch dip?"

"What else is in those bags?" Kendra looked over her shoulder into the backseat, where the plastic bags had morphed into shapeless white heaps on the floor.

"Cookies . . ." Miranda looked sheepish as if she'd been caught with her hand in the jar.

"What kind?"

"Pepperidge Farm. Chantilly."

"The kind with the raspberry filling and the powdered sugar?" Kendra's eyes lit up.

"Oh, wait! Of course!" Miranda grinned. "You were the fries. The rare burger and the onion rings! I'd forgotten—I just figured that since Adam was such a stick about what he eats, that any woman he was interested in would be the same way. I'm so sorry for having misjudged you. Damn. I should have gotten that extra pint of Ben and Jerry's after all."

"There's always tomorrow." Kendra was poking in the bags. "Oh, my God! Krispy Kreme doughnuts! Yes! And a bag of Hershey's kisses!"

Miranda's outlook brightened. The next few days might not be so bad after all.

"You do have good deadbolt locks, don't you?" Miranda had just finished a very businesslike inspection of Smith House.

"Yes. I had them installed when I moved back here last fall. There are latches on all the windows as well."

"No security system, though," Miranda noted.

"We never needed one here. Frankly, no one around here even locked their doors up until a few years ago. I still know people in Smith's Forge who go to sleep at night without locking up."

"Dangerous business these days, but we're locked up tight as a drum here, so we should be fine." Miranda leaned against the kitchen counter. "Do you want to talk about it? I mean, everything that's going on?"

"You mean all these women who have died? You mean the bastard who's been killing them? And the possibility that the man who was convicted of murdering my brother and cousin may not have committed the crime after all? Not to mention the fact that the killer may now be watching me?"

"Yes."

"I can't believe Webster is innocent. He's the most despicable, evil person I've ever met."

"I know his history. He's despicable, yes, indeed he is. Evil? Probably that, too." Miranda nodded. "But that does not necessarily mean that he killed your brother. He may have done a lot of other terrible things, but killing your brother and your cousin may not be among his crimes."

"I can't stand to think that all these years, the person responsible for Ian's death has been out there, and we didn't know." Her voice quivered. "That my mother didn't know. That maybe he's been watching me for a long time and I didn't know."

Kendra shook her head.

"Actually, no, on second thought, I don't want to think about him or why he's trying to get me to notice

him. Would it be crass and insensitive of me to say
that, just for tonight, I'd like to *not* talk about him?"

"No, not at all. We've both been totally immersed
in this for the past few weeks. Me, I don't mind at all.
It's my job. But it isn't yours, not this part of it, anyway. I think a night away from thinking about it isn't a
bad idea at all." Miranda had watched the tension
build in Kendra's face, knew the woman needed a
break. "So I say it's time to break out the pizza and
whip up a few milk shakes and find something to
watch on TV."

"Milk shakes?" Kendra raised a curious brow.
"Wouldn't you rather have wine? Or a beer?"

"Yes, I would. But I'm packing."

"Excuse me?"

Miranda patted herself in the area over her right
kidney. Beneath the bulky red cardigan, there was a
bulge.

"I don't drink when I have it on." Miranda tried to
appear matter of fact, but her gaiety of just moments
before was gone, reminding Kendra that Miranda was
no ordinary house guest.

It seemed to Kendra that Miranda was deliberately
avoiding the use of the word *gun*. Which was okay,
Kendra supposed as she took the frozen pizza out of
the freezer.

"Milk shakes it is," Kendra said. "The blender is in
the cabinet right behind you."

The evening had turned chilly—record cold, the television weatherman had announced—so Kendra lit a
fire in the living room fireplace and pulled out two
afghans that her mother had crocheted when she was

first married. The women curled up at either end of the sofa, watched an "I Love Lucy" marathon, and polished off two small pizzas, a blenderful of milk shakes, and a bag of cookies.

When the eleven o'clock news came on, Kendra asked, "You want a bedtime snack?"

"Sure," Miranda said.

"How 'bout the strawberries? They look pretty good."

"Good idea. After everything else we ate tonight, a little fruit should help balance out all the calories."

"I'll get them," Kendra said when Miranda started to get up. "You throw another log on the fire."

Kendra returned in minutes with a plate loaded with berries.

"Oh, my God," Miranda exclaimed. "You dipped them in chocolate! When did you do that?"

"When the marathon went on break." Kendra passed the plate to Miranda. "I melted some of the Hershey kisses in the microwave. You know, of course, that if you eat chocolate with fruit, the vitamin C cancels out the calories?"

"I'd heard that. Oh, yum, I haven't had these in ages." Miranda took a bite and groaned with pleasure. "Oh, man, that is good."

She reached for another and nibbled it more slowly than she had the first.

"You know, Kendra, you really are quite all right," Miranda nodded. "I wasn't sure when I first met you, that you'd be, you know, quite right for him, but . . ."

"What are you talking about?" Kendra frowned.

"Adam. You know he's nuts about you."

"He is?"

"Oh, come on. Don't even try to deny that there's nothing going on with you two."

"Well, at first I wasn't sure he wasn't just, you know, flirting."

"Adam doesn't flirt." Miranda wiped a bit of chocolate from the corners of her mouth. "He even took you home to meet his family, for crying out loud."

"I thought that was because he didn't want to leave me alone because he thought I was at risk."

"Ummm, Kendra, forgive me for stating the obvious, but you're at risk now, too. He didn't take you to Quantico today. He took you home with him because he wanted to try you out on his family. You met his grandma, didn't you?"

"Well, yes, but . . ."

"That's really key with him." Miranda inspected the plate of berries, hesitated for a second, then said, "Oh, what the hell. After all I ate tonight, one more won't hurt."

"How do you know all this?"

"I've known him for seven years now. I've never seen him really fall for anyone." She grinned. "Not even me, and God knows I tried."

"You did? I thought Portia said she had dated him."

"She did. Well, we both did, only he didn't realize it for a while. He had asked her out, but I was the one who was interested."

"He asked your sister out, she said yes, but you went in her place?"

"After the first couple of dates, when she realized that I was more interested in him than she was, yes."

"And he's still speaking to you?"

"He was actually quite a good sport about it. I finally told him the truth when it occurred to me that he and I could be great best friends but terrible lovers. And we are best friends. He's the best friend I've ever had, after Portia." Miranda sipped at her water. "And for the record, we never went that other route."

"I wasn't going to ask. It's none of my business."

"But you were wondering."

"Ummmm, maybe . . ." Kendra said, then laughed. "You seem to be so close, you and he. I admit I had wondered."

"We are close. But not that way."

"What did you mean, about his grandma?"

"Well, she is one of the most important people in his life. He wouldn't take you to meet her if he didn't have something long term in mind."

"He does seem to dote on her," Kendra mused. "They really seem to have a special bond."

"Did he tell you what they do on his mother's birthday, he and his grandmother?"

"No." Kendra reached for another berry. "What?"

"They spend the day together, Adam and his grandma. His mother is buried in one of those old cemeteries where you can still plant things on the graves? So every year on her birthday, they go there together and clean up the grave site and plant her favorite flowers."

"Wow. Who'd have thought?" Kendra said softly. "Big tough FBI man . . ."

"When I said he was a special guy, I wasn't kidding." Miranda took a deep breath, and said, "Which is my way of saying, please don't mess with him if you're not serious about, well, if you're not looking for a real relationship." She held up one hand as if to ward off protest. "I know it's none of my business, but I'd really hate to see him hurt. If you're really interested in him, that's fine. That's great. Wonderful. Go for it. Just don't mess with him."

"I'm interested," Kendra admitted. "I'm more than interested. It's just been a weird couple of weeks, you know? All of those dead women . . . well, circumstances haven't been conducive to romance, if you know what I mean."

"I know what you mean," Miranda said dryly. "It's the story of my life. It's hard to separate it all sometimes. You work on a case and if you're doing the job right, it dominates your life. And it has to. You can't do this job nine to five. You drop the ball and someone could die."

She took another sip of water, then added, "It's hard to keep a relationship going forward when you're distracted by something else, sometimes for weeks at a time. You really have to be committed to making it work."

"Are you involved with anyone now?"

"No, not now," Miranda replied.

"I'm sorry." Kendra sensed the unspoken "not anymore."

"Well, it was one of those things that would never have worked out anyway. We weren't right for each other." She patted Kendra on the foot that rested on the sofa cushion between them. "But you and Adam, you could be right. And those circumstances that aren't conducive to romance that you talked about? Sometimes you just have to move them out of the way, even if it's only for a night, or a weekend at a time. Otherwise, you'll never get to know what could be. If you wait until there are no other 'circumstances,' you'll lose any chance you might have to find out what the relationship could be. He's not going to give up what he is . . . and neither are you. If you want him, you're just going to have to work around it."

Miranda stood up, then began to gather up the rumpled napkins and empty glasses from the table.

"And those were my unsolicited two cents on the subject. I won't say another word." She started toward the kitchen, her arms laden. "I'll get rid of this stuff, then you can point me in the direction of my bed. You promised me a canoe trip tomorrow morning and I'm holding you to it."

Kendra lay in her bed staring at the ceiling, trying to sort it all out. Her life had taken on the appearance of a canvas onto which the artist had crowded far too many images. Taken as a whole, it overwhelmed. Viewed separately, the components might begin to make sense.

Though she'd initially bristled at having been forced to bring Miranda home with her, she was grateful now that Adam had insisted. Besides the fact that she did feel safer having an armed FBI agent sleeping in the room across the hall—should there in fact be any danger, though she wasn't convinced there was— Kendra couldn't remember the last time she'd spent an evening with a friend eating and watching television and talking about men and laughing and talking and just being, well, just being *girls*. Maybe college, she frowned. Could that be right? She hadn't had a roommate since graduation, and her job had consumed her for years. Come to think of it, the only close friend she had was Selena, and since she started seeing patients at night, there was little time for evening socializing outside of their dinners at the Mission.

She recognized in Miranda a friend in waiting. She'd make certain that she followed through.

Interesting, Kendra thought as she turned over, that Miranda was right on target about her and Adam. They seemed to be in a holding pattern. Maybe, once this case was solved, they could take a few steps forward, instead of the side steps they'd been taking for the past week.

Then, there was the matter of her brother's killer maybe not being behind bars after all, maybe being on her trail at this very minute. Maybe being the same person who seemed to be fixated on her. She pulled the blanket up over her shoulders against a sudden chill. None of the possibilities made any sense to her. Maybe when Adam got back from his meeting he'd have some insights.

At the thought of Adam, she smiled and closed her eyes. So much better to think about him than the man whose face she'd sketched.

Holding on to the image of Adam as he had stood next to his car earlier that day, one hand raised in a half-wave, she finally drifted off to sleep.

* * *

It was almost two when Miranda stole a look at the clock on the table next to the bed in the guest room across the hall from Kendra's bedroom. By nature a light sleeper, every little sound caused her eyes to open and her brain to seek the source of the noise and its possible causes. She'd earlier identified the sound of a log falling onto the hearth in the living room below and a little creaking of the hot water pipes that fed the radiators.

But the sound that she was hearing now . . . she just couldn't put her finger on it.

Instinct caused her to slide her hand underneath her pillow. Fingers sought then closed around the handgun, drew it surely and brought it under the covers, all in the matter of seconds. She lay in the dark, stifling her own breathing while she tracked the sound.

Downstairs. Near the bottom of the steps.

She strained her ears until they ached.

On the steps now, footfalls soft as snow.

Inch by silent inch, she raised herself from a prone position, then slowly moved her feet to the edge of the bed. The door was slightly ajar, and by the nightlight's glow in the hall, she could see Kendra's door. It, too, stood open by several inches. Miranda held her breath, watching through the opening, until the first hint of shadow fell. In one smooth, quiet motion, she was on her feet and opening the door.

"Freeze!"

He turned in one swift motion, and she realized in that split second that she'd misjudged the distance between them. The heel of his left foot caught her squarely in the chest, and she fell back, allowing the intruder access to the steps.

"Son of a bitch . . ." Miranda growled and followed the assailant onto the steps. Three-quarters of the way down, she flung herself forward with both feet, landing a solid kick to the middle of his back. He fell the rest of the way, thudding onto the hardwood floor.

"Miranda!" Kendra yelled from the top of the steps.

"Turn the lights on!" Miranda called back, her gun now held tightly between both hands.

The elbow-punch to the side of her head came from nowhere and sent her spinning, but she managed to pull off two shots before going down and slamming her head against the newel post at the bottom of the steps. Somewhere, far away, a door closed softly. The gun slipped from her fingers, and she surrendered to the darkness.

CHAPTER
NINETEEN

"How is she?" Adam's voice was taut.

"She's okay," Kendra spoke softly into Miranda's cell phone. "She was awake, though foggy, when they came to take her down for more X-rays a few minutes ago. She has a nasty gash from hitting the end of the newel post, and she lost a lot of blood. They're going to keep her for a while, at least until tomorrow. I called Portia, and she'll be here by this afternoon. Fortunately, Miranda has all of her personal numbers stored on her cell phone, so I was able to find her sister quickly. As quickly as I was able to find you."

"And you're all right?"

"Thanks to Miranda, yes. Everything happened so quickly. The commotion on the steps . . . the gun going off . . ."

"She shot him?"

"I don't think she hit him, there wasn't any blood, except for on the newel post, which was apparently hers. It was so dark down at the bottom of the steps. She called to me to turn the lights on, but he must have blindsided her. By the time I got the lights on, he'd hit her in the head and she went down and I ran down the steps and grabbed her gun but he was gone." Kendra swallowed hard. "It all happened so fast. . . ."

"How did he get in?"

"What?"

"I said, How did he get into the house?"

"I don't know. The dead bolts were on, and the windows were latched. Nothing was unlocked. I spoke with the police earlier, right after they arrived, and gave them a quick statement, then drove directly here, to the hospital. Maybe by now they've figured out how he entered, but I've been with Miranda for the past several hours, and frankly, I've been more concerned about her."

"Where's her gun now?"

"The police have it."

"Look, I'm going to be meeting with the profiler at eight this morning, then I'll be on my way up there. I may not get there until tonight. Is there a safe place for you to stay? They've already dispatched agents to your house and to the hospital, but I don't suppose you'll want to stay at the house. I don't know how long you'll want to hang around at the hospital."

"I can go to Selena's," she told him.

"She's right down the road from you?"

"Yes."

"We can have someone watching that house as well. Who's there, who can go with you?"

"What do you mean?"

"Who are the agents there at the hospital?"

"Oh. Well, there's a tall guy with dark hair whose name I don't know, and an agent named Will."

"Will Fletcher?"

"I didn't catch his last name."

"Big guy, good-looking?"

"Very."

"Swell," Adam muttered under his breath.

"What?"

"I said, ask him to go with you when you leave to go to Selena's and just stay there until someone can arrive to stick with you until this is over. John can have someone assigned by this afternoon. We'll send someone to meet you at the house. I suspect Will might want to stay with Miranda but he can spare a few hours to watch over you until a replacement gets there."

"Are they an item?"

"Not in the traditional sense of the word."

"Okay. I'll take Will wherever I go."

"Just be safe, will you, until I can get there?"

"I'm all right, Adam. Nothing happened to me. But I feel so guilty that Miranda was hurt because of me."

"Miranda was doing her job," he replied levelly. "And thank God she's as good at it as she is."

There were voices in the background, and she could tell that Adam had placed his hand over the phone. When he got back to her, he said, "Kendra, I have to take a call. Promise me that you'll stick close and take care until this is over."

"Are you crazy? Of course I will." She hit the end button. She intended on being damn careful.

Kendra stepped onto the elevator, followed by Will Fletcher, her new and somewhat reluctant guardian.

Reluctant, she suspected, only because it was obvious that he hadn't wanted to leave Miranda under guard of another agent, especially an agent he didn't know and trust. But orders were orders, and Will did seem to be making an effort to be courteous and companionable.

Kendra, on the other hand, was impatient to leave the confines of the hospital. With the arrival of Miranda's parents, she felt like a fifth wheel. Add to that the fact that the Cahills' daughter had been injured trying to protect her, and Kendra's level of discomfort had risen throughout the morning. She'd called Selena, but there'd been no answer. She could be seeing patients, as she often did at home. Kendra left a message on the answering machine that she'd be stopping by within a half hour.

"I hope you don't mind stopping at my friend's house," Kendra said somewhat apologetically. "I haven't been able to reach her by phone, and I was hoping to be able to stay with her tonight."

"Not a problem," Will replied. "Where you go, I go. Doesn't matter where. At least until your regularly scheduled guard shows up."

"Do you know who that will be?" she asked.

"No clue." He shrugged as she turned onto her road. "I don't think I've met any of the agents who work in this district. Ordinarily, I wouldn't even be here, except for the fact that Mancini thought that I might want to be with Miranda—that is, with her and her family, since we've known each other since the Academy."

"So you're old friends, then." She slanted a glance in the direction of the passenger seat.

"More or less." He nodded noncommittally and stared out the window.

As she pulled into Selena's driveway, Kendra made a mental note to ask Miranda about Will Fletcher.

Selena, however, was nowhere in sight. Even the gate to the backyard was closed. Usually, when Selena left the house to go to her office in town, she left the gate open so Lola could come and go as she pleased. Today the gate was latched. Kendra searched for Lola for a minute or two before giving up, assuming that Selena had taken the dog with her.

"She must be seeing patients in her office in town," Kendra said as she got back into the car. "I'll try to call her again later."

Kendra drove down the road to her house and pulled in the driveway. Yellow crime scene tape stretched across the back steps, and several police cars were still in the drive. She sat in her car for about ten minutes, watching investigators come and go.

"Want to go see how they're doing?" Will asked, obviously unaccustomed to sitting on the sidelines.

"Sure."

As they walked toward the house, Kendra commented on the number of law enforcement personnel on the scene.

"Yeah, well, you've got your feds, your local police, and your state police." Will nodded. "And looks like some county agency, judging by the van there on the end."

"Why so many?"

"Any number of reasons. You have a federal agent injured, you have a break-in at the home of the daugh-

ter of a former U.S. senator, you'll get the feds. But
you have some local jurisdiction, county, and state.
Everyone wants in on the action." He stopped momentarily to survey the scene. "Hard to tell whose detectives are whose, isn't it? All those tweed-jacket
types look alike to me."

She stood in the backyard and watched the activity
around her while Will tried to find a fellow agent to
check in with.

While she waited, she called Selena's office in town,
but ended up leaving a message there, too.

"Call me. It's very important, *please*." Practically
the same message she'd left on Selena's home machine, but she wasn't feeling very original right then.

A tall man wearing a navy jacket with the bright
yellow FBI across the back came through the open
barn doors and walked toward the house.

"Oh, my God." Kendra shook her head. "Of course.
Why didn't I think of it sooner?"

Kendra started toward the house, looking for Will.
The agent who'd just come from the barn stopped her
before she reached the grass at the edge of the drive.

"Sorry, miss. This is a crime scene," he announced
importantly.

"I know. I'm Kendra Smith."

"Sorry. We're still not permitting anyone inside,"
he told her. "The crime scene crew is still at work. Is
there something you wanted from inside?"

"No. But I need to speak with whomever is in
charge of the investigation." She tried to watch with
detachment, but found she could not. This was her

home, and it had been invaded. "I think I know how he got in."

"I'll get Chief Logan." The agent disappeared into the house.

Minutes later, Chief Logan of the local police department came down the back steps accompanied by Will Fletcher.

"Kendra! You're all right?"

"Yes, Chief. I am."

"Thank God."

Logan took her by the elbow and stepped aside as the photographer emerged from the back door.

"We'll get copies of these to you as soon as they're ready," he told the chief.

"Fine. Great. Thanks." Logan nodded.

"Chief, I think I know how he got in. You may want to keep him"—she nodded toward the photographer—"here for a few."

Logan called to the photographer to wait up, then turned back to Kendra and said, "Go on."

"Well, you know the stories about this house being a stop on the Underground Railroad . . ."

"As many of the houses back here were," he nodded.

"There used to be a tunnel that went from our barn into the basement. There's a trap door in the basement floor."

"Show me . . ."

The steps going down into the basement of Smith House were narrow and steep, only one of a number of reasons why Kendra almost never ventured down. The floor of raised wood planks had been built over years ago by Kendra's grandfather, but prior to that bit of modernization, the floor had been dirt. Smith House, like others in the area, still took in water during heavy storms. The floor, elevated several inches off the dirt, had always reminded Kendra of a boardwalk.

One light hung in the center of the ceiling, but it shed little illumination in the dark, windowless area. Logan turned on his flashlight, shined it around the perimeter, which followed only the later additions to the house.

"Where would this trapdoor be?" Chief Logan asked.

"In the corner on the right." Kendra walked carefully across the wood floor to the far corner. "Here. The boards lift . . ."

She bent down to grab hold of the boards, and Logan stopped her.

"Let me get one of the men upstairs to open it up. I don't want your fingerprints on anything down here that they're not already on."

Two more agents and one of the local detectives responded to Logan's call for assistance. With gloved hands, the detective lifted the trapdoor where Kendra pointed, and shined his flashlight down into the hole. A wooden ladder descended several feet into the earth.

"Let's see where this leads . . ." he said as he lowered himself onto the ladder.

"I'm with you." One of the agents followed.

"Do you remember where in the barn this comes out?" Logan asked.

"Someplace near the back wall, there used to be a door there that opened out right onto the creek. I guess so that the runaways could get out of the canoes and just slip right in the back. Years ago, after one of the fires, the barn was rebuilt slightly closer to the house, and the back door was omitted. I never went into the tunnel. It was too dark and confined and I didn't like the idea of what could be down there with me," she laughed nervously, "but yes, I know where the door is. I'll show you."

Chief Logan and one of the FBI agents followed Kendra out to the barn, cautioning her to wait outside until they confirmed that no one was hiding inside.

"If someone is in there, they won't be hard to spot," she told them as she stood aside the open door. "There's nothing in there to hide behind. There used to be stalls, but after the last fire they weren't rebuilt."

The area declared safe, Kendra stepped inside and went directly to a section where scattered straw still covered the floor.

"At one time, a long time ago, my family had goats. There wasn't enough grass to support cows here, but there was plenty for the goats to eat." With the shoe of one foot, she kicked at the straw. "It should be right around here. There's a broom on the wall there."

She went to lift it and the agent stopped her. Drawing on a pair of gloves, he took the broom and swept in the area she'd designated. A square cut into the floor emerged, and he lifted it to expose a dark hole similar to the one in the basement. He turned on his flashlight, then called to the men who'd gone in from the basement side. A call in response came from the bottom of the hole.

"The floor is dirt," the detective reported as he raised himself from the ladder, "and covered with footprints. Someone has definitely been down there recently."

"So you trampled them good, I suppose." Logan looked pained.

"We tried to walk along the sides of the tunnel to preserve as much as we could," the detective said. "There are plenty to get impressions from."

"Then let's get the team in here for prints. Finger and foot." Logan led Kendra back out of the barn. "It looks as if we're going to be busy here for a bit longer. Where can we get in touch with you if we need you?"

"I was going to stay at Selena Brennan's, but I haven't been able to get in touch with her. I think maybe I'll go over to Father Tim's until she gets back."

"That's good," the chief replied, waving to his small crew of investigators. "Want me to send a car with you?"

"That won't be necessary, thanks. I'll have a guardian, complements of the federal government. He should be here soon, I imagine. Besides, I can't think of any place safer than Father Tim's."

Father Tim spread mayonnaise on two slices of bread and proceeded to stack it high with ham and cheese. A little lettuce, a little onion, and the priest's favorite lunch was ready.

As always, the lunch hour at the Mission of Hope was serve yourself, and at some point between eleven-thirty and one-thirty or so every day, that was exactly what the residents did.

"So, Jimbo," the priest asked as the tall thin man came into the kitchen. "How's the job search going?"

"Not so good," the man they all called Jimbo replied. "But I'm not giving up, you know."

"You never give up, son," the priest agreed. "Peter, how's your mother? She any better this week?"

"She's hanging in there, Father," Peter told him from the doorway. "I appreciate that you let me use a car whenever she has one of her spells. I appreciate it a lot."

Father Tim had picked up his plate. He had a meeting in five minutes with someone who was willing to donate a couple of televisions to the Mission. They weren't new, but they were still televisions. The priest was a big "Survivor" fan himself.

"Well, Peter," Father Tim said, moving toward the doorway where the young man stood, "I know how hard it is to watch a parent go downhill like that. I remember all too well what it was like to watch my own father in the last stages of his illness. You need to be there when she needs you. Anything I can do to lend a hand, I'm happy to do it." Father Tim gave Peter a reassuring slap on the back as he passed him. Peter flinched.

"Something wrong?" Father Tim turned to ask.

"Oh, I . . . I tripped over one of those loose flagstones out by the walk this morning. Fell and hit my back on the gate. I guess I bruised it."

"I'll bet that hurts like the blazes. Why don't you skip the gardening this afternoon and go on upstairs and take a hot bath, then maybe lay down for a while."

"Thank you, Father. Thank you. I think I'll do that." Peter, always soft spoken and humble, nodded.

"Good, good. Nothing like a hot bath. Now, I'll be in my office," Father Tim's voice trailed away as he walked down the hall. "Send Mr. O'Banyon in when he gets here, please. . . ."

Peter made himself a sandwich and ate it standing up, then put away the bread and washed off his knife. Everyone was expected to clean up after themselves here. It was only right, after all. Father Tim was so good to them all.

The car pulled into the drive just as he reached the second floor landing. He glanced out the window as he passed, then stopped, and watched.

Kendra Smith was parking out near the garage. Henry, one of the older men who lived in the Mission and the acknowledged number one gardener, stopped to chat with her. She got out of the car, followed by a tall man who had FBI written all over him. Both of them walked with Henry to the garden.

Peter stood on the landing, debating, his heart beating wildly.

So close. So close.

He couldn't touch her here. Not anywhere on Father Tim's grounds. It would be disrespectful to his benefactor, and without Father Tim's generosity, he reminded himself, where would he have been these past few weeks? Besides, she seemed to have acquired a companion. He pulled the curtain aside and looked out again.

The bodyguard looked like he might know a thing or two about taking care of his charge.

He went up to his room and closed the door, pacing, trying to decide what to do. The time was right, he told himself, but the place was all wrong. And there was that man.

How to get rid of him?

He looked out the window again, in time to see Kendra's friend remove a cell phone from his pocket. He continued to stare, watching as the man first stood, then walked away from the garden. He strolled along the fence, coming closer to the back of the house.

A quiet lift of the windowpane permitted a bit of eavesdropping by those who were so inclined.

". . . probably not much more than another hour or so," the man was saying. "She's found a way to pass the time while we wait, so I'm just hanging loose until my replacement arrives. As soon as he does, I'll head back to the hospital."

The agent turned slightly so that he could see his charge in the garden, then turned back.

"Yeah, concussion. I'll give you a call back after I check in with her doctors." He stood at the edge of the path, the phone in one hand, the other in his pocket. "No, Kendra's just waiting to get in touch with the friend she's planning on staying with."

The agent turned and walked back down the path, and the rest was lost.

The window closed as silently as it had opened.

The eavesdropper walked back down the steps calmly, let himself out by the side door. From there he could see Kendra in the garden, working side by side with old Henry, making rows to plant the corn in.

Looked like she'd be there a while. The man who'd arrived with her sat on one of the benches, just watching.

He slipped off into the woods, taking the path away from the Mission.

Peter was on a mission of his own.

"You're up awfully early, Sheriff," Adam said after the call from Cole Gamble was put through.

"Well, I wanted to make sure I caught you first thing. I told you I'd get back to you after I went through those files again."

"Did you find anything?"

"I think so," Gamble told him. "I'm going to have it checked out today, but here it is. After the Smith kids were discovered to be missing, search parties were arranged to fan out in a twenty-mile radius of the ranch to look for them."

"Right, we talked about that."

"And every one of those search parties was led by a member of one law enforcement agency or another. We had the feds, we had state and county, we had the police from nearby Chaco, since the ranch was located within its jurisdiction. Every one of those officers made a report of his search, where they went, who was in their party, that sort of thing. The sheriff who handled the case before me was real careful to dot every *i* and cross every *t*. He wanted to make sure there was a record of every square inch."

"Smart of him."

"Very smart. Now, the report from the deputy who led the party that went southwest of the ranch indicated that they went fourteen point three miles."

"I thought you said they were supposed to go twenty in every direction?"

"They were, in every other direction. But fourteen miles southwest of the ranch, you run into some hills. You follow the path into the hills, you run into a series of caves."

"Weren't the caves searched?"

"Not all of them. Some of these caves have been taken over by swarms of killer bees that migrated up from Mexico and South America some years ago. Apparently they tried to check a few of the caves, but they weren't successful. The bees swarmed and attacked, scattering the search team. No one ever goes near those caves, Adam. Entomologists who studied several of the hives a few years ago said that, depending on how far back the caves go, there could be millions of bees in any one of those caves."

"Killer bees?" Gamble could almost hear Adam's frown through the wires. "African bees brought over to mate with South American bees as an experiment?"

"Yeah, yeah, everyone knows the story of how the bees escaped and have been moving north, terrorizing everything that threatens their hives."

"What's the point, Cole?" Adam glanced at his watch. He was due in Mancini's office in less than three minutes.

"The point is, the locals refer to these caves as the bee caves." He paused for effect. "Take a piece of paper and write it out. Bee caves."

"Cole, I'm late for a . . ."

"Just write it out. BEE CAVES."

"Okay. Done."

"Now erase the second *e* in bee, and the *e* in caves. And change the *v* to a *u* . . ." The sheriff paused again. "What's that look like to you?"

"BE CAUS . . . Jesus, bee caves. You think that's what Christopher was trying to say? Not *because*, but *bee caves*?"

"I'm betting on it. As a matter of fact, I'm trying to find one of those suits that beekeepers wear, you know, the ones with the hood and the gloves. I'll be checking out the caves myself. The investigators could have missed something, you know? I'm thinking that maybe, after they aroused the ire of the first hive or two, they figured that no one could have gotten into one of those caves to dump a body and gotten out alive. I think they just bagged searching the rest of the caves."

"Can you wait for me?"

"You want to be in on this?"

"I can be there in a few hours. And I'll bring the suits."

It was one hundred five degrees in Tucson when Adam stepped off the plane that had been authorized to transport him to Arizona. By the time he'd driven to Bisbee where he met up with the sheriff, the temperature had climbed to one hundred eleven. It was even hotter when they finally arrived in the hills outside of Chaco.

"It'll start to drop soon, as the sun starts to set," Gamble said of the temperature as he pulled on the specially insulated beekeepers garb. "Of course, by then, we'll be running out of daylight."

"Then we'll set up lights," Adam replied and pointed to the first of the caves that lay ahead of them off the path. "Might as well start with this one."

"The original search team went into that one," Gamble told him. "That one and the next two. They were numbered in the file. I think we should start with the next two, up the ridge. How 'bout if we split up, each take one?"

"Fine, lead on." Adam shoved his gloves under his arms and turned to check on the long breathing tube that trailed behind him like a long, thin, transparent tail.

"You know for a fact, don't you, that this thing is going to be a sure pain in the ass?" Gamble grumbled.

"Yeah, but our experts said that if the bees don't hear us breathing and if they don't smell our breath, they won't bother us, and we'll be able to get through the caves more quickly and with little or no agitation to the bees."

"Well, God knows we don't want the bees agitated."

Adam laughed and headed up the path to the entry to the cave, then lowered his visor and stepped inside. The walls of the inner cave were lined with bees clinging to each other in long, slowly undulating shafts. Careful to keep the light focused on the ground, Adam walked slowly, conscious of the steady hum that filled the air around him. After shining the light low into every corner, and convinced there was nothing to be found, he backed slowly toward the entrance to the cave, ducking slightly as he exited.

"Well, that was different," Gamble greeted him when he stepped outside.

"Nothing in this one," Adam said.

"Here either. On to the next two."

And to the next two after that, but there was no trace of anyone having gone into the caves before them.

"Maybe we should check the lower caves after all," Adam remarked as he removed the hood and took several deep breaths of cooling air. "Maybe something was missed."

"Well, that's not a bad idea." Gamble, too, had removed his hood for the sheer relief of having fresh air—even hot air—on his face. "Since those early search teams didn't have the benefit of these nifty space-age suits, maybe they didn't venture all that far into the caves. Then again, there could be another reason why we're not finding anything."

"What's that?" Adam asked as they headed back down to the lower caves.

"Maybe there's nothing here."

There was nothing in the first cave, but in the second, a ten-year search came to an end.

Here, too, bees were everywhere, and the hum from so many pairs of softly beating wings was incessant. Off to the right of the entrance to the cave, in a slight alcove in the rocks, lay what Adam would later describe as an indeterminate shape. At first glance it appeared to be no more than a pile of rags. But when Adam leaned closer for a better look, he found the rags covered with the remains of thousands of bees. Using a gloved hand to gently clear away the insect carcasses, he uncovered what appeared to be remains of a different sort. As he turned to leave the cave to find Cole Gamble, he tripped over something on the floor. He bent over to investigate, and found a backpack.

"Gamble!" Adam called as he emerged from the cave and stripped off the hood.

"You found something?" the sheriff called back.

"I did. Call in your investigators. We have some remains."

"Think it could be the Smith boys?"

"One of them, maybe."

"Only one?"

"Appears to be. One body. And one backpack."

Gamble called his office to request that the CSI be dispatched immediately, then went into the cave to view the scene for himself.

"There's only one, all right. And it could be one of those boys you're looking for. The body's obviously been there for a long time, and I don't recall that we've ever had reports of anyone else lost out this way." Gamble paused and bit the inside of his cheek. "Wonder which one it is?"

"And if it is one of the Smiths, where," Adam added, "is the other body?"

The crime scene investigators, dressed in the suits previously worn by Adam and Cole, ventured into the cave. The increased activity agitated the hive, and the two investigators were forced to leave until the bees settled down again, and then reentered, one at a time, lest the occupants be overly disturbed.

"I doubt they'll swarm," offered an entomologist they'd called in from a nearby college, "but with a hive that large, I wouldn't want to risk it. I'd hate to anger a colony that large. There's no telling what they'd do. Killer bees are unpredictable as it is, and

I've never even read about a situation like this. I think the smartest thing to do at this point is to irritate them as little as possible, do your investigation around them, as surreptitiously as it can be done, and leave as quietly as you came."

"Works for me," one of the investigators had nodded, and flipped a coin to see who would be the first into the cave.

Several hours later, the remains were finally removed to a waiting ambulance, and the backpack carefully opened. Inside was a wallet. With the utmost care, Adam opened the wallet and withdrew a small white cardboard identification card. He turned it over and read the name aloud.

"Zachary Smith."

"That's him, then." Gamble nodded slowly. "Zachary Smith."

"Well, that's Zachary's backpack. We'll see what the tests come up with as far as the positive ID is concerned."

"You really expect that body to belong to anyone else?"

"Can't think of any reason why it should," Adam admitted, wondering how he was going to tell Kendra that they'd found what could well be her cousin, but no sign of her brother—and just what that could mean.

CHAPTER
TWENTY

"Oh, Miss Smith. There you are."

The young man called to Kendra from the back porch.

"I'm sorry," he was saying, "I looked out before and didn't see you."

"Is something wrong?" Kendra rinsed her hands off under the garden hose. She was grimy and sweaty, but it had been good to spend the afternoon laboring at something. She'd felt out of sorts since leaving her house still in the hands of the police. It would be hours before their investigation would be completed, they'd told her, and it had unnerved her to learn that someone had had full and easy access to her home all along. She, who had always been so careful, so cautious. She'd been lucky to find Henry about to start planting in the Mission's garden, pleased that he was one who enjoyed a little company at such times. It had kept her body moving and her mind occupied, for which she was grateful. Fortunately, Will Fletcher hadn't much cared where they spent the time while they awaited the agent who'd been assigned to stay with Kendra.

A glance at his watch, however, told him that they probably didn't have too much more time before he got there, and that now would be a good time to start back to Smith House.

"Nothing's wrong," the man replied, pushing his glasses up the bridge of his nose, "but I promised Miss Brennan that I'd let you know that she called earlier, looking for you."

"Selena called?" Her face brightened.

"Yes. I'm sorry, I called around, but I guess you didn't hear me." The young man lowered his eyes apologetically. He was so soft-spoken that Kendra had to strain to hear him.

"Did she leave a message?"

"Yes. She said to tell you that she got your message, but that she was tied up this afternoon. She asked me to tell you that she'd meet you at your house around five."

Kendra looked at her watch. It was four-thirty.

"Well, then, I guess I'd better get moving. Thanks. Peter, isn't it?"

"Yes."

"Thank you, Peter." She started in the direction of her car, then stopped and turned back. "Will you tell Father Tim that I stopped by? Henry said he was in a meeting this afternoon."

"Sure thing." Peter nodded from the doorway, then waved as the Subaru made a U-turn.

"Thanks again," Kendra called as she drove past.

"The pleasure was all mine," he said softly.

* * *

The yellow crime scene tape still marked the back porch and almost seemed to glow in the last bit of daylight. Several cars remained in the drive when Kendra and Will arrived, though Selena's was not one of them, and it appeared that most of the investigators were heading in the direction of the cars or packing equipment in the back of the vans.

"Looks like they may be wrapping up," Will said as they got out of the car. "Want to wait here?"

"Sure," she shrugged and leaned back against the car.

Will approached the small gathering of officers and agents who were still chatting in a loose group. Kendra hoped that her new "guardian" was among them. Though he'd been patient all afternoon while she had found useful means of passing the time, Kendra sensed that Will was anxious to get back to check on Miranda's progress.

She glanced at her watch and realized it was a little after five. Selena should be there any time now. Surely she'd be all right for a few minutes alone so that Will could get a ride back to the hospital with one of his fellow agents. She was just debating this when she looked up and saw a man in a dark suit and dark glasses approaching, his hair closely cropped into a dark crew cut.

"Hi," he called to her. "Kendra Smith?"

"Yes." She nodded. "Are you my new bodyguard?"

"I am," he nodded, touching a finger to his mustache.

"I'm so glad you're here," she smiled back. "I was just thinking that maybe I should try to talk Agent Fletcher into leaving, that I could wait alone. I think he's in a hurry."

"Not a good idea." The man shook his head. "But it doesn't matter, does it, since I'm here now."

"Kendra," Will called out as he walked toward them.

"It's okay, Will, you can go," Kendra called back.

"Joe Clark?" Will asked as he drew closer.

"Yes." The newcomer held out his hand.

"Just in the nick of time." Will shook the hand that was offered. To Kendra, he said, even as he backed away, "I'm getting a ride back with one of the others. You have my cell phone number—it's on the card I gave you—so feel free to call if you need anything."

"I won't. I'll be fine," she assured him. "Now go. Everyone's ready to leave. Give Miranda my love."

"Will do," he called back as he hurried across the drive to a waiting car. "Clark, good to meet you."

"Am I allowed to go into the house?" Kendra asked Agent Clark. "I'd like to get a few things to take to Selena's."

"They're done now." The agent nodded agreeably. "They won't be back. Go on in, get whatever you need. I'll wait out here for you."

"I won't be a minute," she told him as she turned for the house, noticing for the first time that he wore brown shoes. He must be new, she thought to herself. Most of the agents she knew dressed pretty well, and probably wouldn't wear brown shoes with a black suit. Old brown shoes at that.

"Take your time," he smiled and strolled down toward the stream.

The fashion eccentricities of her new companion forgotten, Kendra entered the back of the house, and was stunned by its silence. She found herself tiptoeing across the kitchen floor, then laughed nervously. This was, after all, her home.

She ran up the stairs to the second floor and grabbed an overnight bag from her closet. She had just finished stuffing it with the few things she thought she might need for a few days and had started back down the steps when the phone rang.

"Hello?"

"Kendra, where the hell have you been?"

"Adam, hi. I was at the Mission. Father Tim's . . ."

"Has Will's replacement arrived yet?"

"He just did. I came in to pack a few things to take to Selena's. He's waiting outside. Did you need to speak with him?"

"Not really. I just wanted to make certain that he'd gotten there and that everything was all right."

"Everything is as all right as it's going to be, I suppose." Noting the tension in his voice, she asked, "Is something going on that I need to know about?"

"Yes. But first of all, I'm in Tucson, at the airport. My plane will be taking off any minute now, so listen carefully."

"What are you doing in Tucson?"

"I'm about to tell you. But I need for you to sit down."

"I'm sitting." Her forehead creased with concern. "What's happened?"

"I got a call from Sheriff Gamble early this morning." Adam began to reiterate his earlier conversation with the sheriff.

"Wait. What we thought was *because* could mean *bee caves*?"

"That's what Gamble suspected, but someone was going to have to search the caves."

"And that would explain why you're in Tucson. You wanted to be the one to search the caves."

"Yes. Well, Gamble and I searched. I brought some beekeepers gear from Quantico and we went from cave to cave. There were millions of bees, Kendra. Millions, in these caves. God only knows how long these colonies have been there. Several of the caves were simply giant hives." He hesitated, then said, "We found some remains."

"Remains?"

"Remains of someone who'd apparently gone into the cave and was stung to death. The scraps of his clothing were literally covered with thousands of dead bees."

"Oh, my God, that's horrible. What a horrible way to die," she whispered.

"Kendra, there was a backpack found near the mouth of the cave."

"A backpack?"

"Zach's wallet was inside."

"The body . . . do they think the body is Zach's?" Kendra's mind scrambled to process the news.

"The possibility is being considered." Adam appeared to be choosing his words carefully.

"And Ian?" she asked.

"There was no sign of a second body."

"But maybe in another one of those caves, but that wouldn't make any sense. Why would they have gone into different caves?" Her head began to spin. "Farther back, then, in that cave where they found Zach. Maybe Ian had wandered back there."

"Kendra, there is no way anyone could have gotten any farther into those caves without being stung to death. And all of the caves have been checked out. I'm sorry, Kendra, but there's only one body, and we won't know for certain if it's your cousin until the ME is finished."

"But if that's Zach," she said as if she hadn't heard him, "then where's my brother?"

"We're trying to figure that out. In the meantime, I'll be there as soon as I can. Where will you be later tonight?"

"Try Selena's first. She left word at the Mission that she'd meet me here, but she hasn't arrived yet. Here, write down her phone number." Kendra gave him Selena's number.

"I'll give you a call when I'm on my way back."

"Okay." She didn't protest. All of a sudden she missed him terribly. "Any thoughts on what time you expect to arrive?"

"It all depends on when they allow the plane to leave. Can you keep safe until then?"

"I'll do my best."

She rested the receiver down, reflecting on Adam's news. A body had been found, but only one. A backpack had been found. Again, only one. Zach's. If the body in the cave was Zach's, then where was Ian's? And if he hadn't died in the cave with Zach, where was he now? Where had he been for the past ten years?

She was sitting with her elbows on the desktop, her

chin in her hands, wondering what to think, what to believe, when she noticed that the light on the answering machine was blinking furiously. Kendra pushed the play button.

". . . to get you yesterday afternoon . . ." Selena was saying. ". . . before I left, but there was no answer. My sister-in-law broke her elbow—in-line skating with the kids—by the way, remind me to pass on that next time the opportunity arises. Anyway, I drove up here to take care of my niece until things settle down. I expect I'll be back by tomorrow, by then they should have been able to arrange for someone to come in to help out. I brought Lola with me, by the way, because there just didn't seem to be quite enough chaos in my brother's house the last time I was here."

Selena paused, then laughed self-consciously. "There was one other thing. . . . I know you'll think I'm crazy. But, well, I've been having the worst dreams, Kendra. Dark and threatening and well . . . well, the darkness seems to be directed toward you, though I can't pinpoint what or who or why. But it's gathering around you . . . surrounding you . . . I can't explain it and I don't know what it means." She laughed again, the laughter sounding forced. "Okay, yeah, I know. Nutty Selena."

She hesitated, then added, "You know, maybe you're right, maybe I shouldn't have tried so hard to push all of that out of me. Maybe I should have left well enough alone. Maybe I'd know how best to interpret the impressions that I'm getting. Damn, Kendra, I'm sorry if I'm scaring you. I probably shouldn't have said anything at all. If I could figure out how to erase this tape from here, I would. Anyway, you have my brother's phone number. Give me a call when you get this message and I'll deny that I ever said any, well, any of the stuff I just said. I'm sorry. I guess it's just silliness. . . ."

Kendra frowned. Selena must have left that message before she called the Mission to tell her that she'd meet her here at the house at five. Maybe Selena's sister-in-law was released from the hospital earlier than expected.

Kendra stood up and opened the middle desk drawer for her phone book, a small loose-leaf notebook covered in a plaid fabric in which she kept every phone number she'd recorded practically since college. She'd just located the number for Selena's brother when she heard the soft shuffle of a foot behind her.

"Hello, Kenny," a soft voice said from behind.

She looked over her shoulder at the man who stood in the doorway.

"Peter . . . ?" What was he doing here? And where was Joe Clark?

"No, no. Not Peter."

"Where's Joe Clark?" she asked.

He took one step into the foyer, and she noticed his shoes. Brown leather. She knew where she'd just seen them.

"Guess."

She shook her head, confused.

"Oh, come on, now. You can figure it out. We all know what a smart cookie you are." He circled her.

From one pocket he drew out something dark and furry, which he draped over his top lip. "Look familiar?"

He slipped dark glasses on and she gasped.

"Who are you?"

Pausing behind her, he whispered in her ear, "Here's a clue. How many people call you Kenny?"

"No one . . ." Her hand flew to her mouth, remembering.

"Ahhhhh." He smiled with great satisfaction.

"No." She shook her head.

"Say it." He leaned directly into her face. "Ian. Say it. *Ian.*"

Kendra tried to step backward, but the desk was in the way.

"Now, after all the years you grieved for me . . . you did grieve for me, you and Mom, didn't you?"

His eyes narrowed and Kendra tried to peer into them, tried to determine their depth, but she saw nothing. How could these dark, blank eyes be Ian's? Was this his face? It had been so long since that summer day they'd put him on the plane to Arizona. Had the young boy's soft face smoothed into such lean angles?

"How could you be Ian?" she asked, her voice barely a whisper, her brain refusing to acknowledge this face as the face she'd so recently studied, so recently sketched. *No. No no no no no no . . .*

"How could I be anyone but?" He appeared slightly amused. "Well, I suppose I really can't blame you. I have been a bit . . . scarce."

"Why?"

"Why? Why have I been scarce?"

She nodded as if dazed.

"Why did I . . . disappear?"

Again she nodded.

"I'd had enough," he whispered in her ear, as if sharing a confidence. Then the whisper became a hiss. "Enough of her rules and her demands and her school and her arguments and her—"

"My brother never would have just walked away from his home. It wouldn't have happened," Kendra interrupted, shaking her head slightly, side to side. "No. He had no reason to run away, he had—"

"You think only poor kids run away, Kenny? Only poor kids from broken, neglectful homes?" He snickered. "You are just like her, aren't you? You've grown up to *be* her. Just like they say, every woman, eventually, becomes her mother."

"You're not him." She shook her head again. "I don't know who you are, but you are not Ian."

He grabbed her arm and looked deep into her eyes, as if waiting for some revelation. "Well, then, how to prove . . . I know."

He snapped his fingers as if something had just occurred to him. "You can test me."

He crossed his arms over his chest. "Go on. Ask me something. Anything."

She stared at him, wondering how this could be.

"Kenny, this silence is not at all welcoming. Why, one might think that you're not happy to see me. And you should be welcoming me with open arms. After all these years, I can't tell you how disappointed I am." He stared at her through soulless eyes. "You should be happy to see me. You should know me, Kenny."

Kendra stared unblinking at the stranger who demanded recognition. She knew the face, all right. She'd sketched it over and over, several times over the past few weeks.

It couldn't be her brother's face. It just couldn't.

"Where have you been?"

"Well, now, you know the answer to that. You know where I've been staying."

"Before that. Before you went to Father Tim's. If you're really my brother, you would have come here."

"I did want to come here . . . it's my right to be here, same as yours. Smith House. It's mine, too." He stiffened slightly, then said, "But I wanted to be able to see you for a while first. To get to know you, so to speak."

"You were spying on me? Watching me?"

"Every chance I got," he admitted, the smirk still in his eyes, if not on his face. "I admit I found Father Tim's by accident, but once I found out that you were one of the funders of the Mission, well, you have to see the irony of that."

"No," she told him. "No, I don't."

"All these years, I've supported myself. I come back to Smith's Forge and immediately find the Smith money just waiting to take care of me."

"How did you support yourself?" Heart pounding, she forced herself to appear calm. *Keep him talking.*

"Oh, there are lots of ways for a good-looking little boy to earn what he needs. You wouldn't believe all the things I've learned to do for money. Then again, you probably wouldn't want to know."

"Is that what you're here for? Money?"

"You know one thing I missed all these years?" He ignored her question and took a step toward her. "Remember when I was little and you used to make me pancakes in the afternoons when Mom was going to law school?"

Kendra shrunk back, her mind still muddled. As a youth, Ian had been troubled, yes, but had his defiance, his growing bouts of rebellion, concealed something deeper? He had been seeing a child psychiatrist that last year, but her mother had never discussed with Kendra the nature of his problems or what had caused them. There was an air about the young man who stood before her that was sinister, almost unholy. If the seed for such had lain dormant in her brother, could she have been blind to it?

This is a dream, she told herself. *A really, really horrible dream.*

"I never forgot how you used to do that for me." He placed his hands on her shoulders and she flinched from his touch as he turned her around so that she was facing the kitchen door. If he noticed her revulsion, he did not acknowledge it. "I want you to make me pancakes, just like you used to do. That would be the perfect welcome home for me."

He pushed her through the doorway, her feet leaden, her mind numb. "And coffee. I'd really like some coffee."

Kendra stood at the counter, confused. How could she complete such a mundane task?

"Now, you cook, and we'll chat, and I'll tell you everything you want to know," he promised. "We have a lot to catch up on. Of course, I've kept up with you. Big-time sketch artist, eh? I remember when you used to draw people. Remember you drew Mrs. Lentini, that mean-tempered lady who lived across the street, and you made her look so mean? Mom tried to pretend she was horrified but she laughed anyway."

She searched the cupboards for the ingredients for pancakes, her head filled with a loud humming born of nerves and the sheer effort to maintain a composure she was close to losing.

Who was this man?

He seated himself at the kitchen table, facing her where she stood between the sink and the stove.

"You're still skeptical, aren't you. Hmmmm, shall I talk about the old house? The house we grew up in, in Princeton?" Without waiting for her response, his words tumbled out quickly. "It was brick. It had a small front porch with white pillars. Red patterned rugs in the front hallway and big, wide steps that went up to the second floor in a curve. There was a basket on the table near the front door for the mail. There were always flowers on that table, and a lamp with blue swirls on it." He looked up and asked, "Isn't that how you remember it?"

"That house was photographed several times for magazine articles. Anyone could have access to that information. You've proven nothing." She was barely aware that her hands had begun to sweat.

"On to the sunroom, then," he smiled. "Heavy wicker furniture. There was a big round table with a glass top, there were always books stacked on it. She—Mom—always read more than one book at a time. She carried them with her in a canvas bag that had an orchid painted on it. Dad had bought it for her. There was a round pottery ashtray. She smoked cigarettes but prided herself on the fact that she never smoked more than five a day."

He paused, then asked, as if it mattered to him, "Did that change, once she became a senator? I mean, smoking's become so politically incorrect, hasn't it?"

He took a pack from his own pocket, lit one, then tossed the match toward the sink. He missed the mark and she bent down to pick it up. Her hands were trembling.

"You can give me something to use as an ashtray, or I can use the floor," he told her without expression. "It's all the same to me."

She opened the cupboard and took out a saucer, handed it to him.

"Thanks. Now, back to the sunroom." He inhaled deeply, letting the smoke out slowly as if suddenly deep in thought.

"We gave her one of those rock tumblers for Christmas one year. She picked up stones everywhere she went, then, when she had a bunch, she'd put them in the tumbler. It was a very slow process, it would take hours. She put them, those pretty polished stones, all over the house. There was a flat basket filled with them on the table next to her bed."

Kendra's head began to pound.

"The furniture was covered in blue-and-white-and-yellow swirly fabric. There were lots of pillows. The walls were blue, like your shirt."

She closed her eyes and saw the sunny paisley seat

cushions her mother had made for the old wicker furniture she'd bought from the estate of an elderly neighbor.

"These are antiques, Kendra," her mother had said. *"They don't make them like this anymore. See how sturdy?"*

"The dog, Elvis, he was a mix of dachshund and Cairn terrier, the result of an unfortunate coupling of the dogs who lived in the houses on either side of ours—chewed the legs of one of those wicker chairs and she, Mom, was just beside herself." He continued smoothly, his voice a steady and unrelenting stream. "There was a gardener. His name was Mr. Jackson. Mom gave him some of Dad's clothes after he died. He had a brown leather jacket of Dad's that he wore for years. Elvis chewed that, too."

He paused and looked up at her. "Not enough?"

She stared at him blankly.

"Mom almost didn't let me go out west that summer, because I'd been in trouble all year long."

"What kind of trouble had you been in?" she heard herself ask.

"I used to push open the screen in my bedroom window and climb out on the sunporch roof, then up into that big magnolia tree." He grinned at her devilishly. "Want to know what I did then?"

She wasn't sure she did.

"I used to climb up as high as I could go, and just sit there in the dark, waiting for Mrs. Flaherty, our next-door neighbor, to get undressed for bed."

"That's disgusting."

"I didn't think so."

"You were eleven years old."

"I'd been watching her for two years."

Kendra was speechless.

"Not enough yet? How 'bout this? Before I left to go out west that summer, you gave me money from your secret savings stash so I could buy something from an old Indian man who had stuff to sell."

"Where was it? My secret stash." Her voice had grown raspy.

"Under the floorboards in your closet," he said without hesitation.

She sat down across from him at the table, the box of pancake mix still in her hands. He'd thrown so much at her, verbally, that she was having difficulty processing it all. Everything he'd said had been right on the money, hadn't it? Still something nagged at her, begging her recall.

Kendra again studied his face, again tried to re- member her brother's features in detail. What might Ian look like today? The shape of the eyes, yes, the eyes were round, they could be right. The nose, tilted at the end, but as she'd once told Adam, a common enough trait.

If indeed Ian was alive, how might his features have matured?

Time and again, Kendra had aged photographs on paper to determine what someone gone missing for years might look like now, as an adult. But could she mentally age the face of a child whose features she could see only in her memory?

Kendra knew faces. Did she know this one?

"Are you going to make those pancakes for me?"

She rose without answering and continued on with the task he'd given her, all the while concentrating on his features, trying to sketch the child's face within her mind.

"By the way, whatever happened to the Flahertys?" He leaned back with the air of one who was right at home.

"They got divorced."

"I can't say I'm surprised," he nodded, "since she was screwing some other guy every time old Mr. Flaherty was out of town on business."

She turned to look over her shoulder at him.

"I used to watch that, too." His tongue licked at the side of his mouth. "She could sure put on a show, that Mrs. Flaherty. Who'd have thought that Melinda and Mike's mom was such a hot ticket?"

Kendra turned back to the stove.

"And the Cronins, across the street?"

"They're still there."

"Really? Well, that was a pretty desirable neighborhood, from what I recall."

"If you're really Ian, you'd know what happened to Zach." She turned to face him. Would he know about the body Adam said had been found in the cave? And if so, would he know how it came to be there?

"Now, there's a name I haven't heard in years." His eyebrows raised, as if genuinely surprised that she'd asked.

"What happened to him?" Kendra repeated.

"Like anyone cares what happened to Zach."

"I care."

"Do you?" he scoffed. "Why?"

"He's family."

"As if," he snorted. "Zach was a dumb shit who knew nothing about anything and was never going to be anything other than what he was. A colossally dumb shit."

"How can you say that? I thought you were friends."

"Friends? Me and Zach? I couldn't stand him."

"Then why was it so important to you to spend a month with him every year? Two weeks out here, two weeks out there. You always looked forward to his visits."

"Well, if anything ever made me feel like a genius, it was having stupid Zach around," he sneered. "He knew nothing. I mean, *nothing*. Didn't you ever notice how he watched everything we did, before he did it? Or how carefully he listened, to see how things should be said?"

"No, frankly, I did not."

"Yeah, dumb question on my part. You never noticed him at all."

"Why would I? He was years younger than me and was always pretty quiet, as I remember. Frankly, I never gave much notice to any of your friends. You were all so much younger. I was in college that last summer."

He smiled with satisfaction at her use of the word *you*, but did not comment on it.

"That wasn't the reason. It wasn't the age difference. Admit it. He just wasn't . . ." he sighed, "well, let's call a spade a spade. He just wasn't a Smith."

"What are you talking about, he wasn't a Smith? His mother was as much a Smith as my father was."

My instead of *our* rankled, and he frowned, but chose to ignore it.

"His mother was a junkie, Kendra. A junkie whore who didn't give a shit about him. She never did."

"What?" Kendra's jaw dropped.

"Never. Our dear Aunt Sierra shoved a great deal of her share of Grampa's estate up her nose. I can count on the fingers of one hand the number of times I spoke with her when she wasn't stoned."

Kendra sank into the nearest chair.

"When my mother agreed to send Ian out to Arizona, Sierra told us all that was behind her. That she'd been off drugs for a long time. Why didn't we know this? Why didn't you tell us? And if she wasn't treating Zach well, why didn't he say so? Why didn't we see it?"

"Are you crazy? You think Mom would have let me get within a hundred miles of the ranch if she'd had a clue of what was going on?" He laughed. "I liked it, Kenny. It was like nothing I'd ever experienced before. I could smoke more weed in the two weeks I was out there than I could get my hands on the other fifty weeks out of the year."

"You were just a child. . . ."

"Right, and kids don't do drugs?" He chuckled. "Please. Why do you think I went there, Kenny? To share quality family time with my beloved aunt and cousin? To keep the Smith family ties strong?"

Kendra stared at the stranger who sat across from her. She'd never suspected that her little brother had been involved with drugs. Had her mother known? Had that been one of the reasons Elisa had sent Ian for counseling that year?

"Sierra's ranch was one happening place, let me tell you. No restriction, no rules. No one to answer to. We just did what we pleased, went where we pleased."

"If that's all true, I can't believe that no one knew . . . that Zach's father . . ." Kendra tried to comprehend how a child like Zach could have been left in such a situation.

He laughed out loud.

"Zach's father? He could have been any one of a dozen men who stayed on the ranch from time to time."

"But surely someone . . ."

"Someone like who? Zach never went to school, Kenny. Sierra didn't even care enough about him to make the effort to make sure he got to school. She told Mom that he was being home-schooled. What a laugh." He leaned across the table and said, very deliberately, "No one even knew he was alive."

"How can that be?" Kendra held her head in her hands. "Surely, he had medical treatment at some time."

"Holistic," he told her. "There was a woman on the ranch who was part Native American. She grew herbs and treated everyone with some concoctions she mixed up."

"But there were other children there, on the ranch."

"From time to time, yes. No one ever stayed all that long. Except for Zach."

"He was twelve years old that last summer," she recalled. "How could he have lived for twelve years without someone knowing he was there?"

"There was no reason why anyone should," he shrugged. "He was born on the ranch. He told me one time that he didn't even have a birth certificate."

"Poor Zach . . ." Kendra's eyes filled with tears. "Why didn't he tell us? Why didn't you tell us?"

"Maybe he didn't say anything because he was too embarrassed. And frankly, I think he might have been afraid of the consequences. His mother was, well, what she was, but she was still his mother, I guess." He shrugged. "And I didn't say anything 'cause, well, hell, Kenny, what do you think *she* would have done? Gone to court, gotten custody, probably send Sierra to jail."

"If by *she*, you mean Mom, you're damned right she would have." Kendra's voice shook with indignation. "She would have done all those things. She would have fought to bring Zach out here."

"Oh, and wouldn't that have just been swell news for me," he hissed. "No thank you. One Smith son under this roof was just plenty."

"You would permit your own cousin to live like that because you didn't want to share your home with him?" Her eyes widened with incredulity. "You were that selfish?"

"Yes," he said without apology.

"Why did Sierra let him come here, then? Why did she let you go there? And why didn't Mom ever *know*?"

"I don't think Mom gave her much choice. And Sierra, she always cleaned up before she talked to Mom on the phone. I think the first time I went out, she was nervous. But she figured out real fast that I wouldn't tell. She knew I liked it there."

"I want to know what happened to Zach." She repeated the question that had started the conversation.

"Let's just say that Zach," he appeared to choose his words carefully, "won't be heard from again."

"What does that mean?"

"It means, dear sister," he grinned, "that our dear cousin Zachary has gone to that big Smith reunion in the sky."

"How . . . did it happen?"

"You really want to know?"

She nodded.

"We went out camping. He was going to take me to see this old Indian guy so I could buy some things. The third or fourth night out it got cold, so we started looking for some shelter. He went into a cave in the side of the hill." He paused and looked up at her. "You'll never guess what was in that cave."

"Bees," she whispered. "There were bees in the cave."

"Bingo." His brows raised in surprise. "Well, we always knew how smart you were, but I'd have to say, that was one damned smart guess. How'd you come up with that answer, just like that?" He snapped his fingers for emphasis.

"They found . . . remains. In a cave." Her throat tightened.

"What?"

"They found remains that might be Zach's."

"When?"

"This afternoon."

"This afternoon, eh?" He appeared thoughtful. "Well, how's that for timing?"

"What do you mean?"

"Just that it appears the both of us have chosen the same moment to, well, to *resurface*." He smiled charmingly. "Isn't that something? Ian and Zach, together again. Who'd have thunk it?"

CHAPTER
TWENTY-ONE

"Where have you been all these years?" she asked suddenly, her mind processing everything he'd said since he'd started talking.

"Here and there."

"Why?" She searched for words. "Why did you—"

"Pretend to be dead?" He smiled, an "I've got a secret" smile, but still, offered no answer.

"Why didn't you contact me before this? Why now?"

"Well, it isn't as if I haven't been doing my damnedest to get your attention."

Kendra froze.

"What did you say?"

"I said, I have been trying to get your attention for, oh, it's been almost two years, now."

The hairs on the back of Kendra's neck bristled. What was it that someone—Miranda, or had it been Anne Marie McCall?—had said?

I think this guy's been trying to get your attention for a long time.

No, she shook her head slightly, still trying to deny the truth she'd been avoiding since she'd turned and seen him standing in the doorway. It was too terrible, too monstrous.

A wave of nausea washed over her, and her knees buckled. She turned back to the sink and gripped the edge of the counter so tightly her knuckles went white. The hum inside her head became a roar.

No.

"Do they still harvest the cranberries from the bogs down on the other side of the lake?" he asked, as if this were just another day.

"Yes."

"We'll take the canoe down later, after we have pancakes. Though I guess it's way early for cranberries."

"How did you know that Selena was out of town?" She turned to him suddenly.

"Oh, I broke into her house. I was disappointed that she wasn't there—now there's a woman I'd like to get to know better." He smiled as if he were any normal man, expressing a normal interest in any woman, and terror reached toward Kendra's soul. "Anyway, I listened to the messages on her answering machine, and I heard yours."

"What is it you want?" Kendra's heart was pounding, the buzz in her veins louder now, as disbelief and fear continued to swell within her.

"Right now, I just want a friendly reunion with my big sister."

"Beyond that. There must be something more."

"Ahhh, patience, Kendra. That can wait."

"Where's the real Joe Clark?"

"I don't think you really want to know."

She turned back to mixing the batter so that she did not have to look at him.

Whoever this man is, he's severely unbalanced. But is he my brother?

How to gain the upper hand?

"Did you poison Selena's dog?" The thought had not been considered until the words fell from her mouth.

"Well, I tried to." He grinned sheepishly.

"Why?" Kendra's fists clenched. "Why would you do such a thing to such a sweet animal?"

"That dog was a pain in my ass," he stated coolly. "Every time I came around, that damn dog was here. Barking and running along the back of the stream, sometimes I couldn't even get out of the canoe."

"Where did you get the canoe?"

"From Father Tim's." He grinned again. "You know that he highly recommends communing with nature. He thinks it soothes and relaxes. Not that I doubt anything he says, mind you. I'd have been nowhere without Father Tim. Everything I've been able to accomplish, I owe to him."

"And what, exactly, have you accomplished?"

He smiled serenely. "The stuff dreams are made of, Kenny."

"Dreams, or nightmares?"

He shrugged. "One man's dream is another man's nightmare."

"You raped and killed all those women." The words slipped out past her lips.

"Yes." His blithe admission shocked her.

"Why?"

"I had to get your attention in a meaningful way."

"You murdered seven women to just get my attention?" she whispered in horror. Her stomach lurched and she fought back another wave of nausea, bit back the urge to scream.

"Eleven." He corrected her pointedly. "I killed *eleven* women to get your attention. There were four on the West Coast, would have been more, but you moved, and then I had to go to the trouble of finding you all over again."

Knees knocking together, legs weakened beyond their ability to support her, Kendra slumped over the side of the counter, leaned over the sink, and lost her lunch.

He sat, watching calmly, until she had finished gagging. Choking and coughing, she ran the water in the sink until the mess went down, then soaked paper towels to wipe the sweat from her face.

"Are you finished?" he asked without emotion.

When she didn't respond, he shifted in his seat and said, "I asked you a question. Are you finished?"

Still leaning against the sink, she nodded.

"Did you clean up your mess like a good girl?"

She nodded again.

"Sit down, Kendra."

She slumped into the nearest chair, speechless.

"Well, I guess we're going to have to talk about this after all, aren't we? You know, I really hadn't planned on it, at least not yet. Not today. I'd really just hoped for a pleasant reunion in my ancestral home." He stretched his legs out to one side and rested his shoulders against the back of the chair.

"You just remember, this was your idea, okay? So if any of it bothers you, you have no one to blame but yourself. Then again," he smirked, "all those cases you worked on with the FBI, I guess you're not very squeamish, are you?"

He was mocking her and she knew it. He'd just watched her throw up in the sink.

"I mean, I'll bet it takes a lot to gross you out, doesn't it?"

"No," she told him, shaking her head. "Anyone with a conscience—"

"Now, see, I just don't think I have one. I guess that's something you need to understand right up front."

She looked confused, and he laughed.

"Hey, I don't know why." He shrugged. "Must have been something that happened to me when I was a kid. Maybe it was genetic, who knows? Maybe that was something that me and Sierra had in common. Nothing she did ever seemed to affect her either."

His face hardened for a moment.

"But I can tell you," he went on, "that I've never felt the least bit sorry for anything I've done. I can't help it, Kenny. And it isn't as if I haven't tried. I mean, every time, I tried to feel something. Anything. But I don't."

"Nothing at all?" She barely recognized her own voice.

He shook his head. "Nope. Not sorry. Not upset. It didn't even make me particularly happy."

Looking up at her with blank eyes, he said, "I had a friend in 'Frisco. He's the one who taught me how to do it right, where to apply the pressure." He held up his hands, wiggled his fingers. "He liked to watch the light go out . . . you know what I mean?"

He didn't wait for an answer, just kept talking slowly, his voice a monotone, his expression somewhat puzzled, as if for a moment he, too, sought understanding.

"He said that when he put his hands around a woman's throat and squeezed, their eyes stayed open and he could watch the light go out inside them, and when it was happening, he was filled with peace. It made him happy," he said softly. "I thought maybe if I," he sighed, then shrugged, his moment of introspection gone. "Well, it really didn't do much for me, you know what I mean?"

"Then why did you keep doing it?" Her voice was shaky, her eyes burning with tears.

"I wanted you to notice me." He lit another cigarette, intently watched the match burn down before continuing. "I thought it would be fun, you know? You being the big compositor for the FBI," his voice boomed importantly. "The press out there in California made such a big deal out of you, I saw your picture in the paper, and I saw you on TV and I said, Wow! That's Kenny! Well, I have to admit, I was proud to be related to you. I told everyone that you were my sister, not that anyone out there believed me. But then I thought, well, let's see just how good she really is. Let's see if she can sketch me. Let's see if she *knows* me."

You killed all those women just to see if I'd recognize your face? She willed herself not to cry out in horror, to moan with repulsion that this man, this man who claimed to be her flesh and blood, could be capable of such twisted reasoning, of such terrible acts.

"Pretty clever, don't you think? I really thought you'd catch on, Kendra," he said with the same enthusiasm as some others might discuss the plot of the latest mystery novel. "I thought you'd figure it out. Frankly, I was disappointed that you never did. I admit the disguises lately would have made it difficult, but your drawings, right from the start, were too good and I was afraid someone would recognize me, maybe I'd get caught before you caught on." He sighed again. "I was really disappointed when you didn't recognize me."

"How could I have recognized you? I haven't seen you in ten years, and then, you were a *child*! Why would I have even thought . . ." Her mind whirled at the sheer insanity of it all. "You were *dead*. Everyone believed you were dead."

"I thought *blood* would know *blood*." He hissed, and she jumped at his vehemence.

He stubbed out his cigarette and immediately lit another.

"Well, I'm back now, Kendra, and I'll stay as long as I damn well please."

Kendra sat stock-still, watching the face of the man fill with quiet rage as he spoke. There was nothing about him that was familiar to Kendra. Not the rage, not the evil, not the cold eyes, not the man who could conceive of murdering good and innocent women and feel nothing.

Her parents had both been gentle and kind souls,

and had filled their home with love and laughter. How could such a pair have spawned such a monster?

"Yes," she said, "you're back now."

"Home." He dared her to challenge him.

"Yes." She stood on weak legs and turned back to the stove, forcing a calm she didn't feel, wondering how she was going to escape from here. "Home."

"I thought you'd see it my way," he said smugly. "Now, what's happening with my pancakes?"

"Just a few minutes." She turned on the burner under the frying pan to heat it, adding milk sloppily to the mix she'd measured out in the bowl, her mind frozen.

Her stomach lurched as the smell of the pancake batter reached her nostrils.

"Why those women?" she asked sadly, her voice quivering. "Why women who'd leave behind so much? Women who gave so much . . . who loved so much."

"I don't feel like talking about them now. Right now, I want my pancakes and I want my coffee," he said sullenly, pointing out, "You forgot my coffee."

I've been a bit distracted, her whirling mind wanted to scream. But she held on to her composure as she filled the pot with water and measured coffee into the pot, wondering how to gain advantage long enough to get away. To get to her car.

Her purse, car keys inside, were in the front hallway. What excuse could she make to get it?

Or maybe a weapon . . . what could she use as a weapon? There were knives, yes, in the drawer, but could he not turn a knife on her? She was strong and in good shape, but he appeared to be as well, and had the advantage of height and weight. He could overpower her easily.

He pointed to the frying pan. "The pan is starting to smoke."

She poured batter into the pan without measuring.

"How did you meet Father Tim?" he asked. A normal question, the kind a sibling would ask after a long separation. As if there had been no talk of dead women or abused children.

Kendra's stomach turned again. *This can't be happening. It can't be happening.*

"Through Selena."

Focusing her attention on the lone pancake in the frying pan, watching the bubbles rise in the batter, she thought back on days long ago when she stood in front of the stove at the house in Princeton, listening to Ian's chatter about school and that day's soccer or baseball practice. Ian had loved to play soccer.

"Where did you live?" she asked, the thought occurring to her. There'd been so much so fast, she'd hardly had time to think.

"On the streets."

"Where?"

"San Francisco, mostly. That summer, me and Zach were watching TV one night and there was a documentary about these runaways who lived together out there, like a family. It looked so cool, the way they helped each other, like a real family."

"You had a real family." She turned to him with a frown. "Why wasn't that good enough?"

"We talked about that, Kenny," he said calmly. "I don't want to talk about that again."

The first real stirrings of anger began to push aside the fear, ever so slightly, within her.

"You put us—her and me—through hell." She turned on him with a growl. "She never stopped weeping for you. There wasn't a day that passed that she didn't mourn for you. Don't tell me you don't want to talk about it."

His reaction was swift. In less than a blink, he had her by her wrists.

"You're breaking my heart," he snarled. "Don't make me break your arms."

They locked eyes, and he held her still, for another moment. The fury in his eyes was terrifying. Whatever demon drove him was very close to the surface.

"I don't want to hurt you, Kenny." He dropped her hands. "Do not make me hurt you."

He backed up, slowly, his breath coming in ragged spurts as he visibly struggled to regain his composure.

"Turn that over," he said, pointing to the pancake. "It's going to burn. You know I don't like burned pancakes."

He sat down again, lit another cigarette. For a time, the only sound was the ticking of the clock on the wall and the soft rustle of the evening breeze through the large maple tree outside. She turned the pancake onto a plate and offered it to him without speaking.

He pushed the plate back to her, saying, "Keep it warm while you make more. I want a whole stack. And get yourself a plate. I want you to eat with me."

"I'm not hungry." The thought of putting food into her mouth made her blanch. How could anyone eat in the presence of such a monster?

"I said, I want you to eat with me."

She poured more batter into the pan and got out a second plate, wondering how late Adam's plane would be. What were the chances he'd arrive soon?

"There. That's better." He relaxed a bit, resting his arms on the table. "And what's doing with my coffee? Boy, some hostess you are." He chuckled as if sharing a joke.

Kendra opened the cupboard and took out a mug.

"You'll have some, too."

She took down a second mug and placed it next to the first on the counter.

"I take sugar, no cream."

She reached for the sugar bowl and placed it on the table.

"Aw, you're mad at me now, aren't you?" His slender fingers toyed with the pack of matches. "I didn't mean to make you mad, Kenny. Don't you have things you don't want to talk about sometimes?"

Her eyes narrowed.

"I don't know who you are, I swear I don't," she told him.

"She has eyes, but does not see," he mused.

"Who are you?" she demanded.

"I'll have that coffee now." His smile faded and his mouth straightened into a hard line. "And so will you."

She grabbed a mug in each hand. The heat bled through the sides of the mugs into her fingers, and at that second, she knew she might not get a better chance. Reacting before she'd fully thought it through, with a quick twist of her wrists, she tossed the scalding coffee into his eyes.

His scream was angry, surprised, confused. And lethal.

"You bitch!" he roared, coming at her blindly.

No time to search for car keys, she shoved past him and raced down the back steps for the barn and the canoe that rested against the outer wall. As quickly as she could, she dragged the canoe into the water and pushed off, half running alongside the vessel to get as far from the house as possible. Paddling furiously, Kendra made her way toward the lake, her heart pounding painfully in her chest, sobs ripping from her throat. Once she made it to the other side, she could reach the emergency phone in the parking lot where the day-trippers left their cars while they explored the Pines.

But first she would have to make it through the narrow waterways in the dark. Though well acquainted with the creeks, Kendra had never navigated these passages at night. She paddled swiftly, and several times the paddle threatened to slip from her shaking hands. She could not slow down, but she could, she told herself, calm down. She should have paid more attention when she first started out, but the panic was so fresh and the fear so great that she'd paddled mindlessly, escape her only goal. Now that that had been accomplished, she needed to be rational, calculated, if she was to find her way in the dark.

The canoe glided through the shallow channels, but

to what destination she was no longer certain. She rested the paddle across the canoe and drifted just slightly, enough to know she was headed downstream. But which stream? And in which direction?

The cedar grew thick here, the trees standing tall right down to the water's edge. Gnarled roots reached like twisted fingers into the stream from either side, and the treetops met thirty feet over her head in a dense web of branches. She could be in one of two or three places. Without light, it simply wasn't possible to tell. She began to paddle again, thinking that perhaps this might not have been such a great idea after all. But what options had she had? Her car keys were in the foyer, which would have required her to pass the chair the man—she could not bring herself to think of him as Ian—was sitting in. Without access to a weapon that could not be turned against her, the hot liquid had seemed her only choice. But she knew that scalding his face could only be counted on to disable him for the briefest of time, time that had allowed her to escape from the house and from the man.

"Not many choices," she muttered softly as she searched in the dark for something that appeared familiar.

She paddled straight ahead until she emerged from the overhead canopy. Clouds that had drifted past the moon now eased aside, and the faintest bit of moonlight spread through the trees, here where the tall cedars were replaced by pigmy and pitch pines and a lone catalpa tree, last year's long pods still hanging here and there from its branches. Kendra relaxed. She knew the tree—some of the older locals used to call it

Webb's Pub, for the still buried nearby where years ago a man named Jonathan Webb made moonshine out of wild blueberries. It wasn't where she wanted to be by over a mile, but at least she knew where she was now. Through the night she heard the familiar cry of the whippoorwills, and the sound soothed her.

The channel at this point being too narrow and the current being strong, Kendra got out of the canoe and manually turned it around. She'd have to backtrack half a mile or so, then bear to the left to get to the lake. But it was okay now. She let out a deep breath that she'd been holding forever, but could not allow herself to relax. He could be anywhere, she reminded herself. Surely he would have attempted to follow her. How successful he'd be at finding her would depend on how well he'd come to know these waterways.

A chill ran up her spine and she hunched down just a bit, and paddled just a little faster. The short scraggly trees cast dense shadows across the water, and she thought of a movie she'd seen when she was younger, where the trees moved. Several times she thought she saw movement beyond the pines that grew along the water's edge.

"Shit, I am spooking myself," she said aloud.

She paddled on to the place where a pin oak, struck by lightning the summer before, had cracked in half, and she let out a sigh of relief. The lake was three-quarters of a mile to the left. She could make it. She *would* make it.

As she made her way into the turn, her nose caught a whiff of something.

"Smoke," she whispered, looking into the night on

every side to see where the smoke was coming from, but as yet there was no sign of flames.

Fires were so common here, but there'd been no storm tonight to set one off. There could be campers, but they were unusual in the middle of the week, this time of the year. She sat stock-still, her eyes combing the darkness for light where there should be no light, and movement where all should be still. There was nothing.

She heard him only a split second before he leapt at her from the right, from the bank of the stream and the stand of thick laurel where he'd waited while she puzzled over the scent of smoke.

"You bitch," he cursed as the canoe tipped from side to side. "You think I'd let you get away with that?"

He'd landed slightly behind her, and straddled the side of the canoe. Kendra tried to turn quickly to swing at him with the paddle, but he grabbed hold of it and wrestled with her a long minute for its control. She slid from the canoe as it was forced on its side and slapped her head as she fell. Dazed, she sought purchase on the sandy bottom of the stream. She felt his hands, strong and angry, grab the back of her head and force it underwater. Turning her head slightly, she bit into the only part of him she could reach, the soft skin at his ankle.

Howling, he let go of her, and she rose from beneath the surface long enough to gasp a breath before being dunked back under again. She fought and sputtered, her flailing arms trying to reach him, but her struggle only served to deplete her strength.

She felt as if they'd been fighting forever, but eventually her will begin to wane, her energy flowing from her like blood from a deep wound. Inside her head she heard a horrific buzz, and saw great bursts of pearlescent light. The fight forgotten, she turned to it, was drawn into it, her hands floating weightlessly in the tea-colored water.

CHAPTER
TWENTY-TWO

It was dark and still and the air smelled of rotting wood. Coughing and tossing up water, Kendra lay facedown on the ground, desperate to take that first breath. Her back hunched as her lungs spasmed. She couldn't see five inches from her face. She hadn't been really certain whether she was waking in this world or the next until something crawled across her arm and she flinched.

The night, deep and quiet, pressed around her and she shivered, cold and alone, in an unknown place. The first fingers of fear began to wrap around her as pain, raw and silent, rippled across the back of her head. Brain fuzzy and limbs numb, she struggled to focus, to orient herself to time and location, to remember where she had been before the world had crashed down upon her.

Hadn't she been on her way to another place, a place of light?

Whatever had brought her back, into the dark, she was not, at that moment, particularly happy about it.

"Well, I'd say we were just about even now," a voice said, and she opened her eyes, trying to focus.

Not so alone, after all.

"Why didn't you kill me?"

"Because I'm not done with you yet."

He sat six feet away from her, his back leaning against the side of the burned-out shell of a barn that had been lost to fire sixty years ago.

"McMillan's," she rasped, her throat sore and raw, though she could not remember quite why. That she had recognized the locale, however, gave her a tinge of satisfaction.

"What?"

"McMillan's barn."

"Oh, right, McMillan's barn," he said sarcastically. "As if it matters."

"What do you want from me?" She shivered in the cool air of dawn. Her clothes and hair, she realized, were wet and damp, her jeans clinging to her legs like soggy plastic wrap.

"Nothing, not anymore. All that talk about how much you care about family, it was just bullshit. The first chance you got, you tried to hurt me." His voice was indignant. "You *did* hurt me. My eyes still burn. My face is burned. That wasn't nice, Kendra." He got down on one knee and growled into her face. "That . . . was . . . not . . . nice."

She turned her head, and with his hand, he turned it back again.

"Do not look away from me when I am speaking to you."

She looked up and blinked, still trying to focus. There were two of him, she was pretty sure. Both had angry red blotches where the coffee had scalded his skin.

Good. She hoped it hurt like hell.

She blinked again, and there was only one.

She tried to sit up a little more, but the pain shot through her head and she leaned back upon the ground again.

"Have a little headache, do we?" he asked.

"I'm cold," she said, ignoring the question.

"Tough. This little outing was your idea."

"Where's the smoke coming from?" she asked weakly.

"It's your house, stupid." He laughed and for a moment, pleasure lit up his eyes. "You left the burner on under the frying pan. Careless of you."

"Oh, my God . . ." She tried to sit up and he shoved her back with one hand. "We've got to—"

"No, we don't. Besides, it's only what you deserve," he hissed at her. "It's what you get for hurting me. I wasn't going to hurt you, Kendra. I only wanted what was mine."

"What do you mean, what was yours?"

"You owed it to me, all of you did."

"What are you talking about?" Her teeth were beginning to chatter as the cold continued to seep through her wet clothes and spread like thin ribbons throughout her body.

"Half of everything should be mine."

"You mean Dad's estate?" Her cheeks too numb to smile, she tried unsuccessfully to force a laugh. "Well, that might take some doing. Mom had you declared dead after seven years."

"It figures, doesn't it? Bitch." He stood up and started to pace, his hands moving restlessly. "Well, then, I'll just have to have myself declared alive again."

"How will you do that?" She struggled to sit and wrapped her arms around her chest in an effort to warm herself. "You can't just walk into the police station and announce that you're not dead after all."

"I can tell them . . ." His fingers slid through his hair, front to back, in one smooth motion. "I'll tell them that I had amnesia. Yeah. People get amnesia. I read about it."

"You'll still need to prove somehow that you are Ian. You'll have to take some tests."

"No. No, I don't. I don't need any DNA tests. I can prove I'm Ian. I have proof right here." His hands slid into his back pocket and pulled out a wallet. "See. I have the picture."

He held it up and she squinted to see it in the growing light of dawn. It was Ian's seventh-grade photograph.

"You kept that wallet all these years?" she asked, puzzled. "Why?"

"So I could prove I was Ian." He looked at her as if she were stupid. "Why do you think?"

His voice had taken on the tone of a man younger than the one who stood before her.

"That's not going to prove it to the police."

"It's always proved it. I showed it to everyone. Everyone knew I was Ian Smith."

"Who's everyone?" The sun was starting to come up, but she was getting colder by the minute and she began to fear hypothermia. She could no longer feel her fingers or her toes. From somewhere sirens shrieked through the stillness.

"Everyone in San Francisco. Everyone on the street. They all knew I was Ian. The police will know, too, when I show them the picture."

"I'm freezing. You have to take me back to the house. I have to get warm."

"I can't take you there now. Didn't you hear the sirens? I'll bet they're there already, to fight the fire. What? You thought I was kidding about that?" He laughed at her. "Ladybug, Ladybug, fly away home, your house is on fire . . ."

"I'm really cold," she told him, the status of her beloved home suddenly secondary to the immediate matter of her lack of body heat.

"There are blankets there behind you. You can use one of those." He sat cross-legged on the ground in front of where she sat but made no move to assist her. "I brought them when I used to come to watch you through the windows. Sometimes I watched even after the lights went out."

"You came inside, too. You were in my room," she said, remembering the feeling of someone watching her while she slept.

"Just a few times. The house always smelled funny. Like a pipe or something. I hate that smell."

She stopped and turned to look at him. "You don't know what that smell was?"

"Tobacco, I guess. I didn't know that you smoked. I never saw you smoke." He pointed toward the small pile of blankets and said, "Don't take the blue one. That's mine. Give it to me. I'm a little chilly now, too."

"Which one?" She stopped abruptly and turned to stare at him.

"The blue one."

"This one?" She lifted the corner of a green plaid quilt.

"No, the blue one. The other one. What's the matter with you, are you color blind?"

She tossed him the blanket.

"No, I'm not." She gathered the quilt around her and shivered into it, wondering how long it would take for her to warm. "But Ian was."

Adam drove over the crushed stone drive behind Father Tim's Mission of Hope and turned off the engine. He'd been calling every fifteen minutes on his drive from the airport and was more than a little concerned that he'd gotten no answer at Selena's house, but he'd been unable to get past Father Tim's answering machine and the recorded message that cheerfully announced that the Mission closed at nine P.M. but would reopen at eight in the morning. Emergency calls could be made to a different number, which Adam had tried several times without success. He glanced around as he got out of the car, looking for Kendra's old Subaru, but it wasn't in the lot. Maybe she'd come with her friend Selena, he thought, recalling the cars that were parked out on the street.

The back-porch lights were on, Adam noticed as he walked toward the house, and inside several lights were on. He tried the back door, then tried the knob when his knock was unanswered. It opened without hesitation.

"Kendra wasn't kidding about people around here leaving their doors unlocked at night," he muttered, frowning, as he stepped inside.

A shadow passed through the hall.

"Father Tim?" Adam called out to the figure.

"Father Tim isn't here." An elderly man who appeared to be missing several of his front teeth stepped from the darkness. "Who are you?"

"I'm a friend of Kendra Smith's," Adam explained. "I thought she might be here."

"Kendra's friend, eh?" The old man turned on the kitchen light. "If you're her friend, how come you're not over there fighting the fire with Father Tim and everyone else?"

"What fire? Over where?"

"Fire down the road. Father Tim and the others went down about an hour ago, right after we got the call. Thought it could be the Smith place. Hey, we're all volunteer firemen, you know, Father Tim insists on it. Way to do a little for the community, you know, while we live here. Though these days I mostly man the fort. But I drove many a pumper when I was younger, fought many a fire back here in the Pines."

Adam took off through the back door while the old man was still talking.

Given all he'd learned that day, Adam could not get there quickly enough. He hoped he'd remember the way, and he prayed he wouldn't be too late.

"What happened to my brother, Zach?" Kendra asked.

He stared at her thoughtfully. Finally, he said, "That gave me away? The blanket thing?"

She nodded.

"But up until then, I had you convinced, didn't I?"

"I admit I was wavering."

"Then I'm pretty good, huh? Of course, I've been Ian for ten years now." He nodded, a touch of pride in his voice. "I've got it down pat."

"You've *been* Ian?"

"Yup. You ask anyone on the streets in San Francisco. They all know Ian Smith." He laughed and added, "Hell, I've been Ian almost as long as *Ian* was Ian."

"What happened to him, Zach?" Shielded from the cold by the quilt, she rubbed her hands together hoping to regain lost circulation.

"That little shit." The smile curled into a snarl. "And he was a little shit, Kendra, make no mistake about it. Your precious little brother was a first-class prick." He leaned forward, close to her, and she drew back instinctively.

"Look, Ian could be an annoying little kid sometimes, and yes, he could be a pain in the ass, but—"

He grabbed her arm. "I hated him. Hated every one of you. Self-righteous, sanctimonious, better-than-everybody-else bastards."

Kendra stared, wide-eyed and dumb. She hadn't known that a body could contain that much hatred without exploding. It whipped around her like a blinding wind and pounded at her with its fury.

"All of you, patronizing me. Oh, our poor little cousin Zachary. Let's bring him out for a few weeks in the summer so he can see how the real Smiths live. Stupid little Zach." He looked at her with eyes now filled with the remembered pain of the child he'd been. "I wasn't stupid. I just never got to go to school."

"Zach, it was never like that. Nobody thought you were stupid." She sought to quell the storm she saw building within him, knowing if it was released, there would be no chance to survive its fury.

"Do you know that the great state of Arizona didn't even know I existed until they thought I'd *died*? They never knew I was there until my mother called them in when I didn't come home for days." He snorted. "And even then, she told them I'd been home-schooled. *Home-schooled*," he repeated for emphasis. "Want to know what I learned in my home school?"

His voice quivered with hot anger.

"I learned how to cultivate weed and how to sober up a drunk. I learned how to avoid the advances of my mother's girlfriends—and sometimes her boyfriends, too. I learned that if I didn't get away, I was going to die there long before I ever got to live."

He tossed his cigarette on the ground and crushed it under his heel.

"I could have been just like you. Just as good as you. *She* had inherited just as much money as your father had. I used to see the checks. But it all went to drugs and liquor and supporting that flophouse she called a ranch. Everything she had went into the ranch, into having fun with her friends."

Tears formed in the corners of his eyes and began to slide down his cheeks.

"And then I'd come East every year for two weeks,

and see what it was like to be a Smith. A big, beautiful house that was always clean, always smelled good. I remember everything about that house. Everything." He closed his eyes for just a second. "There was always good food. We went places. Places I'd never even heard of. Museums. Amusement parks. We watched television. We did things. For those two weeks I was just like you. Only not as good. Never as good."

Zach felt in his chest pocket for his cigarettes. The bitter, brittle words came ever more quickly, and his hands were beginning to tremble. How long before the rage boiled over?

"I had to watch you to see how to act, listen to how you spoke, so that I'd know how to speak right. But Ian knew. And Ian never missed an opportunity to remind me. Made fun of me because I didn't talk as good as he did. Because I didn't know about all the things he knew."

"For God's sake, Zach, why didn't you say something?"

"Say what? Hey, Aunt Elisa, did you know my mom's a junkie who's putting all that Smith money up her nose?"

"Yes." She looked him directly in the eye. "Yes, that's exactly what you should have said. Ian should have told us if you couldn't. I don't understand why he always painted such an idyllic picture of the ranch."

"Don't you get it? Don't you understand? Ian loved that little walk on the wild side he got to take for two weeks every year. And he loved that he was younger than me, but that he knew so much more. That he was so much smarter." He looked up at Kendra smugly. "I guess, in the end, he wasn't so smart after all, was he?"

"What did you do to him?"

"You really want to know?" He smirked.

"The body they found in the cave . . . that's Ian, isn't it?"

"Of course it's Ian."

"What happened?" she asked again. After all these years, Kendra needed to know. She would have begged him for the truth if she'd had to, but it seemed that Zach was now as eager to tell as she was to listen.

"Ian was so hot to trot to find this old Indian guy. He wanted that Cochise bow, let me tell you. He wanted it in a big way."

"Was there really a bow?"

"What do you think?" He looked at her as if she had sported an extra head.

"Then why did you tell him?"

"Because I needed him to have money with him. And I knew he wouldn't be able to resist something like that. It was the only way I was going to get out of there, don't you see? I couldn't stay there any longer. That TV program I told you about, I saw it the first night I was at your house that summer. All those kids, living together on the streets. It looked better to me than what I had. And I got the idea to go there. I figured I had nothing to lose. But I needed a little something to take with me."

"So you got Ian to bring money out so you could kill him and steal it."

"No, no, you gotta understand this. I never planned on killing him. I was just going to take his wallet, that's all. I figured I could make him believe that he'd dropped it someplace on the trail, that it fell out of his backpack or something. The other stuff . . . it just sort of, you know, happened. I mean, like it was fate."

"What exactly happened?"

"It was cold. I said I'd make a fire, but he didn't want to sleep outside again. He went up the hill. I saw him going into the cave. For a minute, I almost called to him to not go in there." Zach swallowed, remembering. "But as soon as he got past the mouth of the cave, he started to scream. Man, did he scream. I never heard anything like it." A look of triumph crossed his face, as if he was reliving that moment, savoring Ian's agony. "It seemed like he screamed forever. I thought he was never going to stop."

"And you did nothing to help him?" A horrified Kendra shivered.

"Hey, what could I do?" Zach shrugged cavalierly. "The minute he went in there, he was as good as dead. If I went in, I'd have been stung to death, too. What good would that have done?"

"So you just stood there and listened to him scream."

"Couldn't avoid it, Kendra. He was *loud.*"

"And you left him to die."

"Couldn't avoid that either."

"So that you could take his money." Kendra swallowed hard.

"Yeah, well, his wallet was in his backpack there on the ground, so I figured, what the hell? I wasn't looking that gift horse in the mouth. I took the backpack with his stuff in it, threw my old pack into the cave with him, and just walked away."

"What about Christopher? Was he there?"

"Christopher? Oh, you mean the kid from the ranch? Yeah, he was there," Zach said. "He followed us. We let him camp with us, but sometimes he had trouble keeping up. I told him to go back to the ranch, but he didn't. He'd followed Ian up the hill, he was maybe twenty or thirty feet behind Ian when he went into the cave. He just stood there with his hands over his ears, whimpering and crying, all the time Ian was screaming. He was still crying the next morning." He paused for a moment, reflected briefly, "I wonder if he ever stopped crying."

"No," Kendra said softly. "He never did."

"How do you know?"

"I saw him when I was in Arizona recently."

"You were in Arizona? Did you stop at the ranch?" She nodded.

"See, that's another thing. That ranch should have been mine, but she left it to her friends. I always knew she cared more for them than she did for me. She cared for everybody more than she cared for me. She was one damned poor excuse for a mother, Kendra. I deserved better. I deserved more." His jaw settled hard again. "It should have been mine. She should have left it to me. I wasn't even in her will."

"She thought you were dead, Zach," Kendra pointed out.

"Even after she found out I was alive, she wouldn't change it." He jammed his hands in his pockets. "Bitch. Why couldn't she have done that much for me? She never did a damned thing for me my whole life. And you know what the first thing she said to me was, when she saw me? She said, 'Where's Ian?' " He sniffed and wiped at his nose with his shirtsleeve. "Five years I'm gone, and the first thing she says is 'Where's Ian.' "

"What did you tell her?"

"Oh, I showed her. Showed her where the cave was. She wanted to know how I pulled it all off."

"What did you tell her?"

"Same thing I've been telling you."

"You didn't finish the story."

"There isn't anything left to tell."

"Where did you go after Ian? How did you get there?"

"I walked most of the night. I figured I could hitch a ride and get to California once I got out to the road. The kid followed me, but I had to leave him when I got a ride with some college kids who were on their way to Sacramento. He was still crying but I told him someone would come along and pick him up and take him home. These kids, they took turns driving straight through the next couple of days, and after they dropped me off, I got a ride with a trucker to San Francisco. I lied and told him my dad lived there. And once I got there, I found a lot of kids, just like me, and that's where I stayed, mostly. And then I was Ian. No more Zach."

"There's a man serving two consecutive life sentences in prison in Arizona who was convicted of killing you and Ian," she told him.

"Yeah, I read about that." Zach laughed dryly. "Dumb shit pedophile. I know all about what those guys do. You have no idea what they . . ." He shuddered, as if something terrible had touched his soul. "He belongs in a cell. They all belong in jail. I hope he rots there."

"He may belong in prison, but not for the crime he was convicted of."

"So what? What difference does it make, what crime he's in for? He hurt little boys, you have any idea what that means? You think he deserves to be out walking the streets?" Zach took on a decidedly righteous expression.

"It matters, if he's being held for a crime he didn't commit. It's wrong, Zach."

"I don't care. They're all creeps and they all deserve to die."

"Why didn't your mother call us after she found out that you were still alive?"

"Because by that time she, too, had gone to that big Smith reunion."

"What do you mean?"

"I mean that right after she and I had our little chat," he glared at her, his eyes blazing, "she took a little tumble off the side of the hill."

"You pushed her." Kendra shook her head. She'd begun to think there was nothing Zach could say that could shock her after learning how he'd gleefully listened to her brother's agonizing death. How many more terrible secrets could this man possibly harbor?

"Let's just say accidents happen and leave it at that."

"Why? Why would you do such a thing to your own mother?"

"Sierra, as you now know, was hardly June Cleaver," he said coolly. "Not exactly Mother of the Year material."

"But all those other women you killed, *they* were." Kendra's stomach lurched every time she thought of the beautiful young women, the loving young women, who had been so devoted to their children, so brutally taken from them.

"Yeah, and you think those kids appreciated them? Those kids had everything. They got to do everything, go to school and everything. They got to play baseball. Soccer. Had friends to play with. Bikes to ride. They had nice houses to live in." His voice rising, he turned to her with the eyes of an angry, spiteful child. "I watched them. They did not appreciate what they had, Kendra. And you know what happens when you don't appreciate what you've got, don't you? It's taken away from you, that's what, because you don't deserve to keep it. They didn't deserve." His words began to free-fall from his mouth in a jumble. "They did everything for their kids, you know that? Everything."

Fat tears began to roll down his face.

"Why couldn't one of them have been mine?" The howl of pain was sharp and clear. "Why couldn't she have been like that? Why was everything always so wrong for me, and everything always right for everyone else? It just wasn't fair."

The tears stopped as another wave of anger washed over him.

"I went to her. I thought maybe she'd be glad to see me again. But she hardly seemed to even care that I was alive. Like it didn't matter. So I figured, okay, it doesn't matter to me either. Just give me what's mine and I'll go away again. But then she told me about her will, how everything was already set up and she wasn't going to change it, not even about the Smith trust being set up to support the ranch and her friends. She offered me a couple thousand dollars to go away again. A couple of thousand dollars!" The words fell from his mouth in a tumble. "It wasn't fair, Kendra. All that money, the ranch . . . she wouldn't put me— *me,* her only child!—back in her will. She met me in the hills the next morning and gave me the cash—five thousand dollars, can you believe that? Well, it just wasn't right. She had to be punished for being so mean to me. So she took a tumble and I took her money and I left, figured I'd go back to San Francisco. What the hell, I'd lived all those years on the streets, I'd probably die on the streets."

His focus wandered for a second or two. "I hitched back to California, got stranded overnight and got a room in a motel on Route Ten. Got some dinner, got a shower. Laid down on the bed to watch TV. Well, who do you think I saw on the TV that night? Can you guess?"

He jammed his hands into his pockets and rocked back on his heels, enjoying the telling, building up to the moment.

"My beloved Aunt Elisa! Right there on 'Larry King Live'! All those years I'd been away, she'd gone and gotten herself elected to the goddamned United States Senate! I thought, well, shit, Sierra cut me out as Zach, let's see what I can get from Aunt Elisa as Ian. I mean, we had so many of the same features, who's to say we wouldn't have looked alike when we grew up?"

"You went to see my mother?" Kendra whispered, incredulous. Finally, something to truly shock, when she'd begun to believe that he had no secrets left to tell.

But her mother had never mentioned that she'd been contacted by Zach. Surely she'd have told Kendra if he had.

"Why not? Oh, you should have seen her face when I walked into the house. Let myself right in the back door. She was in the library, reading, and I stood in the doorway and said, 'Hello, Mom.' "

Beneath the blanket, Kendra's fists began to clench, her body quivering now from something other than the cold.

"I almost had her convinced, too."

"You told her you were Ian? You let that woman think that, after all those years." It was almost too terrible to speak the words. No one knew better than Kendra how her mother had suffered the loss of her son.

"Sure. I thought I could cash in with the happy reunion thing. But she wasn't having any of it." The sneer returned to his face. "After the shock of seeing me wore off, she knew I wasn't Ian."

"A mother would know her own child," Kendra's voice was still a whisper.

"Now, see, that's just what she said. *Exactly* what she said," he told her, the sneer turning into something uglier. He stubbed out his cigarette in the dirt. "Right before I put the gun to her head and pulled the trigger."

"You . . ." the words stuck in her throat. "You . . ."

"Well, damn, Kendra, I'd had about enough, you know? My mother turns me down, my aunt turns me down . . ."

She flew at him so fast, with such fury, that he barely saw her coming, had no time to even brace himself before she slammed into him and knocked him backwards. He fell over a fallen branch and slammed headfirst into the dirt. Her mind now as numb as her body had been, Kendra raced to the canoe and grabbed the paddle, but this time she chose not to flee. She came back at him, the paddle raised over her head, held in both hands, and she smashed it across his face even as he tried to stand.

"Bastard!" she roared, and slammed his face again. Blood ran from his broken nose and his mouth.

"You bastard!" she screamed, and hit him across the shoulders when again he sought to rise.

Every emotion that had been tucked away inside her since her mother's death exploded. The torment she'd suffered, the double pain of loss and the terrible business of dealing with the aftermath of a loved one's suicide, the overwhelming sense of guilt, of not having done enough, not having been enough, to have kept her mother tethered to this world—all surfaced in one massive, unstoppable swell. Wild-eyed, she fought him furiously until the paddle cracked, then broke, and even then she fought him with her hands and her fists, until he fell back, his head cracking against the side of the burned-out barn.

Her breathing labored, her lungs in agony, her face wet with tears, she stumbled, exhausted, to the canoe and untied the rope from the bow with rapidly swelling fingers, several of which were broken though she was not yet aware of the pain. Adrenaline had carried her beyond her physical limits, but was beginning to abate. Still, she could not, would not, permit him to get away. Staggering back to where he lay, she rolled him over and tied his hands behind his back in a tight knot. She tried dragging him to the canoe, but he was too tall and too heavy for her to budge him.

"Hell with it," she mumbled, and walked on unsteady feet to the canoe. Zach could awake in the dirt, as she had earlier, and wait for the police to come for him.

With the broken paddle and bloodied hands, she headed for home, weeping as she thought of her mother's last moments, stunned by the unexpected confirmation that she'd been right all along, that Elisa had not taken her own life, had not chosen to leave her. Now she had proof. Kendra clung to this unexpected treasure, this newly found truth, and it warmed her and gave her the strength to keep on moving toward her home.

What, she wondered as she found her way through the ever-thickening smoke, would she find when she got there?

CHAPTER
TWENTY-THREE

The flames licked at the roof of Smith House, plumes of water chasing them higher as hoses trained on those not-yet-ignited parts of the house sought to contain the blaze. Drawing water from the stream, the firefighters did their best to douse the fire and to save as much of the historic house as possible.

Adam had arrived as the first pumper had set up and the hoses were being brought to the water's edge. The sight of flames shooting from the roof of the beautiful old house saddened him, but that it was Kendra's house, the house that symbolized all she had left of her family, sickened him.

But where was Kendra? His eyes scanned the landscape again, but she was nowhere to be seen.

He'd started across the yard when he was struck by the unthinkable. Was Kendra in the house?

He threw his jacket on the ground and rolled up his sleeves as he crossed the yard, yelling to the crew frantically attempting to put out the fire that had spread to the back porch, limiting their access to the source of the blaze.

"Is she here?" Adam demanded of the first man he reached.

"Haven't seen her" was the reply.

"Are you a friend of Kendra's?" A man wearing a black shirt and a worried expression grabbed Adam's arm.

"Yes. Have you seen her?" Adam tried to push the man aside.

"I'm Father Tim." The priest sought to calm him. "I'm a friend, as well."

"What are the chances she's inside?" Adam fought to control his emotions.

"We don't know." The priest shook his head and continued with his tasks. If Kendra was inside the burning house, the best thing they could do for her— the only thing they could do for her—was to extinguish the fire and get her out. "Pray that she isn't."

A frantic Adam drew as close to the house as he could, seeking a possible safe entry, but as yet there was none. He grabbed a portion of hose and held on as the water pressure built before hitting the house with a blast. When enough of the flames had been subdued, he started up the back steps with the clear intent of kicking in the door, at which time several of the firefighters directed his energies to helping hold the hose. Without the proper gear and lacking training, Adam could be more of a hazard than a help.

"If she's in there, they'll find her." Father Tim grabbed Adam by the arm. "They know what they're doing. You don't. You're getting in the way. Let them do their job."

Only the thought that his well-intentioned efforts

could impede Kendra's rescue kept Adam from entering the house. He stood near the rear of the property, watching the men struggle to take control of the conflagration, his mind nearly paralyzed with the fear that she could be trapped in the inferno. After all, her car was in the drive, and there'd been no sign of her or Selena.

Had Selena's car been parked at her house? Adam realized he hadn't even noticed as he'd flown up the road, following the smoke and flames.

"Anyone check Selena's?" he asked Father Tim. "Maybe Kendra's there with her."

The priest shook his head. "Selena's still at her brother's up around Trenton. As a matter of fact, it was she who first alerted us to the fire."

"How could she have known about the fire if she's out of town?" Adam frowned.

"She saw it in a vision," Father Tim told him without giving any sign that he found that even the least bit questionable.

"A vision? You brought the fire trucks down here because someone had a vision?"

"No, but I did drive out here to check after she called. As soon as I made the turn off the main road I could see the smoke. *Then* I called in the fire. Good thing I did, wouldn't you say?" Father Tim pointed to the house, where the flames were just starting to subside.

Adam was still pondering the probability of anyone rousing himself in the middle of the night because someone had had a vision, when movement from the corner of his eye drew his attention to the stream that ran behind the house. He turned just as the canoe stopped at the water's edge.

"Holy Mother," he whispered.

The woman was covered with blood and moved on shaking legs that appeared barely capable of taking the next step. In three strides, Adam had covered the distance and gathered her into his arms. She collapsed against him, sobbing and muttering something indistinguishable.

"Kendra . . ." His arms tightened around her. "Dear God, what happened to you?"

"McMillan's barn," she sobbed. "The barn . . . Zachary. He killed Ian. . . . He left Ian to die in the cave. . . ."

"I know. The report came back from the medical examiner. They'd checked the dental records on the body they found. It's definitely Ian." Adam stroked her back as if to comfort her.

"Zach tried to be Ian," she said, clinging to his neck like a child, "wanted to be Ian."

"Is he armed, Kendra?" Chief Logan asked.

"Don't think so."

Logan sent three officers into the stream toward McMillan's.

"She didn't do it, Adam," Kendra sobbed. "She didn't do it."

"Didn't do what, sweetheart?" He smoothed her hair, thanking God that she was here, that she was all right. That she was alive. "Who didn't do what?"

"My mother . . . my mother . . ." she said, her last words before passing out.

The ambulance took way too long to arrive, in

Adam's opinion, and he paced restlessly, Kendra still in his arms, until the first emergency vehicle arrived. He reluctantly relinquished her to the gurney, then climbed in the back with the EMTs and rode with them to the nearest hospital emergency room, which was twelve miles away. Once there, his FBI badge notwithstanding, he was relegated to the waiting room, where he paced some more.

He'd filled out her admission forms, printing his own name on the "next of kin" line. It wasn't a lie, he thought. Who else did she have? From where he sat, she had him, and she had Selena, and that was about it.

Bless Selena. If she hadn't called Father Tim when she did, they might not be worrying about who Kendra Smith's nearest and dearest were.

Later, at the hospital, Selena would tell Adam, the vision had blasted through the shield she generally invoked whenever she had the feeling that something was trying to get through. She could see Kendra's house, clear as day, flames spilling from the kitchen windows. Through the smoke, she could see Kendra, in water, struggling. Selena had awakened from sleep shaking, cold, coughing, and sputtering, as if she'd been drowning. She'd not stopped to think before picking up the phone and calling Kendra's house. When the operator came on the line and told her there were problems with the line, Selena knew. She called Father Tim, who went to check Kendra's house and rallied the volunteer firefighters as well as Chief Logan, and within minutes, a line of cars and trucks were screaming through the night in the direction of Smith

House. Chief Logan and two patrol cars had pulled into the drive just minutes before Kendra had stumbled onto the bank and all but collapsed into Adam's arms.

Kendra had been barely recognizable, her hair hanging down her back in one long wet tangle, her face and shirt covered with blood. Her jeans had been wet and torn and she'd been weaving with fatigue. It had taken Adam's brain only a split second to realize that the woman teetering toward them was Kendra. How she had come to such a state had yet to be determined. Had Zach attacked her and set her house on fire? Adam had seen the bruises on her neck and on her arms, seen the broken blood vessels in her eyes, and his fists clenched at the thought of Zach's hands around her throat.

"Mr. Stark?" The young doctor stood in the doorway of the waiting room.

Adam jumped to his feet.

"I'm Dr. Brady," she smiled. "You're listed as next of kin for our patient."

"Kendra Smith, yes," he nodded. "How's she doing? Is she going to be okay?"

"She's going to be fine. But I'm afraid she won't be able to come home for at least another day."

"What exactly—"

"Well, she's suffering from hypothermia, exposure, and broken bones in both hands."

"Her face?" he asked, recalling all of the blood.

"A few cuts and bruises," the doctor told him.

"But all the blood." Adam frowned.

"Apparently it wasn't hers."

"Really." He pondered this.

The doctor shrugged. "I have no idea whose blood

it is, but it isn't Ms. Smith's. Oh"—she tapped the clipboard that she held—"she does have bruises around her neck."

"And broken blood vessels in her eyes." Adam muttered curses under his breath. "Evidence of strangulation."

"Yes. We will be calling in the local police," she told him.

"They already know." Adam took out his badge and showed it to her. "Chief Logan should be along real soon."

"I'm confused." The doctor frowned. "Are you here because she's the victim of a crime, or because—"

The double outside doors slid open automatically and a gurney, accompanied by three EMTs, emerged.

"Got another one. Shit, you'd think this was a weekend night in the summer," someone complained from the other side of the emergency room.

Chief Logan appeared in the doorway, and signaled to Adam.

"When can I see her?" Adam asked.

"You can come back with me now," the doctor told him, "she'll be down here until her room is ready and the paperwork is done. She'll be going to X-ray soon."

"Great, thank you." Adam turned then toward the gurney and the new patient who was being wheeled in.

"Says his name is Ian Smith," the chief told him. "What do you think of that? Kendra's brother, after all these years."

"It's Zachary Smith," Adam said. "Kendra's cousin, after all these years. Ian Smith is dead."

The man on the gurney breathed heavily through a broken nose, and his face was encrusted with dried blood. He looked up at Adam through puffy eyes.

"She do this to you, Zach?" Adam said, pleased at the extent to which she'd fought. He leaned down and said, so that only Zach could hear, "I'll bet you never figured her for a fighter, did you? She do all that when you were trying to strangle her?"

"You're the FBI agent who's doin' her, aren't you?" Zach's swollen mouth smirked, and Adam fought an urge to break the man's nose from the other side.

Instead, Adam stood up and back, allowing the orderlies to take the gurney into the emergency room.

"We'll be here when they're done with you, Zach," Adam told him as they wheeled him away. "The chief and I will be waiting."

"What do you think you have to hold me on?"

"We can start with the attempted murder of your cousin," Adam said calmly.

"She told you I tried to kill her?" Zach yelled.

"No, but I'm betting she will."

"And it's Ian. She's my sister." He tried to sit up. "And I want to press charges against her. For assault."

"Save it," Adam muttered in disgust.

"He's been insisting since minute one that he's Ian," one of the police officers noted.

"His name is Zachary Smith. He's the son of Sierra Smith, who was the sister of Kendra's father. We know he tried to kill her." Adam watched the gurney disappear behind the curtains of one of the examining rooms. "We're also going to want to question him about seven recent murders in Pennsylvania. And God knows what else he's done."

"We'll keep an eye on him," the chief nodded.

"Mr. Stark, if you're ready." Dr. Brady dropped some paperwork off at the receptionist's desk. "I'll take you back to Ms. Smith now."

"How is she?" Chief Logan asked.

"I guess I'm about to find out," Adam told him as he followed the doctor to the door of the fourth examining room on the right.

Adam stood in the doorway and looked at the figure that lay upon the bed. Most of the blood had been washed from her face and her bloody clothes had been exchanged for a worn blue-and-white hospital gown. She rested back against the pillows, an IV drip in her right arm, her eyes half-closed.

"I heard him," she said without opening her eyes. "He's here. Zach . . ."

"Yes, he's here." Adam pulled a chair over to the side of the bed. She looked so small and so pale, so . . . wounded. The sight of her wrenched his insides.

"He did it all," she murmured. "You were right. Miranda was right. He killed those women."

"Did he tell you that?"

She nodded.

"He wanted to see if I could sketch him. If I'd know him." She swallowed hard, her throat tight and raw. "It was all just a game. Just to see if I'd know him. All those lives ruined, all those beautiful young women dead . . . how sick do you have to be to do such things?"

"Or how evil." Adam wanted to take her hands in

his own, to give her some small comfort, but both were heavily bandaged. He rested a hand gently on her forearm, to touch, to reassure. To make some contact, however slight.

"And Ian . . . he let him die. Call Sheriff Gamble. Webster. . . . they'll have to let him go. . . ."

Her voice was so faint now that he could barely make them out. "Sierra. Not an accident."

She partially opened her eyes, and he was surprised to find the faintest trace of light, a smile.

"Adam, she didn't do it," Kendra murmured. "She didn't do it. I knew she didn't do it . . . told you she wouldn't."

"Who?" Adam leaned forward, wondering if they'd given her medication for pain, and if it had confused her. "Who are you talking about?"

"My mother," she said, only the very corners of her mouth curving into the barest hint of a smile. "Didn't kill herself."

"She didn't?"

"No," she sighed as she drifted off to sleep. "Zach did."

CHAPTER
TWENTY-FOUR

While Kendra slept, Adam made phone calls. The first was to her stepfather, Philip Norton. The second was to John Mancini.

Philip Norton had been the first to arrive. Adam sat with him in the lounge and drank several cups of terrible coffee from the vending machine while he related to the widower of Senator Elisa Smith-Norton what Kendra had told him about her mother's death.

"Yes." The tall man with the New England accent had nodded his graying head, and wept openly. "Yes. It would have had to have been like that. My wife would not have left her daughter in such a way . . . wouldn't have left me. Kendra and I have never believed for one second that Elisa had taken her own life, regardless of the evidence, of the official reports."

"I've already spoken with the Bureau and requested a copy of the files on the senator's case. I want to see what they had, how they could have missed that someone else had pulled the trigger."

"I've seen the file." Norton raised his head and looked Adam in the eye. "There's nothing there to suggest that anyone else was in the house. He must have been very clever."

"How were you able to—?" Adam started to inquire, then remembered that the man who sat before him was Philip D. Norton, Ph.D., a former White House press secretary with connections that reached all the way to the Bureau's director, a man to whom many favors might be owed. No doubt, where his wife's death had been concerned, he'd called in every one. "Never mind."

"Did he, Zachary Smith, tell Kendra exactly how he'd managed to . . ." Even now, almost four years later, Norton could not say the words.

"I don't know how much detail he gave her. But since he's in custody, I expect that sooner or later we'll get the whole story."

"In custody, eh?" Dr. Philip Norton's eyebrows raised with interest. "Your custody, Agent Stark?"

"Right now he's in the custody of the New Jersey State Police. That's subject to change, once the jurisdictional issues are ironed out," Adam told him. "New Jersey isn't the only state that will want a piece of Mr. Smith. I suspect that Washington, California, and Arizona will want to chat with him, after Pennsylvania and New Jersey, of course. And God knows who else. There are federal issues to be dealt with, as well. The killing of a United States senator . . ."

"Do we know what happened to Ian Smith?" Norton cut him off.

Adam brought him up to date on what had been found in a cave in the southern Arizona hills.

"What a terrible, terrible way to die." Dr. Norton

shook his head sadly. "And this fellow was, what, not even in his teens when he permitted his own cousin to go to a certain death? A pitiful start to what's obviously been a pitiful life."

"Kendra alluded that the 'accidental' death of Zach's mother may not have been an accident, after all."

"Good Lord," Norton muttered. "His own mother. His cousin. His aunt."

"And we've yet to tally up how many women he killed while trying to attract Kendra's attention. Seven out here, and several . . . I'm not sure if anyone knows for certain how many out on the West Coast."

"Trying to get Kendra's attention? He told you that?" Norton appeared horrified.

"He told her that; I've yet to speak with him about it." Adam nodded. "But apparently it was all part of some game he was playing with her."

"To what end?"

"Does it matter? Regardless of whatever twisted explanation he gives, whatever excuse he offers, could what he did ever make sense, ever be justified?"

"Of course not." Dr. Norton appeared surprised at the question. "Evil, like beauty, is its own excuse for being."

The hospital corridors were quiet when John Mancini, head of the FBI's special task force on abductions, stepped off the elevator on the fourth floor. One hand held a huge file tucked under his arm, the other hand held a worn brown leather briefcase that was bursting at the seams. He located the room he sought, nodded a silent greeting to the agent who sat outside, and stood in the doorway, his handsome face creased with concern as he stared at the young woman who lay on the bed with IVs in both arms and casts on her hands.

In the course of his career, he'd seen more than his share of violence. Its victims never failed to affect him.

The woman in the bed turned to the door and raised one casted hand.

"John," she called to him in a low, raspy voice, "you looking for Adam?"

"No." He forced a smile as he stepped into the room. "I was looking for you."

"I got your flowers," she said, pointing in the direction of a large spray of pink roses and blue hydrangeas that sat on the window ledge. "Thank you. That was so sweet."

"Yeah, well, don't let *that* get out." He smiled again, genuinely this time. "And thank Genna when you see her. The flowers are her thing."

"Well, then, I hope I do see her again so I can thank her in person," Kendra said, fondly recalling her acquaintance with Genna Snow, an agent with whom she'd worked her first case, who just happened to be John Mancini's fiancée. "Maybe I'll get lucky and get my name on that guest list for the wedding."

"I've seen that guest list, and I believe your name is on it."

"Hopefully by the time your wedding rolls around, I'll have use of my hands again."

"What are the doctors saying?"

"Four weeks in the splints, then therapy," she told

him. "Not so bad, when you consider that he could have killed me. He almost did kill me," she said, recalling those moments right before she'd lost consciousness, when, her head held underwater, she'd fought for breath. "I'm not sure why he didn't, unless he wasn't finished bragging about all he'd done."

"I'm going to want to talk to you about that, as soon as you're ready."

"I'm ready," she rasped.

"I don't think so." He patted her foot. "We'll give you at least until tomorrow."

"You'll be speaking with Zach, though, won't you." It wasn't a question.

John nodded.

"Then you should speak with me first," she told him. "I can give you information so your people will know what to ask him about. He's not going to volunteer anything, so you need to know what to ask. There are so many families who need to know."

"Kendra, your voice is almost gone."

"I don't care," she insisted. "If my voice goes, I'll whisper. There are things you need to know about this man."

Adam returned to Kendra's room shortly after Mancini began to record her recollection of the events of the past twenty-four hours. He offered to assist in the interview, but John was already into it, and he waved off Adam's offer.

"But if you wouldn't mind," Kendra's voice was noticeably weaker than it had been earlier that morning, "could you check on my house for me? Chief Logan says the damage is all to one side, but I'd feel better if you went out and actually looked things over for me."

"If you know who your insurance agent is, I can call him for you. I think you're going to need to report this as soon as possible."

"Jess Webb is my agent. He's also one of the volunteer firemen, so I'm guessing the report has already gone in."

"I'll just run out, and take a look then," Adam said, though he made no sign of moving. He seemed almost reluctant to leave her, even in the company of his own boss.

"Were you planning on doing that today, Stark?" John asked without turning around.

"Ah, yes sir, I was." Adam still stood at the foot of Kendra's bed. "You're okay? You don't want to wait until tomorrow to talk about what happened?"

She shook her head no. "I want to do it now."

"She's in good hands, Stark." This time John did turn to face him. "I'll take good care of her, I promise. And she'll still be here when you get back."

"Sure." Adam nodded, backing toward the door. "Sure. I knew that."

Not happy at having been dismissed, but understanding that John might want someone other than Adam, whose interest in Kendra was clearly more than professional, to conduct the initial interview, Adam drove back to Smith's Forge.

He could smell the remains of the house long before it came into view. From the moment he'd turned onto Kendra's road, the odor of charred wet wood hung in the still midday air. He drove slowly down the dirt road, almost fearing his arrival at Smith House. The house was all Kendra had left of her family, her connection to them and to her past. Her sanctuary. If the house had been destroyed, what might that do to her?

Three cars were already parked in the drive. One was Kendra's, the other Selena's. The third was an unknown.

"Hey," Selena called to him as he got out of his car.

Adam waved as he walked toward her, wondering where the driver of the third car might be.

"How's Kendra?" Selena asked, her eyes dark with concern.

"She's going to be fine," Adam nodded.

"I thought I'd stop back again this afternoon, after I finished up here with Jess."

"Jess?"

"Jess Webb. He's making a report for the insurance company. His dad, Oliver, was an old friend of the Smiths. He left a message on my answering machine, telling me what happened, and when Jess would be here. He thought someone should be here for Kendra, since she clearly wasn't going to make it." Selena's eyes filled with tears. "It's just all so terrible, so terrible."

Adam put an arm around her shoulder and let her cry.

"As terrible as it's been—and yes, Kendra had a really bad time and I suspect she'll tell you all about that—there's been good come of it."

"What good could come from this?" Selena scoffed, gesturing toward the old house, with its roof caved in over the kitchen and God knew what damage inside.

"As despicable as Zach Smith is—and I suspect we

have a long way to go before we discover just how despicable he is—he gave Kendra something that no one else could have given her.".

"What are you talking about?"

"Zach told Kendra that he killed her mother."

Selena's jaw dropped.

"He . . . killed . . ."

"Yes."

"That means, she didn't commit . . ."

Adam nodded.

"Kendra was always so certain, and I'd always felt she was right." Weak in the knees, Selena leaned back against her car. "Oh, God, this must have lifted such a weight from her soul. . . ."

"Exactly."

"Oh, my." Selena shook her head, pondering this news, and what it might mean for her friend, as the insurance agent came around one side of the house, a clipboard in his hand.

Selena waved to him, then introduced him to Adam.

"Is it safe to go inside?" Adam asked.

"Yeah, the floors are soaked, but they'll hold you. I wouldn't recommend going in before the adjuster gets here, though."

"How bad is the damage?"

"It's mostly contained to the kitchen area," he shook his head, "though how the rest of the house remained untouched, I'll never understand. That was some nasty fire."

"Well, if the kitchen's the worst of it, I guess it's not so bad," Selena said. "Kendra's been saying for months that she wanted a new kitchen. Guess now she'll be getting one."

"What about the contents? The furniture, books, carpets, that sort of thing?" Adam asked.

"Water and smoke to the upholstered pieces in the front room, seems to be the worst. Then there's smoke damage upstairs, some water there, too. But as I said, the kitchen took the worst of it," the agent explained. "I called this in first thing this morning to the company and asked for an adjuster to be sent out right away. I expect someone along any time now, I just came out a little early to see for myself what we needed to concentrate on."

He turned to Selena. "You let Kendra know that it's being taken care of."

"I'll do that." She smiled at him, and the young man blushed. "And maybe I'll call Karen Hill over at Antiquities to see what needs to be done to restore any of the antique pieces that may be damaged. I know just about everything Kendra owned was passed down through her family."

"I already called Karen to give her a heads up," Webb told her. "She'll be here at two to meet with the adjuster."

"Well, then, I'd say you thought of pretty much everything," Adam said. "Kendra's lucky to have someone looking out for her interests right now."

Jess Webb blushed again and muttered something about the responsibilities of a good agent.

Minutes later, the adjuster arrived, and Selena and Adam prepared to leave.

"I feel so responsible for all this." Selena stood next

to her car, the driver's door open, one foot already inside the vehicle. "If I had paid more attention, if I hadn't been so willing to slough it all off."

"Selena, that's ridiculous. No one could have known."

"I did." She looked up at him, eyes blazing now. "For weeks I've been sensing that something was not right. For days I've seen the clouds gathering around her, and I didn't stop it."

"You couldn't have stopped it."

"I could have warned her." Selena's eyes filled with tears again. "I saw the clouds, and I saw the flames and I saw her in the water."

"While it was happening?"

Selena nodded.

"Then how could you have stopped it?"

"If I hadn't tried so hard to block it out, if I'd let myself be more receptive instead of ignoring what I felt." She sighed deeply. "When I was a little girl, I used to get these . . . feelings, I guess, is the best way to describe it. I could sense what people would say, or what they would do. I could see things in dreams, and then they'd happen. I'd tell my mother, and she'd flip out. 'Don't talk crazy,' she'd say, 'Don't ever, ever tell anyone. People will think you're crazy like your grandmother Brennan.' So I didn't tell people. Just a few. Kendra knew."

"Did Kendra think it was crazy?"

"No. She always believed. She thought it would be fun, you know, to know what people thought, what they were going to say before they'd say it." She shook her head. "It wasn't always fun. Sometimes the visions, the dreams, scared me. Sometimes it was terrible to hear the thoughts other people had in their heads."

She pressed her hands to the sides of her head.

"Sometimes it just hurt too much to hear. To see." She closed her eyes. "So I just refused to let it in, as much as I could refuse. As much as I could block it from my consciousness, I did. But sometimes something got past me. This man—Peter, he called himself at the shelter—got past me. I knew there was someone at Father Tim's who was bringing all the darkness, but I'd blocked out the ability to see and to hear for so long, I couldn't trust what I saw."

Selena looked back at the house. "Until I saw the flames around the house, saw Kendra's face in the water . . . then I trusted."

"And by calling Father Tim, you saved her home from being totally destroyed."

"None of it should have happened at all."

"Maybe there are some things that no one could have prevented." Adam shook his head. "You've nothing to regret, Selena. Nothing to feel guilty about."

She stared at him for a long moment, then got into her car, and turned around in the dirt driveway, her tires sending up a cloud of dust as she headed for the road.

Adam watched her drive off, then turned back to the house for one last look. Kendra would want to know everything, he knew.

He walked around the house, taking note of the broken windows here, the unbroken ones there, wishing there was something he could salvage for her at

that moment, something tangible to bring to her to reassure her that her family home still stood. He'd
started toward his car when the breeze picked up and
the woody arms of the lilac that grew near the front
corner of the house began to wave, as if beckoning him.

Sections of the bush were covered with debris, and
several long branches were crushed on the ground,
where ladders had been pushed up against the side of
the house and firemen had trampled whatever was
necessary to put out the blaze. But the branches farthest from the window still bore flowers, and Adam
reached up a long arm to bring a few of the tallest ones
to eye level. The blooms had just opened, and he had
to hold them right up close to his nose to catch the fra-
grance over the stench of burnt wood. With his Swiss
Army knife, Adam cut as many branches as his arms
could hold, and carried them to his car.

It was all he could find to bring to her that had not
been damaged. He hoped it would be enough to set
her mind at rest.

"Mancini still in there?" Adam asked the agent
who sat outside Kendra's door.

"Left about ten minutes ago." The agent nodded
toward Kendra's room. "I think they gave her something to make her sleep."

"Swell," Adam muttered under his breath as he
opened the door and walked into the darkened room.
The drapes had been pulled over, and all the lights
were out except those directly over the bed. In their
glow, Adam could see that Kendra's eyes were closed.

She smiled and sniffed the air as he drew closer to the bed.

"Oh!" she exclaimed, her voice still little more than a gasp. "Lilacs!"

She opened her arms as far as she could without knocking out the IVs, held up her casted hands, several fingers in splints, and reached for the flowers.

"I didn't realize I'd cut so many," Adam told her apologetically.

"I want them," she said, and he lowered the enormous mound of branches into her outstretched arms. She gathered them to her body and buried her face in the blooms. "Oh, they're wonderful. You're wonderful."

"I cut them from the tree next to your house."

"The one near the front?"

"Yes."

She raised her eyes, and he could see they were beginning to glisten.

"Thank you," she whispered as the tears flowed more quickly. "Oh, thank you."

She hugged the flowers closer.

"My father planted that lilac for my mother the year they were married," she told him, her tears now flooding her face. "I was so afraid it had been destroyed. That my house . . ."

"Your house is going to be as good as new." Adam leaned over the side of the bed and brushed a strand of hair back from her face. "Jess Webb is out there with the guy from the insurance company, and someone . . . I forget her name . . . is going to look at your antiques."

"Karen Hill," Kendra said, sniffing, annoyed that her nose was beginning to run.

"Yes, that was it. She's going to meet with Jess and the adjuster today and see what needs to be done. So there's nothing to worry about. The kitchen took the brunt of the fire."

"Because I forgot to turn off the pancakes."

"Pancakes?" Adam frowned.

"It's a long story," she said, her voice almost faded away completely.

"You can tell me later," Adam said, taking the chair by her bed, "we have all the time in the world."

"John's not making you go back to Virginia today?"

"I'm not leaving," he told her, and she opened her eyes just the tiniest bit. "The last time you needed someone, I wasn't there for you. I waited too long to come back. I'm not making the same mistake again. This time, I'm not going anywhere. There is nothing that could make me leave Smith's Forge now."

She smiled and closed her eyes, and drifted off to sleep.

"That might make things a bit awkward," said a voice behind him.

Adam turned to see John Mancini leaning against the doorjamb.

"What would make things awkward?"

"Well, you sticking around here while she's in North Carolina. I'd have thought you'd want to be with her, but hey, that's just me."

"John, what are you talking about?"

"She didn't tell you? I offered her a job. No more freelancing. When she's not in the field, sketching, she'll be lecturing at the Academy. She's a superb investigator, always asks the right questions. And I've never met anyone who has a better talent for homing in on physical descriptions."

"She's going to be working for the Bureau?"

"Yes. The doctors all said she could leave in a few days, and since she doesn't have a house to go back to right now, I thought I'd send her down to Nags Head. We've been asked to assist on a series of child abductions. Miranda Cahill's already on her way down. She couldn't wait to get back to work, so I thought we should accommodate her."

"Do you think either of them—Kendra or Miranda—can handle working so soon, after everything that's happened?"

"As I said, Miranda is restless. And of course Kendra can't draw anything just yet, but the doctors all feel her hands and fingers will be good as new with therapy. And I think with her ability to pry descriptions out of witnesses, I can send another artist along to do the actual sketching if I have to. I have someone in mind, he might learn from the experience of working with her. It'll be interesting to see how that works, don't you think? And she can get the therapy she needs for her hands down there, there's a good clinic."

Adam merely nodded, and tried not to frown.

"Now, when you get down there, the first person I want you to speak with is . . ."

"When I get down there?"

"Sure. Someone has to be in charge. You're senior on the team, aren't you? Now, come on downstairs to the cafeteria and we'll grab some lunch, and I'll fill you in on this case." John's voice dropped. "It's pretty nasty."

"They've all been nasty lately," Adam said without thinking. "It's been a nasty couple of weeks."

"It's the nature of the job, Adam."

"Is Will Fletcher assigned to this investigation?" Adam's fists visibly clenched.

"No." John was not oblivious to the tension. "I need him in West Virginia right now. Besides, I wanted to give him a little breathing room. He blames himself, you know, for what happened to Kendra."

"As well he should. If he hadn't left her there alone with Zach—if he'd had the presence of mind to check the ID of the man who claimed to be Joe Clark . . ."

"And how many IDs did you check, the night of the fire? Did you ask to see any?"

Adam met his boss's stare with silence.

"That's what I thought."

"So you think it's okay, that Fletcher just let Zach walk off with Kendra?"

"Of course not. But at the same time, I think the circumstances need to be taken into consideration. There were several law enforcement agencies at the scene. I doubt that anyone checked anyone else's ID. Who would have thought the killer would walk into the midst of them, pretend to be one of them? Brilliant on Smith's part, if you ask me."

"Kendra could have been killed, John."

"Well, then, consider this. We not only caught our killer, but Kendra has finally found peace of mind. She knows now what really happened not only to her brother, but to her mother, as well. Ask her if she'd rather it had played out any other way."

Adam looked over his shoulder at the woman sleeping on the bed behind him. He knew without asking what her answer would be.

"You go on down," he told John. "I'll join you in just a few."

John patted Adam on the back and said, "She's going to be fine, Adam. I know it's tough when it's someone you care about, but she's going to be fine."

Adam nodded, and returned to the side of the bed where Kendra lay, her breathing more regular, her vital signs as recorded by the monitors above her bed just fine. He watched her for several long minutes, fussing over her slightly, moving a branch or two from her face, straightening her blanket out just a bit.

"I'll be back," he whispered to her sleeping form, "and then we'll talk about Nags Head. For starters, anyway. We have a lot to talk about, you and I. . . ."

How long did they think they could keep him tied up like this? Where the hell was his lawyer, anyway? Isn't this cruel and unusual punishment, shackling a guy to the bed? Where did they think he was going to go?

He smiled to himself. He knew where he'd like to go.

She was still here, right up two floors from him. He'd heard the nurses talking about her. How brave she was; how she'd broken both her hands trying to get away from her attacker.

Bullshit.

She was lucky, that's all. She wasn't brave, she was scared shitless. And she broke her hands beating the crap out of *him*. So why all the sympathy for her when he'd clearly gotten the worst of it all?

Bitch. Did she think she was going to get away with this? Damn near killed him, that's what she did. Beat him till he could barely move, couldn't run, though he'd tried. Took him nearly ten minutes to slip the ropes she'd tied him with. Tough to make ground with a broken leg. He'd tried swimming but he'd been disoriented and he swam right into the arms of the three police officers sent to bring him back.

One could say that his stars had been poorly aligned last night. He'd certainly had a run of bad luck.

Of course, he reminded himself, he shouldn't complain. After all, look at all the good luck he'd had over the past few years. He pondered this for a while. He had been inordinately lucky. Why, he'd never even come close to being caught. Until now. And if it hadn't been for her, he'd still be free.

Free.

How long, he wondered, before he'd be free again?

Maybe never, he whispered softly.

Maybe, he smiled, pulling on the cuffs that bound him to the bed. They couldn't keep him locked to the bed forever. Sooner or later they'd have to uncuff him.

Maybe sooner than later. A good lawyer, a good plea. Was insanity a defense in this state? In any of the states that would want to try him? He thought about this. If he could plead . . . and get himself into the right facility . . .

If one was very, very clever and very, very alert, well, who knew if—and when—the right opportunities might present themselves? He'd just have to be alert, that's all. Alert and smart and willing to take a chance or two.

Just like he'd been doing for the past ten years.

Smiling, musing on the possibilities that could come his way, he closed his eyes, and drifted off to sleep.

Read on for a sneak peek of

DEAD WRONG

the wonderful new novel from Mariah Stewart

Oh, sure, I heard the little one crying. And the middle one, too. Only one I never heard was the older one, the boy. They ain't lived here long—maybe a month or so. I never saw much of them. Oh, once in a while I'd pass the boy on the steps. He never had much to say. No, never saw the mother bring men home. Never saw her much at all, though, don't know when she came or went. Heard her sometimes, though. God knows she was loud enough, screaming at them kids the way she done. No, don't know what she was doin' to 'em to make 'em cry like that. No, never saw no social worker come around. Don't know if the kids went to school. Did I what? No, never called nobody about it. Wasn't none of my business, what went on over there. Hey, I got troubles of my own. . . .

Mara Douglas rubbed her temples with the tips of her fingers, an unconscious gesture she made when deep in thought or deeply upset. Reading through the notes she'd made while interviewing the elderly, toothless, across-the-hall neighbor of the Feehan family, she was at once immersed in thought and sick to her stomach. The refrain was all too familiar. The neighbors heard, the neighbors turned a deaf ear rather than get involved. It was none of their business what a woman did to her children, none of their business if the kids had fallen through all the cracks. In neighborhoods as poor as this, the tenants all seemed to live in their own hell. Who could worry about someone else's?

Mara rested her elbow on the edge of the dining room table, her chin in the palm of her hand, and marveled at how a child could survive such neglect and abuse and so often still defend the parent who had inflicted such physical and emotional pain.

Time after time, case after case, she'd seen the bond between parent and child tested, stretched to the very limit. Sometimes even years of the worst kind of abuse and neglect failed to fray that connection.

She turned her attention back to the case she was working on now. The mother's rights were being challenged by the paternal grandparents, who'd had custody of the three children—ages four, seven, and nine—for the past seven months. Mara was the court-appointed advocate for the children, the one who would speak on their behalf at all legal proceedings, the one whose primary interest—whose only interest—was what was best for the children.

As their champion, Mara spent many hours reviewing the files provided by the social workers from the county Children and Youth Services department and medical reports from their physicians, and more hours still interviewing the social workers themselves, along with neighbors and teachers, emergency room personnel, family members and family friends. All in an effort to determine what was best for the children, where their needs—all of their needs—might best be met, and by whom.

Mara approached every case as a sacred trust, an opportunity to stand for that child as she would stand for her own. Tomorrow she would do exactly that, when she presented her report and her testimony to the judge whose job it would be to determine whether Kelly Feehan's parental rights should be terminated and custody of her three children awarded to their deceased father's parents. It probably wouldn't be too tough a call.

Kelly, an admitted prostitute and heroin addict, had been arrested—again—for solicitation. Her nine-year-old had stayed home from school to take care of his siblings until Kelly could make bail. Unfortunately for Kelly, her former in-laws, who had been searching for the children for months while their mother had moved them from one low-rent dive to another, had finally tracked them down. After calling the apartment several times a day for two days in a row and having grown suspicious when their young grandson never seemed to know where his mother was, the senior Feehans had called the police. Their next move was to take temporary custody of the children, who were found to be bruised, battered, and malnourished.

Over time, it became apparent that Kelly wasn't doing much to rehabilitate herself. She'd shown up high on two of her last three visitation days, and the grandparents promptly filed a petition to terminate Kelly's rights permanently. Total termination of rights was a drastic step, one never made lightly nor without a certain amount of angst and soul searching.

After all, Mara knew all too well the torment of losing a child.

In the end, of course, the decision would rest in the hands of Judge McKettrick, whom Mara knew from past experience was always reluctant to sever a parent's rights when the parent contested as vehemently as Kelly Feehan was doing. Much would depend on the information brought to the court in the morning. The responsibility to present everything fairly, without judgment or embellishment, was one that Mara took very seriously.

With the flick of her finger, the screen of Mara's laptop went blank, then filled with the image of a newborn snuggled up against a shoulder covered by a yellow and white hospital gown. The infant's hair was little more than pale fuzz, the eyes closed in slumber, the perfect rosebud mouth puckered just so.

Another flick of a finger, and the image was gone.

Mara's throat constricted with the pain of remembrance, the memories of the joy that had filled her every time she'd held that tiny body against her own. She abruptly pushed back from the table and walked to the door.

"Spike," she called, and from the living room came the unmistakable sound of a little dog tail thumping on hard wood.

"It's time to go for a walk."

Spike knew *walk*, but not *time*, which was just as well, since it was past one in the morning. But once the thorn of memory began to throb, Mara had to work it out of her system. Her conditioned response to emotional pain was physical. Any kind of sustained movement would do—a walk, a run, a bike ride, a trip to the gym, anything that got her on her feet was acceptable, as long as it got her moving through the pain so that she could get past it for a while.

Mara pursued exhaustion where others might have chosen a bottle or a needle or a handful of pills, though there'd been times, in the past, when she'd considered those, too.

By day, Mara's neighborhood in a suburban Philadelphia college town was normally quiet, but at night, it was as silent as a tomb. She walked briskly, the soles of her walking shoes padding softly on the sidewalk, the occasional street lamp lighting her way, Spike's little Jack Russell legs keeping the pace. Four blocks down, four blocks over and back again. That's what it usually took to clear her head. Tonight she made the loop in record time. She still had work to do, and an appointment in court at nine the next morning.

The evening's earlier storm had passed through, and now a full moon hung over her small house and cast shadows behind her as she made her way back up the brick walk to her front door. She'd let Spike off the leash at the end of their drive, and now stood watching as the dog sniffed at something in the grass.

"Spike," she whispered loudly, and the dog looked up, wagging his tail enthusiastically. "Come on, buddy. Time to go in."

With obvious reluctance, Spike left whatever it was he'd found on the lawn and followed his mistress to the front steps. Mara unlocked the front door, but did not go immediately inside. She crossed her arms and stared up at the night sky for a long moment, thinking of her own child, wondering once again where in this vast world she was at that exact moment, and who, if anyone, was standing for her.

On the television screen, the earnest five o'clock news anchor droned on and on, his delivery as flat as his crew-cut hair. Mara turned the volume down to answer the ringing phone.

"What's for dinner?" Mara's sister, Anne Marie McCall, dispensed with a greeting and cut to the chase.

"I was just asking myself that very thing." Mara grinned, delighted to hear Annie's voice.

"How 'bout a little Chinese?"

"You buying?"

"And delivering."

"You're home?"

"I'm on my way."

"What time will you be here?"

"Thirty minutes, give or take. I'm just leaving the airport. If you call in a take-out order at that little place on Dover Drive, I'll swing past and pick it up."

"Perfect. What do you want?"

"Surprise me."

"Done. I'll see you soon."

Pleased with the unexpected prospect of Annie's company, Mara found herself whistling while she hunted up the menu. She called in the order, then set about clearing the kitchen table of all the mail that had accumulated over the past several weeks while Mara had worked on the Feehan case. That case having been heard just that morning, Mara could pack up the materials she'd reviewed and return them to the courthouse in the morning. She wondered where Kelly Feehan had gone that night to drown her sorrows, her parental rights having been severed by Judge McKettrick until such time as Kelly successfully completed a rehabilitation program and obtained legitimate employment, at which time she could file for visitation rights. The odds that Kelly would follow through were slim to none, but the option was there. It had been the best the judge could do for all involved.

While the decision was clearly in the best interests of the children, it still gave Mara pause to have played a part, however small, in another mother being separated from her babies, even though she knew full well that Kelly had brought her troubles upon herself. She'd wanted to shake the young mother, shake her good and hard, for having put herself and her children in such a situation.

You had a choice, Mara had wanted to shout at the sobbing woman as her children left the court room with their grandparents. *We don't all get a choice. . . .*

Mara scooped dry dog food into Spike's new Scooby Doo dish, then gave the dog fresh water. She turned up the volume on the television, hoping to catch the weather forecast for the morning. She'd been looking forward to her early morning twice-weekly run with several friends and was hoping that the earlier prediction of rain had been revised.

". . . and in other news, we have a somewhat bizarre story of two women who have the same name, who lived in the same town, and who met with the same fate exactly one week apart." The anchorman spoke directly into the camera. "Jason Wrigley is standing by at the Avon County courthouse with the story. . . ."

Headlights flashing through the living room window announced Annie's arrival. Mara had just begun to open the front door when a face appeared on the screen.

"This is Mary Douglas," the reporter was saying as he displayed a picture of a white-haired woman in her early sixties.

Mara watched in fascination as he held up a second photograph of another woman and said, "And this is Mary Douglas. What do these two woman have in common besides their names?"

The reporter paused for effect, then faced the camera squarely, both photographs held in one hand, the microphone in the other.

"Both of these women lived in Lyndon. Both women died in their homes in that small community, in exactly the same manner, exactly one week apart, the body of the second victim having been found earlier this afternoon. Local police have admitted that they are clearly baffled as to motive."

Video played of a prerecorded press conference.

Spike ran to the door and barked when he heard Annie's heels on the walk, but Mara's attention remained fixed on the television.

". . . without divulging the manner in which the women were killed, we're investigating the possibility that the first killing was an error. That the second victim may have been the intended target."

The police spokesman paused to listen to a question from the floor, then repeated the question for those who had not heard.

"Do we feel it was a contracted killing, was the question. I can only say at this point that anything is possible. It has been suggested that perhaps the killer had only known the name of his victim—no description, no address—and that after killing the first victim and perhaps seeing some news coverage or possibly reading the obituary in the newspaper, he realized that he hadn't killed the right woman. According to friends and family of both victims, neither Mary Douglas had an enemy in the world. Both women were well liked, both lived somewhat quiet lives. So with no apparent motive, we can't rule out any scenario yet."

"Mara . . . ?" Annie called from the doorway.

The face on the television was taut with concentration as he spoke of the victims.

"Yes, then we think he sought out the second Mary Douglas and killed her, though we do not know why either of these women would have been targeted, for that matter. . . ."

"Mara . . . ?"

"This is bizarre," Mara shook her head.

"What is?" Annie set the bag she carried on the coffee table.

"This news report . . ." She was still shaking her head slowly, side to side. "Two women named Mary Douglas were murdered one week apart. Killed in the same manner, though the police aren't saying how they were killed."

"Wow. Doesn't that give you the creeps?" Annie frowned. "That the name is so close to yours? Mary Douglas. Mara Douglas . . ."

"A little, yes," Mara admitted, "But what makes it really freaky is that there's a woman who works in the D.A.'s office at the courthouse—she's administrative staff—named Mary Douglas."

"Was she . . . ?" Annie pointed to the television.

"One of the victims? No, thank God. I was holding my breath there for a minute, though. She's such a nice person—a real ray-of-sunshine type. Friendly and a good sport. Not a day goes by when each of us doesn't get at least one piece of mail meant for the other."

"You don't work in the D.A.'s office."

"Right, but very often the mail room will mistake Mary for Mara, or vice versa, and we get each other's mail. And if something is addressed to *M. Douglas,* it's anyone's guess whose mailbox it ends up in." Mara watched the rest of the segment, then turned off the television. "I feel sorry for the families of the two victims, but I can't help but be relieved that the Mary Douglas I know wasn't one of them."

"Odd thing, though," Annie murmured as she pulled off her short-sleeved cardigan and tossed it onto a nearby chair. "Two victims with the same name. That can't be a coincidence. . . ."

"Intrigued, are we?"

"Hell, yes."

"Itching to know more?"

"What do you think?" Annie carried the fragrant

bags of egg foo young and chicken lo mein into the kitchen.

"Maybe you'll get a call."

"Well, it's early yet. Only two victims. Have they given out any personal information about them?"

"The first victim was a retired school librarian. Sixty-one years old, lived alone. No relatives. By all accounts, a lovely, pleasant woman without an enemy in the world."

"And the second victim?"

"Attractive woman in her midfifties, two grown kids. Yoga instructor at the local YMCA. Husband died two years ago."

"Boyfriend?" Annie leaned against the door frame, her expression pensive.

"They didn't say. According to the news report, she was well liked. Active in the community, spent a lot of time doing charity work. They haven't been able to come up with a motive for either of the killings."

"There's always a motive. Sometimes it's just harder to find. They need to do a profile on the victims."

"I was waiting for that." Mara watched her sister's face, knew just what she was thinking.

As a criminal profiler for the FBI, Annie's experience had taught her that the more information you had about a victim, the more likely you were to find the perpetrator of the crime.

"Can't help it. It's my nature." Annie waved Mara toward the kitchen. "Come on, dinner's going to get cold. Do I have to be hostess in your house?"

Mara got plates from the cupboard while Annie

removed the little white boxes from the bag and arranged them in a straight row along the counter.

Mara nodded approvingly and handed her sister a plate. "Buffet is good."

They chatted through dinner, but Mara could tell her sister's attention was wandering.

"Hey, I'm talking to you." Mara waved a hand in front of Annie's face.

"Sorry."

"You're thinking about those women. The Marys."

"Yeah. Sorry. Can't help it."

"You're wondering if the FBI will be called in."
Annie nodded.

"And if so, if you'll be assigned to the case."

"Sure."

"You know where the phone is." Mara pointed to the wall.

"Maybe I should just . . ."

"Of course."

"And actually, I have my own phone." Annie reached in her bag for her cell phone, then paced into the small kitchen while the number rang.

Somewhere, deep in FBI headquarters, the call was answered.

"This is Dr. McCall. Anne Marie McCall. I'd like to speak with John Mancini. Is he available?"

Damn, but didn't that just beat all?

The man spread the newspaper across the desk so that he could read the article that continued below the fold.

He shook his head, bewildered.

Unbelievable. He'd screwed up not once, but twice!

He ran long, thin fingers across the top of his closely cropped head, laughing softly in spite of himself.

Good thing I don't work in law enforcement. Sloppy investigative work like this would've gotten me canned. And better still that I wasn't getting paid for the job.

Not that he'd ever done work for hire, of course, but even so . . .

What, he wondered, *was I thinking?*

He picked at his teeth with a wooden toothpick and considered his next move. He really needed to make this right.

He folded the paper and set it to one side of the desk. He'd have to think about this a little more. And he would. He'd think about it all day. But right now he had to get dressed and get to work.

He'd been lucky to find a job on his second day here, even if it was only washing dishes in a small diner on the highway. It was working out just fine. He got his meals for free on the shifts he worked and he made enough to pay for a rented room in a big old twin house in a run down but relatively safe neighborhood in a small town close enough to his targets that he could come and go as he pleased.

Of course, he'd had only three targets in mind when he arrived.

The fact that he'd missed the mark—not once, but twice, he reminded himself yet again—would prolong his stay a little longer than he'd intended. His rightful target was still out there somewhere, and he had to find her—do it right, this time—before he could move on.

And he'd have to be a little more cautious this time around, he knew. Surely the other M. Douglases—there had been several more listed in the local telephone book—might understandably be a bit edgy right about now. It was his own fault, of course. He'd gotten uncharacteristically lazy, first in assuming that the only Mary Douglas listed by full name, the kindly woman who lived alone on Fourth Avenue in Lyndon, was the *right* Mary Douglas. Then, to his great chagrin, hadn't he gone and *repeated* the same damned mistake? He'd gone to the first M. Douglas listed, and in spite of having confirmed that she was in fact a Mary, she was, alas, *still* not the right woman.

Not that he hadn't enjoyed himself with either of them—the second Mary had been especially feisty—but still, it wasn't like him to be so careless.

He was just going to have to do better, that was all. Take the remaining M. Douglases in order and see what's what. Check them out thoroughly, until he was certain that he had the right one. The next victim would have to be the right victim, else he'd look like an even greater fool than he already did.

He shuddered to think what a panic a third mistake could set off among the *other* M. Douglases, and though that in itself could be amusing in its own way, well, he didn't really need the publicity, what with the inevitable horde of reporters who would flock to the area. After all, this wasn't supposed to be about *him*. This was all about someone *else's* fantasy.

Oh, he'd fully understood that it had all been a lark as far as the others—he thought of them as his *buddies* now—were concerned. It was supposed to have been just a game, just a means of whiling away a few hours on a stormy winter day, locked in a forgotten room with two other strangers. But then the idea had just caught hold of him and clung on for dear life, and damn, it had caught his imagination. What if he went through with it? What if he played it out? What would be the reaction of his buddies? Would they, each in their turn, pick up the challenge and continue the game? Would they not in turn feel obligated to reciprocate? To continue on with the game, whether they wanted to or not? Wasn't it a matter of principle? Sort of a new twist on the old, *eye for an eye . . .*

His fingers stretched and flexed, as if remembering his Marys.

He smiled to himself, trying to imagine what the reaction of his buddies would be when they realized what he'd done. Shock? Horror? Pleasure? Gratitude? Amusement?

It sure would be interesting to see how it all played out in the end.

As for him, well, Curtis Alan Channing wasn't about to strike out a third time.

He snapped off the light on the desk and tucked the little notebook into the pocket of his dark jacket and headed off to work. He wanted to be early today, to give himself a little time to go through the phone book and jot down a few addresses and numbers before clocking in for his shift. He needed to set up a little surveillance schedule to focus on the right target. This time, there would be no *uh-oh* when he turned on the

TV or opened the newspaper. There simply would be the sheer satisfaction of having completed his task and completed it well, before moving on to the next name on the list. Which he would most certainly do in short order.

After all, it was his honor that was at stake.